HOW TO
SOLVE
YOUR OWN
MURDER

HOW TO
SOLVE
YOUR OWN
MURDER

A NOVEL

Kristen Perrin

DUTTON

DUTTON

An imprint of Penguin Random House LLC
penguinrandomhouse.com

LIBRARY OF CONGRESS CATALOGING-IN-PUBLICATION DATA
has been applied for.

ISBN 9780593474013 (hardcover)
ISBN 9780593474037 (ebook)
International edition ISBN: 9780593719800

Printed in the United States of America
4th Printing

This is a work of fiction. Names, characters, places, and incidents
either are the product of the author's imagination or are used
fictitiously, and any resemblance to actual persons, living or dead,
businesses, companies, events, or locales is entirely coincidental.

For Tom

HOW TO
SOLVE
YOUR OWN
MURDER

Castle Knoll Country Fair, 1965

"YOUR FUTURE CONTAINS DRY BONES." MADAME PE-
ony Lane looks somber as she delivers the opening line of a
fortune that will dictate the rest of Frances Adams's life.

Frances is quiet, her eyes fixed on the woman in front of
her, though her two friends giggle at the terrible theatrics.
From the gaudy beaded curtains adorning the tent to Peony
Lane's tacky silk turban, the whole thing screams Holly-
wood kitsch. Peony Lane herself can't be more than twenty,
though she's adding a rasp to her voice in an attempt to seem
ageless. It isn't quite working. It's all so flimsy that none of
them should take her seriously, and almost none of them do.
Except for Frances.

She takes in every word as if it's gospel. And with each
new line of her fortune, her expression tightens just a bit.
Like hot water teasing out its boiling point, giving off steam
but not yet ready to erupt.

When the girls leave the darkness of the psychic's tent,
Frances doesn't even blink in the bright August sun. Her hair
is long and loose, and it glows red-gold. A man selling toffee
apples gives her a lingering glance, but she doesn't notice
him. She doesn't notice much of anything after the grim prediction she's just been handed.

Emily takes Frances's left arm, Rose joins at her right, and the three girls walk like a chain of daisies, weaving in between stalls selling antiques and trinkets. They turn their noses up at the butcher selling sausages, but stop to look at silver necklaces warmed by the sun's intensity. It's just a trick to get Frances's mind on something else, but Emily buys a delicate chain with a bird on the end. It's a good omen, she says, because her last name is Sparrow.

It's Rose who tackles the issue head-on.

"Frances, you look like death has already found you," she says. Rose elbows Frances to try to jolt some life back into her, but Frances's stern expression simply deepens. "It's all rubbish anyway, you know? No one can see the future."

Emily ties her long blond hair up with a ribbon, and then fastens the bird necklace around her neck. It flashes in the sun—a tiny echo of the knife blades gleaming on the hunting stall behind them. Emily sees Frances eyeing the necklace in horror.

"What?" Emily asks. Her voice is innocent but her expression isn't.

"A bird," Frances says, her eyes narrowing. "The fortune-teller said, 'The bird will betray you.'"

"Then I've got the perfect remedy," Emily says. She dashes off into the crowd and returns several minutes later. Two more silver bird necklaces glint in her palm. "For you and Rose," she says, smirking. "That way you'll never know which bird will betray you. You could even betray yourself." She laughs, and it's wild and open, like Emily herself.

Frances looks desperately at Rose for some understanding, but Rose is laughing too. "I mean, I think it's a good idea actually. Take your fate into your own hands!" Rose fastens her necklace on, as if in demonstration.

Frances hesitates, and finally puts the necklace in her skirt pocket. "I'll consider it."

"Oh, cheer up, Frances," Emily says. "If you keep sulking like this, I'll be forced to murder you myself." The corners of Emily's eyes are creased, as if another laugh is bubbling beneath the surface, and she rejoins her arms through theirs.

"Can you both stop ignoring how creepy that was?" Frances lets go of them and comes to a halt. She wipes her sweaty palms down the simple cotton skirt she's wearing, and then crosses her arms. The rectangle of her miniature notebook peeks out from her skirt pocket, and she's got ink stains on her fingers from fiercely scribbling down every word the fortune-teller said.

Rose covers the distance between them in two tall strides and wraps an arm around her shoulders. She's close enough that her short black bob brushes Frances's cheek. "I think that woman was just messing with you."

"But *murder*, Rose! I can't ignore that!"

Emily rolls her eyes. "Oh, honestly, Frances! Let. It. Go." She bites off each word in the sentence like a crisp piece of apple, and with Rose's Snow White looks and Emily's golden glow, Frances suddenly feels as if they're all fairy-tale characters. And in fairy tales, when a witch tells you your fate, you listen.

Emily and Rose each take one of Frances's arms again and they continue to browse the fair, but things are quieter now, as if the day has been stuffed with cotton wool. The sun is still blazing, and ale still flows from kegs in pop-up tents. The air is sticky with burned toffee and the faint smell of smoke, but Frances's footfalls have become heavy and purposeful. Under her breath, she repeats her fortune again and again, until it's burned into her memory.

Your future contains dry bones. Your slow demise begins right when you hold the queen in the palm of one hand. Beware the bird, for it will betray you. And from that, there's no coming back.

3

But daughters are the key to justice, find the right one and keep her close. All signs point toward your murder.

It's such an unlikely prediction that she should laugh. But those words have planted a seed in Frances's mind, and small but toxic roots are already spreading through her.

The three girls make the best of their afternoon, and soon the laughter isn't so forced. The jokes and gossip and little things that decorate their friendship creep back in. At sixteen, ups and downs are as natural as breathing, and these three girls have breathed deeper than most.

But if anything is unlucky for them, it's the number three. Because in a year's time, they won't be three friends any longer. One of the girls will disappear, and it won't be Frances Adams.

There will be an open file with the local detective, the only evidence in a small plastic bag stapled to a missing persons report that's far shorter than it should be. A small silver chain, with a tiny bird clinging to it.

CHAPTER

1

IT'S ONE OF THOSE HEAVY SUMMER EVENINGS WHERE the air feels so thick you could swim in it. When I surface from my journey on the Piccadilly Line, even the staleness of Earl's Court Station feels like a breath of fresh air. By the time I make it up the three flights of stairs to street level, I'm winded and rummaging through my backpack for my water bottle. All I find is a Thermos full of stale coffee from this morning.

Slim men in suits sail past me like urban gazelles while I gulp down the dregs. It's as disgusting as I anticipated it might be, but I need the caffeine. My phone buzzes and I pull it from my pocket, resisting the urge to check my email and instead answering the call flashing across the screen.

"Jenny." I let all the exhaustion finally leak out into my voice. "Please tell me you're on your way. I can't face Mum's basement again without backup. Last week when I was cleaning it out there were spiders. Huge ones."

"I'm already here," she says. "But Annie, I'm staying on the front step until you arrive, because I don't feel like being dragged around the house by your mum while she tells me which walls she's knocking down."

"Good call. Also, I don't think she's allowed to knock down walls in that house; we don't even own it."

"That's a good enough reason then. And I imagine she's on one of her design rampages, with her private exhibition at the Tate looming."

I wince. Mum's a painter—quite a famous and successful one actually. Or she was, until interest in her work dried up. Unfortunately, this career slump coincided with the loss of the fortune she made from her earlier work, so for most of my life we've walked a fine line between living like squatters and being frugal because it's bohemian and arty. "I mean, Mum's design rampages will keep me from endlessly check-ing my empty inbox, so I'm actually on board with whatever she wants me to do. I have a backpack full of paint swatches and lots of pent-up frustration. I'm ready to tackle this base-ment. Except for the spiders—those have your name on them."

"Aw, my very own army of spiders," Jenny coos. "Just what I've always wanted." She pauses for a beat, as if she's con-sidering her next words carefully. "Why is an empty inbox bothering you? Have you sent out more writing?" Jenny's been my best friend since we were nine. Last month I was made redundant from my low-paying office job, and she stepped up as the perfect mix of shoulder to cry on and motivational life coach. She made a great case for me using this as an op-portunity to follow my dreams and pursue a career writing murder mysteries, because not every struggling writer has a mum with an eight-bedroom house in central London who'll let you live rent-free in exchange for help with odd jobs.

It's not the typical setup for a twenty-five-year-old who's had to move back home, though it does come with the baggage of dealing with Mum's moods. Since that's something I'd successfully escaped by moving out in the first place, this does feel like a step backward. But I have my own floor in the Chelsea house, and the place is falling apart in a rather romantic way. My childhood bedroom has its own chandelier, dust-covered and missing several of its crystals, and it casts a ghostly light over the antique typewriter I found in one of the cupboards. I don't actually write with it; I just sort of clunk the keys now and then for some atmosphere. It has a tartan-patterned plastic case and a 1960s vibe, which I love.

"I started sending out my latest manuscript to some literary agents," I say, and bite my lip when Jenny doesn't reply. "It's only been a week since I emailed the first few." I wipe the sweat from the back of my neck. I'm walking up Earl's Court Road, darting across traffic where I can. My backpack weighs a ton, but the library was having a sale and I couldn't resist. And I can justify buying seven hard copies of Agatha Christie books as *research*. "But I'm already starting to feel like my book is actually terrible."

"It's not terrible."

"No, it really is. I just couldn't see it until I actually *sent* it to people to *read*."

"But you were so confident about this one!" Jenny says. I can hear the bubble in her voice; she's getting ready to go into cheerleader mode.

I cut her off before she can really get going. "I was, but I'm wiser now. You know when a toddler randomly walks up to you, and the kid's mum is beaming at it and assuming you'll find it just as cute as she does? But the toddler's got a gooey nose and old food stuck to its clothes?"

"Ugh, yeah."

"I'm that kid's mum, and I've just sent it out into the

world with a gooey nose, thinking people will see it the same way I do."

"So wipe its face. Introduce it to people when it's cleaner."

"Yeah, I think that's what editing is for."

I hear Jenny suck in a breath on the other end of the line. "Annie, are you telling me you sent a book out to literary agents and you didn't even *edit* it?" Jenny laughs long and hard, and it's infectious. I can't help it—I'm smiling broadly as I turn onto Tregunter Road.

"I just got so excited!" I wheeze, letting a laugh escape. "I did a thing, you know? I wrote many words, and they all culminated with THE END."

"Yes. And I'm proud of you. But I think you should at least let *me* read it before you send it out to any more agents."

"What? No!"

"If you won't let me read it, *why are you sending it out to strangers?*"

"Hanging up now, I'm nearly at the house." I shuffle to the end of the road, where Jenny is sitting on the steps waiting for me.

Mum's house sits miserably at the end of a posh row of terraces, like Halloween attending a garden party. I wave to Jenny as she dusts off her chic skirt and runs a hand through her long black hair. Her fashion sense is impeccable, and I smooth a hand down my voluminous summer dress and reconsider having bought this monstrosity. For some reason, I just seem drawn to dresses that make me look like a Victorian ghost. My pale skin and blond curls only contribute to this impression, so I might as well stop fighting it.

Like Mum, Jenny and I studied art at Central Saint Martins. Her parents moved to London from Hong Kong when Jenny was a baby and are some of the loveliest people you'll ever meet. I'd never tell Mum, but sometimes when I craved a nice stable atmosphere that included a dad and siblings, I'd head to Jenny's after school instead of going home, even when Jenny was at tennis lessons or out somewhere. Her parents would let me sit and do homework and I'd chat with the whole family while the smells of actual home cooking filled my nose.

When Jenny graduated, she landed so firmly on her feet that she's already in dream-job territory. She turned down a job in set design at the Royal Albert Hall to become part of the team that does the window displays at Harrods. She lives for it, and creates masterpieces, especially at Christmas.

"Well," she says, linking her arm through mine, "should we see what your mum's basement has in store for us?"

We both take a moment to stare up at the house. Two sets of grimy bay windows frame the large stone steps leading to the front door. A long time ago the door must have been green, but the paint has been shedding itself in layers over the years, and the wood's a bit warped. I do love it, though. Four stories of whitewashed former grandeur loom upward, and most of the old velvet curtains still shroud the windows.

"Thanks for doing this with me," I say. I'm not even sure what I'm thankful for, because this is the house I grew up in. And even though it was just Mum and me, it's always been a happy place to be. I think I'm just grateful that Jenny shows up when I call her, even when the call is just something like, *Hey, want to clean out an old basement with me?*

"No problem," Jenny replies. "And you already did the hard bit last week, right?"

"Ugh, don't remind me. There were so many boxes and trunks. And the removal men I hired were complete cowboys; they just threw everything into their van. I think I heard glass shatter on a few occasions. But I signed my name on the dotted line and had it all shipped over to Great Aunt Frances's weird mansion in Dorset. I hope she doesn't get too angry when a bunch of her old junk shows up unexpectedly, but Mum is insistent on converting the basement into a studio."

"Frances is the aunt who technically owns this house, right?"

"That's the one."

"Why haven't I heard more about her? Or met her?" Jenny's voice is open, but there's a small hint of a sting to her tone, as if she suspects I've left her out of something important.

"Don't take it personally," I say. "I've never met her either. Apparently she doesn't like London, or traveling. And she's so wealthy that she doesn't bother checking up on this place. I think she even sends Mum a bit of money each week. It's sort of silly and old-fashioned, like a weekly allowance from a parent, but Mum's not too proud to take it. Once I asked Mum why Great Aunt Frances sends money, and she just brushed it off and shrugged."

"Huh," Jenny says, and I can see her chewing on all this new information, not ready to let it go. "This sounds macabre, but what happens when she dies? Does she have kids who'll kick you guys out?"

"Nope, Mum is set to inherit everything." I brace myself for Jenny's reaction, because this is the sort of fact that your best friend of sixteen years should probably already know. And I wasn't keeping it from her; it's just something that honestly never came up. Great Aunt Frances is so distant that my default mentality is that the house really is ours. I forget she exists until I have to do something like sort through all her old stuff.

But Jenny just whistles under her breath. "Family money," she says, rolling her eyes. "I thought the concept was fake, like something that's just in movies."

We push open the stiff front door—unlocked, of course. Mum never locks it; she says if someone's going to choose a house on Tregunter Road to rob, it won't be ours. My eyes sweep over the exposed brick of the hallway, half the plaster still lingering in patches. Mum's right—any burglar would take one look at the layers of peeling wallpaper in here and determine there's nothing worth stealing. They'd be wrong, though, because most of Mum's art is worth an absolute fortune. She'd never sell any of the early work she still has around the house, though; she's far too sentimental about it.

"In here!" Mum's voice echoes from the kitchen, which is deep in the back of the house. We tiptoe through two vast rooms that most people would use as sitting rooms but that Mum uses as studio space. Huge canvases lean against the walls, and the floor is covered in paint splatters. Mum gave up using dust sheets for the floors decades ago. The light that comes through the two sets of bay windows is yellow and musty, fighting its way through at least twenty-five years' worth of city grime. Never once in my life do I remember Mum having the windows cleaned, but I'm so used to the light being this way that I think if she did, it would feel too harsh and shiny—like taking your sunglasses off on a bright summer's day.

Mum has swept her ash-blond hair on top of her head with a green bandanna and has a nearly empty glass of red wine in her hand, with two full ones waiting on the table. She's hovering over the massive range, sautéing onions, which is her sole culinary skill. Something's in the oven, but I suspect it's ready-made and soon to be garnished with the sautéed onions.

"There's post for you on the table," Mum says without turning around.

"Hello to you too, Laura," Jenny says to Mum. Her tone is

teasing, but Mum looks a bit chastened as she turns around and gives Jenny a quick kiss on the cheek.

She moves to say hello to me, but instead hands me the nearly empty glass she's holding and then takes a full one from the table.

I taste gas fumes on the back of my tongue, but Mum beats me to it. "Cooker's gone out, just a sec." She lights a long match from the ring under the frying pan, then twists a knob on the cooker to the *off* position and wrenches open the oven door. The cooker's so old you've got to lean all the way inside and light it with an actual flame, risking certain death in the process. I know better than to bring up replacing it, because it's a discussion we've had too many times over the years. Mum thinks it's retro and cool. I, on the other hand, work hard not to think of Sylvia Plath every time I look at it.

I slump into the hard wooden chair next to my bag and pick up the thick envelope with my name on it. My heart pounds for a second, because I recently entered several fiction-writing competitions. But no one has replied by post to those for years; it's all online these days. My brain is just doing silly things with the expectation that someone might notice me for something I wrote. I throw back the remaining swig of what is most certainly supermarket-brand table wine. It already tastes like a headache.

I slide open the heavy flap of the envelope and pull out a letter printed on headed paper:

Miss Annabelle Adams,

Your presence has been requested at the offices of Gordon, Owens, and Martlock LLC for a meeting with your great aunt, Ms. Frances Adams. Ms. Adams would like to discuss the responsibilities that will come with being sole benefactor of her estate and assets.

I pause there. "Wait, this is from Great Aunt Frances's solicitor," I say. "Looks like he mislabeled this letter, and it was supposed to say Laura. It's about the inheritance."

Jenny leans over my shoulder and skims the letter. "It does say *great aunt*," she says, and points to the words on the page. "That doesn't seem like a mistake."

"Oh, she *didn't*," Mum snaps. She crosses over to the table and snatches the letter out of my hand. She stares at it long enough for the onions to give off a burned caramel smell, then tosses the letter onto the table and returns to the stove. Mum moves the cast-iron frying pan off the hob before the whole thing catches fire.

Jenny mumbles the rest of the letter's contents as her eyes scan the typeface again. *"Please present yourself at the offices of blah blah . . .* it's just instructions for the meeting. It's in a couple of days, somewhere in Dorset called Castle Knoll. Oh my God," she whispers, "an estranged aunt in a sleepy countryside village? A mysterious inheritance? This is a serious case of life imitating art."

"I'm sure this is meant for Mum. Apparently Great Aunt Frances is superstitious to the extreme, so I doubt she'd just change her mind about something like this and disinherit Mum. Though actually," I add slowly, "given the stories I've heard about Great Aunt Frances, this might be the kind of thing she'd do." I look at Jenny's awestruck expression and decide that I owe her a real deep dive into the weird background of Great Aunt Frances. "It's family lore," I say. "I've really never told you?" Jenny shakes her head and sips from the remaining glass on the table. I look over at Mum. "Do you want to tell the story of Great Aunt Frances? Or shall I?"

Mum goes back to the oven and wrestles with the door again, pulling out an aluminum tray of something unidentifiable. She takes the cast-iron frying pan and scrapes the singed onions onto the top of it, grabs three forks from the basket where she keeps loose cutlery, and sets the whole thing between us, forks stuck in at odd angles. Then she sinks into a chair and takes another drink of wine, shaking her head at me slightly.

"Okay then," I say, and I try to put on my best storytelling voice. Jenny takes the wine bottle and fills my glass. "Great Aunt Frances was sixteen, and it was 1965. She and her two best friends went to a country fair and had their fortunes read. Great Aunt Frances's fortune came out something like this: *You're going to be murdered, and end up a pile of dry bones.*"

"Ooh, very over the top, I love it," Jenny says. "But if you're going to write mystery novels, Annie—and I say this with all the love in my heart—you need to work on your delivery."

Mum has the letter again, and studies it as if it's evidence of some crime. "That wasn't the fortune," she says quietly. "It was: *Your future contains dry bones. Your slow demise begins right when you hold the queen in the palm of one hand. Beware the bird, for it will betray you. And from that, there's no coming back. But daughters are the key to justice, find the right one and keep her close. All signs point toward your murder.*"

I stab one of the forks into the thick cream of what I suspect is potatoes dauphinoise from the Tesco freezer section. "Right. Anyway, Great Aunt Frances has spent her whole life convinced that this is going to come true."

"That's . . . I can't figure out if that's tragic or very savvy of her," Jenny says. She turns to Mum. "So, Annie's really never met this lady?"

Mum sighs and picks at the onions. "Mostly we just let Frances live in her big house and get on with things."

"Wait, so you have an aunt with a country estate and you just ignore her?"

Mum waves a hand to swat Jenny's comment away. "Everyone ignores Frances. She's nutty. So much so that she's a local legend—the weird old lady with a huge country house and piles of money, just digging up dirt on anyone who crosses her path in case they might turn out to be her murderer."

"So are you going to call this solicitor about the mix-up?" I ask.

Mum pinches the bridge of her nose and hands me the letter. "I don't think it *is* a mix-up. I'd come with you to Dorset, but that date is deliberate."

I look at it again. "Your show at the Tate," I say slowly. "She's trying to make sure you can't come?"

"Frances may be nutty, but she's very calculating. And she likes to play games."

"Okay," I say. My shoulders sag at the thought of missing Mum's Tate exhibition, but it looks like this meeting concerns our livelihood. I'll just have to hope the opening goes well, so that there will be others. "But then, why me?"

Mum lets out a long hiss of air before she speaks. "She lives her life by that fortune, and for years I was her sole benefactor because of that line—*but daughters are the key to justice.* I'm the only daughter in her family; my father was Frances's older brother."

"The second part of the line," I muse. *"Find the right one and keep her close."*

Mum nods. "It looks like Frances has decided that I'm not the right daughter anymore."

CHAPTER

2

The Castle Knoll Files, September 10, 1966

*I'M WRITING THIS ALL HERE BECAUSE I JUST KNOW
there will be things I've seen that might matter further down the
road. Some details that seem small now will turn out to be extremely important, or the other way around. So I'm keeping
everything together, and I'm making careful notes.*

*Rose still thinks I'm bonkers for fixating on this fortune. But
she doesn't know the reason I believe in it so fiercely.*

*Because someone's been threatening me even before we saw
the fortune-teller.*

*I found a piece of paper in my skirt pocket that read "I'll put
your bones in a box." That threat gives me shivers when I think
about it, but I have to keep it close in case there's something I can
learn from it. Some clue that might help me stop whatever ill fate
is already in motion.*

*And then there was my fortune—"Your future contains dry
bones." Two mentions of bones—it can't be a coincidence. And
then Emily, vanishing a few weeks ago, almost exactly a year after that fortune was told.*

When the police interviewed me, I could tell they didn't fully believe what I said. They even asked me if I was feeling like I needed some attention, now that all the focus is on finding Emily.

So I didn't bother to tell them the rest. I decided then and there to take matters into my own hands. Because the last people I want knowing about this past year are the police.

CHAPTER

3

IT ONLY TAKES THREE STOPS FOR MY TRAIN TO nearly empty—all the commuters leave before the city bleeds away. In two hours the patchwork green of Dorset's rolling hills comes into view, and I feel excitement pooling in my stomach. I take out one of the empty notebooks I brought with me and try to jot down some descriptions of the scenery. This train doesn't go all the way to Castle Knoll, so I've got to find a bus from a town called Sandview, and there's only one per hour.

Finally, the train lurches to the end of the line, and I see that my connection is a classic open-top double-decker bus—the kind designed for tourists heading to the seaside. I sit right at the front of the top level like a little child, and it rattles through a constellation of obscure villages before it finally approaches Castle Knoll. By then I've inhaled the heady scent of manure mixed with distant sea air for a full forty minutes, but the dappled light and country lanes that accompany it make the smell seem charming rather than offensive.

The village of Castle Knoll is like a picture on a biscuit tin—all narrow lanes and dry-stone walls, with a tall hill at one end that holds the crumbling ruins of a Norman castle on its shaggy shoulders. Sheep even graze its slopes, and I can hear the odd bleating from my seat as we navigate the road around the castle.

I'm a few minutes early to this meeting with Mr. Gordon, so I head up the cobbled high street to poke around. As I hoist my backpack up a little, I wonder if I should have brought more books. Or maybe that fourth notebook—the one bound in blood-red leather.

It's such a small village that I can see the whole thing by simply turning in a circle. The castle ruins loom at one end, with an ancient-looking pub called the Dead Witch at the foot of the hill. It looks suitably haunted. Its slate roof slopes as if its sides are too tired to hold it up anymore, and the whitewash on the thick walls is sun-bleached and peeling. The rest of the village is spotless—to such an extent that it feels like a film set. An old-fashioned sweets shop is already bustling with tourists at ten A.M., and a Victorian train station takes up a good portion of the street adjacent to the pub. Steam drifts from the engines waiting there, and families line up to buy tickets to the trains' only destination—the neighboring seaside town.

On the other end of the high street is a sweet little stone building that stares down the road at the Dead Witch. The words CRUMBWELL'S DELI are painted across a bright red sign in gold lettering, and it bookends the high street like a jolly antithesis to the Dead Witch. Near the deli is the Castle House Hotel. It looks like the kind that's boutique, immaculate, and posh, and it probably charges the earth.

Eventually I swing open the door of Gordon, Owens, and Martlock, which is really just the ground floor of one of the terraced cottages that line the high street. It's an open, airy room that's surprisingly cheerful given that they've crammed four desks in what was once a small sitting room. The glow of green banker's lamps competes with the light streaming through the glass in the front door. There's a round-faced man at a large desk in one corner, but all the other desks are empty.

"Excuse me," I say. "I'm looking for Mr. Gordon?"

The man looks up and then blinks at me a few times. He checks his watch and then looks up again. "I'm Walter Gordon. Are you Annabelle Adams?"

"Yes, that's me, but just call me Annie."

"Lovely to meet you," he says. He stands up to shake my hand but doesn't come out from behind the desk. "You know, you're the spitting image of Laura."

I laugh weakly, because I hear that so often it's old news. But it does remind me that Mum grew up near here, and that there are people in Castle Knoll who knew her when she was younger. I wish she'd brought me here when I was little, but she didn't get along with her parents and always said London was the only place we needed.

"I've just spoken to Frances on the phone," Mr. Gordon says. "I'm afraid we're going to be moving this meeting to Gravesdown Hall. She's having some sort of car trouble. We'll just wait for everyone to arrive and then we can all make our way up there together."

I help myself to the chair opposite his desk, and he notices too late that he's been rude not to offer me a seat. I'm not old-fashioned this way, but Mr. Gordon clearly is—he's wearing a rumpled suit but has made the effort to include a pocket square, and he glances at the desk next to his and mumbles something about a secretary and tea. "You said 'everyone.' Do you mind if I ask who we're waiting for? I was under the impression I'd just be meeting with you and Great Aunt Frances."

"Oh." He looks a little flustered and starts shuffling some papers across his desk. He's trying to look official, but I can tell he's nervous. "Frances has made some rather, erm, *creative* changes to the future plans for her estate. So we're meeting with Saxon and Elva Gravesdown, who will be late—they always make a point to be."

I'm torn between asking who Saxon and Elva Gravesdown are and keeping my mouth shut so that I don't reveal how cut off I am from the great aunt who has suddenly decided I'm going to inherit her fortune. If Gravesdown Hall is Frances's house, I'm guessing these people are relatives of her late husband.

"And my grandson, Oliver, should be back any minute," Mr. Gordon continues. "He's included in the meeting too. Ah, speak of the devil."

I turn in my chair as a profile appears through the glass in the door. The person on the other side struggles with the handle because he's balancing a tray full of takeaway coffee cups. Mr. Gordon jumps up to help, and a blast of late morning light throws a golden stripe across me as the door opens. Oliver Gordon finally makes it across the threshold, and he's magazine-gorgeous. If anything, he's a little *too* put together, in that "dress for the job you want" sort of way. His shirt is a light blue obviously chosen to match his eyes, with one button open at the collar instead of a tie. He's wearing gray suit trousers and has a leather laptop bag slung over his shoulder.

In one hand he holds a cardboard tray with several coffees in it, and in the other an elaborate-looking cake box. The words *Castle House Hotel* flash gold across the top.

"Annie, this is my grandson, Oliver," Mr. Gordon says, his voice holding the notes of pride that seem specific to

21

all grandparents. "Oliver, this is Laura's daughter, Annie Adams."

"Annie Adams," Oliver repeats slowly, and one side of his mouth curves upward a little. He tilts his head as he says my name, letting his caramel-colored hair slide just a little bit across his forehead. It looks like a well-practiced move, which makes me immediately determined to be immune to it. "That's a great name," he says. "Like a comic book name."

"Sorry?"

"You know, like Lois Lane, or Pepper Potts." He lifts his very full hands slightly, as if he's tipping his hat to me but with takeaway.

"Nice to meet you," I say, and I feel my face crack into a smile. I like that there's a secret nerd lurking behind his attractive facade. He catches himself then, and I watch a businesslike mask slip back into place. "No Frances yet?" he asks Mr. Gordon. "I wanted to make an entrance with coffee and cake. I thought she'd appreciate the gesture."

Mr. Gordon raises an eyebrow. "You did? Or Rose did?"

A more natural smile moves across Oliver's face. "All right, Rose did. She ambushed me outside the Castle House Hotel and shoved all this at me. I think it was her way of reminding Frances that she wanted to be included."

"Why would someone give out free cake if they're angry about being left out?" I say. "That seems like the opposite of what you'd do."

Mr. Gordon gives me a half smile. "True, but Rose is the type of person who demands attention by being overly kind." He smooths a hand across his pocket square, but all the gesture does is rumple it further. "Well, Frances can talk to Rose about that in her own time. We'll be taking those cakes on the road, I'm afraid, because Frances can't get to town. The engine in her old Rolls-Royce is playing up."

At this point, an elegant woman glides up to the door.

"Oh God," Oliver mumbles. "I didn't know we'd be dealing with Elva today."

The woman saunters inside, looking slightly over our heads as if we're not who she's here to see. Her silvery hair is swept up in a neat ponytail. I'd guess she's in her mid-fifties, but she has that kind of ageless face that makes me wonder if there's actually somewhere people can get Botox in Castle Knoll. She's wearing a cream blazer that matches her trousers. If Jenny were here, she'd be able to tell if it was Chanel or Dior.

"Walter." She makes Mr. Gordon's name a statement, a clipped greeting that gives the immediate feeling that she's in charge.

He rises from his desk and does his flustered shuffling of papers again, as if he's been caught doing something he shouldn't. "Elva, hello. Feel free to take the chair next to Laura here," he says.

"Annie," I correct him, and the woman snaps her chin in my direction, birdlike in her curiosity.

"Yes, of course, forgive me, Annie," he says.

"Well." Elva crosses her arms and takes a step closer to me, her lips pursed in an odd expression of satisfaction. "You're Laura's daughter? Typical. She's sent you here to deal with the bad news instead of coming herself."

"Bad news?" I say. I feel like I'm walking into some kind of trap, but I want to know what she's talking about. "All I know is that Great Aunt Frances sent for me." The words sound old-fashioned coming out of my mouth, as if I'm a character in a Jane Austen novel where people are *sent for.*

She turns and addresses Mr. Gordon again, and my shoulders unclench a bit. It feels as if the arctic blast of an air conditioner has shifted away from me and is now being aimed across the room. "Yes. Frances has changed her will. And she's changed it to exclude Laura. She told me personally a few days ago." Elva says this so matter-of-factly that it's almost clinical. Like the voiceover on a nature documentary narrating the horrible carnage of a lions' feast in a dull monotone. "Is she coming to explain it all to us? I've got an important lunch at twelve thirty in Southampton, so I can't hang around here all day. And Laura's daughter needn't be here, if Laura's been cut off."

A surprised snort escapes from me as Mr. Gordon stammers, "Elva, really! Frances isn't even here, so please stop speculating. She'll explain everything shortly, when we see her. Where's Saxon?"

"Saxon's stuck doing an autopsy at Sandview Hospital. Once he finishes he's got an hour's drive ahead of him, and that's assuming he gets the ferry on time. So he's told me that everyone should just carry on without him, and I'll catch him up on the details later."

"Frances might not like that," Mr. Gordon says, sinking into his chair again.

There's a tense moment while we wait for Elva to react, her expression settling into a mask of haughty disdain. For whatever reason, the Elvas of the world don't tend to find me threatening, which is a distinct advantage in situations like this.

I snap on a bright smile and say, "I'm sorry, I didn't hear how you're related to Great Aunt Frances. Are you a cousin of some sort?"

"My husband, Saxon, is Frances's nephew," she says smugly.

Mum never mentioned that Great Aunt Frances had any other relatives, I suppose because she was always the only one in the will. I open my mouth to ask about this, but Mr. Gordon leans my way.

"Saxon was Frances's husband's nephew," he says, mostly to me. "Lord Gravesdown took Saxon in when his parents died, and Saxon went to boarding school soon after Frances married his uncle. She's taken care of him financially, over the years, the same as she's done for Laura. . . ." He throws a sideways glance at Elva, who's examining the wall next to Mr. Gordon's head as if the noise he's making is just nonsensical buzzing and she's trying to find out what's causing it. "But they've never been particularly close," he finishes.

"And as for Laura," Elva continues, as though no one else has been speaking, "Frances thankfully saw sense with all that. The Chelsea house has been in the Gravesdown family for years, and it should remain so. And when I was up at the estate last week, I saw that Laura had sent over some of Frances's old trunks for no reason at all. That just sealed it for Frances. She intends to evict you both."

Unease twists my stomach. "That was me," I say slowly. "I sent the trunks to Gravesdown Hall, and my name was on the removal invoice that Frances would have signed. Wait—is that why she's suddenly so interested in me? Why would that convince her to name me the sole benefactor of her estate?" My brain stutters a little because I don't understand.

But also, what if Elva's right? What if getting those trunks from Chelsea has convinced Great Aunt Frances that it's time to evict her long-term house sitters?

Elva looks like she's about to explode, which confirms she was bluffing about knowing Saxon would inherit. Clearly she made assumptions after hearing Mum had been cut out of Great Aunt Frances's will.

"All of this can be addressed when we meet with Frances," Mr. Gordon answers. Another layer of weariness settles over him, and I realize he's older than I first thought. He must be in his seventies, and working past retirement.

"I'm confused again," I say. "Is this a meeting where Great Aunt Frances just tells everyone to their face what she's written in her new will? Is that . . . normal?"

"Frances does what she likes," Mr. Gordon says, and sighs heavily.

"You mean she lives and dies by that bloody psychic reading from 1965!" Elva snaps. "That horrible old bat!" My eyes widen a fraction, but I'm riveted. Elva is losing it, and seeing someone so carefully composed come undone is quite satisfying to watch. "Did you know, Frances refused to pay for our wedding unless we changed venues? We had our hearts set on the Queen Victoria Country Club, but Frances wouldn't hear of it! Something about how their logo had a drawing of Queen Victoria on it, and how all the napkin embossing and wineglass engravings meant she might *hold the queen in the palm of one hand* all night. It was ridiculous! She had a *visceral* reaction to all potential palm-size queens!" The way Elva says the word *visceral* makes me recoil a bit, as if we're all about to be flayed.

Elva suddenly turns and looks at Oliver, like she's only just noticed him standing there. "Why is your grandson here, Walter? This is Gravesdown family business."

Mr. Gordon takes out his pocket square and mops at his forehead. "May I remind you, Elva, that Frances has asked Saxon, Annie, and Oliver to come to this meeting. She didn't ask for you."

"Oliver?" Elva doesn't try to hide the shock on her face. "Why not ask *you*, if she wants to leave something to the Gordon family? The Chelsea house and Gravesdown estate for Saxon and me, and some sentimental odds and ends for you, Walter. That makes sense."

Mr. Gordon pinches the bridge of his nose. "Elva, will you

please stop trying to *guess* the nature of Frances's last will and testament? How many *times* must I say—"

Oliver is holding his car keys and nods in my direction. "I can give you a lift. Let's get a head start, shall we? Don't bother with your bag," Oliver says as he glances at the leather weekend bag I've set in the corner. "You can come back and get it after the meeting."

We flee the office like it's on fire, not even bothering to mutter a *see you soon* to the others.

CHAPTER

4

The Castle Knoll Files, September 15, 1966

THEY'RE DREDGING THE RIVER DIMBER, WHICH RUNS *from the next county over, through the Gravesdown estate, and down into the village.*

They're only focusing on the deep parts, because by the time the river reaches the village, it's shallow enough to see the bottom. The deepest bits are on the Gravesdown estate, and I can't stop thinking about that too.

Because that's where it all started, really. And it was Emily's idea that we sneak onto the estate at night—she's reckless that way.

I have to put this book away for a bit because Peter's here and he's arguing with Mum. No one can stand that Tansy woman he's married, but now that they've got the baby I suppose there's no going back. They've wanted a baby so desperately. Maybe she'll be a nicer person now that she's not worrying so much about that.

It's odd being an aunt at seventeen, but I suppose that's what happens when your brother is nearly ten years older than you. Though I have to admit, little Laura is the sweetest thing. One month old and making cute gurgles when I see her. She does look like her mum, though, which is a shame.

CHAPTER
5

OLIVER'S FACE IS UNREADABLE AS WE WALK TO HIS car. My brain feels like a messy room after meeting Elva, so I let myself focus on his sharp jawline while I think of something to say that might bring the comic book references back out.

He clicks the key fob in his hand and the parking lights of an immaculate-looking BMW blink. He's parallel parked it off the high street so that it completely blocks the sidewalk. We get several glares from people stepping into the road to get around his car, but he either doesn't notice or doesn't care.

There's an awkward silence as Oliver starts the engine up and pulls away. He rolls his window down a little so that the summer air hits our faces, and any tension I've been feeling is blown away. We turn off onto the lush country lanes, and I want to lean out the window to breathe in the green of the leafy tunnels above our heads. I resist, however, because I'm not a golden retriever.

"So, what do you do in London?" he asks me. The way he

takes the bends should make me nervous, but he has an air of confidence, like he knows the roads well.

I pause because this is when I'm supposed to say, *Oh, I'm a writer.* Jenny says I should tell people it's my job when they ask, because it is technically what I'm doing at the moment. I'm just not getting paid. Or noticed. I bite my lip when my empty inbox flashes into my mind.

"I'm between jobs," I say, which is not technically a lie. "And I'm using the time to explore several creative projects." I'm met with silence again, so I immediately rush back into small talk so we don't delve any deeper into the nature of my "creative projects." "What about you? Do you live in Castle Knoll? I mean, you handle these roads like a local." I smile, but my comment makes his eyes narrow a fraction.

"Oh, no. I live in London, too, and I work for Jessop Fields." He pauses like I should know the name, but I draw a blank. I think of similar company names to deduce what kind of industry he's in. Jessop Fields sounds like Goldman Sachs, or PricewaterhouseCoopers. . . . "Finance?" I guess.

He snorts, and I know I've lost the game. The sweetness of the comic book comment must have been a fluke. Oliver might be attractive, but I already get the feeling that he's kind of a dick.

"Property development," Oliver says finally, deftly changing gears to tackle a hill that I could swear has no room for more than one car to pass. "Jessop Fields is *the* largest property development firm in London. But we've got projects all over the country. All over the world actually." The breeze ruffles his hair slightly, and the sandy blond waves drift upward at odd angles before settling again. I stifle an urge to laugh.

He seems angry that I assumed he lived in Castle Knoll

and I don't understand why, so I decide to ask more questions. "But Mr. Gordon's your grandfather, right? So did you grow up here? Or spend some nice summers visiting him?"

He slithers away from the suggestion, covering up any connection to Castle Knoll with details of his privileged upbringing. "I did, but I spent a lot of that time at boarding school. I went to Harrow, same as Saxon Gravesdown," he declares proudly. "Then there was Cambridge, and then I moved straight to London and started working for Jessop Fields. So it's hard to say I grew up here really, when I spent so much time in other places."

I think of my childhood, which was London through and through. Me and Mum spending weekends pinging around tube stations like silver balls in a pinball machine. I always assumed people who were raised in the countryside had *roots* of some sort, but hearing Oliver talk about his lack of connection to Castle Knoll tells me that I'm the one with roots. Something about that makes me feel momentarily mollified. My ramshackle upbringing with Mum might have been unconventional, but at least it was happy. But thinking about our life in the Chelsea house makes me worry anew—*What if Elva knows something I don't?* I swallow hard, my throat constricting at the thought.

"So you don't feel connected to Castle Knoll at all?" I ask, not bothering to keep the incredulity from my voice. "You didn't run wild through those castle ruins when you were little, or take packed lunches on the steam train?"

Oliver just shrugs.

"I find that a bit sad," I say.

"That's because you're not from a small town. Castle Knoll might seem like a quaint place to you, but living here is really quite boring. I personally would rather be anywhere else."

32

"Only boring people get bored," I counter, which is one of Mum's favorite sayings. "But don't worry, if you had a dull childhood, I can invent a better one for you." I pause and watch the scenery for inspiration, determined to really wind him up. "That hill over there," I say, "is where you broke your wrist falling from your bike when you were eight. And that school over there"—I point to a building in the distance—"is where you had your first kiss after a year-eight disco while waiting for your mum to pick you up."

"That was not my school," Oliver says tightly. "I just told you I went to boarding school." He's irritated, but I like him better this way, because at least his irritation is authentic.

"And over *there*"—I point to a field full of tents, where families are camping—"is where you lost your virginity the summer you visited home after your first year at Cambridge. Bit of a late bloomer, but that's okay. I'd blame the comic books, but I think it just took you a few years to come out of your shell."

"Are you quite finished?" Oliver snaps.

My smile broadens, and I tip my head back. "For now," I say. I close my eyes and watch the dappled light through the red-gold of my eyelids.

BARELY FIFTEEN MINUTES later, Oliver's car is pulling off the lane and through the jaws of an imposing gate. The white gravel drive is a bright stripe that slices a rolling lawn in half, and it's so long I can't see Great Aunt Frances's house yet.

We wind around a gentle bend, and finally the house—Gravesdown Hall—comes into view from behind a veil of dark green cypresses and the clipped clouds of hedges. It's a sandy stone building that's stately and somehow gloomy, even in the bright August light. Three stories of windows glint in the sun, diamond-latticed and elegant. I can tell the house sprawls back quite a bit—it has the feeling of depth as well as a grand facade. A lone gardener is working on one side of the drive, pruning the expansive hedges into rippling shapes. They're tasteful but also kind of creepy. We park right at the front of the large circular drive, where the only other car I can see is an antique Rolls-Royce, its engine exposed as if someone was working on it and got called away suddenly.

Oliver and I stand for a second in front of the tall oak doors, and I run a hand over the ornate carvings on them. Vines, brambles, and intricate scrollwork come together in a way that makes my mind feel like I'm falling into a maze. I'm nervous to finally meet this elusive great aunt who suddenly summoned me after twenty-five years. But it's an excited kind of nervous, like waiting for the results of a job interview where you felt you did really well.

When I press on the brass doorbell, a complex pattern of chimes resonates from deep within the bowels of the house. A silence stretches out that feels too long, so Oliver tries the heavy cast-iron door knocker. Three rich thuds echo from it, booming so loudly they could almost be gunshots. The moments that pass by make it seem very unlikely anyone is coming, so he tries the handles of both doors. They're locked.

"Should we ask the gardener?" My voice comes out shakier than I expected, because the house is making me uneasy. "I mean, do you think he'd have a key?"

Oliver arches an eyebrow at me, and it's maddening how good the expression looks on him. "Hey, Archie!" he calls, without looking away from me. The corners of his mouth twitch in a sly smile. Of course he knows the gardener, *he grew up here*. I want to roll my eyes, but I can't seem to look away from Oliver's steady stare. "I'd better help Archie down the ladder," he says quietly, wearing a full smirk now. "He's got a bad knee, you know. He dislocated it eighteen years ago, pulling me out of the River Dimber when I fell off a rope swing."

I can't tell if this is a lie, but I know it's Oliver's way of continuing our sparring match from the drive.

Behind us, the gardener is still clipping hedges, the rusty snip of his shears the only background noise to our staring contest. It's me who looks away first.

It's true, the gardener does seem too old to be climbing a rickety wooden ladder, and my jaw clenches just watching him. The man turns around and shields his eyes from the sun, blinking a couple of times before he recognizes Oliver.

"Oliver Gordon," he says slowly. "Back so soon?"

I turn to Oliver. "Back?"

"Oh, I was here earlier," he says casually.

"Why?" I ask plainly.

He stares at me. "What does it matter? From what I hear, you've never even met Frances. Now you're suddenly her personal secretary?"

I take a step backward at that, but I'm instantly angry at myself for giving ground. "I'm here because I'm interested. Because I want to meet her. I just asked why you were here earlier because—"

"You were being nosy," he cuts me off.

I wince. "I was being curious."

Archie the gardener has gone back to trimming a few stray twigs from the hedges, and every snip of his shears feels louder as Oliver scrutinizes me. Finally he says, "Frances had some property questions, and she invited me for breakfast and we went over some old ground plans together."

I don't have time to ask any more about that, because Archie starts making his way down the ladder, struggling to balance his long pruning shears in one hand. Oliver puts his hands in his pockets, and only when I clear my throat does he reluctantly pull them back out and move to help Archie. I don't think Archie does have that bad knee.

"And who might this be?" Archie's feet hit the gravel, and he starts mopping his forehead with a small cloth. He's the storybook version of an old gardener, from his worn-out overalls and work boots to the deep folds in his face, leathery from a lifetime spent outside. Silvery wisps of hair escape his tattered canvas flat cap and sweat trickles down his neck.

"I'm Annie Adams," I say, and his handshake is dry like cracked earth.

"Archie Foyle," he says. "Pleased to meet you."

"Are you the only gardener here?" I ask, looking around at the hedges and lawns. "This looks like a huge job."

Archie smiles and his eyes crinkle further. "I'm the only *real* gardener. But the truth is that Frances lets me take over what I like. Really, she's got some professional landscaping team that swans in once a week with their ride-on mowers and leaf blowers. I do the delicate stuff because I like it, and she leaves me to it. But these days the farm takes up most of my time, so I mostly just work on the hedges when I've got a spare moment."

My gaze sweeps down the row of rippling hedge, twice as tall as I am and running at least a hundred yards down the drive before it turns to cypress. "They're very impressive," I say, and I mean it. Looking at them more closely, they don't seem creepy to me now. The whole effect is of green undulating waves, and as someone who's seen a lot of art, I feel well qualified to say that this is some of the best. This gardener is a sculptor of plants.

"Thank you. They're my pride and joy. No one touches these hedges but me, not until I die. And even then, I've asked

Frances if I can be buried under them, so my ghost can haunt anyone who tries to change them." He laughs a little at his weak joke, but when his eyes find Oliver, he stops abruptly.

My brain jumps back a step, because I sense something going on under the surface here. Oliver, property development, breakfast with Great Aunt Frances, and ground plans. "Did you say farm?" I ask, trying to defuse the sudden tension.

"That's right, Foyle Farms." Archie points to a brick-walled garden off to the side of the house. "Beyond the formal gardens and about half a mile down are my fields, my farmhouse, and all sorts. That is, it used to be Foyle Farms, before the Gravesdown estate swallowed it up. But my granddaughter tells me it's good for her business to have the estate on the labels of all the cheese and jams and things she sells. She runs the deli in town, Crumbwell's."

Our conversation is cut off by the sound of tires sliding on the gravel, as Elva Gravesdown takes the bend of the drive too fast. She ignores us and parks the car as close to the house as possible, as Mr. Gordon's modest Renault lumbers up behind her. He's driving through the clouds of chalky dust her wheels kicked up, and if a car could cough, I feel like that poor Renault would have.

"Archie," Oliver says slowly, "do you think you could let us into the house?"

"I can't," he says matter-of-factly. "Don't have keys."

We watch as Elva and Mr. Gordon repeat the process we went through earlier—ringing, knocking, ringing again. The minutes stretch out, and no one comes.

"Should we be worried?" I ask. "Is Frances the kind of woman who sets up a meeting and then forgets?"

"Maybe she's on the phone," Oliver suggests.

"Or the toilet," I wager. Oliver shoots me an annoyed

glance, but I shrug. "It's a legitimate reason not to answer the door."

Another five minutes pass, and Elva clearly starts to get impatient. I look over at Archie, who is watching with a worried expression.

"It looks like Walt has keys, though," Archie says, his tone curious.

We turn to see Mr. Gordon unlocking the door, so Oliver and I hurry to catch everyone else up. I give Archie a nod and another wave as we hurry across the drive and into the gloom of the hallway, and he watches us intently the whole way in. Only the closing of the heavy door cuts off his persistent stare.

The house feels dark after the bright white gravel of the drive, and our steps echo across a tiled entryway. Everything smells of furniture polish and old rugs.

"Frances?" Mr. Gordon calls out, but his voice is tired and doesn't carry.

"Frances, it's me, Elva." The singsong of Elva's voice has a shrill edge that travels much farther. It reverberates down the hall and finds its way under my skin. I shudder and follow Mr. Gordon through a doorway into an enormous rectangular room. It's old—so old that there are two massive stone fireplaces, one at each end of the room, and the floor is lined with worn flagstones rather than wood or tiles. With its vaulted ceilings and dark beams, and the long shining table with its high-backed chairs, it has the feel of an old banquet hall. I picture bards performing while elegant people dine on pheasant and tarts, but there's also a grayness to it that makes me shiver. It looks like Great Aunt Frances felt this too—flowered curtains hang around the tall windows, and sets of armchairs in matching upholstery are arranged around each fireplace to make it feel a bit more welcoming. A huge chandelier hangs from the ceiling, sparkling with hundreds of crystals that point down like daggers.

There are flower arrangements dotted around the large hall, with about seven of them lined up in a row. It seems a little odd until I notice they're labeled: *To be delivered to church.* There's a show-stopping arrangement at the center of the table that must stand at least four feet tall. "These are beautiful," I say. "Does Great Aunt Frances rent the house out as a wedding venue or something?"

"No," Mr. Gordon says casually. "Frances's primary hobby is flower arranging. She's such an avid amateur florist that she has Archie bring in fresh flowers from the gardens every morning. These probably *are* for a wedding, though, as Frances does all the flower arrangements for the church."

"Wow," I say, because they really are quite something.

We step through a door at the far end of the room, into a library that's cozier than I expected, its walls lined with dark leather-bound volumes. The large square windows let in a flood of light that's tinted green from the leaves of the wisteria that hangs outside.

There is a strange feeling of tension in the air as I follow the others farther in. I spot Mr. Gordon frowning at a disheveled-looking bunch of roses sitting on a large wooden desk in the center of the room. They seem out of place compared to the well-arranged vases found everywhere else. We're all stepping lightly without realizing it, our feet making no noise on the green patterned carpet.

"Frances?" Mr. Gordon calls again. The silence in the room is oppressive.

And then we see it, all our eyes somehow falling on it at once—a hand on the floor peeking out from behind the desk. It's pale, except for the trickle of blood crossing the palm and dripping onto the carpet.

CHAPTER
6

The Castle Knoll Files, September 21, 1966

THE FIRST NIGHT WE WENT THERE WAS IN MARCH, *when it still got dark early and we'd had months of being so bored we thought we might die. But Emily had already scouted the place out and found a perfect spot in a tumbledown section of the gardens where we could drink and smoke and have some fun. So of course she was smug as hell leading us around the brambles and through the weak spot in the fence.*

John's hand was warm in mine, and he kept looking at me in the moonlight. His sandy hair and freckles were washed out in the flat glow, bringing out his handsome silhouette. Walt Gordon was up ahead, an open beer in one hand and the other catching Emily around the waist from time to time. He had two joints tucked behind one ear and walked with that lazy swagger of his. Here and there Emily would lean in and whisper something in his ear, her voice low and urgent. Knowing Emily, it was probably something scandalous.

Rose brought up the rear, and she was extra quiet that first night. She'd had a string of boyfriends through the winter, but she always cast them aside for any old reason. Archie Foyle's breath smelled, and he was too forward. Plus, he was living in a foster home and was a bit on the dangerous side, though Walt liked him because he was his main weed supplier. Then there was Teddy Crane, but Rose said his acne was too bad.

"Do you know how Lady Gravesdown died?" Emily asked with her usual dramatic flair. "God, what a name." She laughed her musical laugh. "This family has always been doomed." Em's voice became low and husky—she was going to tell either a gruesome story or a rude joke.

She had her hair long and loose, with a single pearl comb sweeping a section of it across her forehead. I was annoyed because not only was it my pearl comb, but that was my signature hairstyle. Since January—no, further back than that—she'd been doing little, deliberate things to imitate me. At first her imitations came with compliments: "I just love your cotton skirts! Can I borrow one?" or "I wear the lavender hand cream because it reminds me of you," all said with her winning smile. But I've known Emily all my life, and her smile is never simple. Everything she does means something.

"Which Lady Gravesdown would that be?" Rose asked. "Didn't most of the family die in a car accident a couple of years ago?"

"Only a few of them." Emily waved a hand as if three lives meant nothing. Three years ago, Lord Gravesdown's eldest son was driving his sports car, with his father and wife as passengers. He took one of the hairpin turns near the estate far too quickly, rolling the car and killing them all instantly. Rumors abounded as to why he was driving at that speed around the curve, and everything from alcohol to heated arguments were bandied about as theories. The most popular explanation was the most tragic— that the eldest Gravesdown brother had rolled that car on purpose, because of an affair between his father and his wife.

No one will likely ever know the truth, but the youngest Gravesdown brother, Rutherford, was suddenly not just the heir to the Gravesdown title and lands at the tender age of twenty, but guardian to his then seven-year-old nephew, Saxon. So Rutherford did what he thought he was supposed to do. He married, and quickly. But that didn't last either.

"If you're talking about the most recent Lady Gravesdown," Rose said, "she didn't die." Rose's breath came out as clouds in the cold air. "She left. It happens more and more these days; it's the oldest story around. She met some bloke she liked better, and that was that."

"Oh, there's far more to it than that," Emily said. "And when I was here before, I found the proof. Do you want to see?"

"I do," John said. His hand pulsed around mine in a playful squeeze, and I leaned closer to him while we walked. He smelled like aftershave and peppermints—smells that meant he planned to get close to me that night. I squeezed back and smiled in the dark. He helped me over a fallen tree, while up ahead Walt held back some branches so that Emily could pass through. He let them go with perfect timing, and they hit Rose in the face.

"Walt!" I screeched, but they'd already gone up ahead. I stopped to help Rose pick pine needles out of her collar, and John stepped up and held the branches back for both of us.

"That bastard," she muttered, smoothing her hair. Normally Rose would have shouted at Walt, but she seemed tired tonight. I felt bad for her; I think Em and I had nabbed the only interesting boys in Castle Knoll. John leaned in and kissed the space just under my ear, and I was glad I couldn't see Rose's face in the shadows. I could feel her eyes on us even in the dark.

We caught up with Emily and Walt again, and I decided that getting interested in Emily's ghost story might keep them from picking on Rose.

"The whole village knows that the most recent Lady Gravesdown—Rutherford's wife—left her husband," I said. "What proof do you have that she didn't?"

John lit up at the idea of playing detective. "The whole village does know," he said, "not that anyone's ever heard it from Rutherford. He never socializes with anyone in Castle Knoll; he's one of those rich people who lives in a country house but only goes to parties in London."

"You're right," Rose said quietly. "He even keeps a fancy house, on a posh road in Chelsea."

Emily rounded on Rose. "How do you know that?"

"Archie Foyle told me," Rose said, and she squared her shoulders, daring Emily to question this. It was fascinating to watch, like a tennis match. "He used to live on the grounds of the Gravesdown estate, in a farmhouse."

"Ah, I forgot." Emily grinned. "Rose's bad boy Archie has all the gossip then. So did he tell you what happened to the wife?"

"Just that she left," Rose said plainly.

"Oh, she left all right. . . ." Emily paused for dramatic effect. "She left this mortal coil." Walt cackled at her flimsy joke, and chose that moment to wind himself around her. She let out a small moan as he kissed her neck, and then reached for his beer and took two long swigs. Behind us, Rose lit a cigarette, and there was a momentary flash of orange as her lighter flared.

"She was stabbed." Emily said the words in a serious voice that made us stop and pay closer attention. "Killed with an antique knife that has a ruby in the handle. I've seen it. It's hidden on the grounds. And then he dumped her body in the River Dimber."

"Very dramatic, Em," I said, shaking my head. A twig snapped loudly in the woods off to the left, and I let out a nervous laugh.

John took a cigarette from Rose, and when her lighter sparked again, I screamed.

The momentary glow cast by the lighter had illuminated a face in the darkness. It was a child's face, a boy with a steady gaze, watching us. When John sparked the lighter a second time, keeping the small flame bouncing atop it, the face was gone.

Walt turned in worried circles, looking for the boy. Rose came close and grabbed my arm, clearly alarmed as well. But Emily's reaction was strange, and so was John's. It was then that I should have known, but I had adrenaline coursing through me and I only put the clues together later, when I started looking back. When I'd already found out.

Emily's expression was unsurprised. And John's face was angry.

"Where are you, you little creep?" Emily shouted. "Come out, come out, wherever you are!"

John dropped my hand and headed toward where we'd seen the face peering at us moments ago. He ducked farther into the trees, and the sound of more twigs snapping punctuated the darkness.

"Ow, hey, let go!" a voice chirped. John emerged from the trees dragging a boy who couldn't have been more than ten. John had him roughly by the arm, which was strange, because it now occurred to me that I knew exactly who the boy was. We all did. And you did not drag around Saxon Gravesdown as if he were a stray cat. Little might be known about his uncle in the village, but everyone knew the family was wealthy and titled. And those things are powerful, whether you've met someone before or not.

"John," I said, "what are you doing? Let him go."

Saxon noticed me then and gave me a calculating look. His eyes darted from John to Emily and back again, and his pale face twisted with something that might have been anticipation. John let him go and walked back over to me, placing a protective arm around my shoulder.

Saxon dusted off the arm John had been holding, as if wiping away a bad stain.

"He's a horrible little snoop," Emily hissed, making sure Saxon could hear.

Saxon scoffed, but his face split into a grin. "I live here, and I do what I want. You're all the ones trespassing. Should I tell my uncle about this?" He took a couple of steps closer to me and John. "I think I should. I know your name." He looked at Emily, then at the rest of us in turn. "I know all your names."

"You do not," Rose countered.

Saxon stepped around John until he was standing right next to me. I was trying to get the measure of him, but I couldn't quite. His mannerisms were odd. He seemed like an older person trapped in the body of a ten-year-old boy.

"I'm not afraid of you, Saxon," I said calmly. "And I don't care if you tell your uncle we sneaked onto your land. That was our choice, and it's got nothing to do with you."

"That," said a smooth baritone voice, "is a refreshing thing to hear." And out from the depths of the woods, as if he'd been an actor waiting in the wings for the right moment, stepped Rutherford Gravesdown.

CHAPTER

7

MR. GORDON FRANTICALLY RUSHES AROUND THE desk, but the rest of us stay back as he kneels in front of Great Aunt Frances. She's crumpled like a marionette that's had its strings cut, and her eyes are open and staring. I'm gulping small mouthfuls of air, trying to push down the panic that's creeping up on me. I can sense flutters of movement from the others, but the edges of my vision feel fuzzy. It's as if everything in this room is out of focus except the lifeless form in front of me.

Other than the blood on her hand—on both her hands, I notice—she doesn't appear to have been injured. But her hands are a mess. They aren't cut, but *punctured.* Small blood-filled holes dot her palms like sinister constellations.

My breathing is getting frantic, so I try to slow it down. I drag my eyes away from Frances's body to the mess on the floor next to her. Near her hands are several long-stemmed white roses. She must have been clutching them as she fell. I imagine the kind of terrible spasm that would cause someone to squeeze the thorny stems so hard they'd puncture their hands, and I feel my throat constrict.

I am not good with blood. And by *not good*, I mean that I tend to feel faint around blood, needles, injuries of any kind, and often just the general atmosphere of hospitals and surgeries.

And this is most definitely not a minor injury. I feel myself start to back away toward the window seat, nausea and dizziness gripping me in tandem.

"Oh my God," Elva breathes. "Someone's actually done it. Someone's *actually* murdered her. After all these years, she was right about her fortune." A laugh barks out of her and then she covers her mouth, horrified. I notice that her eyes are watery, and her hands shake a little.

Mr. Gordon bends down and gingerly tries to take Frances's pulse, and shakes her by the shoulder, but it's all just feeble attempts at action in the face of something irrevocable. Because it's clear that there's nothing anyone can do to help my great aunt now.

I feel hot sweat start to trickle down my neck, and I sit in the window seat, reaching up for the lever to open the window behind me. Air. I need air.

Elva collects herself and starts coolly dialing a number on her phone. Oliver has turned away, and his hands are on his hips as he paces. He breathes deeply and is so far into his thoughts that I doubt he'd even hear me if I called out to him.

It's me that Mr. Gordon looks up at, his eyes as wide as a small child's.

"I . . ." he says, then stops.

"She's dead, isn't she?" I say, my voice a hoarse whisper.

Elva angles in front of me, and I take the chance to close my eyes for a few deep breaths. She addresses Mr. Gordon as if he's the only one in the room. "I've called an ambulance. They're about fifteen minutes away."

"Did you call the police?" I ask, still trying to control my breathing. I feel my palms start to sweat, and then I think of the bloody dots on Great Aunt Frances's hands and— What am I supposed to do when I panic like this? Count things around me that are blue? Or five things I can smell? I don't want to do that, because all I can think of is the coppery smell of blood. Which is absurd, because right now I can only smell the roses, mixed with the floral din of the other arrangements in the room. I focus on those so that I don't have to look at the body on the floor.

"No, I just asked for paramedics," Elva says. The shake in her voice is gone, but there's a tautness to her tone that I can't decode.

"Why?" I choke out. I'm still looking at the flowers, trying to calm down, and it's helping. I spot ranunculus in yellows and oranges blending with off-white and peach roses. I take a deep breath and turn back to Elva. "Weren't you the one who just said she'd been murdered?"

Elva gives me a pitying look, like I'm a small child. "That was an overreaction. I was in shock. But looking at her, she clearly had a heart attack or some kind of stroke. She's only bleeding because she must have spasmed and squeezed those roses too hard before she fell to the floor."

"Surely that's something the police should decide," I say, narrowing my eyes. If I were writing this as a novel, Elva's decision not to call the police would be flagged as suspicious behavior.

"I don't know about the rest of you," she says, as if I've not spoken, "but I'm not keen to spend my time standing over a dead body." She gives Mr. Gordon a pointed look. "If you need me, I'll be in the next room." She heads for a small door in the corner of the library, tucked so neatly behind the iron staircase that leads to the upper gallery that I hadn't noticed it.

Oliver looks up, then follows her through the door without a word. I look back at Mr. Gordon, not sure what the right thing to do is. "Should we . . . stay here with her?" I ask. I'm still light-headed, and it gives my voice a butterfly flutter.

Mr. Gordon stands, his hands braced on his knees as he does, because it's an effort after crouching for that long. He shakes his head sadly. "I suppose there's no need; we can't help Frances. And I'd like to keep Elva in my sight, if possible."

I open my mouth to ask what he means, but he heads through the door before I can form the words. I can't help it—I look back again at Great Aunt Frances lying there on the floor, roses scattered next to her. Half the arrangement is still strewn about limply on the desk, the other half in a vase at the center of it.

Finally, I turn my back to her, because Elva has a point. I don't like sitting here with a dead body either. I get up and hurry through the little unimposing door in the corner of the library. A door that, it turns out, leads to a room devoted to Great Aunt Frances's obsession—predicting her own murder.

The air in the little room is so thick it feels sinister, as if it has folded in on itself and contains every single theory and paranoia that Frances collected over the years. There are no windows, but someone has flicked on the lights to stave off the dimness. The feeble flourescent bulbs flicker and buzz, so when I notice some candlesticks and a box of long matches I strike one and light the wicks. But lighting the candles only seems to make the ambience worse—the whole place feels saturated with sadness.

When I finally take a good look at the far wall, that feeling only amplifies.

I let out a low whistle under my breath, because Great Aunt Frances even has her very own murder board. It stretches from floor to ceiling, with her name and picture at the center. Colored string reaches out toward old photos that are pinned all over the wall, and Post-its, notebook paper, and newspaper clippings fill nearly all the gaps in between.

"Well, this is taking it a bit far," Elva mutters, looking at the murder board. Her previously ageless face is suddenly lined with scorn, and she reaches out and whips a Post-it from the wall. She skims it, then scoffs as she crumples it up.

I really hate this. I press my palms against my eyelids until the pressure gives me starbursts.

I love murder mysteries. But standing here in this room, facing my great aunt's obsession with her own murder after only just finding her dead body . . . I feel with full force that this isn't just a story, and murder isn't just a puzzle. It's a selfish, final, complex act.

"Annie, are you okay?" Oliver tugs at my elbow and it snaps me out of my spiral. Mr. Gordon spares me a glance, then goes back to examining the murder board.

"Yeah," I say, but my voice is shaky. "I just really don't want to be in this room right now. But I don't want to be out there either. Is there anywhere else we can go?"

"We should all stay together," Mr. Gordon says. "We can make our way to the kitchen, that might be better. . . ."

"I'm staying here," Elva says, and she whips another Post-it off the wall. "There are all kinds of lies written here, and I'm going to sort this out."

"Don't touch that!" I say, and my words are forceful. My head is clearing a bit, and I'm frustrated with Elva for messing with the board. I look at the floor to see if Elva has thrown the crumpled Post-its there, but there's no sign of them. I clear my throat and narrow my eyes at her. "What if she was actually murdered? What if things on that wall are evidence?" I ask.

Elva hesitates, then tears another piece of paper off the wall anyway.

"Look at it this way, Elva," Oliver says evenly, "interfering with Frances's notes makes you look rather guilty."

Elva crosses her arms and gives us all a defiant look. "Fine," she says. "But I'm still staying put. There are things on here about you too," she says, giving Mr. Gordon a long look.

Mr. Gordon looks intrigued rather than worried, and he takes a closer look at the murder board. Oliver points to another wall, where more pictures and string hang in a smaller arrangement. "It's you as a teenager," he says to Mr. Gordon. "I'd recognize this photo anywhere."

I take a moment to look at the rest of the room as I wander to where Oliver is standing. Books are crammed on every shelf, and it looks like these comprise Great Aunt Frances's own special murder-themed collection. Plant encyclopedias sit next to chemistry textbooks, and true crime volumes abound. Books on psychology, puzzles, poisons, and weaponry are arranged in no order I can understand.

A well-worn leather armchair sits under a tall Tiffany-style lamp, but it isn't facing the books—the chair faces a smaller collage of colored string, photographs, newspaper clippings, handwritten notes, and police reports. An old photograph of a girl with hair the color of bleached straw is at the middle of all this organized chaos, with her name scrawled carefully on a piece of paper underneath.

Emily Sparrow, last seen August 21, 1966.

It's another murder board.

Oliver picks the photo he mentioned off the wall and hands it to me. It has *Walt Gordon, October 1965* written along the bottom of the picture. He's thinner and smilier, with longish brown hair that makes him look a bit like one of the Beatles, and he's sporting a questionable-looking tight-fitting high-necked jumper. A smile sneaks onto my face.

Mr. Gordon comes our way and looks at the photo, but he only gives it a half glance. He looks down at his watch as if he can track the ambulance with it, but it's clear he just wants to look anywhere but at the walls of the room.

Elva is now tugging on the drawers of the filing cabinets, finding every one of them locked. A spark of satisfaction ignites within me: I like the fact that Elva is locked out of Great Aunt Frances's deeper secrets.

"Who's Emily Sparrow?" I ask Mr. Gordon.

Mr. Gordon is quiet for a moment, while Elva is looking around with a disgusted twist to her face. Oliver is trying to appear interested, but he keeps checking his phone.

"She was a friend of Frances." He coughs lightly and then continues. "And a friend of mine. She went missing when we were seventeen."

Just underneath the picture of Emily is another, more dog-eared one. Three girls stand with linked arms, and I recognize the blond girl, Emily, on the left. Emily's slender frame and blond hair are contrasted with a young Frances beside her. She is striking, with loose hair the warm color of autumn leaves falling to her waist in waves, swept out of her face by a glinting gold comb. Light freckles dot her face, and her high cheekbones make her look regal. Most teenagers are spotty and awkward, but these three were favored by fate. From this picture I can tell they were girls who were the queens of their school, noticed everywhere they went.

Someone I don't recognize is linking arms with Frances on her other side, a girl with sharp features and a dark bob. She's perfectly outfitted in a way that makes me think of a 1960s secretary rather than a teenager, though she looks the same age as the other two. The inscription reads, *Emily Sparrow, Frances Adams, Rose Forrester, 1965.*

Under that is the same looping handwriting that's covering the wall.

Your future contains dry bones. Your slow demise begins right when you hold the queen in the palm of one hand. Beware the bird, for it will betray you. And from that, there's no coming back. But daughters are the key to justice, find the right one and keep her close. All signs point toward your murder.

"The famous fortune," I say. "I wonder why she was so convinced it was true?"

I raise a finger to trace the words written on the wall, and it's then that I notice the handwritten marks next to some of the sentences. "She's ticking things off," I say. "Like a checklist."

Oliver crosses his arms while he looks at the wall. "Maybe those are the things that she thought came true."

"She's ticked off *Your slow demise begins right when you hold the queen in the palm of one hand*, and *Beware the bird, for it will betray you*. The ones about daughters and murder are left with question marks. But here—*Your future contains dry bones*. She's ticked that one too. And it looks more recent; it's a fresh thick Sharpie mark while the others are faded. Like she was convinced it came true, but only recently. What kind of bones could that mean?"

My brain starts to work through the fortune immediately. What kind of queen can you hold in the palm of one hand? My immediate thought is a coin—the queen's profile is on every single one. But that seems almost too commonplace.

I think there was a chessboard in the library, but why would Great Aunt Frances have one of those, if she was so superstitious about her fortune? If it were me, I'd want any palm-size queens far away from me.

Beware the bird, for it will betray you. My eyes land on the label of the photograph. Emily's last name is Sparrow. I wonder what kind of a betrayal there could have been, but there's no way I'll ever know without being able to ask Great Aunt Frances. I look at Mr. Gordon, who is standing at the smaller murder board. He gingerly reaches out a finger and touches Emily's photo.

I might not be able to ask Great Aunt Frances what the betrayal was, but I wonder if Mr. Gordon knows. The details of it might not matter, however. From my perspective, all that's important is that she saw things in that fortune coming true, the most recent one being *Your future contains dry bones.*

And then she either died of natural causes, or she was murdered.

My thoughts are cut short by a faint "Hello?" that echoes from somewhere else in the house, and Elva calls out, "In here!" We shuffle rather reluctantly back into the library, just as two paramedics make their way through the door. There's a woman who looks to be in her sixties, with blond roots growing out of dark purple dye, and a tall man about Mum's age. He might be a little younger, though, maybe late forties? He's lean, with dark curly hair that has no signs of gray in it, and his face has that windburned look that comes from spending a lot of time outdoors.

"Magda, Joe, thank you for coming. It's Frances," Mr. Gordon says, as he takes them over to where she's lying.

Seeing Great Aunt Frances's body a second time tips me over the edge and I start to feel the ground swim under my feet. I can tell that if I don't get outside I'm going to faint.

The paramedic named Joe feels for her pulse in a few places. "Yes, I'm afraid she's dead," he says gently. "Did you call the police when you phoned for us?"

Mr. Gordon's brow creases and he shakes his head. "It was Elva who called, and none of us understood she'd only asked for paramedics until you were already on your way. And in the upset of the situation, her point sounded like a good one—other than Frances's hands, which look to have been injured by the rose thorns, there's no sign of foul play. Were we wrong?" Mr. Gordon looks stricken. "Should the police be here?"

"We have to call them now that I've confirmed she's dead," Joe says. "It's protocol. But this looks like natural causes to me. Of course, an autopsy will make certain of that, and I'm sure Saxon will make quick work of it."

I swallow hard. Saxon? Frances's nephew is the coroner? I vaguely remember Elva saying something about him being tied up at an autopsy earlier. My hands are starting to feel numb. I have to get some air.

Joe notices as I reach out to steady myself on the window frame behind me, and he takes me by the elbow and leads me outside. I sink down on the stone steps in front of the big doors and put my head between my knees, taking in steady, slow breaths. It takes a minute, but eventually the dizziness subsides.

"I can get you some water, if you need it," he says. He's sitting next to me with his hands resting on his knees, looking out at the bright green of the lawns. Archie Foyle has stopped his hedge clipping and is nowhere in sight.

"I'll be okay now," I say. "Thanks, though."

"You should stay here. I'm going to pop in and help Magda if you're feeling better."

I nod, and he's gone.

Fifteen or so minutes later, two uniformed police officers arrive, but they're in and out quickly as I blink dazedly at the view from the steps of Gravesdown Hall. Soon after, I'm joined on the steps by Oliver and Mr. Gordon, though Elva takes her time and doesn't come out until the cloth-covered gurney is wheeled through the front door. We all look away, but Elva's following it like the funeral procession has already started.

"You're sure no one killed her?" I manage to ask weakly as the paramedics pass me.

"It doesn't look like it," Joe says. "Do any of you know who her next of kin is, so we can notify them?"

"Well, that would be Saxon, obviously," Elva says.

The paramedic with purple hair—Magda—cuts in before Mr. Gordon can speak. "Really, Elva? Because I'm pretty sure the whole village knows Frances chose her niece, Laura, to inherit, and that's been in place for years." The two women give each other icy stares, but then Magda's gaze snaps back up as Mr. Gordon clears his throat.

"Magda, before you attempt to call Laura, perhaps her daughter, Annie, should be the one to break the news about Frances?"

"I, um . . ." My voice holds the sandpaper scrape of disuse, even though I haven't been silent for very long.

Joe stands with the driver's side door of the ambulance

open, and it's like he's seeing me for the first time. "You're Laura's daughter?" he asks, and there's a pause that's longer than I expected. "Of course you are," he answers his own question. "Now that I look at you, I can see Laura all over your face. It's the hair—those curls are a dead giveaway." He smiles, but it's a little sad.

"I get that a lot."

"It's nice to meet you. I'm Joe Leroy," he says. He walks over to me and extends a hand, though his grip is a little weak. I shake it, wondering if I should repeat my name, even though he already knows it. "I knew Laura a bit, years ago." He's quiet for a moment, but then gives me a solemn look and says, "I'm sorry about your great aunt." He gets into the driver's seat and pulls down a radio receiver and says something I can't make out.

"You've had a bit of a shock," Magda says. "You should go back to the village and have some food. Or just a nice sit down. The hotel is a good place for that, and Joe's mum— Rose—owns it. She would probably like to meet you. Rose was a great friend of Frances's."

I think of the photograph, of the three of them linking arms—Great Aunt Frances, Emily Sparrow, and Rose. Rose is now the only surviving member of the trio.

Joe's attention is back on us, and his expression looks a little pained. "Please," he says, "if you do go over there, don't tell Mum about Frances just yet. I should be the one to tell her."

"Of course," I say.

Mr. Gordon jangles his keys inside his trouser pocket. "I need to get back to my office," he says quietly. "Annie, do you plan to stay in Castle Knoll for a while?"

I draw in a deep breath, taking in the sweeping gardens in front of me. Elva is already behind the wheel of her car,

starting the engine and looking like she's ready to be anywhere but here. Oliver is off in the distance talking on his
mobile and looking surprisingly cheerful given the grim experience we've all just had.

"Yeah," I reply finally, and with conviction. I have the
overwhelming sense that I have things to do here, regardless
of whatever inheritance issues there are now. I picture Great
Aunt Frances's murder board and find that I desperately
want to know who she really was, and what drove her obsession. "I think I'll see if the hotel has any rooms."

"Magda," Joe calls, starting up the ambulance, "we need
to get moving."

"Right," she says. She hops into the passenger seat and
nods to Joe. "It was nice to meet you, Annie. And I'm sorry
about Frances." The blue lights on the ambulance flash silently as they head back down the gravel drive.

Oliver gets in his car while still on his phone and doesn't
even bother to check if I need a lift back to the village. Outrage bubbles in the pit of my stomach, and I want to know
what his deal is. Something's going on with him. And whatever it is, it's on the other end of the line. Mr. Gordon and I
watch as Elva's car follows the ambulance down the drive,
with Oliver taking up the rear.

"Um, do you mind giving me a lift?"

Mr. Gordon's eyes crinkle at the edges as he smiles. "Of
course. I just need to lock the house back up."

We both pause, looking at the carved wooden doors. He
searches his pockets for the keys and comes up empty. "I'll
just be a moment, Annie," he says. "I must have left them in
the house somewhere."

"I'll help you look," I say. I can't think why, but I don't like
the idea of being outside alone, staring at Archie Foyle's
hedges. The whole estate feels menacing now.

We make our way back through the long entrance hall, through the echoey stone dining room, and into the library. The flowers are still scattered on the big desk at the center of the room, but everything else is so orderly that you'd never guess that only minutes ago a dead woman lay on the floor.

Mr. Gordon ducks into the little antechamber while I take one last look around. There's a small green leather-bound notebook sitting on the edge of the desk, and when I crack it open I notice the same spidery writing I saw on the walls in the little room. My eyes take in the words *Walt Gordon was up ahead, an open beer in one hand and the other catching Emily around the waist . . .*

It's a journal. The first page is dated *September 10, 1966.* I deliberate for a moment, then decide to slip it into my backpack. Technically I'm not stealing, if I'm supposed to be Great Aunt Frances's beneficiary. And even that small glimpse of the words inside tells me this book might give me context I don't have.

The messy bouquet on the desk grabs my attention again. Great Aunt Frances must have pulled half the contents from a nearby hedgerow to construct it. Wildflowers and lacy cow parsley mingle with long-stemmed white roses in a way that is, quite frankly, rather hideous.

The other arrangements, near the window, are done like something from a country living magazine. They all match, and the colors remind me of a sunset against pine trees, perfectly balanced.

I absent-mindedly pick at one of the pieces of foliage dripping off the flower arrangement on the desk. Someone has put the long-stemmed white roses that were on the floor back up there, and they sit on top of the stray bits of wildflowers scattered around.

The arrangement is oddly transfixing, probably just because it feels so *wrong*. This vase even has clover in it, and bright orange wild poppies glowing like neon balloons. Half of it falls limply over the side, especially the clover, which has no structure at all and is in such haphazard clumps that it weighs everything else down. Everything except the roses, which stand up in defiant spikes, their thorns glinting in the light through the window.

I look closer, and the thorns on the white roses look back at me with such a fierceness that I finally see what's wrong. The detail that has been nagging at me since I first saw the arrangement.

I hear the jangle of keys as Mr. Gordon comes back through the small door, but I don't look up.

"Something's wrong with the roses," I say.

"What do you mean?" He reaches over to pluck out a rose.

"Stop!" I lean forward and grab his wrist before he can touch it.

"What?"

"The roses . . . there are . . . are those needles?" I say, my voice not sounding like my own. "There's something metal coming out of the thorns. All of them."

Mr. Gordon's breath comes out in a steady stream as he leans in, curses mingling in the rush of air. He's looking at the arrangement as if it's suddenly sprouted tentacles. "I . . . yes. They are. I don't know how it's possible, but those are needles." He runs a hand though his few remaining wisps of hair.

I pick up one long stem very carefully. When I hold it up to the light I can see how carefully the tiny sharp metal pieces have been inserted through each thorn so that they come out at the ends in perfect alignment. I swallow hard. We definitely need a detective now.

CHAPTER

8

DETECTIVE ROWAN CRANE IS SITTING IN THE BACK corner of the small office of Castle Knoll Police Station, drinking coffee in long sips and staring out the window. Mr. Gordon gave me his name and told me where to find him before he rushed back to his office.

It's early afternoon, and there's a lazy feel to the atmosphere in the station. Aside from a rather snippy receptionist, the detective is the only one here. Since he hasn't noticed me yet, I quickly take stock of him. He's dressed casually, in dark jeans and a T-shirt with a light brown blazer over it that doesn't quite work. He looks to be in his early thirties and has a mess of dark hair that would look unruly if it weren't for the neatly trimmed beard balancing it out. It makes him look rugged in a fashionable way, but he gives the overall impression of someone who does just enough in the mornings to get out the door.

He turns and notices me, and I'm instantly treated to an assessing look of his own. It's the kind that lasts only a second but seems to take in details you don't mean to give away. The detective has deep brown eyes with surprisingly thick lashes, and his focus moves in a quick pulse from my messy blond bun to the pen stains on my fingers to the plastic carrier bag they're clutching, and finally lands on the needle-studded roses poking out of it.

None of his attention is judgmental, but I feel like I'm being cataloged as evidence before I even have a chance to say why I'm here. The palms of my hands start to itch, and I distractedly wipe one hand on my jeans.

"Can I help you?" he asks. He's got a resonant voice, which gives off an air of authority that I instinctively like. And then my guard snaps firmly into place. Whenever I meet someone like this (which is rare, because who has a quietly commanding presence these days, outside of classical literature?), I make it a point to be careful. Just because a fluke of genetics makes someone sound reassuring doesn't mean you should be reassured by them.

"Detective Crane?" I ask, even though his name is on a little rectangular plaque on his desk.

"That's me." His eyes dart to my hands again as I switch the carrier bag to the other hand.

"My name's Annie Adams, and I'm here because my great aunt has just died, and I found something strange that I think you should see."

The chair opposite his desk scoots out seemingly of its own accord, and it takes me a moment to realize he's nudged it my way with his foot. "Perhaps you should start at the beginning. What's your great aunt's name? And when did she die?"

I shrug off my backpack and perch on the edge of the chair, which is one of those uncomfortable plastic ones. "We only just found her a couple of hours ago?" I make it a question, because time feels as if it's running in strange circles.

"The paramedics took her away, but a couple of police officers came too."

He looks thoughtful for a second, and then picks up a pen, only to tap it absently on a stack of papers in front of him. "There wasn't a call that came through this station," he says slowly. "But I suppose the paramedics might have alerted the police in Little Dimber, if they were nearby and between calls." He uncaps the pen and writes something down, but his expression doesn't give much away.

"The paramedics said it doesn't look like there's anything suspicious about her death, and . . ." I stop and try to turn my explanation into less of a ramble, but it doesn't really work. "I mean, Great Aunt Frances was rather elderly. Frances Adams, that's my great aunt."

His pen falls from his hand when I mention Great Aunt Frances's name.

"Oh God," he says, leaning back slightly. "I'm very sorry. I liked Frances, even if she tended to phone about every little thing. She was interesting."

"*Interesting* is one way of putting it," the receptionist barks from her desk near the door.

"That's enough, Samantha," the detective says evenly. "Frances has just died, and her great niece is here. Have some respect, please."

Samantha swivels around in her chair—one of those rolling office ones—and scoots it forward a few feet but doesn't get up. She's got an immaculate gray perm and doesn't look much younger than Great Aunt Frances.

"Respect? Like Frances had for us? That woman wasted more police time and resources than children pulling pranks on Halloween."

"Samantha." There's a warning in Crane's voice now, but Samantha is apparently not the type to care.

"Remember when Frances phoned to tell us she was being held at gunpoint? But it turned out her gardener had pruned a tree into an odd shape and the shadow of it looked like a man with a rifle? A *shadow*, Rowan. A car was stolen in the town center while half the PCs were up at the Gravesdown estate dealing with a *shadow*."

"Samantha—" Detective Crane winces, but Samantha just keeps going.

"No, it needs to be said! Her relatives should know what her mad fixations cost this village! And you should be on my side, *Detective Crane*, given how she treated you."

"Great Aunt Frances mistreated the detective?" I blink in surprise. "You'd think with how worried she was about being murdered, she'd have wanted to keep him on her side."

"She had a thing against bird names," Samantha snaps. "She was awful to the whole Crane family because of it."

"Oh, right," I mutter, thinking of her fortune: *Beware the bird, for it will betray you.*

Detective Crane pulls a hand down his jawline and pauses as if he's about to give Samantha a piece of his mind. But a businesslike expression settles over his features, and he turns away from her instead.

Samantha shrugs and wheels the chair back to her desk.

"Can you tell me what happened, and the names of everyone present? You said *we* when you mentioned finding her."

I give him the exact details of my morning, and I find that telling it like a story from a book makes me feel more removed from it. It's like I'm someone else, looking through a window, watching another Annie find her great aunt dead on the floor of her fancy house.

I stop short of explaining the bouquet, and instead I hand the whole mess in the plastic bag to the detective, not wanting to look at the needles again. As I do, my palms throb. For a quick moment my mind goes directly to Great Aunt Frances's fortune—words about demise linked to holding things in the palm of one hand come to mind—before my thoughts shuffle forward and it hits me.

"Oh, *shit*," I hiss. I don't remember touching the roses. In fact, I know I didn't. I was really careful.

Wasn't I?

But when I look at my hand, I can see small blisters forming across my palms and between a couple of my fingers. I definitely touched *something.* I swear again, this time with more conviction.

Detective Crane leans forward, concern creasing his forehead.

"That looks nasty," he mutters so quietly it could almost have been to himself.

I rush to get the rest of the words out. "There are needles in those roses! She was clutching them when she died, and her hands were all cut up from them! It's why I came here!"

Detective Crane is annoyingly calm as he reaches into a drawer and comes out with a surgical glove, snapping it on like a doctor would. I feel like I'm half crime scene, half emergency room patient as he gently takes my wrist and tilts it toward him, examining my palm. With his other hand, he gingerly lifts the bouquet out of the bag, using another surgical glove pinched between his bare fingers. He places the flowers on the desk and turns back to my hand.

"Did you hear what I said?" My voice rises, and the squeak of the wheels on Samantha's desk chair make me want to run out of the police station. I get the impression that she's about to accuse me of *causing a scene*, like the mad aunt who came before me. This makes me even more determined to be taken goddamned seriously. "My Great Aunt Frances is dead," I shout, "found clutching roses full of needles, which I've somehow also touched! Why is no one calling an ambulance right now?"

"Because I recognize a plant in that bouquet *and* the rash you've got," Crane says evenly.

"Yes, I think we all recognize roses and cow parsley," I snap.

Detective Crane looks carefully at me, still holding my wrist lightly between his thumb and forefinger. He looks back down and angles my hand under the light of his desk lamp.

"That's not cow parsley," he says, jutting his chin toward the mess of plants. "It's a weed that irritates the skin, and Castle Knoll has an epidemic of it every summer. We'll get you to a doctor anyway, for some antihistamine cream to help clear it up."

"What exactly is it then?" I ask. I'm still not entirely calm, but he's so certain about all this that I feel my shoulders start to unclench.

He treats me to another assessing look. I can see him registering how pale I am, and how my hands shake slightly as they sit palms up on his desk. "It doesn't matter," he says dismissively.

"Would it matter to Great Aunt Frances?" I ask coolly. I can tell when someone's hiding information from me so that I don't panic. I'm annoyed, but I hold on to the feeling because it's helping me think more clearly.

He doesn't say anything; he just snaps off the desk lamp and gets up from his chair.

"Great Aunt Frances spent her whole life convinced someone was going to kill her, and then she's found dead with *this* on her desk?" The words tumble out of me; I'm full of frustration that I've just handed a detective a bouquet riddled with needles and some kind of skin-irritating weed, and he's not really making much of it. "So are you going to investigate the bouquet?" Detective Crane is leading me out of the police station now and gives a curt nod to Samantha as we head through the door.

"A family of amateur sleuths, aren't you?" he mumbles. "When was the last time you spoke with your great aunt?" he asks, not answering my question.

I don't want to admit that I've never actually spoken to her. "I'm here from London to attend a meeting with Great Aunt Frances. Walter Gordon spoke with her on the phone not long before we went to her house—he was probably the last person to speak with her."

Crane doesn't say anything; he just furrows his brow and nods. I try not to look at my palms, but I can't help it, and I feel myself sway a little.

Crane has me by the elbow and leads me gently down the twisting little alleyways of Castle Knoll. The sandy stones of the buildings are all lit up in the golden glow of late-afternoon light, but I'm too busy talking to pay much attention.

Even though he's not given me all the facts about whatever it is that I've touched, Crane isn't making me feel fragile—the opposite, in fact. He's quietly listening to me air my theories, playing devil's advocate here and there.

"I saw the arrangements Great Aunt Frances made. They were stunning. Like professional wedding flowers."

"Well, she did flowers for a lot of weddings in Castle Knoll. And the arrangements for the church every week," Crane says.

"Yes. Mr. Gordon mentioned that," I say. "We saw a bunch of arrangements lined up to be delivered to the church. But the bouquet that had those roses in it looked messy, as if it was pulled from a hedgerow. I think someone sent it to her knowing she'd take it apart."

"Unless her death occurred while she was in the act of putting it together herself," he says lightly. "You assume the bouquet was *for* Frances. What if it was *from* her? Intended for someone else?"

I sputter. "Do you really think anyone would send something that sinister to someone's wedding? Or to *church*?" I ask.

"I don't know, maybe someone there made her angry. Frances didn't forgive easily," he adds.

I file that information away for later; it feels significant.

"What did she have against the church?" I ask.

"She certainly had a past with the vicar," Crane says. He winces, as if he couldn't help saying it but understands too late that he shouldn't have.

"A *past?* As in—"

"Forget I said anything, Annie. We're nearly at the surgery."

"Had this past recently come back to haunt her, do you think?"

"I said drop it, Annie, it was forever ago." His voice has a mild heat to it, and the fact that he's issued me a command makes me even more eager to ignore it.

"Forever ago? Like . . . 1965 forever ago? Back when she got her fortune told?" The wheels in my mind are turning furiously now. "Or a month ago? Some kind of argument over flowers got blown out of proportion, and then . . ." I try to think of a way Great Aunt Frances arguing with the vicar could be related to dry bones and give her a reason to tick off that part of her fortune, but I draw a blank.

"Like 1965 forever ago. I have a family member who knew Frances back then, so I know what I'm talking about when I ask you politely to leave this alone." He stops for a second, and the look he gives me is so stern that I shrink back from him a little. "And before you get any ideas—and I can tell that you will, you're the type—leave the poor vicar alone. John's been through enough."

Interesting, I think. And I have a new name to consider if I'm riddling out the mystery of these flowers. *John.*

I look away, and it's only then that I notice we've arrived at an unimposing doorway painted a cheerful green. It's set in a terrace of stone houses that look so ancient they must have been built when the castle was still whole. Detective Crane raps his knuckles on the door, and even his knock sounds highly professional. There's a sign next to the door announcing the doctor's surgery, headed up by a Dr. Esi Owusu.

A woman in a lab coat answers the door. "Esi," Detective Crane says apologetically, "do you have time to see an unexpected patient?"

The doctor looks slightly annoyed but gives me the type of sympathetic glance that decent medical professionals can muster even on their worst of days. "I suppose," she says, beckoning me in. "I don't normally see patients on Tuesdays; it's paperwork day. But I've been rushed around, suddenly needing to do urgent autopsies and all that." She gives Crane a pointed glance, and some electric spark of village knowledge passes between them. I feel my eyes widen. Why would a local GP be doing an urgent autopsy? Surely this couldn't be Great Aunt Frances? Certainly it's far too quick?

"Please, Esi," Crane says. "I really don't want to have to take her up to the emergency room. Just quickly?" My hands are pulsing with pain now, and the rash is spreading.

"All right," she says. She opens the door wider and waves us through. "Now, what is it that's got you needing a doctor so urgently?" Dr. Owusu's voice is gentle but steady. My mouth feels dry all of a sudden. The fluorescent lights of the doctor's surgery just make my head swim more, and the pain in my hands is playing an echo game with my rising panic.

The rustle of the plastic bag sounds far away as Crane carefully extracts the bouquet. Dr. Owusu prods at it, then says something to Crane in a low voice.

I hear his resonant voice say the word *hemlock*, but my head swims. I feel faint and unnatural and strange, before my bones seem to melt and an arm pulls me into a chair.

The word *hemlock* echoes again before everything goes dark.

CHAPTER

9

The Castle Knoll Files, September 21, 1966

"I COULD ASK YOU WHAT YOU'RE ALL DOING HERE," Rutherford said, and his eyes fell on each of us in turn. He looked at Emily, still holding Walt's beer, Rose with her cigarette, and me with John's arm draped across my shoulders—it was as though he could see through all of us. "But I suspect I already know." His mouth twisted into a small smile, as if he was thinking of a private joke.

He was younger than I expected, but then, according to town gossip, he'd only be twenty-three now. He was broad-shouldered, and considerably taller than any of us. I couldn't see his eyes clearly, but his jawline had a formidable cut to it, and I imagined if he were pressed into a fist fight, he could take a surprising number of blows before emerging victorious. I wondered why he'd already been married, but then again he was handsome and wealthy, and finding someone to marry isn't hard when you're both of those things. And I suppose he was saddled with his nephew and a title at barely twenty years old. I wouldn't want to be alone in that either.

Emily straightened her shoulders, not bothering to hide the beer, but I could tell it was false confidence. Her eyes darted meaningfully to me, then back to Lord Gravesdown. She looked him in the eye, and I swear I saw her shake her head slightly. I felt strangely on display, like there was an in-joke floating around and I was the punchline.

His eyes settled on Emily for a long moment. "And who might you be?" he asked.

Emily made a small noise of surprise but covered it with a step forward and a smile. "Sir, I'm Emily, and this is Walt. That's Rose, and John, and John's girlfriend." She pointed to all of us in turn, and I was miffed that I only got the title of "John's girlfriend."

"I see. And what are you doing on my estate late at night?"

Emily cleared her throat, and everything was suddenly a perfect performance. "We're very sorry, but you know how it is, right? No one in the village understands how harmless our fun is." She cast her eyes down for a second, then brought them up and looked straight at Lord Gravesdown. She took two more steps away from Walt and tilted her head a little as she walked so that her hair fell over one shoulder, and she brushed a strand of it behind her ear with a nervous look on her face. Emily is anything but nervous, but she's very good at getting out of scrapes by pretending she is. By my guess, we were possibly a minute or two away from false tears and promises of attending church.

He cut her off with a palm in the air. Em let her face crumple a little further, but her audience had lost interest.

"Stick to the wooded areas and the Grecian temple ruin on the eastern side of the estate, and don't leave any mess behind," he said. I saw one corner of his mouth twitch upward, and I thought maybe the gaps between us weren't all that large. Had he come here with friends to party in recent years, before he'd had so many responsibilities? Otherwise, I couldn't see a reason why he

didn't just order us to leave then and there. Perhaps we represented a past he didn't get to have.

"Stay away from the formal gardens and any of the open
space near the house, and you are not to go near the abandoned
farmhouse for any reason. The waterwheel is broken, for one,
and it's extremely dangerous. I don't want to be pulling any
bodies out of the River Dimber." He turned and gave me a long
stare, and I felt John stiffen his shoulders. "Saxon tends to
wander." He gave his nephew a stern glance. "So if you see him
again, please bring him back to the house. You—What's your
name?"

I had to clear my throat before I could mutter a small
"Frances."

"Frances," he repeated. He gave me a soft smile, and I got the
impression that he appreciated me not shouting at his nephew
for being a demon-child earlier. Blood flushed to my cheeks as I
remembered that we'd been talking about Rutherford's wife only
seconds before he'd emerged from the woods, and there was
enough moonlight where I was standing that I knew he could see
me blushing.

His expression changed, and his smile became cavalier—the
kind of smile that comes from someone who knows just how
much power they have, and how to use it. He crooked a finger at
me, beckoning me closer. I was tempted to lean farther into John.
Suddenly everything felt like a trap, but I walked closer to Lord
Gravesdown anyway.

"Frances," he said, more quietly this time. "Do you like riddles?"

I was so taken aback at the absurdity of his question that I let
out a small indignant snort. What was he, some kind of sphinx
standing guard before his fallen columns, testing my worth? If
there were ruins here, they'd be like all Grecian temples erected by
aristocrats in gardens—fake. This whole interaction felt off to me.

My heart sped up as I was overtaken with a sudden boldness.

"No," I said. "I don't like riddles. Outside of myth, they're just an excuse for people to broadcast false cleverness."

A laugh erupted from him, and he threw his head back in amusement. When he looked at me again, it was with steady approval.

"I like you," he said.

Emily scoffed in the background. Maybe she was annoyed that her theatrics weren't as entertaining to Lord Gravesdown as my defiance, or maybe it was just simple jealousy that I was suddenly his focus.

There was a long pause, and I realized I was supposed to say something. I didn't know if he was complimenting me or merely speaking his thoughts, but I said, "Thank you, Mr., um, sir. And thank you for not sending us away, or being angry," I added hastily.

His smile broadened and his straight white teeth gleamed in the moonlight. "Please, call me Ford." He looked at me so steadily that for a moment I half believed Emily's stories about a ruby knife and the River Dimber. It was just a look, but I felt hunted.

Emily made her way into the gap between us, and his attention shifted. "Don't worry, Ford," she said his name easily, as if they'd been friends for years. I was still going to call him sir if I ever saw him again after that night. "I know we might seem a little wild," Emily continued, abandoning her nervous mask as easily as she'd put it on, "but we're really very respectful."

He didn't reply to her; he just nodded thoughtfully. "Come, Saxon," he said finally.

As Saxon passed Emily, I heard him whisper something, his quick words hissing through the air. "Be careful," he said. "We like wild things." Then he grinned and followed his uncle back through the bare trees.

None of us moved for what felt like an eternity. Finally Emily's laughter exploded out in all directions, and the ice that had settled over the moment shattered.

"What a weird family!" she said.

Rose bounded a little up the path ahead, her chin darting this way and that, and she finally came back looking a bit calmer.

"They're definitely gone, right?" Walt said.

"They're gone," Rose answered. After our encounter with the Gravesdowns, she looked a little more like herself. It was as if our having a small adventure together woke her up a bit.

I admit, I felt more alive too. It was a narrow escape, a mystery, and a free pass all rolled into one.

John hitched one strap of his backpack up a little higher and grinned at me while the others whispered about what had just happened. He took my hand again, and we started down a small dirt track in the trees, opposite where Saxon and his uncle had gone.

"So where's this Grecian temple ruin then, Em?" I called behind me. John was walking onward with sure steps, leading me through the dark by the hand.

I heard Emily snort out a laugh, and she said, "Follow the path to the right, John!" But John had already headed that way.

Finally we reached a clearing, and the moonlight was so bright that I could see why someone had chosen to build a secret structure there. Woods closed in on all sides, creating a screen of pine and birch, but if you looked up, the sky and the stars looked huge. It was a clear night, and I could see the Big Dipper.

"Get your head out of the sky, Frances," Walt teased. "Let's blow off some steam." I heard the hiss of another beer being opened, and looked to see Emily and Walt settling themselves on a fallen Grecian pillar.

All around us were mock ruins—stones placed carefully by some garden designer to make it feel like a mysterious feature that was really just a seating area in disguise. "So what do we all want to do?" Walt asked as the smell of his joint filled my nose.

Emily's eyes narrowed as she took a drag. "The obvious

choice. You and I are going to smoke, Rose is going to sulk, and John and Frances are going to sneak off and have sex."

"Oh, way to kill the mood, Em!" Walt elbowed her and laughed.

John's jaw tightened just a fraction, but he didn't respond to her. It was just like Emily to cheapen everything this way. She'll take things that are supposed to be unsaid, pull them out into the light of day, and suck the heart out of them by making everything seem like a joke. But I wasn't going to let my relationship be a farce.

I squeezed John's hand again and set my shoulders back. I found my best smug expression and said, "Well, whatever we get up to, at least we won't be wasting time with you losers." It wasn't the most cutting reply, but it was the best I could muster.

But Emily's posture tightened, like I'd declared war. A wicked smile crawled across her face.

"Don't worry, Frances," Emily said softly, almost cooing. "I know it must be hard being the last virgin of the bunch. Good ol' John's got experience, though, so you're in great hands."

"Don't listen to her, Frannie," John whispered. "Let's just leave, we don't need her shit."

I gave him a long, slow kiss, just to make it seem like I couldn't care less what Emily said. And he led me off down another path into the dark.

We walked in silence for a minute or two, John leading the way. His backpack was bulging with the blanket and the bottle of wine I knew he'd stuffed in there. I hadn't told Emily about our plans, and I doubt John had, but I suppose we were a bit obvious. We certainly couldn't go to either of our parents' houses, and neither of us had a car. Walt had driven us all here, parking a mile up the road so we could walk and sneak in under the weak spot in the fence Emily had found.

In my head it had seemed romantic, but as we walked over

76

dead branches and looked for a place in the woods that wasn't studded with brambles or wet leaves, it started to feel like a means to an end. I swore under my breath. That was just what Emily was trying to get me thinking.

"I'm starting to really hate her," John said, as if he were in my thoughts.

"Me too," I said. Neither of us talked about it any further, but it was kind of nice to agree on that.

We finally found a sheltered spot under a massive pine tree, where the ground was soft with fallen pine needles and the branches swept low enough to hide us. As soon as we were under the shelter of the tree, I felt the tension leave my clenched jaw. This place was hidden and safe. Perfect.

John must have felt the same, because he smiled at me and kissed me, and then opened the backpack and spread the blanket out. He pulled the cork from the wine bottle—half-empty already and from his parents' cupboard, I suspected—and took a long drink before passing it to me.

I laughed as red wine dripped down my chin when I took too big a gulp, and he wiped the drip with a finger before setting the bottle aside. When he kissed me again he was serious, and our movements became more urgent. I tried not to think of Emily's words as I noticed how confident John's hands were with the buttons of my blouse, or how he'd undone his belt so quickly I hadn't noticed him doing it. All the fumbling was from me, and I hated Emily all over again when I felt embarrassed that I somehow wouldn't be good enough for John, that my nerves would make me seem immature and then neither of us would enjoy it.

And I hated her for making me think of this in a new way—it became a finish line, not the slow pleasure I'd imagined. I just wanted to pass the milestone and have this done with.

John's kisses went down my neck and into the unbuttoned cavern of my blouse, and I finally started to relax. I looked at the pine branches sweeping down next to us, and the earthy smell all around us made me decide that Emily couldn't touch this. My eyes were starting to close, and a sigh of pleasure finally fluttered out of me, my fingers twining in John's hair. But a pale streak through the branches snapped them open again.

"Shit," I said. "John, it's that kid."

John's face surfaced and I closed my blouse with a flush of feelings—anger, shame, disappointment, need.

John was still hovering over me, belt flapping but everything else still tucked away. I hastily buttoned my blouse, but it was clear what this scene was about. Saxon wasn't moving, which made the whole thing even creepier. Why didn't he run away? He just stared at us through the branches, his face impassive as I put on my wool coat.

As John turned away and fastened his belt in quick angry movements, I could tell that something in his usual calm demeanor was starting to boil over. His shoulders were suddenly tight, his jaw set, and he stood up with such force that I worried he might actually go after Saxon.

"Get out of here, Saxon," I yelled, my voice halfway between exasperated and worried. Creep or not, he was still a little boy.

That seemed to break the spell, but as Saxon turned and ran, John ran after him. I hastily jumped up to follow, tripping over the blanket and sloshing the dregs of the wine bottle over it as I fell.

I sprang up again quickly, the brambles leaving thorns in my palms, as I heard Saxon scream through the trees ahead of me.

Not ten feet away from where John and I had been lying, the line of trees abruptly ended and gave way to the rolling lawns of the estate. I hadn't understood how close we were to all that open space, and it made me shudder to think that my intimacy with John was potentially so exposed. I hated everything about the Gravesdown estate in that moment. It was a twisted, seductive place that I never wanted to see again. I hugged my arms to my chest and hunched my neck farther into my wool coat, trying to disappear. But I could hear Saxon crying now, so I hurried forward to where I saw him lying on the grass, John looming over him.

"What did you do?" I shouted to John as I ran up behind him.

John turned, his hands in the air. "Nothing, Frannie, I swear! I was just going to give him a telling off, and he tripped!"

I looked at Saxon, who was hugging his knees to his chest now, his cheeks shining with tears in the moonlight. One of the knees in his trousers had torn through, and I could see he'd skinned it. I reached out a hand to help him up, and he took it. I didn't feel a whole lot of sympathy for him—he was such a strange boy—but seeing him crying with a skinned knee made me wonder if he was just a child who needed better things to do with his time. He should have been skinning his knees climbing trees in the summer sun with friends, not skulking around in the woods on his elusive uncle's estate.

I thought about how horrible it must have been to lose his parents and his grandfather in a car accident so young. I hoped he didn't know about the village gossip.

"Come on," I said to him. "We'll walk you back up to the house."

Saxon sniffed and clutched my arm. "I'm not going with him," he said, narrowing his eyes at John. "He pushed me!"

"That's a lie and you know it!" John spat back. I trusted what John said, but I really didn't feel like being a referee between him and Saxon. I was tired, and my emotions about all this—John and me missing our moment, Emily and her twisted words, even the mystery of what was bothering Rose lately—felt like they were right under the surface, waiting to spill out in every direction.

I sighed. "Come on then," I said to Saxon. "John, I'll meet you back with the others once I've delivered Saxon home."

John caught my elbow and pulled me away from Saxon. "No,

79

Frances," he whispered. He leaned in and spoke low in my ear so we weren't overheard. "I saw the way Lord Gravesdown looked at you. This whole thing has a stink to it. I don't like it."

I whispered back, "I'm just taking him to the house. I won't go in."

John looked worried, then angry again. "I'm going to follow behind you." I felt like I didn't recognize John, and for a second I really wondered if he'd actually pushed Saxon.

My anger flared, and the strangeness of the evening finally tipped me over the edge. I looked at John then—really looked at him—and it occurred to me that the Gravesdown family weren't the only people acting oddly tonight. "You'll do nothing of the kind," I said, keeping my voice even.

"Frances, I—"

I cut him off with a glare. "Something's going on with you," I said. "Emily's comments earlier . . ."

"Don't let her get to you! You know how she is." He took a step forward and lightly took my hand. Saxon was watching us from under a nearby tree, his bright eyes suddenly clear of all tears. He now looked like the type of boy who would throw a stone into a flock of pigeons, just because.

I closed my eyes for a second, and let the breath leave my lungs in a slow stream. I probably was being too sensitive; it's a constant problem with me. I'm the person who believes in fortune-tellers, for Christ's sake. John was right. Emily could wind me up far too easily, because I let her.

"I'm sorry if I'm being overprotective," John said, "but the thought of you alone with either of them—the uncle or the nephew—makes me so worried."

I kissed him quickly and said, "I'll be fine. Just . . . show me you believe I can look after myself by waiting with the others? I don't know what's going on with Saxon, but I'm tired and I want to make sure he's safely tucked away at his house."

John hesitated, rubbing one hand on the back of his neck.

"John," I said, when he refused to look at me, "you're not my dad!"

Finally he nodded. "I'll meet you back at the temple ruins, with the others."

"Thank you."

I walked up the path toward where Saxon stood. "Let's be quick about it," I said to Saxon. "It's cold, and honestly, I want to go home."

We walked in silence for a good minute—Saxon Gravesdown isn't the sort of person who makes silence feel friendly. I also had the guilt of those moments with John hanging over me, and anger at having been watched.

"You shouldn't spy on people," I said eventually, as Saxon and I walked across the lawn. "And whatever you saw, it wasn't something that children—"

"Oh, I know all about the birds and the bees," he said. "But I did you a favor. I know you think I'm a creep, but your boyfriend's worse."

"Excuse me?" I sputtered.

"He probably told you that you aren't safe coming to the house with me. But really he just doesn't want you talking to me."

"That's ridiculous," I said. We were nearing the house, heading for a back door with brightly lit stained-glass windows on either side of it.

Saxon shrugged. "Believe what you want. I'm just trying to help." He turned the handle on the door and looked over his shoulder. "Come on then, Uncle Ford wants to speak with you."

CHAPTER

10

WHEN I COME TO, CRANE IS GONE AND DR. OWUSU IS handing me a paper cup filled with cold water.

"There, you're starting to look a bit better," she says. Her voice is warm, with the smallest hint of a West African accent. She's probably in her mid-forties, and when I look around I notice that her surgery is immaculate, with just the right touches of comfort to make it feel personal. The magazines look new and there's a TAKE ONE, LEAVE ONE shelf of used books that boasts some rather good titles. A box of children's toys sits beneath a fish tank where goldfish reflect the overhead lights in flashes of copper. I focus on the trickle of the filter, and it helps me shake off my sudden exhaustion.

"I'm sorry," I say weakly. "But did I hear the detective say *hemlock?*"

"You're going to be fine," Dr. Owusu says. "It seems that you did touch a bunch of hemlock—it was in that bouquet you brought to Rowan to investigate. But it's like he told you, hemlock just causes skin irritation when touched, and the rash is easily dealt with."

Relief rolls through me and I nod slowly. My limbs all feel drained. That's the thing with panic attacks—I feel totally depleted afterward. I should probably find a good therapist.

Dr. Owusu has a tube of some kind of cream and is rubbing it into my palms. "Hydrocortisone cream," she explains when I look at it and bite my lip.

"I thought hemlock was really poisonous," I say. "You know, Socrates and all that."

"It is if you ingest it," Dr. Owusu says. "Or if it gets into your bloodstream somehow. But you'll be fine; you've only touched it. It happens with surprising frequency in the summer. Hemlock isn't that common, but it does grow wild in the area." Dr. Owusu pauses and then adds, "I'm very sorry for your loss," and pats the back of my hand lightly.

"Thank you," I say, and I feel almost fraudulent, having not known Great Aunt Frances personally. I don't deserve the creases of concern that have formed on Dr. Owusu's forehead. But if there's one thing I *have* learned about my great aunt in my brief time in Castle Knoll, it's that she'd be outraged at being murdered. And who wouldn't be? But she was hyperfocused on exactly this inevitability, so it feels like I'm doing her justice when I bring my mind back to that particular puzzle.

"Hemlock is only deadly in your bloodstream," I murmur. "What if the needles themselves weren't poisoned, but whoever put the needles there did it so that Great Aunt Frances would cut her hands, and the hemlock would get into her bloodstream? Although . . . wouldn't she have been able to tell the difference between hemlock and cow parsley?"

"Probably not actually," Dr. Owusu mused. "She only arranged flowers; she didn't grow or pick them. From what I understand, her gardeners kept her in constant supply of fresh-cut flowers, and I doubt anyone at the Gravesdown estate would ever let any weeds pop up there. Cow parsley *or* hemlock."

I'm quiet for a minute, thinking. Dr. Owusu knows an awful lot about Great Aunt Frances's flower arranging. Maybe this is an "everyone knows everything in a tight-knit community" sort of thing? But she's perceptive and catches my thoughts before I even voice the question.

"Frances did the funeral flowers when we buried my late father," she says. "She was very compassionate, and talking to her about the arrangements sort of took my mind off my grief for a moment." Dr. Owusu sighs. "A lot of people in the village will tell you stories about how bizarre Frances was, and . . . there *was* that side to her. I had every reason to dislike her, with how often she called me in a panic over some murder plot or other."

"I understand that was a habit of hers. A woman named Samantha at the police station had a lot to say about that," I add.

"Those of us in, shall we say, murder-adjacent professions got a lot of calls from Frances. Myself, several individuals at the police station, Magda and Joe, who are paramedics—"

"Yes, I just met them, when . . ." I trail off.

Dr. Owusu nods. "The funny thing is, Frances actually expanded my knowledge of local and household poisons greatly. Don't look at me like that." She gives me a shy smile. "I know how that sounds, but when Frances used to call me, it was because she was worried she'd ingested something toxic someone had given her. I spent so many hours examining her for different symptoms at her request—lead poisoning, poisoning by bleach, fertilizer, and pesticide. She once thought there was hand sanitizer in her wine, but it was just an old vintage that was corked. Anyway, there was an incident when Frances thought someone had slipped one of those tiny single-cell lithium batteries into her food, and I was ready to finally lose my patience with her. But we went through all the symptoms of having swallowed one, got her to the hospital, had her X-rayed, and found it was just very bad heartburn. Probably from stress."

"That sounds frustrating," I say.

"It was, but I would never turn a patient away just because they have a history of this type of behavior. And that incident ended up saving my niece's life. The very next day, I was at my sister's house, and her one-year-old was suddenly very ill. There was no reason to suspect she'd swallowed a lithium battery, and the thing with ingesting those is you don't have much time. They are deadly very, very quickly. Maybe it was just because my mind was still immersed in Frances's worries, or some instinct, but we rushed my niece to urgent care and were able to save her life because I insisted they check to see if she'd swallowed one of those batteries. And it turned out that she had. I'm not superstitious, but something clicked for me that day. I understood how scared Frances was, and how few friends she had. The least I could do was continue to believe her, while the rest of the village whispered behind her back."

"Wow," I breathe. Some of the tiredness is leaving me. "I'm sorry to hear about your niece, but I'm glad she's okay."

Dr. Owusu draws herself up, as if her thoughts have been floating around the room and it is time she made them behave.

"I can see you're worried about those flowers," she says. "But please, you can trust Rowan and me to handle this. I had an agreement with Frances that when she died, I'd be the one to perform her autopsy, and that it would be done as soon as possible after her death was declared."

"That sounds like a strange arrangement," I say slowly.

"But from what you've told me, she trusted you, when she didn't trust many people."

"I know it sounds strange," the doctor admits. "But . . ." she trails off, not wanting to say more.

"She was making significant changes to her will when this happened. And I think there's been foul play," I say. I want to trust Dr. Owusu, and knowing that Great Aunt Frances trusted her helps me make that leap. Although this is Dr. Owusu *telling me* that my great aunt trusted her. But still, something about the way the doctor talks about Frances feels honest to me.

"Well, all I'll say is that Frances said it was imperative that her body not be sent to the coroner. A conflict of interest, she said. And I found that I agreed with her on that."

"Saxon's the coroner," I said. "Isn't he?"

"Yes." Her voice is quiet, and she's not looking at me. Dr. Owusu finishes with the cream and sits back in her chair. She reaches for some gauze and medical tape and patches up my palms until my blisters are well-hidden.

"When will you have the results of the autopsy?"

"It usually takes a few days," she says after a long pause. "There are things that need to be processed in the lab at the hospital; I don't have the facilities here to run certain tests. But if there's not a backlog at the lab, it's possible those results will be back as soon as tomorrow. And before you ask, I'm not at liberty to discuss my findings. Not until I can make my report. And if there are any signs of foul play"—she gives me a meaningful look—"that report will go directly to Detective Crane."

"Is there any way you can update me too? As her next of kin?"

"I'm not sure you're listed as next of kin, Annie. She might not have updated her records. I'll check for you, though, and get back to you." She chews her bottom lip when she sees my shoulders sag. "But I *can* tell you that you're going to get a call from Walter Gordon soon. Or perhaps your mother is. I'm not familiar with your family situation."

The door opens before I can reply, and I recognize Magda the paramedic breezing in. "Hi, Dr. Owusu. I had an extra question after my appointment this morning. Do you mind if I pick your brain?"

"No, come in," Dr. Owusu says. "Annie, you should be completely fine. Come back if it doesn't clear up in a day or so, and keep applying the cream as per the instructions on the tube." Dr. Owusu takes the tube of cream and puts it in a small white paper bag and hands it to me.

"Thanks," I say. Magda gives me a weak wave and I turn back to Dr. Owusu. "I thought you didn't see patients on Tuesdays," I say. "When Detective Crane knocked on your door, you said you kept Tuesdays for doing paperwork."

"Oh." She looks at Magda and then back to me. "I make exceptions for other health professionals," she says quickly. Her smile turns strangely tight around her eyes.

There's nothing more I can say without wading into someone else's private medical issues, so I head for the door. Dr. Owusu leads Magda into one of the practice rooms at the rear of the surgery, and I hear the door shut and low voices talking. I hear a muffled laugh, and the din of more conversation follows.

There's an open appointment book on the small reception desk across the little waiting room, and I can't stop myself.

Dr. Owusu's schedule for today is right there, and it's not appointment-free.

Magda is in the appointment book twice. Once this morning, at 9:30, then again at 11:45. That alone is confusing to me, because who books a follow-up appointment so soon? Even more strange is that at 11:45 Magda would have only just left in the ambulance with Great Aunt Frances's body. Our meeting was supposed to be at 10:30 at the solicitors' office and, thinking over the morning, I would guess we found her body at around 11. In order for Magda to make that appointment, she'd have had to come straight here after collecting the body.

Unless she was instructed to bring Great Aunt Frances's body here? But then why put Magda in the appointment book? Especially if it was already so empty?

But there's something else in the diary that's a bit more concerning to me. At 9:45 is an appointment for Frances Adams.

Of course, it's possible that Great Aunt Frances never went to the appointment because of her car trouble. But it's also possible her car trouble started after she got back and tried to head to the village again for the meeting. And where would her meeting with Oliver factor in to such a busy morning? Something isn't right here.

I like Dr. Owusu, and I want to trust her. But I take my phone out of my pocket and snap pictures of the appointment book. I pull up my notes app and dash off my thoughts about the timings, including some questions I have after my chat with Dr. Owusu.

Because I know of four people who saw Great Aunt Frances shortly before she died: Oliver, who was at her estate to go over some property issues, as confirmed by Archie Foyle; Archie, who Mr. Gordon said delivers fresh flowers from the gardens for Great Aunt Frances to arrange every morning; and now Magda *and* Dr. Owusu, provided Great Aunt Frances actually made it to this appointment.

Putting aside the fact that I don't know enough about

these people (or Great Aunt Frances for that matter) to determine if any of them had reason to kill her, something important about the flowers occurs to me.

It doesn't matter if the murderer saw her the day she died.
That's the brilliance of the hemlock-and-needles bouquet. It
could have been sent while the person who made it was
safely miles away. It could have been given to her at any time,
and maybe it took her hours or days to be disturbed enough
by the ugliness of it to tear it to pieces and rearrange it.

The flowers would be impossible to trace this way. Frances herself might not even have known who they came from.

Except. "She didn't throw them away," I say out loud to
myself. "The only reason someone that good at making their
own flower arrangements would keep something so hideous
is if the person who gifted it meant something to them. If
she knew there was a chance they might stop by and notice
its absence."

So that took some of the anonymity out of things. It had
to be someone in Castle Knoll, and it had to be someone
close to her. Someone who knew her well, judging by the fact
that Frances did in fact pull the needle-studded roses out. A
plan like that could never be a sure thing, unless the person
really knew Great Aunt Frances.

I hear the doorknob to the practice room squeak as
someone turns it, so I hurry back to the front door and try
my best to time the *click* of closing it with the other door
opening. I don't know if I really manage, so I lose myself in
the maze of Castle Knoll's back streets as fast as I can, the
bells of the church chiming as I finally tumble back onto the
high street.

CHAPTER

11

The Castle Knoll Files, September 21, 1966

I HESITATED AT THE DOOR, DRAWING BREATH TO SAY A polite good-bye to Saxon now that I'd seen him home safely. But a housekeeper came to greet us and ushered me inside with such efficiency that I was through the door before I could protest. Her presence made me feel a little better about following Saxon into the strange house uninvited, and everything inside was brightly lit and warm, so I relaxed a tiny bit.

The house was so big my footsteps echoed as I walked through the hallways, and everything was polished and gleaming. I slowed a little under the sparkling chandelier in the big dining room, but Saxon skipped ahead of me, his scraped knee forgotten. I felt the need to keep up, because I didn't want to be caught gawking.

Saxon led me into the library, where his uncle was sitting in a leather armchair with a book in his lap. He had one foot resting across his knee, and his chin balanced on a fist, as if the book was terribly boring but he had to read it anyway. It made him look even younger, which I admit caught me off guard.

His expression brightened when he saw me, and it was so

different from the long, unsettling glances he'd given me earlier that I wondered if I was just being skittish when we first met. It was probably the tricks of the shadows outside and the jolt of being caught trespassing—it had given me worries that weren't real.

"Frances, hello!" he said. He stood up to greet me, as if I were an honored guest and this was a cocktail party or something. "Thank you for bringing Saxon back to the house, I do appreciate it. Won't you sit down? I can have some tea brought."

Words rather failed me then, and I couldn't think of a reason to refuse. I should have just said I needed to get back to my friends, but he was already gesturing at the housekeeper to come over. Saxon settled himself at a small table in the corner and started moving pieces on a chessboard, so at least I wasn't alone with Lord Gravesdown. A roaring fire was throwing an orange glow over everything, and the whole scene felt almost homely.

Not wanting to be rude, I said, "Thank you, Lord Gravesdown, that would be lovely."

He held a hand out for my coat, so I shrugged it off my shoulders and the housekeeper whisked it away.

"Please, call me Ford," he said.

I was led to an armchair that was across from Saxon rather than next to his uncle. "Do you play?" Saxon asked me without looking up from the pieces.

"I'm afraid not," I said. Ford left my side for a moment, and appeared a few seconds later with a small wooden chair he must have brought from a hallway or kitchen. It was easier to think of him by his first name suddenly, because he gave off an air of such nonchalance. He sat on the chair backward, up against the side of the small table between me and Saxon. It made him seem like just another boy I'd met at a dance. He could have been Teddy Crane or Archie Foyle, or one of Rose's casual dates who still hung *around sometimes. I could see his profile in the firelight, his dark hair slicked back in that old-fashioned way, like they did ten years ago. It should have reminded me of my dad, but on Ford it didn't. He was clean-shaven, and his hard jawline softened a bit as he rubbed it, thinking. His eyes were fixed on the chessboard.*

With the three of us around the little chess table it felt—this is so strange to describe, because less than an hour before, I hated this big creepy estate and swore never to come back here again—like I'd been plucked out of a bad dream and shown how silly I was to be afraid of imaginary things. And sitting there with Saxon and Ford, it felt friendly. They were a little family, and they'd decided to let me in for a moment.

Ford reached out and moved a piece—I think it was a knight, but I couldn't be sure, I didn't know the rules then—and sat back and watched Saxon thinking. Finally, Saxon made his move and watched his uncle expectantly. When Ford spoke to me again, he was still staring at the board, his voice quiet.

"This is just my opinion," Ford said, "but I don't think your friends are good enough for you."

I opened my mouth to reply, but it was such a startling thing for him to say that I was quiet for a moment. I remembered his odd question in the woods, asking if I liked riddles, and I felt as if he was trying to trip me up all over again. So I said the first thing that came to my mind, rather than the more polite thing you're probably supposed to say when you're drinking tea with a lord. "And how would you know that?" I asked, while I tried to keep my eyes on the chessboard. "You barely know me. I could be the worst of the lot." I stole a quick glance up at him and noticed he was looking at me.

A broad smile spread across Ford's face then. "Very true," he said. He let his eyes drop back to the chessboard, and moved another piece. "But something tells me you're not like them at all."

I decided not to reply, but then Ford leaned closer to me and whispered, "This is the part where you tell me that I don't know them either."

I felt a rebellious streak growing inside me, brought out by Ford being so sure he had the measure of me, and I liked it.

"Perhaps the next time I visit, you can give me the script in advance. That way I can arrive having all my lines memorized." I finally met his eyes and smiled sweetly.

A laugh rumbled from deep in his chest, and I couldn't compare him to the village boys anymore. As I looked around the library, I recognized that he came from another world entirely. His world included expensive art to be bought on a whim and London society parties. Rare volumes of Shakespeare and travel to places I would only ever read about in books. My confidence faltered a bit, because how could I ever be interesting to someone like this?

And then I felt very conflicted, because I really did want him to find me interesting. I wanted that desperately.

I told myself to snap out of whatever silly spell was dragging me under, and when I looked at Saxon, his expression helped clear my head further. His eyes were darting between me and his uncle, his features cold.

"We don't like your friends," Saxon said. "We haven't liked them any of the times we've met them."

"I don't understand. Any of the times? Wait," I said slowly. "Did you see Emily when she was here before?" The question was out of my mouth before it occurred to me that I was dobbing Emily in for snooping around the estate. But it didn't matter; neither of them reacted .

When Ford finally looked at me, there was something soft in his face. Not pity so much, but a look as if I'd said something innocent or endearing. I suddenly felt younger than him again. "They've all been coming here for weeks."

"Weeks?" I sputtered a little, and my eyes darted around the library as if I could find some answer in the hundreds of books on the walls. I noticed cups of tea steaming on a silver tray next to us. "They all acted like they'd never been here before. I mean, Emily said she had, but the others . . . Why lie about something silly like that?"

Ford was quiet, but his eyes glittered as he watched me thinking. I didn't want to impress him anymore, because I didn't like being toyed with.

"And you . . ." I replayed the scene in the woods when we'd all "met" him earlier. "Why did you pretend you didn't know them? Singling me out, and asking me about riddles? Is this all just a game to you?" I could feel my temper flaring, and I made no effort to keep it in check.

Ford didn't react to my outburst, but he didn't change the subject either. He idly picked up a chess piece and rolled it between his thumb and forefinger. "I like a good game," he said finally. "I saw an opportunity to teach a lesson to your friend Emily, so I took it."

"Teach her a lesson? Why? And how?"

My mind raced with potential times the whole group could have slipped away here, and excuses Emily had made over the past weeks found their way back into my memory. Days when Emily said she had to look after her young cousins, or she told me Rose was feeling unwell. Times Emily said Walt and John were in trouble with their parents again and weren't allowed out after dark. The excuses always came through Emily, and I always believed them. How much of that had been lies? But more than that, why? Why leave me out? What had I done?

I'd been meaning to get back to them quickly so they wouldn't worry, but hearing about their betrayal made me decide to stay as long as I liked. I'm not a rebellious person generally, but my thoughts seemed to be turning more that way since I'd set foot in Gravesdown Hall. I suddenly felt like making a few choices without my friends. Even if they turned out to be bad ones.

94

Ford shrugged when Saxon moved his piece on the board. "Maybe they lied because they didn't want you to feel left out," he said, sounding disinterested.

"You didn't answer my question about teaching Emily a lesson. Why Emily specifically?" I didn't like just being a pawn in a scheme against Emily. If she had been here visiting, I had no doubt what her ambitions with this attractive millionaire would be. The question wasn't what Emily would try, the question was whether she'd succeeded.

His uncle may have been disinterested, but Saxon was the opposite. He was almost bouncing in his seat, and he had the look of someone dying to spill some good gossip. It was yet another strange adult imitation for the ten-year-old, and I was starting to feel unnerved by how ageless he could seem.

"Your friend Emily got on the wrong side of Uncle Ford a few times," Saxon said. "I think she hoped he was looking for a new wife." He rolled his eyes and snorted, finally acting his age. But he stopped abruptly when his uncle gave him a sharp look.

Saxon had an odd way of speaking, and seeing him with his uncle made me finally grasp why that was. If his uncle was his only companion, and he'd suffered such a horrible tragedy in losing his parents, it was no wonder Saxon spoke like a miniature adult.

"They really aren't that bad," I said finally. It felt a fraction safer to side with my friends over an eccentric lord who liked playing games. And excluding me felt like a typical plan of Emily's, so I'd take that up with her later. It also explained why Rose had been so unlike herself recently. She's fiercely loyal, and clearly this whole thing had made her uneasy. "Emily and Walt cause a bit of trouble sometimes," I continued. "And I don't mind admitting we're drifting apart. But Rose and John are really nice people. I've known them all my life."

"I'm sure they are," Ford said. He sounded thoroughly bored

now. It was stupid of me, but I was angry at being used to make Emily jealous, and the longer I stayed, the clearer I could see that's what was happening here. They seemed well matched in that, Emily and Ford. I don't know why, but lately Emily saw me as a threat—and all her copying me over the past months, the clothes she borrowed and never returned, it wasn't flattery. It was some kind of game. In that case, she and Ford deserved each other. I've never been very good at games.

I thought about leaving, but Ford had already accomplished whatever point he wanted to make to my friends by keeping me here and taking up my time. And the thought of going back to face the awkwardness with John and the puzzling atmosphere among the others . . . Maybe I wasn't any good at games, but I could dabble. "So, tell me about chess then," I found myself saying.

This was, apparently, the right thing to say. Ford made brief eye contact with Saxon, and Saxon smiled back and swept the pieces away, resetting the board.

"Here," Ford said, and handed me a chess piece with friendly laughter in his eyes. "You hold the queen." He grinned at me as though he'd put a crown on my head.

I held the chess piece in one hand and lazily took a teacup from the tray next to me. The tea was still lovely and hot, and the cup was delicate bone china.

It wasn't until I looked at the queen there, sitting in my palm, that ice slid down my spine. The words of the fortune-teller came back to me in a rush—Your slow demise begins right when you hold the queen in the palm of one hand. But I couldn't panic, not here with Ford looking at me with such intensity in his eyes.

My mind raced, and I thought of all the types of queens I might have held in the palm of one hand recently, as if tiny queens being commonplace would take away the power of the words. Coins—those are everywhere, and hadn't I played cards with my brother just last week? I knew I'd held a queen then. It was like

Emily said when she bought the bird necklaces: Making it or-dinary did make it seem sillier.

I took a deep breath, feeling more in control. But looking back, that was the moment my world began to change. A piece of my fortune, locking into place.

"Before we go through the rules and the basics," Ford con-tinued, "I'd like you to understand something about chess. People love to look at chess as a philosophy, which isn't entirely wrong. It can be an allegory for life, and most often chess gets compared to war. I think that misses some of the more delicate aspects of the game, but we'll get into that another time.

"While there are many old adages and phrases comparing chess to this or that element of the human experience, there's only one that I think stands above them all, and it's something I al-ways come back to."

"What's that then?" I asked, feeling my shoulders loosen.

He reached out and gently took the queen from my fingertips. My fortune rang in my ears again, but this time I felt relief. Maybe Ford taking the queen back could save me. I looked at him and felt something shift in my chest. He held the queen up between us so that our gazes had a focus while he spoke.

"My favorite chess saying is very simple: You can play without a plan, but you'll probably lose." *His smile broadened, and he put the queen in her place on the board.*

"Do you have a plan, Frances?" *Saxon asked me.*

"I didn't realize I needed one," *I said. I got the impression we weren't entirely on the subject of chess anymore.*

"Well then," *Ford said, and he put his hands on the back of the chair and relaxed his shoulders. He gave me a thoughtful look and finally said,* "It's lucky our paths have crossed."

"Something tells me luck had nothing to do with it," *I said.*

And he lifted his chin to me almost imperceptibly, like I'd won a point.

CHAPTER

12

I'M ABOUT TO CHECK IN TO THE CASTLE HOUSE HO-
tel when Mr. Gordon rushes in. It's a good thing, because I
realize then that I'd forgotten I'd left my weekend bag in his
office.

"Oh, Annie, I'm glad I caught you." He takes his rumpled
pocket square and uses it to mop his brow again, which
seems to be a nervous habit of his. "Frances's last wishes are
that you should stay at Gravesdown Hall in advance of her
will being read tomorrow morning. I've got a taxi waiting
just outside to take you up there, if you don't mind?"

"I . . ." I clear my throat and follow Mr. Gordon out to the
high street, where the taxi is idling. "This sounds rather
childish, but the thought of staying in that big house alone,
right after Great Aunt Frances . . ."

"Completely understandable," Mr. Gordon says. "But Frances's will also names Saxon and Oliver, so they'll both be
staying as well. I imagine Elva's already there, as she sees herself as an extension of Saxon, and . . . well, you met her. Just
be on your guard." He gives me a meaningful look, and I nod.

"I'm afraid I've got to stay and finish up some work," he says, bundling me into the taxi. "But I'll see you in the morning."

I throw my backpack into the backseat next to me and the taxi pulls away. I wish I could say I'd traveled light, just throwing a few essentials in a bag, but my backpack is bursting with notebooks, novels, Post-its, notecards, far too many pens, my tired laptop, and several unread books on how to write a novel.

I notice the leather weekend bag that I've filled with a minimal assortment of clothes and toiletries is already in the car. I found it in the basement of the house in Chelsea and only notice in the taxi that it bears the initials RLG. What was Great Aunt Frances's husband's name again? Yet another thing I should know, if I am in fact *the right daughter*. My shoulders sag as my own inadequacy starts to sink in. I feel like I don't deserve to be here, because even though I'm technically family, I've been chosen by Great Aunt Frances for reasons that don't make sense to me.

I'm calling Mum before I really think things through, because I want my feet back on familiar ground. She answers on the second ring, just as I remember it's the evening of her Tate exhibition and I shouldn't be bothering her on such an important night. I'm honestly surprised she answers at all, but the fact that she does sends a warm pulse through me. Maybe she needs to hear a familiar voice too. This probably isn't the time to tell her about Great Aunt Frances's death, I think.

"Annie, hi," she says. Her voice has that forced breeziness to it that she gets when she's trying too hard to fit in somewhere she's unsure of. Mum and I may have our ups and downs, but I've never felt more in sync with her than when I hear that tone.

"Hi, Mum," I say. "I'm sorry to bother you, I only just remembered it's your opening. Congratulations!" The forced breeziness makes its way into my own voice as I say this, and I feel like her echo. "How's it all going?"

I can hear the din of voices in the background, punctuated by the odd clink of champagne glasses. I picture her exhibition room, the walls lit carefully to show off new canvases in signature Laura Adams style—work that appears messy at first but reveals layers as you look at it, much like Mum herself. Her subject matter has always been decaying urban spaces, which she paints as being reclaimed by the natural world in a way that's quite vigorous.

"It's going really well," Mum says. "There are a lot of critics here that I recognize, and people are saying nice things about the paintings, and the show's already selling out."

"Oh, Mum, that's fantastic!" I say. And my excitement for her is genuine. I know how much recognition means to her, especially after she's had such a dry spell since her heyday in the nineties. And even though she knew she'd inherit from Great Aunt Frances, money was always tight because the windfall from the sale of those early paintings disappeared with my dad. "Don't let me keep you," I add.

"No, I like hearing your voice. How are things going with you? Is Aunt Frances as mad as ever?"

"Um," I pause, trying to find a way to skip over the news about Great Aunt Frances, but somehow she catches the weight behind my silence.

"Annie? Is everything okay?"

"I didn't want to tell you this right now. I honestly forgot it was your Tate exhibition when I phoned," I say slowly.

Mum sighs, but she's not angry. "Don't worry about upsetting me, Annie. If there's bad news, there's bad news."

I bite my lip and nod, even though she can't see me. "Great Aunt Frances is dead, Mum. I'm really sorry."

There's a pause. "Do I need to come to Castle Knoll?" If Mum's upset, she's hiding it well. She's always been able to do that, and I know she'll get through the rest of the evening showing the world the best side of Laura Adams. I feel terrible, though, being the messenger that brings Great Aunt Frances's ghost to her opening night.

"Not at the moment," I say. "Please don't worry, everything's in hand. And if I need you, I'll let you know." I wince inwardly as I say this, because Mum and I both know that's not true. If I need Mum for anything, I always ask someone else, or muddle through myself. She's wonderful in her way, but she's never been a lifeline. The honest version of that statement would be, "If I need you, I'll call Jenny."

"Okay," Mum says. There's a pause again, and this one's awkward. "Annie, can you do me a favor?"

"Um, sure."

"Aunt Frances kept a really detailed set of files. They're in a little antechamber off the library. Can you get one of the files for me? It's just . . . it's important that no one else gets their hands on it."

My thoughts lurch forward, then sputter out. "I . . . yeah, sure. Which file do you need?"

Another sigh flows down the phone, and this one sounds tired. "Sam Arlington."

Dad.

I run a hand through my hair, forgetting it's still piled on my head in a messy bun, so I tear the elastic band free and let it spill down in all directions. I should have some feelings about Great Aunt Frances having a whole file dedicated to my dad, but I find all my feelings are directed at Mum for knowing the file's there in the first place. And presumably knowing what's in it. Mum suddenly doesn't feel like such familiar territory after all.

"Annie? You still there?"

"Yeah," I say. "I'm here. I'll get the file for you."

"Thanks," she says, and she sounds relieved. "Read it or don't read it, it's up to you."

I bristle at this, because it would have been up to me anyway. I'm the one here in Castle Knoll, rooting through Great Aunt Frances's life. And now Mum's.

"I'll let you get back to your show," I say, reminding myself that I've just told Mum her aunt is dead, on one of the most important nights of her professional life. As usual, I pack away the mix of emotions she's left me with, to take out and deal with later.

"Yeah, I'd better go."

"I am sorry, about Great Aunt Frances. And about the timing of all this."

We hang up, and it's then that I notice that the taxi driver keeps looking at me in his rearview mirror.

"Rutherford Lawrence Gravesdown," the driver says, when he meets my eyes in the mirror.

"I'm sorry?"

"The initials on your bag," he adds. "I put it together since I'm taking you up to the Gravesdown estate. Family heirloom?"

"Um, yes." I take a moment to study the taxi driver, because I've been traveling with my London mindset, where drivers are all anonymous and plentiful. But this is Castle Knoll, and I just had a very personal conversation with Mum within earshot of someone who could very well gossip about it at the local pub.

I can't see much of him from the backseat, but he looks

about Mum's age, with close-cropped hair that's gone fully gray. He's got broad shoulders and smells strongly of cigarettes.

He pulls into the circular drive and stops in front of Gravesdown Hall. I get out once I've paid the fare, and walk up to where he's rolled the driver's window down. He's giving the house a proper glower, which makes me back up a step.

But when he sees me, his features shift back into a pleasant mask. "You're Laura's daughter, aren't you?"

"I am," I say. I'm wary of him, but the reflex not to be rude is strong.

He grins. "We had a bit of a thing," he says. "Me and Laura, way back when. In our teens." He glowers back at the house again. "Frances meddled and put a right end to it. I don't want to speak ill of the dead, but don't you worry about Laura being broken up at her death. There was no love lost there."

I can't help it—my jaw drops. This man not only eavesdropped on my whole conversation, but he's Mum's exboyfriend? And now he's just happy to jump right into my business? Who the hell does he think he is?

He keeps talking, and I just stand there, blinking at him. "You look just like her." He smiles. "Tell her Reggie Crane says hello."

"Did you say Crane? As in, Detective Rowan Crane?"

Reggie nods. "That's my son. I bet you've met him already."

"Yes," I say blandly. "I have." I *cannot* match the steady detective to this nosy taxi driver, but then I suppose it's normal for people to be quite different from their parents, in both looks and demeanor.

It's not until the taxi is crawling back down the drive that the words of Samantha the police station receptionist come back into my mind.

She was awful to the whole Crane family.

I wonder just how horrible she was, and if she was horrible enough for them to want her dead.

CHAPTER
13

"HELLO?" I SAY WEAKLY AS I PUSH OPEN THE LARGE front door. "Elva?"

Archie Foyle surprises me by poking his head through the nearest doorway. "She's over in the village," he says, almost cheerfully.

I give him a long look. "I thought you didn't have keys," I say.

"I don't. But my granddaughter Beth does. She's in the kitchen. She wanted me to bring over some fresh produce from the farm. She cooks for Frances sometimes, did I mention that? She normally doesn't come in on a Tuesday, but given the circumstances . . ." He trails off, thoughtful for a second. His dark eyes snap back into focus as if he's only just seen me there. "Walt told us the will is going to be read tomorrow morning, so Beth's going to put on a nice brunch for you all. Frances would want that."

"I see." The words come out slowly, and more suspicious-sounding than I mean them to. I should really work on my poker face. It seems most likely that Archie gave Great Aunt

Frances those flowers, although my only reasoning for this is that he's the gardener, and he brings her fresh flowers every morning, which all seems a bit too convenient.

Something occurs to me then—Archie's just come from the doorway that eventually leads to the library. Not only did the group of us who found the body this morning probably trample on all sorts of important fibers or hairs, but whoever was responsible for Great Aunt Frances's death would have even more reason to contaminate the scene. The idea of the library being unexamined and open for anyone to wander through makes me worry. "Archie, have the police been here?"

"Yep, a whole team of them. Even the detective—Teddy Crane's grandson—was here with some other people doing all their forensic stuff. Library's been locked since they left, and Walt has the only key to that. But you've already seen the library; I can show you around the rest of the place if you like."

"Maybe another time," I say, and I give him a weak smile. "I'd like to wander on my own and find a room. I'll introduce myself to Beth when I'm settled."

"Suit yourself," Archie says, and whistles as he wanders away toward the back of the house, where I assume the kitchen is.

I keep my backpack on but leave the overnight bag in the hallway and make my way through the large dining room, to the door of the library. I'm not planning to break in, but Archie having popped out as if he'd come from this direction makes me uneasy.

I try the handle, and it isn't locked at all. The door swings open easily, with no sign of police tape or anything else indicating a sealed crime scene. Either Archie was mistaken or he was lying.

I step through the door and notice that everything looks

immaculate inside, and smells faintly of pine. Across the room, the door to the little antechamber is slightly ajar, and I think again of Archie going to the extra effort to explain to me that the library was locked. The antechamber is empty when I get there, and looks just as it did earlier.

Great Aunt Frances's filing cabinets loom against one wall like a group of sulky teenagers, and I feel the hairs on my arms stand up as I walk toward them. I make a point not to look at the fortune written on the wall, but my eyes catch the words *palm* and *hand* just as my own palms throb under the dressings, and the connection feels spooky.

In total, there are ten metal filing cabinets. They look like they've been here since about 1980, but this might just be me being judgmental. They're painted that old-fashioned avocado color, for one, but they're so well used that the paint along the seams of the drawers isn't just chipped but worn smooth down to the silver underneath.

Each cabinet has been numbered using one of those black typeface label makers. The very top drawer on the far left is slightly open, with a set of keys hanging from the metal lock at its top. Two large skeleton keys hang from it as well, which I guess must be keys to the house and some outbuildings. But it's the collection of small keys on the ring that makes me tilt my head to one side as I run my fingers through them. They clink together like tiny wind chimes. They're identical, and they're all numbered to match the filing cabinets. They weren't here when Elva, Oliver, Mr. Gordon, and I were waiting for the paramedics earlier. The police must have found them after that. It's interesting how they've just left them here.

I start with the first drawer, since it's unlocked and I assume the files are alphabetical and my dad's name—Sam Arlington—will be in there.

It isn't, but there's a whole jumble of other people's names. I can't see any real order, and I start to get frustrated and flip through names to see if I recognize anyone's.

Finally I come across my own.

I pull out a flimsy file, and in it is a photo of me and Mum from my graduation at Central Saint Martins, and a few random pages of things I can't believe anyone would ever find important. Some of my old school reports, a CV I once posted on LinkedIn, and then, finally, a photocopy of the invoice from the removal company I used to send Frances the trunks from our basement. My signature swoops neatly at the bottom of it, and I wonder why she'd keep a copy of something so random.

None of the rest of my family have files in here; there's nothing on Mum, or on my grandparents Peter and Tansy. Everyone else in here is a stranger to me. Finally, I notice the piece of thick card at the front of all the files, and the words *Secrets TBD* written at the top of it.

I quickly pull out the next drawer and find several pieces of card dividing it, with increasingly alarming headings. The first one reads *Arson*, and surprisingly, there are three files behind that one. No name I recognize, thankfully. The next headings are *Assault* (a worrying number of names under this one), then *Bankruptcy*, and on and on it goes.

So, it turns out her system *is* alphabetical. But it's alphabetical by secret.

My stomach twists, and I feel worse with every drawer I open. I don't know whether to feel angry at Great Aunt Frances for reducing her friends and neighbors to their indiscretions, or sorry for her for spending a lifetime swimming in a sea of such distrust.

Finally I get to the letter *I*, and there he is—Sam Arlington, right under *Infidelity*. I pull the file out carefully and find it's as thick as a novella. The *Infidelity* category takes up the entire drawer, and I get a sour taste in my mouth thinking of all the broken hearts that must be connected to these files. Did Great Aunt Frances have a hand in revealing any of these secrets? Or did she just dig them up in a bid to root out some unknown enemy? I don't know what ended my parents' marriage; it was before I was even born, so it never mattered to me. And Mum never explained, so that was that. We lived our lives without my dad.

I blink my way out of these thoughts as my eyes catch on the name Crane near the back of the drawer. I instinctively reach in and pull that file out too. It's thick—full of even more paper than my dad's. I don't open it to see which Crane this concerns, but I'm surprised to find myself hoping it's not the detective.

I didn't notice him wearing a wedding ring when I met him, and I suppose if he's guilty of infidelity that's his business. Unless Great Aunt Frances made it hers. There's a file for *Gravesdown* too, but my arms are already overloaded. Could this be Saxon or Elva? Or possibly Frances's own husband?

I think of Elva and her insistence on ripping Post-its off Great Aunt Frances's murder board, and I kneel down and place the Crane and Arlington files on the floor. I wrench the Gravesdown file out, open it quickly, and flip through the contents. There's a lot—but it all seems to concern other Gravesdowns I don't know. There's no mention of Saxon, Elva, or Rutherford. But it does have separate files contained inside it. Someone named Harrison Gravesdown, another named Etta Gravesdown, and finally a third person named Olivia. It looks like the Gravesdown family were not a particularly faithful lot.

I return the Gravesdown file and shut the drawer, deciding

it's time to find a room so that I can have somewhere private to think through just how much I want to know about these infidelities.

When I get upstairs, I notice the others have already claimed bedrooms—Elva's white designer blazer is suspended on a hanger from the grand four-poster bed in the first room I look into. It's not like me, but I dash in, making a beeline for the blazer. Perhaps it's the fact that I've just spent time rooting through the secrets of half the town, but I feel no shame in turning out Elva's pockets.

My fingers find the Post-its she tore from Great Aunt Frances's murder board, as well as another folded-up page. I stuff it all in my own pockets and quickly exit the room, shutting the door quietly behind me.

Through the next door along, I see Oliver's empty laptop bag thrown across the bed of another very spacious room overlooking the rose gardens. But I think I've reached my threshold for snooping. And aside from being a bit of a prat, Oliver strikes me as relatively harmless, so I leave his things be. Next to the scandalous Gravesdown family, he actually seems rather boring.

I wander farther down the hall, my feet silent on the deep red carpet that runs along the middle of the polished wood floors. Finally, I find a small room with a big window, and I throw my backpack on the iron-framed bed that sits against one wall. The window has a stained-glass border around it, which casts cheerful shapes of color on the floor as the last of the evening glow comes through.

I wonder who used this room. It's far smaller than the others, and the bed is plain compared to the elegant four-posters I saw in the other rooms. The floor is made of simple whitewashed boards, with a tidy little rug in the center. A housekeeper's room, possibly, or some other household staff?

When I sit cross-legged on the bed, the files in front of me ready to be cracked open, I finally notice that my overnight bag has been carefully placed near the small wardrobe across the room.

I blink at it in surprise for a moment. It was probably just Archie trying to be helpful, but all the same I feel slightly unnerved by the gesture. I'm certain there are more rooms, so how did he know that I'd pick this one? Or he was making a statement: *This is where you belong, tucked away in a staff room. This house isn't yours.*

I think my brain is starting to frazzle a bit, which isn't helped by the fact that I'm also extremely hungry. I haven't eaten all day, not since the train. To be honest, I haven't been hungry until now, but I'm suddenly so ravenous my stomach feels like it's digesting itself.

I put the files in my backpack, sandwiched snugly between Great Aunt Frances's green diary (yet another thing on my reading list of Castle Knoll secrets) and my stack of notebooks. I slide the whole thing under the bed, even though I'm certain that if anyone came snooping, that's the first place they'd look. But I can't just leave everything out in the open.

I head back downstairs, and it doesn't take me long to find the kitchen. I can hear Archie whistling, and the low hum of conversation. I wonder why Beth is here cooking if it's brunch she's planning for the morning. But I do know that if you're baking bread there's a lot to do the night before.

The kitchen is enormous and full of light. It's easily the size of most people's entire flats in central London. There's a big Aga against the far wall, and a huge island across from it, topped with thick wood. The other end of the room has a fireplace so large I could fit inside it, with two armchairs arranged in front of its stone hearth. I notice a purple cardigan on the arm of one of the armchairs, just as the woman at the island turns around and spots me.

Beth Foyle looks about ten years older than me, with dark curls and one of those faces that's beautiful in an unconventional way. She has a hawkish nose and is extremely tall, and her choice to accentuate rather than hide these features makes her go from pretty to striking. She's dressed head-to-toe in 1930s clothes, and her red lipstick and deep blue tea dress look like the most normal outfit one could wear for baking. Even her Oxford heels don't seem out of place. She has an apron tied around her dress that looks like it's from the 1950s, or is possibly handmade to look that way. She's carefully kneading dough on the flour-covered island, but she stops when she sees me.

"Oh!" One hand flutters to the side of her head, and even the gesture seems vintage and perfectly timed, like she's Ingrid Bergman about to kiss Humphrey Bogart good-bye. "You're Laura's . . . you're Annie, aren't you?"

"Hi, yeah, I am." I give her a half wave, but she walks around the island while wiping dough fragments on her apron, looking for a formal handshake.

"I'm Beth."

Archie isn't here, even though I could swear I heard him whistling just now. Maybe Beth whistles the same tune.

"It's nice to meet you." My stomach growls loudly, and I decide to get straight to the point. "Archie says you're planning a brunch for tomorrow. Any chance there's something I can eat now?" I ask. "I know it's rude of me, but I'm ravenous."

"Of course!" Beth says. "But I'll do you one better. Do you like soup? I made minestrone and some crusty rolls for Grandad's lunch, and he barely made a dent in it." She's already over at the large refrigerator, where she pulls out a cast-iron pot—an expensive Le Creuset one—and then puts it in one of the Aga's many compartments. I notice the Aga looks brand-new, and the cherry-red enamel matches Beth's lipstick perfectly.

"Thanks," I say. I walk over to the Aga and admire the shiny chrome handles.

"Do you like it?" she asks. "Frances let me pick it out specially when the old one needed replacing," she says. Beth's face falls at the mention of Great Aunt Frances, but everything about her is so carefully contained that it's hard to read what she's really feeling. Even though she's embodying the primness of another century, I don't get the feeling that she's like Elva, where everything is a performance. I'm honestly not sure what to make of her.

"I'm sorry," I say. "You must have known her well. Today has probably been terrible for you."

Beth gives me a watery smile. "I've been cooking my way through my feelings. I find that helps," she says. "But thank you."

Eventually she removes the warmed soup from the oven, ladles me a bowl, and sets it in front of me. I tuck into it, and it's truly excellent. When I'm nearly through the bowl, I look over at the empty armchairs.

Beth follows my gaze to the purple cardigan hanging on the arm of one of them and sighs.

"Frances's," she says. "I didn't feel right moving it." Her eyes well up again and she looks away. She busies herself pulling something out of the oven, and when she looks back at me she's got an expression on her face that's a little too bright.

I think about what Archie said, about their farm being on Gravesdown land, and I wonder what Great Aunt Frances's death means for their future. I debate with myself for a moment, but then decide it wouldn't be rude to ask about the farm. She might even be glad that someone's thinking about her family.

"Beth, I was just wondering," I say. "What will happen to your family's farm, with Great Aunt Frances gone?"

Beth wipes her hands on her apron again, and her brow creases. "Oh, it's up to whoever inherits, I suppose." She's putting on a casual tone, but it's clearly forced. "I'll admit, it would have been nice if Frances had chosen to leave the farm to us, but Mr. Gordon has already notified us that we're not included in the will."

"I'm sorry," I say. And I really am. It seems unfair that Great Aunt Frances wouldn't protect the farm and keep it with the Foyles. This estate is huge enough already; why would anyone need the farm too? I wonder if there's more to this story.

Beth nods lightly and gives me a grateful smile. "Well, let's just hope it all comes out okay," she says. She busies herself dusting the countertop with more flour, and kneads another large ball of dough.

The shrewd part of my mind wonders if that's what her brunch tomorrow is really about—to stay close and keep tabs on her future. I probably would, if I were in her position.

It's then I notice that we're being watched.

To the rear of the kitchen is a big open conservatory, sunken down by a few steps. *Conservatory* isn't the right word for something this grand—I can see it goes back quite far, but the lushness of the plants hides its depth. It might be called a solarium, or an orangery perhaps. The early evening light is trickling through tree ferns and palms, casting everything in a syrupy glow. It's the first part of the house I'm properly tempted to explore (other than the library, but I've got mixed feelings about that room now). And I would, if there weren't a face pressed up against the glass pane nearest the kitchen.

"There's a frail-looking woman watching us," I say to Beth slowly. "Should I let her in?"

Beth's eyes widen, and then she spots the face. Another sigh escapes her, but this sigh is frustrated rather than sad. "Rose," she says carefully, raising her voice so she can be heard through the glass. "Would you like a cup of tea?"

Rose. My brain goes back to that photo—Great Aunt Frances, the missing girl, Emily Sparrow, and their third friend, Rose Forrester. She's Joe the paramedic's mum, so she must have married to become Rose Leroy at some point. Rose is the one who owns the Castle House Hotel.

The face leaves the window, and I hear the rattle of a glass door from somewhere within the jungle of plants. There must be a back door through the conservatory leading out to the gardens. Rose emerges from the ferns, a pink hibiscus bloom in one hand and a knotted handkerchief in the other.

She looks just like the photo, only older. She's still got her signature bob, and even her blouse and blazer seem cut from 1960s polyester. Her hair is salt-and-pepper now, but it suits her sharp features. Her cheekbones have grown more pronounced, and it makes her brown eyes look wider. Looking at Rose, I'm reminded that Emily and Great Aunt Frances would only be in their seventies now, and that seventy isn't actually that old.

But the second she spots me, Rose's features change. Anger lines her eyes, followed by alarm. She starts to work the handkerchief in her hand in small circles, and finally I see grief settle in as she looks over at the empty armchairs.

"Rose, come in and sit down," Beth says gently. She leads Rose to one of the armchairs, and then goes to the sink to get her a glass of water.

Rose closes her eyes and breathes in deeply through her nose, inhaling the scent of fresh bread that's starting to fill the large room. Finally, she says plainly, "You must be Annabelle. It's nice to meet you. Forgive me, for a minute there I was surprised by the sight of you. But I knew to expect you. Frances has mentioned you."

"It's nice to meet you too," I say. "Great Aunt Frances mentioned me? I didn't think—" But Rose's sniffle cuts me off.

"I'm sorry," Rose says, dabbing her eyes. "I'm really not myself. As you can see, the loss of Frances has been . . ." Rose's voice cracks, and one hand flies to her face suddenly, like a small bird startled from its hiding place. She sniffs and then pinches the bridge of her nose, as if she can contain her tears that way.

"I'm sorry for your loss," I say. "I know you were a friend of Great Aunt Frances."

"I was her *best* friend," she says fiercely. I start at the change in her tone, but I know that grief is a funny thing, from what little I've seen of it. People can go from sad to angry in moments. I suddenly feel very young.

"Rose," Beth says gently, "is there anything we can do for you?"

"I just . . . I needed to see—" Rose chokes on a sob, then recovers somewhat. "When Joe told me Frances was gone, I felt so guilty! None of us believed her." Her voice shakes, angry. "And she was *right*! All these years, and she was right about being murdered."

"No one knows that for sure," Beth says.

I decide that now is not the time to share my theories. This poor woman has only just learned that her best friend is dead. To tell her that someone in her town, someone Frances must have known, probably killed her . . . that just seems cruel.

"But they'll find out," she says quietly. "I have faith in Frances. She spent sixty years preparing for this. The police will find out who did this, won't they?" She looks from Beth to me and then back to Beth again. "Frances valued justice—we can't have her murderer going unpunished!"

"There are detectives looking into it," I say. "They'll do right by her, I'm sure." I'm not actually sure, but this seems like the right thing to say. Rose calms down a bit and nods while blowing her nose.

"Annie," Beth says, over Rose's head. "Do you mind finding my grandad and seeing if he can give Rose a lift back to the village? He's just out in the gardens, I can see him through the glass there."

Rose narrows her eyes. "I'm not ancient, I drove my own car up here!" she snaps.

"All the same," Beth says, "I'd like it if Grandad rode back with you. You're very upset, and accidents can happen in circumstances like this."

"I've done enough riding in cars with Archie Foyle," Rose mumbles.

Beth gives me a pointed look, and I nod and head out to find Archie.

He's pruning roses—deep crimson ones that are falling to pieces. When we come back into the kitchen, Rose is more collected than I've seen her thus far. She smooths a hand over her hair, and the handkerchief has vanished.

"Hey there, Rosie," Archie says. "Could you give me a lift to the pub? My workday's finished."

"I suppose," Rose says. As she stands, she gathers the purple cardigan from where it rests on the armchair and squeezes it before draping it over her own shoulders.

Archie holds out his arm to her as if he's leading her to the dance floor, and I watch them slip back through the ferns.

CHAPTER
14

I EXPECT TO SPEND THE EVENING GOING THROUGH the files I stuffed into my backpack, but when I reach my little room after Beth's warming soup, the exhaustion of the day catches up with me and I can barely keep my eyes open. I don't wake up until Oliver knocks on my door in the morning, telling me to be downstairs in ten minutes for the reading of Great Aunt Frances's will.

I scramble to make myself presentable, but I only have one spare dress, and it doesn't feel quite right for this sort of thing. Still, my only other option is to wear the clothes I had on yesterday, which is decidedly worse. At least the dress is a castoff from one of Jenny's Harrods spending sprees, so it's designer. The top half is close-fitted before flaring out at the skirt, which makes me feel far more exposed than I do in the voluminous fabrics I usually hide behind. I pile my hair on top of my head again and check my reflection in the full-length mirror on the wall.

I'm pleasantly surprised. Maybe it's because I spent yesterday hearing how much I resemble Mum on a constant loop, but this dress looks sleek and elegant, and I feel like someone new in it. I take a deep breath and smooth the navy silk before heading out of the room and down the stairs.

With the reading of the will looming, everything feels solemn as Mr. Gordon leads us through to the library. The air inside is stuffy, but there are some subtle changes from when I was in here yesterday. The flowers have been removed, even the nice displays by the windows, and it makes the place feel a little less claustrophobic. Early morning light streams in through the windows, and the lawns look dewy and ready for the sun to bake them free of their droplets. I notice that Beth has laid out a brunch spread on a long table off to one side, and I feel slightly bad that no one's touching it. Someone has shuffled the chairs around, and Mr. Gordon sits behind the big wooden desk at the center of the library while the rest of us—except for Saxon, who isn't here yet—sit facing him. It's all very formal, and it's just how I'd picture the reading of a very wealthy person's last will and testament to be.

Elva Gravesdown sits to the far left, with an empty chair next to her for her husband. I'm on the other side of the empty chair, with Oliver Gordon on the end. His phone keeps buzzing in his pocket, and he's been angling his shoulders away from me to check it every time. By his haggard expression, I deduce that it's either his boss or he's got a very controlling girlfriend.

One interesting addition to our group is Detective Crane, though he's not sitting with the rest of us. I'm surprised to find myself rather glad to see him. He makes everything feel a little calmer, a little safer. He's got an important-looking file tucked under one arm and is leaning against one of the window frames, quietly taking us all in. He gives me a small nod when I sit down, but other than that he keeps to himself. I'd bet almost any amount of money that the file he's got with him is the results of Dr. Owusu's autopsy, and I'm beyond curious to know what's inside.

Mr. Gordon clears his throat and pointedly checks his watch before giving Elva a meaningful look. "I don't understand how Saxon can be late to a meeting that's taking place at the house *in which he is currently staying.* Elva, if he's not here in five minutes, I'm going to search all the rooms and drag him down here."

Elva looks mortally offended, and it's the kind of reaction that feels like it needs stage lights and an orchestra. Nothing about her feels natural; she's a complete one-woman show. "Don't be ridiculous, Walt. This is Saxon's *own* home. He grew up here. For God's sake, have some compassion, he's probably taking his time dealing with old ghosts."

"I'm aware of that, Elva," Mr. Gordon says quietly. "But you forget that I have experience dragging Saxon out of hiding places, and I wouldn't be surprised if he'd never grown out of his childhood habit of spying on a situation before making his presence known."

My curiosity is piqued, but no one elaborates, and I feel weird about asking.

Elva just opts to change the subject. "Why is Oliver here?" she asks.

I've been wondering this myself. I know Great Aunt Frances mentioned him in her will, but the reason why remains a mystery. I'm secretly glad Elva's willing to ask questions I find too uncomfortable to voice.

"That will be explained shortly, when we get to reading the will," Mr. Gordon says.

I can feel Detective Crane's solid gaze from across the room. Everyone but the detective startles when the door to the library slams, and, as if on cue, a man with a thick head of oyster-colored hair strides through the library. "So sorry, everyone," he says, giving the room a warm smile.

"Saxon, finally," Mr. Gordon says.

Saxon is wearing an expensively cut gray suit that sits well on his slim frame. He's probably a few inches shy of six feet, and he radiates confidence in a way that already feels more genuine than Elva's ceaseless performance. He's got a square jaw and green eyes, and I can already hear Jenny calling him a "silver fox" in my head. He notices me staring and takes a step back.

"You're not Laura," he says plainly. But the smile remains, and he doesn't make the comment that I look just like her.

"No," I say. I sit up a little straighter, summoning the feeling I had when I looked in the mirror in this dress a few minutes ago. "I'm not."

"Saxon, this is Annabelle Adams. Annie. Laura's daughter," Mr. Gordon says. "She's now included in all this"—he looks down at the papers in front of him and frowns hard enough that his whole face sags—"mess." He mutters the last word to himself, but his feelings toward the will seem pretty clear.

Saxon comes around and sits in the empty chair next to me. He leans my way and says, "It's nice to meet you, Annie. Hopefully all this will be sorted out fairly and easily, so poor Walt won't collapse from the stress of it. And I appreciate Elva might not have made things feel very welcome for you yesterday, you'll have to forgive her. I think she was taking the bad feelings she has for Laura out on you."

I don't know what I was expecting when I met Saxon, but it wasn't this. A mirror of Elva, possibly. Or someone too busy and important to acknowledge my existence, given his late entrance. But Saxon sits calmly next to me, giving off an air of being extremely reasonable while also understanding how awkward this situation must make me feel. It's a very pleasant surprise.

"Thank you," I say.

I momentarily wonder what Mum might have done to upset Elva, but from what I've seen of Elva so far, they're pretty much chalk and cheese. Mum would probably make a game of upsetting her, and I feel a wave of affection with that thought.

"Right, well, I'll just lay this out plainly for you all then." Mr. Gordon puts on a pair of reading glasses and picks up the stack of papers in front of him. "Frances has not divided up her estate; it is to remain intact. This includes the house in Chelsea and the farm and land attached to the Gravesdown estate, as well as the entirety of the estate itself and the surrounding lands. It also includes the sum of forty million pounds."

Elva claps her hands together and draws in a breath but quickly tries to cover this with a cough. Saxon tuts at her quietly, and Mr. Gordon gives her a stony look over the tops of his reading glasses.

Everyone remains quiet, so Mr. Gordon continues. "Saxon, Oliver, and Annie—recently replacing Laura—are the remaining beneficiaries, but this is where the complications start. The best way to explain this is to read to you directly from a letter provided by Frances:

Dearest Saxon, Annabelle, and Oliver,

I'd wanted to do this in the normal way, believe me. I'll get to Oliver in a moment, but first I'll address Saxon and Annabelle. I've long known that my life would end by murder, and therefore I leave my estate—the entirety of it, including the funds in all my accounts—to the person who successfully solves my murder.

For years I've been mistreated in this town, just for something I believe deeply. Everyone is so uneasy about the secrets they've been keeping, and my skill for finding them out, that they've worked hard to discredit me as a kook. But I've always known that something isn't right in Castle Knoll, and that the secrets stuffed into the crevices of our streets, our church walls, even my own house, are rotting us to the core. I've known all along that these secrets would prove deadly. After all, they have before.

My last act on this earth is to make believers out of both of you, and hopefully, in the process, make believers out of the entire town.

May the best among you inherit my wealth, rather than my fortune—

My jaw drops as I try to make sense of Frances's words. I feel the prickly hand of fate yet again, because ever since we found Great Aunt Frances, this is exactly what I've been try-ing to do. What I can't seem to *help* doing. I feel like I'm a part of Great Aunt Frances's fortune, like I might be the right daughter.

At this point Elva splutters, "Excuse me? Can she do that? Make us jump through hoops like that?" shooting a look at Detective Crane.

Detective Crane is looking down at the file in his hands, and it's unclear whether he's heard anything Elva has said.

Mr. Gordon clears his throat again. "Elva, there is no *us*. This involves Saxon and Annie. And Oliver and the detective here, but I'll get to that if you let me finish."

There are rules, of course. I don't want you hanging around doing nothing while my corpse is rotting in the ground and

justice isn't served. I'm giving you one week. If, at the end of
this time, you haven't managed to solve my murder, then all
my properties will be sold off piece by piece, care of our
young property developer, Oliver Gordon, and his employer,
Jessop Fields. I don't care if the estate becomes a shopping
mall or a quarry; if you fail at this, the whole village will feel it
for generations. The money from the sales, and the rest of my
fortune, will go to the Crown—

I can't help it—it's me who interrupts next. "But what
would happen to the farm, to Beth and her grandad and
their business?"

Mr. Gordon gives me a long look, and I can't tell if he's
grateful someone is thinking outside the confines of their
own gain, or tired because I've reminded him that this will is
set to send shock waves through the village like a bomb. He
doesn't reply but just keeps reading.

But I also don't want you hastily putting together false answers
to get what you want. So your findings must be verified by
Detective Crane, and an arrest or a positive conclusion
reached. Walt will have the final say as to whether he feels this
has happened. He also has the power to disqualify either of
you if you're handed a prison sentence for any reason—

"So we can murder each other, so long as we get away
with it," Saxon says dryly. "Very elegant, Frances." Saxon
leans my way again and adds, "Don't worry, Annie, I'm not
going to murder you."

"I appreciate that, Saxon," I reply. "I'm not going to murder
you either." And then we both smile, because this is such a
strange thing to say ten minutes after meeting someone for
the first time.

"Actually," Walt says, "it *is* an elegant addition to the will. It will lead you to keep an eye on each other. Frances wouldn't have wanted her estate going to someone who is unworthy." He lifts the letter back under his nose and keeps reading.

I'm not going to put any contingencies in here for death by natural causes, such is my conviction and belief in what will come to pass. And believe me, if I had an inkling of who is planning to kill me, I'd have filed a report with the police in advance. (Detective Crane can verify—I've attempted to do this several times.) I've been trying to riddle out who my eventual murderer will be for years, but it is challenging to solve a crime that hasn't happened yet, so I must leave that part to you.

I tried to play this game with a plan, but it looks like I lost anyway. So I've set my plan to continue without me.

Good luck,
Frances

We sit in stunned silence for what feels like several minutes, until I decide to break it.

"What happens if we solve it together?"

"Or what if one of us did it?" Saxon asks.

Detective Crane turns to look at Saxon, and the corner of his mouth pulls upward a fraction. "Why? Are you confessing?"

"Just purely from an academic perspective," Saxon replies. "I want to know how far Frances thought this through. It is really quite a stunning scheme." Saxon seems amused more than anything, as if this is all just an interesting game.

Oliver has been tapping on his phone this whole time, but snaps his head up and says, "Not that I'm trying to help solve this murder, seeing as I'm only here as insurance . . ." The look on his face could curdle milk, and I'm suddenly aware that he's livid. "But since the lovely Frances has decided that my career prospects are just toys to be played with from beyond the grave, and I'd rather not get murdered in my sleep when this all gets too cutthroat"—he spares a glance at Elva—"I'd like to point out that we're all cleared based on Frances's time of death, as we were all in the same office in Castle Knoll when she was killed. Well, everyone but Saxon."

"That doesn't matter actually," I say. "Those flowers could have been given to her at any point recently, giving the murderer plenty of time to get away."

Detective Crane gently pushes himself away from the window ledge he's leaning on. "The flowers didn't kill her," he says quietly.

"They . . . what?" I blink a few times, trying to understand how hemlock in someone's bloodstream wouldn't kill them.

"So she was wrong? She wasn't murdered?" Saxon asks.

"I didn't say that," is all Crane says. He's watching Elva and Saxon very carefully, measuring their reactions. Saxon stares back, aware that he's being assessed by the detective. Elva seems oblivious.

"Well, we were all together in Mr. Gordon's office when she died," Elva replies. "Didn't Frances call you about moving the meeting? So she was alive while we were all there. And Saxon was coming back from the hospital—he would have been on the ferry."

"I have a ticket, if anyone needs to see it," Saxon says evenly.

"No one's talking about the elephant in the room," Oliver cuts in, the snap of his voice surprisingly harsh.

"Which one?" I blurt out, because I can genuinely think of multiple elephants in this room.

Oliver ignores me and turns to address the detective. "What was the cause of death, Detective Crane? Or are you not intending to tell us, even though I can see you're holding the autopsy report?"

"Oh, that elephant," I say.

Detective Crane doesn't move. He just stares at Oliver and smiles slightly.

"Fine," Oliver says. "But what happens if she really did just drop dead of her own accord?"

"What, you mean you think she'd kill herself just to make us do this whole song and dance?" Elva says, as if she might actually think that could be true. I don't like to judge, but I'm coming to think Elva Gravesdown is not particularly clever.

"No, I mean what if she had a heart attack? Or went into diabetic shock or something, I don't know! What happens then?" Oliver asks.

Detective Crane finally steps forward. He walks over to where Mr. Gordon is sitting and places the file on the desk. "She did have a heart attack," he says slowly.

Oliver groans and reaches into his pocket for his phone again.

"But it wasn't a natural one," Detective Crane says, opening the file. "Frances was right. Someone killed her."

CHAPTER
15

The Castle Knoll Files, September 23, 1966

JOHN WAS BEING DISTANT, DODGING MY QUESTIONS about the Gravesdown estate and what they'd all done there when they'd gone without me. Saxon's warning still wafted around me like a bad smell: "I know you think I'm a creep, but your boyfriend's worse."

But for every question John dodged, he came back with some sweet gesture: a perfume ordered all the way from London, a copy of my favorite book. He carved our initials into trees and told me he loved me. And slowly, over the course of the next week or so, the ice between us began to thaw.

And thankfully John agreed that the woods on the Gravesdown estate weren't the most romantic spot in the world. He came up with all kinds of other ideas for us to be together for the first time, like sneaking to the castle ruins in the dark, or borrowing Walt's car for an evening. But ever since my time with Ford and Saxon, I'd felt a bit uneasy about my friends.

Emily still insisted that the Gravesdown estate was the most exciting place we could possibly hang out, which was only rein-

forced when the police kicked us off the village green at seven P.M. one night for being too noisy. As usual, it was Walt making all the noise. He decided to piss against a tree while singing "You Really Got Me" by the Kinks, telling us all that he could piss as long as the song and no longer. Walt's always doing things like that—he's such a child.

Rose was back with Teddy Crane after I convinced her that his acne will clear up, and that once it does he's going to be really handsome. I wasn't lying; he's got a nice face under all the spots. Dark hair and strong features, and a sort of steady presence that feels a bit protective. I just think Rose doesn't see things in the long term sometimes.

When John and Teddy went to buy more beers, just before Walt's singing attracted the police, I finally had a chance to chat with Rose about all my conflicting feelings. It had been two weeks since we'd sneaked onto the estate, and I'd been playing the whole experience in my head on a constant loop. Part of me knew I should watch out, because my friends were deceitful and I didn't want to be played for a fool. But I also find it exhausting to hold on to mistrust or anger for any length of time.

I sat myself down on the picnic blanket next to Rose and tucked an arm through hers. I had two jumpers on, because Emily had borrowed my wool coat and was refusing to give it back.

The way she wore my coat made it look like it had always been hers, somehow. I looked across at her for a moment, laughing and talking to Walt. It looked better on her—the double rows of gold buttons and bell cut of it were too mod for me anyway. I did feel a pang about those buttons, though, as they were the reason I'd chosen it in the first place. So unique—they had leaping stags on them, and I've never seen another coat with that detail.

"God, you must be freezing, Frannie," Rose said, and she rubbed my free arm to help me warm up.

129

"It's not too bad," I said, but it was still just the start of April and pitch dark, so that was a blatant lie.

"I'm going to put my foot down and get your coat back," Rose said. "This has gone on long enough."

"What, Em borrowing things? It's just how she is, you know that. Besides, I don't lend her anything without knowing I might lose it forever."

"Can't you see? It's more than that. The way she imitates you is really intense. You're too kind, you just gloss over everything, but it's . . . she's really calculating."

For a moment, all the feelings of the past two weeks welled up inside me. But I shook my head, tired. "You're giving her far too much credit," I said, but I thought about Rose's words. They were an echo of my instincts, my darkest worries that Emily had declared me to be her enemy. She was calculating, we all knew that about her. I just wasn't sure why her calculations had suddenly started targeting me. Normally, they always had to do with boys.

"Frances, just . . ." Rose ran a hand through her hair and bit her lower lip. For a moment it seemed like she was going to tell me something, but then she looked down and said nothing more.

I could see John and Teddy having a cigarette in front of the off-license, so I chose my moment. "Rose, why didn't any of you tell me you'd been sneaking onto the Gravesdown estate without me?"

Rose winced as if I'd poked her with a thorn but still didn't look up. "I'm sorry, Frannie, it was Em. You know how she is. She threatened me if I told you we'd been there."

"All right," I said firmly. "Then why did you go along with them in the first place?"

Rose looked at her hands, then back up at me. "I was only there the first time, and I didn't understand until later that Emily

130

lied to me. She said you were home feeling ill. I never went back with them after that, I promise."

"Okay," I said slowly. "But I still think there's something you aren't saying. Ford said he'd met Emily before, and he tried to warn me off you all. What exactly happened on that first visit?"

Rose looked over at the off-license, where Emily and Walt were buying some beers. "John, Walt, and I were up to the usual stuff. But Em disappeared for a while, and only popped back up when it was time to go home. Walt got a bit angry about it, and they argued, because it was clear where she was going."

"She was going up to the house," I said. I don't know why the realization deflated me, even when I'd suspected as much. I'd only spent an hour there chatting and drinking tea. But officially knowing Emily had been there first left a sour taste in my mouth. Saxon's comment floated to the top of my mind: "Emily got on the wrong side of Uncle Ford a few times. I think she hoped he was looking for a new wife."

The group was heading toward us across the green, and I watched Emily in my wool coat. She swayed and laughed on Walt's arm. With her blond hair cutting through the dark, he watched her as if she were a falling star, a streak in the night sky you only see a few times in a lifetime.

Walt had cut his hair and it mirrored John's now, which was neatly trimmed—he'd lost the mop he'd had only a few weeks earlier. It was curious, because Walt had loved his hair. He loved the sour looks he got from old ladies who muttered "ruffian" at him under their breath, and he loved how girls at the beach stopped him to tell him he looked like George Harrison. I just assumed fashion was changing and I was out of the loop.

It was an easy conclusion to come to, because I'm always the last to know. What I should have asked myself was why Walt was suddenly trying to look like John?

"I've got the best surprise game," Emily said as she approached, smiling widely and sitting herself next to me. She reached into one of her (my) coat pockets and pulled something out, something that was all dull metal and strange curves cloaked in the darkness of the evening.

Teddy swore, and Rose grabbed my arm to pull me farther away from Emily.

"What the hell, Em?" I shrieked. The revolver sat in her palm, almost innocent, like a prop in a play. "Where did you get that?"

"And why?" Teddy added. Rose just sat there, quietly terrified.

"I found the key to my dad's gun cabinet," Emily said, and swallowed a laugh so that it became an indignant snort. "It wasn't hard. And as for the why"—here she gave Teddy a narrow-eyed stare that practically screamed killjoy—"why not? So. Ever played Russian roulette?"

This was when Walt started his tree-pissing Kinks-bellowing racket, which thankfully attracted enough attention from the neighbors that they shouted that the police were on their way.

Emily sighed in a world-weary way that I felt she hadn't earned. Acting like a rebel around Castle Knoll didn't make her any more grown-up than the rest of us.

"Another time," she huffed, shoving the revolver down into her pocket again. "Let's all pile into the car before we're chased with pitchforks."

Emily sauntered back over to Walt, and the moment her back was turned, Rose reached into her own coat, just inside the collar.

"She's gone too far," Rose said, and I saw the thin chain on the bird necklace give off a small glint, like a feeble cry in the night, before Rose reached her hands behind her neck to unclasp it.

Finally she got free of the necklace and threw it out onto the green. "You should chuck yours too, Frances," Rose said.

I really did consider it. But the history Emily, Rose, and I have—well, it's the glue that's held us together for so long. Sure, that glue was thinning, but I felt I had to remind Rose it wasn't gone entirely.

"We know Emily, Rose. Think—when she acts like this—"

Rose cut me off. "She's never acted quite like this before."

"True, but she's come close. And Rose, you know why that was. This time is probably no different."

Emily's mother, Fiona Sparrow, has always been the picture-perfect woman. She's beautiful and traditional, and has extremely high expectations for Emily. Her father is the local councillor, and they're the kind of people who everyone in town wants to impress because they're so charismatic.

Emily's older sister ran away to London when she was just fifteen, and her name is never spoken in their house. Emily is treated like an only child, but the gap her sister left just means that Fiona is all the more determined to succeed with Emily where she failed before. Fiona is controlling in the extreme, choosing every item of clothing Emily wears, dressing her like a living doll.

I looked at Emily through the darkness and noticed that she still wore Fiona Sparrow's signature heels, and stockings with seams up the back, which you can't even get in shops these days.

I was in smart cigarette trousers, and I felt rather bold because I'd found some gingham fabric—the lining of a raincoat from a jumble sale—and made them after I saw them in a magazine photo. Mother had helped me, and we had a right laugh tearing the coat to pieces to make the trousers à la Audrey Hepburn.

Emily looked my way suddenly, and it was almost spooky, as if she could read my mind.

I thought back to when we were ten and I unexpectedly popped in to say hello to Emily. Back then, Rose, Emily, and I had the kind of friendship that was simple and easy. Making rope swings over the River Dimber in summer and filling up on blackberries in

August. Believing that the wild rabbits that popped out of hedgerows could speak to us, and that we could tame them. And Emily always came up with the best games, the most creative ideas.

I suppose, in a way, it was me who unmasked all the layers of Emily's life. I wonder if she blamed me for it.

That day the front door was cracked open, to catch any hint of a breeze in the stifling summer air. Emily had books balancing on her head, as if she were in finishing school, and was failing to set teacups down silently enough for Fiona. I could hear Fiona's words traveling across the room in a loud hiss: "How will you get anyone to love you if you can't even do the simplest things? You're going to be stuck in Castle Knoll forever, in this life! You're pretty, Emily, if you don't ruin it by opening your whiny mouth. And being pretty is the only currency you have, because everything else about you is unexceptional. You've got to learn to use your looks so you don't become an embarrassment to this family."

The cup clattered again, and chipped this time because Emily's hand shook so badly.

Fiona swept the entire tea set off the table, and it shattered against the wall before peppering the floor, and Emily just sat there silently, staring at it.

"You'll spend the rest of the day gluing this back together, thinking about your clumsiness," Fiona had said. "Men from good families do not want graceless wives. You wouldn't snare a Foyle, never mind a Gravesdown, with your sloppy manners."

Emily knelt on the floor and started scooping up the shards. Outrage was flowing through me, and I had my hands in fists at my sides. Fiona had her back to me, but Emily's eyes flicked to where I stood in the doorway. She looked hurt and ashamed, and then an angry determination settled over her face. She shook her head almost imperceptibly, as if to say, Frances, don't you dare get involved.

And so I didn't.

But after that, Emily's games got darker and more intense. Not all at once, but gradually, and in a way that was thrilling at first. Our early teens passed with Emily inventing the best scary stories, and leading Rose and me in summoning ghosts or dabbling in made-up black magic. We spied on people in the village and gossiped together when we uncovered secrets that we knew were half-invented. But we never hurt anyone, and we never hurt ourselves.

"We can't blame Fiona for everything Emily does," Rose said. "She's not here, making Emily's choices."

"Maybe not," I said. "But I sometimes wonder whether Emily toys with us just to feel she has some control over her life, outside of Fiona's reach. Or perhaps it's a way of punishing us for knowing too much."

Teddy was sitting there silently, very tactfully pretending to be transfixed by the clouds rolling in over our heads. There was just enough moonlight to reveal their stormy edges in the darkness. Someone shouted for us to get a move on, so we made our way across the green, more unsaid thoughts about Emily hanging between us.

I felt it was fate when the toe of my shoe caught on Rose's necklace, and I carefully untangled it from the grass.

"You know, the bird will betray you, Frances," Rose said softly as I tried to hand the necklace back to her. She refused to take it, so Teddy reached out and took it instead.

"I thought you didn't believe in my fortune," I said.

"I'm starting to," she said. And I felt a chill take me then. I wanted to stand by Emily through her horridness, but my fortune was starting to shake my trust in everyone and everything around me.

Crane, Sparrow, queens on chessboards, bank notes and playing cards—I felt like I couldn't beat this fortune on my own. I wanted someone to help me. I felt so very, horribly lonely right then.

And then I thought, Ford. Ford knows how to plan. He knows how to play games and win. *After that, I couldn't stop thinking of him.*

CHAPTER

16

SAXON WALKS UP TO THE DESK AND TAKES THE FILE with a small *Do you mind?* lift of his eyebrows. The detective nods, and Saxon brings the file back to where we're all sitting. I suppose we're all entitled to know the results written there now, and Saxon has the proper expertise to interpret them.

"How did that autopsy get done so fast?" I ask Crane.

"The coroner from the next county over was available to work in tandem with Dr. Owusu, and it turned out there wasn't a backlog in their labs like there usually is in Sandview. Autopsies only take about four hours. It's the paperwork and the lab results that can hold off the formal reports. But in this case, all the right people were free, so it was processed quickly."

"Oh, okay. So what happened to her if it wasn't the hemlock? That bouquet... Dr. Owusu said hemlock can be deadly if it gets in the bloodstream, and Great Aunt Frances had cuts all over her hands."

I decide to move away from Saxon, who is muttering to

himself while Elva hovers at his shoulder. I get up and walk over to Crane, who has gone back to his perch by the window. Mr. Gordon stays where he is, making it clear that he's heard this already.

"It wasn't the hemlock that killed her. That appears to have been an unrelated incident," Crane says.

"Unrelated? Even if the flowers didn't kill her, they were certainly a threat. That makes it relevant," I say.

Crane leans in a little and gently touches my elbow. He says evenly, "I'm looking into it, Annie. Let me do my job." He's so quietly authoritative that it's disarming. With a jolt, I realize that this is his thing—and *disarming* is exactly what he's doing. Great Aunt Frances has created a hornet's nest for him professionally, by pitting the group of us against one another to solve her murder. We're going to meddle with whatever investigation he'll be trying to conduct, and whatever happens . . . it's going to be difficult for him to come out of it looking good.

The ticking clock has put my brain into overdrive, and I'm already doing mental gymnastics trying to get ahead. I take a breath to steady myself. On paper I have a week to figure out what's going on, but really, Saxon and I each have as long as it takes the other to solve this.

This means that for me, there are several levels of motivation now.

Me solving this murder would mean that Mum could have the Chelsea house. The house where she's always been happy and inspired. Leaving that house might upset her already fickle process for painting, especially because it was there that she created the early work that did so well. And watching Elva take it over would break both our hearts.

And I can't bear the idea of Oliver and Jessop Fields destroying the land on the Gravesdown estate to make car parks and cinemas. Gravesdown Hall might be spared if it's a listed historical building, but it would undoubtedly be sold to a hotel developer. The woodland would certainly be leveled for a housing estate, and while I understand people need blocks of flats, I am certain there are better places to build them.

But above all, I want to solve this puzzle. And I've been called on to do just that, the one thing I can't help doing already. *I'm needed.* Me. Annie Adams, aspiring murder mystery writer. And I get the sense that something *happened* here. Not just with Great Aunt Frances yesterday, but a story spanning decades.

Oliver's drawl cuts through my thoughts. "What happens if Detective Crane solves the murder first?"

Saxon's head snaps up, and everyone looks at Mr. Gordon. "If the detective solves the murder first, then the estate gets sold through Oliver." Mr. Gordon's expression is cloudy, as if there's a thunderstorm brewing inside him and he's doing his best to hold it back. Castle Knoll is his home, and from what I gather, his grandson has done his best to spend as little time as possible here. I very much doubt Mr. Gordon is happy about the idea of Gravesdown land becoming a block of flats or a car dealership.

"So," Oliver says slowly, "I get the choice of being on the detective's team, or—"

"We are not a team," Crane cuts in without missing a beat.

Oliver ignores him. "Or I just sit around here waiting for these two to fail?"

Saxon and I look at each other then, and I can almost see the other shoe dropping for him. He's finally worked out that our competition isn't just with each other—both Oliver and Detective Crane have professional stakes in this. Oliver just needs us to fail, and Crane isn't going to want us making a mess of his investigation. And we will. The most logical thing for Saxon and me to do is to keep any significant discoveries or evidence away from the police. I look at Crane again and find him already watching me. I get the feeling he's always five steps ahead, and it makes me uneasy. He's got police resources, and I find him too charming for my liking. If I were him, I'd try to get one of us on his side, and I can tell it's not Saxon he's going to work on.

There are so many variables that it's overwhelming. Mr. Gordon isn't entirely neutral either. That green leather-bound book I took yesterday floats to the top of my mind, and I decide to read it as soon as I have a quiet moment.

I feel my jaw set with determination. I need a notebook; I should be writing this down. It's a very good thing I have several blank ones waiting for me up in my room.

I feel Crane's hand on my elbow again, and he leans in and says, "Are you okay?"

"No one's injured. I'm not going to keel over," I say through clenched teeth.

"I just wanted to check," he says. Oliver is watching us, his gaze cool and calculating. And standing between them, I get the feeling I've been identified as the weak link here. Annie Adams, recently redundant admin assistant by day, wannabe writer by night. Prone to fainting at the worst possible times. Daughter of Laura, the modern artist out of touch with reality.

Saxon walks over to me with the autopsy in his hand and passes me the file. Like me, he's weighing up all these dynamics, but his face is carefully blank.

"It's rather brilliant, what she's done. I hate it, of course, but it's a very fitting game. Uncle Ford would have been proud of her."

From a certain perspective, if I can't solve this murder,

Saxon is probably the next best choice. Perhaps I can make some kind of deal with him if he wins, and he'll let us keep our house. I'm still determined to do the best I can, but it's smart to consider all the possible outcomes. The property development company just sounds like a horrible way for this to end. And there it is—another stroke of Great Aunt Frances's genius.

The whole town will give us whatever information they can, once they find out what will happen if we fail. Aside from the murderer, of course. But it's extremely cunning. Great Aunt Frances really has forced everyone who ever doubted her to take her seriously now.

I look at the file in my hands. "So what are we looking at? How did she die?" I ask him in a low voice.

Crane takes a couple of pages from my hands. He gives me a questioning look, and my anger flares again at the gentle treatment he's offering me after my fainting episode yesterday. "I can handle it," I say, giving him a level stare.

"She was poisoned, but in a way that would have been almost impossible to trace. Luckily Dr. Owusu was very thorough, and because Frances was her patient, she noticed something that a lot of doctors wouldn't have."

"What kind of poison is nearly impossible to trace?"

"The kind that isn't usually poison. Frances was seeing Dr. Owusu for a series of vitamin injections. She was extremely deficient in B_{12}, which needs more than tablets to correct when your levels get too low. But some vitamins and minerals can be lethal in high doses."

"What, like B_{12}?"

"No, like iron. And that's what caused Frances's heart attack. The level of iron found in her bloodstream was lethal, and Dr. Owusu found an additional injection site on Frances's body, so it seems someone injected her with iron.

But here's the confusing part: That amount of iron isn't easy to come by. No doctor's surgery will just have syringes of iron on hand."

"Then where would it come from?"

Crane puts the papers back in the file, which is still open in my hands. "That's what we're still trying to determine."

Saxon suddenly looks eager to leave. He glances at Elva, and she's by his side. Before they go, Saxon turns to me.

"Annie, I'll give you a leg up, to level the playing field." His smile seems genuine, but it's more tightly contained than it was when he first said hello to me.

"Why?" I ask. I'm unsure how the dynamic between Saxon and me is going to play out. Are we going to be adversaries, fighting to win an inheritance? Or teammates, making a deal to share the estate, to have the best chance of saving the whole thing from the clutches of Oliver and Jessop Fields?

"Since you're new here, and don't know this town the way I do, I feel it's only fair." His voice is even and businesslike. It seems Saxon is taking this game seriously, and I feel the air between us click firmly into adversarial territory. But at least he's coming at this from a perspective of fairness, which I'm certain is more than Elva would do.

Saxon taps the autopsy folder in my hands. "Crane's right, no GP would have syringes containing that dosage of iron on hand. But there's someone else on the Gravesdown estate who would."

"What?" I blink in surprise, because I can't think who Saxon might mean.

"Beth's wife, Miyuki, is a large animal vet and has a clinic on Archie Foyle's farm. And based on the level noted in the autopsy, Frances was injected with enough iron to dose a horse."

CHAPTER
17

The Castle Knoll Files, September 26, 1966

WHEN WE GOT KICKED OFF THE VILLAGE GREEN, WE ALL piled into Walt's car and Emily slid behind the wheel. If she hadn't been driving, maybe we would have ended up somewhere else, but she took us back to the same broken spot in the fence on the edge of the Gravesdown estate.

"If we have permission to hang out in the woods, why keep up this sneaking through the fence malarky?" I said.

"Malarky," Emily sneered in a singsong voice. "You talk like my grandma."

"Leave Frances alone, Em," John said, and he sounded tired. I was sitting on his lap because the backseat of Walt's car only had room for three, and Rose and Teddy were still in that awkward phase where they were skirting around each other, waiting to see how they got on. I know for a fact that Rose lost her virginity to Archie Foyle in that exact backseat, and I wondered if Teddy had heard that gossip. It's the sort of information Emily would drop at the worst possible moment, just to see what sort of trouble it would cause.

I could tell Rose was trying to like Teddy; she always talked about how we were going to find the two best-looking boys in Castle Knoll and get married and have babies at the same time. Emily would be off doing something glamorous in London, and things would be more peaceful for those of us who were happy to stay in Castle Knoll.

"I don't want to hang out in the woods," Emily said. "I told you before, I've got proof that Ford killed his wife." Her smile was like the Cheshire Cat's, and I felt like Alice down the rabbit hole, stumbling around in a world where everyone knew the rules but me.

"You seem on rather friendly terms with him," I said, and Rose gave me a sharp sideways glance. "In fact, Em, I wouldn't be surprised if you'd been up to the house before." I waited to see if she'd deny it, and Rose stiffened and got a worried look on her face. I suppose by baiting Emily this way, I was throwing Rose under the bus, but really it was Ford who'd told me they'd all been hanging around without me, and if it came to it, I'd tell Emily that.

Emily's grin only got wider. "And how was your visit with Ford, Frannie? Did he have tea brought and teach you about chess? Did he warn you that your friends are no good?"

I felt as if I'd had a bucket of ice tipped over me. I hadn't told the others any details about the hour I'd spent up at the house, just that I'd chatted with Ford and Saxon, then left.

I tried to come up with something to say to Emily, but my mouth just stuck open as though I'd run out of air. John's grip tightened around one of my wrists, and I felt strangely as if I'd been caught doing something wrong. "What's this proof you have then?" I said, refusing to take her bait. "That Ford killed his first wife. Do you even know her name?"

"Of course I do. It was Olivia Gravesdown. I'll show you my

proof, but only once we're inside the abandoned farmhouse. You'll have to see it to believe it."

Walt let out an annoyed groan and put a hand on the seat behind Emily's head. *"Em, come on! We don't need to hang out in some falling-down building. We'll have much more fun out in the open. And Ford said not to go there. He practically called it a death trap."*

"Why do you think he's so keen for us to stay away?" she asked. *"Don't you want to see what he's hiding there? I'm positive it's his dead wife. . . ."*

"You are so dramatic, Em," Rose said. *"But I'd like to see you play the fool for once. Let's go then, off to this damp old building full of nothing but rats and your lies."*

"Wow, Rose, when did you grow a spine?" Emily crowed. She looked pleased, though, as if Rose was stepping in and filling a role Emily wanted someone to play.

Rose didn't answer. But when Emily parked the car and we all got out, there was a small moment where they stared each other down, an unspoken challenge between them. It was Rose who looked away first and started to squeeze her way through the hole in the fence.

It began to rain as we picked our way through the woods, and we had to make a mad dash across the lawns to get to the north side of the grounds, where the edge of the farm started. The house was a black spot in the night, squatting there like a toad on the riverbank.

As we approached it, I was surprised to see that it wasn't falling down, just eerie and still. It was rather sprawling for a farmhouse, and made of the white stones that come from the nearby quarries. But it was so moss-covered and overgrown with ivy that it looked almost completely green. The door was unlocked, and the inside was nothing like I'd imagined. Emily produced a small *pocket torch, and everyone but me shook water droplets off their coats. I shivered in my now-damp jumpers, watching Emily in my coat, looking snug.*

It was curious, though—there were no broken windows or rotting floorboards here. This was well-kept and . . . not dangerous at all. Why did Ford not want us coming here?

"This is someone's home, Emily," John whispered as we tiptoed inside. He was right—the house wasn't empty. It held nice furniture, lamps, a clock—even dishes in a china cabinet on one wall. It was as if someone had just popped out and would be back any minute.

"We shouldn't be here," Rose said. I was feeling the same—collectively, we'd changed our minds about the place the second we'd stepped through the door. All of us except Emily.

"Just wait," Emily said. She led us farther into the house, her torch bouncing off mirrors and shining back at odd angles. The room she took us to was a study, but I could see why it had captured her grim imagination. It had been utterly torn to shreds, as if someone with a violent temper had declared war on the walls themselves.

Glass from shattered photo frames was all over the floor, and books were in heaps, along with splintered chairs. Even the wallpaper had huge strips taken out of it, and I had visions of a knife fight happening here—every missed stab recorded on the walls forever, like violent fingerprints.

"This," Emily said dramatically, "is where he killed her."

Rose freed a photo from a shattered frame, and her forehead was all creases as she tried to make it out. "This was Archie's house," she said quietly. "And no one was killed here, Emily. The family got evicted, Archie told me that. He never told me he lived here, just that he used to live on a farm. And then his father left, so Archie was stuck in foster care."

"Wait, who is this? Shifty Archie?" Teddy asked.

"Oh, yes, Rose has a history with bad boys. Sorry, Ted," Emily cooed. "But they got evicted because Archie's dad was a drunk and a gambler, and he was having an affair with Ford's wife. Ford told me he smashed some of the rooms up. He said it was a good place to get his anger out after he kicked them both off the estate. But I don't think he just smashed up the rooms. . . ." Emily said.

"You don't know anything," Rose said. "You're making a whole history up when you have no idea."

"Do I not?" She threw us her best innocent face. "Ford likes me. He says he can talk to me."

Walt's expression was thunderous.

"I need some air," Rose said.

"I'll come with you," I replied, and I linked arms with her as she headed for the door.

Outside the rain was still falling, but it had eased into a gentle drizzle. "Rose," I said carefully, "do you actually have some feelings for Archie Foyle?"

"Not really," she said slowly. "I mean, yes, but more in that way you get when someone's had a sad life and you feel sorry for them. Archie's had a really rough go of things. But I've no idea what actually happened here."

"I do." Saxon's voice cut through the dark.

"Saxon! Jesus, you scared me!" I hissed. "You really do like to pop out of nowhere, don't you!"

"Sorry," he said, and he actually sounded it. "But you shouldn't be here. It's not dangerous—my uncle lied about that—but this place is sort of personal to him. Anyway, you'd better leave before he figures out you're here. He has a weird knack for knowing about anything that's happening on our grounds."

"I'll drag Emily out," I said. "The rest of them will go wherever she goes. Rose, you wait here with Saxon, and then we can take him back up to the house."

Saxon gave us both a considering look. "Before you go in, let's play a game."

"Saxon, really! We don't have time for games," I said sternly.

"You have time for this one. It's very simple." Saxon's face was carefully blank. "It's called A Secret for a Secret. And that's what it is—I'll tell you a secret, and you tell me one back."

"Neither of us has any secrets," Rose said.

"She's right, and I bet you know about five times as many secrets as we do, with all the spying you do."

Saxon grinned, because of course that was the point. The gossip that was burning him up on my last visit—he just wanted an excuse to tell it.

"Fine, Saxon. I'll tell you a secret," I said. "But you tell me yours first."

"Your friend Emily's got a whopping big secret." He emphasized his point by miming a rounded belly on his front. "A secret she got from your boyfriend, right here in these woods."

CHAPTER
18

"RUN THIS BY ME ONE MORE TIME," JENNY SAYS. I'M sitting on the bed of my little room, back in my jeans and T-shirt from yesterday. I've sprayed an extra layer of perfume over myself, but soon things are going to get desperate and I'll need to take a bath and find some new clothes.

At this point I'm getting tired of explaining the bizarre situation in which I find myself, so I let out a snort of exasperation and just say, "I'm a contestant in Great Aunt Frances's murder games."

"Right," Jenny says. "That part I got. The part that's throwing me is the alphabetical secrets, and why you haven't opened the file about your dad."

I look at the two files laid out on the bed in front of me. "If I'm completely honest," I say slowly, "I'm actually more interested in what's in the Crane file. I looked at the first few pages of Sam Arlington's file, and he just feels like some man I don't know. There are bank records in there, tax documents, probably things that prove he had some kind of affair while Mum was pregnant with me, but all that stuff feels like

Mum's story. Maybe I'll be interested at some other point in my life, but right now I want to focus on who killed Great Aunt Frances."

"Okay, that's fair," Jenny replies, and changes the subject. "You're the murder mystery fan, so where are you starting? Suspects? Motive? I'd be your Dr. Watson if I had any useful skills in this department, but I'm afraid the best I can do is make you a miniature murder scene if you need one."

"If this were a locked-room scenario, I'd be all over that," I say.

"Well, if TV has taught us anything, it's that the murder rate in small villages is disproportionately high. So you'd better keep me on standby, because I'm sure there's a locked room in your future."

"I'm just warning you that from now on I'm taking any predictions about my future extremely seriously," I say. And I'm only half joking. Great Aunt Frances's fortune is starting to get under my skin. "But thinking like a TV detective isn't a bad place to start. In most crime shows and murder mysteries, there's a time just after the victim dies, when whoever is investigating asks several standard questions. They're usually some variation of, *Did she have any enemies?* and *Was there anything odd about her behavior before she was killed?* and *Who was the last person to see her alive?*"

"Ooh, also *Who found the body?*" Jenny says, her voice excited.

"Yes, good one. If we start there, we've got Elva, Mr. Gordon, Oliver, and me. But now that we know Great Aunt Frances was killed with an injection of iron rather than poisoned by the roses, it makes it seem less likely they could have murdered her. But both Elva and Oliver arrived late, and looking at the time of death . . . it's a fifteen-minute drive to the village from the Gravesdown estate, so it's a narrow window, but it's possible." I pause and rummage in my backpack for a notebook and a pen. I pull out a notebook that has friendly illustrations of woodland mushrooms on it. Just for the sake of being thorough, I write down all those names and cross out Mr. Gordon, citing my reasoning in the margin. Something about that flower arrangement still gnaws at me, so on the opposite page I write *The flowers—who sent them, and why?* under the heading *Unanswered Questions*.

"What about Frances's own investigation into her future murder?" Jenny asks. "Who did *she* suspect?"

I think of Great Aunt Frances's murder board, all its crisscrosses of colored string and the different photos there. She suspected the whole town of having a reason to kill her, and seemed completely oblivious to the fact that her suspicions and incessant digging probably *gave* them those reasons to begin with.

It occurs to me that I've got even more reason to suspect Oliver, because of his breakfast meeting with Frances, when they went over the Jessop Fields plans for the estate.

"I need to have another look at her murder board," I say. "It was very involved; I should photograph it."

"Make your own list first," Jenny suggests. "That way you won't let her paranoia bias you."

"Easier said than done," I say. "If her paranoia drove someone to kill her, one of the most useful things I can do is try to understand the way her mind worked."

There's a friendly silence while I write down a few more names of people I think are potential suspects. I find Rose's surname from when I met her son, Joe, earlier, and find Beth and her wife Miyuki's by doing a quick Google search of their businesses. The top half of my list reads:

~~Walter Gordon~~
Oliver Gordon
Elva Gravesdown

I read out the next set of suspects to Jenny: "Saxon Gravesdown, Archie Foyle, Beth Takaga-Foyle, Miyuki Takaga-Foyle, Detective Rowan Crane, and Rose Leroy."

"Not to state the obvious, but if Silver Fox Saxon told you that Beth's wife probably supplied the iron, I'm immediately doubting it was her," Jenny says.

"He said he was playing fair," I say.

"Uh-huh. Because it totally makes sense to *play fair* with the relative from London you've never met, who stands to take away your childhood home," Jenny deadpans.

"Okay, fine," I relent. "I'll admit we shouldn't necessarily take Saxon at his word. But at least we know he was on the ferry coming back from work at Sandview Hospital. He even produced a ticket when the detective asked him to verify his whereabouts."

Jenny groans. "Did you learn nothing from the Andrew experience?"

And I immediately see her logic. Andrew was an art student with Jenny and me at Saint Martins, and I fell head over heels for him in our first year. I finally uncovered his scheme of lying about seeing another girl behind my back when I realized the parking passes he bought when he went to "work" were a scam. As in, he paid for parking, but that wasn't where his car was.

"Just because Saxon had a ticket," I say slowly, "doesn't mean he used it."

"Exactly," Jenny says.

Remembering cheating Andrew from university draws my mind back to the files in front of me.

"Speaking of cheaters," I say, "care to hear which member of the Crane family Great Aunt Frances suspected of infidelity?"

"I was wondering why you had Sexy Detective on your suspect list," Jenny says.

"I never used that adjective to describe him," I say evenly.

"I know. I just colored in the lines for you."

"Well, you can put your crayons away," I tell her.

I open the file and a stack of papers slides out. It's everything from receipts for rooms at the Castle House Hotel to surveillance photos. I instantly recognize Reggie Crane, my taxi driver and the detective's dad, in a car with a blurry blond woman late at night. In the photos they appear to be arguing, but the emotion on Reggie's face is plain. This isn't the kind of intensity you have in an argument with just anyone.

I keep flipping, and I see papers that look much older. I startle when I recognize a photo of Mum—this one's from a newspaper clipping from when she first made it big. She's at some kind of event, but there on her arm, in that awful nineties fashion of suit jackets with three buttons, is Reggie Crane.

There's nothing else in there on Mum and Reggie, but I remember him saying that they dated in their teens. When the dust has settled on her new exhibition, I'll ask her about him.

"Hello? You still there?" Jenny's voice echoes down the phone.

"Yeah, sorry." I flip back to the beginning of the file and notice that I skipped the first few pages by mistake. There, the words *Cease and Desist* practically scream at me in bold at the top of the page. "It's just . . . I found a very angry letter threatening Great Aunt Frances with legal action if she doesn't leave the Crane family alone."

"Let me guess, the embittered taxi driver tried to get a restraining order, and when your great aunt wouldn't stop, he took matters into his own hands to silence her?"

I wince. "This letter isn't signed by Reggie. It's from Detective Rowan Crane."

"Huh. But you said the detective seemed genuinely sad when you told him Frances had died. He said he liked her, right?" Jenny asks.

I feel small lines of disappointment crease my forehead. "From the tone of this letter, it looks like he lied."

I absently underline Detective Crane's name in my notebook, and my *Unanswered Questions* heading catches my eye again.

"Those flowers," I say. "They can't be a coincidence. Sending them is such a horrible and specific threat." I can't let go of the idea that the flowers must be connected to the murder in some way. And if my instincts are right, then another name needs to be added to my list of suspects.

"The vicar's name is John something," I muse. "I'm adding him to my suspect list because of what Mr. Gordon said about Great Aunt Frances doing the flowers for the church every week, and because Crane mentioned that she and John had a past." I can hear background voices on Jenny's end of the line, and I'm guessing her coffee break is over. I hastily add *John (Vicar)* to my list.

"I've got to head back to work," Jenny says. "But I want regular updates, okay? I'm taking this Dr. Watson thing seriously."

"You got it," I say, and hang up. I don't surface from my thoughts, though, because Jenny saying the word *doctor* reminds me that my suspect list still needs a few more names.

I remember my visit to Dr. Owusu's surgery, and the appointment book. Supposing Great Aunt Frances *did* make it to the appointment she was penciled in for, then the doctor's surgery suddenly looks very suspicious. I can't think of a reason Dr. Owusu would want to kill Great Aunt Frances, but I might be able to find one if I dig around in Frances's files long enough.

I add:

Dr. Esi Owusu
Magda (paramedic)
Joe Leroy (paramedic)

I want to find out John the vicar's surname, so I open the browser on my phone and do some searching. On the church website, there's a photo next to the name John Oxley. He's standing in front of the church's open doors with a smile on his face, as if he's welcoming you inside. He looks slim-built and immaculate in the way that clergymen usually are. In his picture, he has a soft grip on a Bible and wears his clean, pressed robes like a doctor wears a lab coat. Delicate wire-rimmed glasses and neatly combed white hair give the impression of the type of person who has a favorite armchair.

I consider using another notebook to elaborate on each person, as if they were characters in a story. I lift my stack of notebooks toward me and let my fingers flutter over one covered in cork. I notice that the green book I stole yesterday has found its way into the pile and I pull it out carefully, trying not to get my hopes up. I know Walt's name was in there, but the rest could be flower identification, or horoscopes, for all I know.

But it's not. The first page bears a heading—*The Castle Knoll Files, September 10, 1966.* She begins: *I'm writing this all here because I just know there will be things I've seen that might matter further down the road.* At barely two pages in, I find

myself gripping the sides of the book, bewitched by her curling teenage handwriting and the account written inside. An
hour later, I'm still reading it. I'm about a third of the way
through—Saxon has just revealed that Emily is pregnant—
when I'm pulled away by my phone ringing again.

By then I've underlined one name on my list several
times: John Oxley. Right now he seems like the suspect with
the most motive.

One question I haven't asked yet is, *Why now?* Frances
had presumably been a busybody ever since her worry about
her fortune really took hold. For the past *sixty years.*

So what happened recently that finally secured a fate
sixty years in the making?

CHAPTER

19

The Castle Knoll Files, September 26, 1966

SAXON MIMED A PREGNANT BELLY FOR THE SECOND *time, just to be sure I'd understood.*

My eyes widened and my jaw set, but I kept my composure. This could all be complete lies. Rose, however, looked mortified but unsurprised, so I drew myself up and said, "Fine then, we'll see."

I strode through the farmhouse door and back to the wrecked study, where Emily was commanding the attention of the boys with some ridiculous story. "We need to go," I said, "and I want my coat back." Emily's face turned stony when she saw Saxon and Rose behind me. My mind was racing when I thought of John that first night—his reluctance to let me walk alone with Saxon, and Emily's taunts about John's experience with women. Had she been talking about experience with her? I wanted the truth, and I wanted it now.

Emily looked me right in the eyes and said, "No, I'm going to keep it."

"Give me my coat back, Emily," I said again. My voice was

hard, my expression furious. "I'm cold." Emily and I stared at each other, and we both knew this conversation wasn't about a coat.

"No, you're not."

I strode forward, and before I knew it, I had a handful of the wool fabric and was wrenching the buttons apart while she screamed in my face. She called me every horrible name she could think of while she clawed at my arms, and the others stood quietly, letting it all happen. The coat was stylish but cheap, so a couple of the buttons popped open easily. Something heavy was in one of the pockets, and it thunked against my leg as the coat flapped open. My eyes flew to her abdomen.

"Is it true?" I screamed. "Are you pregnant? Is it John's?" Everyone else had retreated several steps to stand behind me.

Emily straightened her shoulders, and the small bump of her midsection became even more prominent. "I suppose it was only a matter of time before the whole thing became obvious," she said. Her voice was so calm it almost sounded lazy.

"What the hell, Emily?" Walt screamed, coming out from behind me and closing the distance between them. "All that garbage you fed me about 'women's troubles,' all those excuses to suddenly stop getting close to me?"

"You'll get over it, Walt," she said. She sounded almost smug, as if this was a nice plan of hers that we'd all just stumbled into. I was breathing sharply through my nose, my breath ragged, watching her.

"So I'm guessing," I growled, "based on the fact that Walt's looking like he might strangle you, that he's sure this isn't his baby." My words came out like drumbeats, and my throat was hot with anger and betrayal. I couldn't look at John. I wouldn't. He was silent behind me, like some slinking shadow, and the fact that he hadn't stepped in to defend himself or to try to talk to me at all spoke volumes.

"We haven't been together that way for months," Walt said,

his face pinched in a mixture of confusion and shame. "Like a fool, I believed her when she said she was having some kind of health issues, gaining weight, feeling down. I worried that she was losing interest in me, but I thought she'd come round again." His eyes turned glassy, and his expression started to shift between rage and despair, as though both emotions were so big he couldn't feel them at the same time. "And really it was just that she'd been going behind my back." Walt's eyes shifted to a point over my shoulder. "With my best friend!" His voice was a roar as he went for John, but Teddy Crane blocked him and it seemed to knock some of the fight out of Walt.

"Here." Emily tossed the coat at me. "Take your bloody coat."

I caught the coat, and out of some bizarre impulse to take back something that was mine, I put it on. My hand found cold metal in the pocket, where the heaviness had caught me just a minute ago. My mind couldn't make sense of what I was touching until I pulled the revolver out.

And then it all happened so quickly.

Walt flew at Emily—fun-loving Walt, always up for a laugh, always following Emily around. He hit her, actually hit her, and before I knew it I was screaming at them both, the gun sweaty in my hand as I squeezed too hard.

A shot hit the wall, another scar of violence for that old farm-house.

Emily's nose was bleeding from its collision with Walt's fist, and people were talking to me, but I couldn't hear them. My ears were ringing too badly, and tears blurred my eyes.

So I ran, and I didn't even think about where I'd put the gun until much later. I was choking on sobs, my face messy and my hair slicked down with rain, when Ford answered the door.

"Let's get you inside," he said.

I didn't tell Ford about any of it; my teeth were chattering so badly that even if I'd wanted to, I couldn't have. He took my coat and sat me by the fire, and his housekeeper brought me a towel to dry my wet hair.

He sat patiently with me and waited for me to calm down. When I finally felt at ease, I started apologizing and couldn't stop. This whole thing was such a mess! What the hell was I doing here?

But Ford didn't make me feel silly. He effortlessly steered the conversation toward easy topics that didn't concern my friends. He showed me a backgammon set he'd bought on his travels to Afghanistan, and I sank into the intricate patterns of it. The beautiful inlay of abalone shell and mother-of-pearl next to deep black onyx was transfixing in the firelight.

"Afghanistan," I breathed as I ran a finger over the fine lacquer. "What's it like?"

"It's a beautiful country," he said. "The food, the people, there's fantastic art there too. Do you like art, Frances?"

"I'm not very cultured," I admitted, "if that's what you're asking. But I love to learn new things." I gave him a smile, and I think I managed to make it only half-sad.

Suddenly he looked up, and the housekeeper was back. She had a bedraggled Rose beside her, with Emily—red-eyed and puffy-faced—bringing up the rear. Em was actually hiccupping, and her distress looked genuine. The blood from her nose was still running down her face, and she had one arm underneath it, in an attempt to keep it from dripping on the floor.

I felt rage tighten my arms, and I gripped a cushion as my hands curled into fists. Ford leaped into action, because he only saw what was happening on the surface—Emily bleeding and crying, Rose looking lost. He asked the housekeeper to get some warm flannels for Emily's face, and installed her and Rose by the fire. He motioned me onto the sofa next to him, and it was the first time we'd sat that close. It wasn't even close, really, there was enough space for both of our hands to fall by our sides without touching, but I still felt acutely aware that he was near. I was reeling over John, hating him and Emily, and feeling wretched, but sitting by Ford made me feel anchored somehow. And in the way he had arranged us all, I had the odd sense of having been chosen. When I looked over, Rose and Emily were watching us as if they were watching a film.

"Where is the rest of your group?" Ford asked. His voice was casual, but some of the menace I thought I saw in the dark that very first night was creeping back. But when he looked at Emily, there was very nearly laughter in his eyes. It was unsettling.

I suddenly wished I'd used my time alone with Ford to ask him about Emily's previous visits to Gravesdown Hall, instead of talking about Afghanistan.

"Teddy drove Walt's car back to the village, with Walt in the backseat and John up front," Rose said carefully. "He told us he'd come back and get us once he'd dropped them home, but that it wasn't a good idea for us all to travel as a group, given the . . . fight that broke out."

"I see," Ford said. He stood up, and even that was rather elegant—like a fern uncurling. "I'm going to go and check on Saxon—I can hear his muddy boots clomping in the hallway. When I get back, we can decide whether you'd like me to give you all a lift to the village, or if you'd prefer to wait for your friend to collect you."

We listened to Ford's shoes clip on the flagstones in the next room, until they faded away.

"Emily, what the hell?" I finally shouted. "It's like everything I have, you want." I rose from the sofa and went to face her, speaking in harsh whispers. "John loves me, he actually does," I hissed. But a quiet voice of doubt slithered through me. Does he? He didn't say anything when the confrontation happened earlier.

"I know he does," she said quietly.

"Then why?" I shot back. "Why do this? It's so unbalanced when I think about it! My hair combs, my coat . . . was my wardrobe not satisfying enough for you? You had to take my boyfriend as well?"

Emily was quiet, but she met my eyes unflinchingly.

"Well, you can have him," I spat. "And what then? When I don't want John anymore, are you going to sniff around at my heels, waiting to see who I go out with next?"

Finally she spoke, and the sweet smile on her face turned my stomach. "For once, Frannie, it's the other way around." She leaned in and dropped her voice. "This time, I found the best man first. You watch, I'm going to be lady of the manor." She grinned, and it made all the emotions I'd had about Ford swirl back up again—and they felt tiny, and silly.

"You stupid slut," I fired back. "Who exactly is the father of this baby?"

Emily said nothing, but her coy comments about my evening with Ford the other day rang back in my mind like church bells. Perhaps she'd told me this already.

"Have you decided how you'd like to return to the village?" Ford's voice was quiet from the doorway, but his steely gaze was directed at Emily.

"I'd like a ride back, if you don't mind, please, Ford," Emily said.

"I'll wait for Teddy," Rose said. She'd been remarkably quiet through the whole exchange, but then, what was there for her to say? This was between me and Emily. It seems it always was, even when it was just about a hair comb. "Is that okay? I don't want him coming all the way back just to find us gone. Especially when he was only trying to help."

"Of course, Rose," Ford said. "That's thoughtful of you. You can have some tea and wait here by the fire if you like. The housekeeper will fetch you when he arrives." Ford looked at me. "Frances, are you staying with Rose, or getting a lift with Emily and me?"

It was oddly like being asked to choose between my two closest friends. But even before all the drama of the evening, I'd have always chosen Rose. Something in me hesitated, though, and I was back in the game I couldn't stop playing.

"I'll go with you and Emily," I said. "In case I have more I need to say," I muttered, half to Rose. As an explanation, it was rather weak, but I felt I needed to justify this strange impulse to get in the way of whatever Emily had planned.

Ford handed me my wool coat, and Emily gave me a long look as I slid it over my shoulders. The revolver was still in the pocket, and if Ford noticed, he chose not to say anything.

We stepped out into the rain and walked to a smart Mercedes that was parked in the drive. Emily automatically reached for the handle to the front passenger's seat, but Ford got there first.

"Frances will sit in the front," he said coolly. I blinked my surprise, but the rain was falling so steadily that I trusted my expression was well-hidden.

"Of course," Emily said, and she smoothed a hand over the rounded shape of her belly, small but obvious in the tight jumper she was wearing. I wondered if she'd planned to wear it specially for tonight. She'd been waiting to give Ford this news, and to show him just how real it all was. For the last few weeks all she'd worn were bell-shaped dresses, hidden under the looseness of my coat, presumably to disguise her changing figure. But tonight she had dressed as if she wanted everyone to see.

The skirt she'd paired with it had an elastic waist, which I knew well. I'd sewed it myself, adding extra-deep pockets out of the lush corduroy I'd used the last of my savings on.

I didn't even recall lending it to her. In fact, I'm sure I hadn't.

Ford studied a spot in the distance as Emily walked around

the front of the car, stepping through the glow of the headlights as if to underline the way her skinny frame bulged in one telltale place.

We drove in silence, but when I stole a glance at Emily in the rearview mirror, she was smiling.

CHAPTER

20

DETECTIVE CRANE'S NAME FLASHES ACROSS MY phone's screen, and I reluctantly put Great Aunt Frances's diary down.

"Hello?"

"Annabelle. This is Rowan Crane."

"Yes." I smile slightly at his awkward phone manner, before I remember his signature on the cease and desist letter sent to Great Aunt Frances. "Can I help you?" I ask, my voice a touch frostier.

"I'm coming back to the Gravesdown estate. Not to alarm you, but I'm a bit unsure how safe things are there. Can you lock the door to the room you're staying in?"

"Why? Has something happened?"

"I checked CCTV cameras for the eleven o'clock ferry, to verify Saxon's alibi."

"Let me guess," I say, thinking of cheating Andrew again. "He wasn't on that ferry."

"No, he wasn't. He was on a much earlier one, and his car

is also on CCTV in the Castle Knoll area around the time Frances was killed."

"I knew he was lying," I say.

"How?" Crane asks.

"I'm good at spotting liars." I let this phrase hang in the air, hoping that maybe Crane will feel a twinge of guilt. Because the more I think about it, the more *I'm sorry to hear about Frances, I liked her* doesn't match up with him threatening her with legal action.

"Well, I'm on my way. I'll question Saxon, but please don't confront him, no matter what this inheritance might make you feel you should do. He may have some other excuse—a different reason for telling Elva that story about being at an autopsy in Sandview. And then when the murder happened, he had to stick with it."

"What, like an affair?" How much infidelity can there be in one small village? I'm skeptical, but maybe I'm being a bit naive.

"You never know, but just don't do anything until I get there. Lock your door and wait for me, okay?"

Even though I know that Saxon is now a strong suspect for Great Aunt Frances's murder, I don't like the detective telling me what to do. And I certainly didn't get the impression that Saxon would actually hurt me. This feels like a convenient way to intimidate me into *not* investigating—almost as if Crane doesn't want me wandering around the house and digging into things he might suspect are hidden here.

"I won't talk to Saxon, not if I can help it," I say. I keep my words very specific, because underneath my growing suspicions of absolutely everyone around me, there's a tiny hope that Crane isn't involved in anything more than sending an angry letter to protect his dad. So I want to keep my conscience clean and not start lying to him. Yet.

When he hangs up, I pack away my laptop and slide the diary into my backpack. I head down from my bedroom into the cavern of the main house, and straight for Great Aunt Frances's files.

When I get there, I find Saxon and Elva already at work. I feel a twinge of alarm, because the number of files spread across the floor with their paper guts pulled out tells me there's information I'm not going to be able to get my hands on easily. I feel like I've arrived late to a wedding buffet, and the only food left is limp salad and dry potatoes.

There's tension in the air at my arrival, but Saxon gives me a polite hello when he sees me. Elva ignores me entirely and is digging so deep into one of the drawers that it's threatening to swallow her whole.

I decide not to try to elbow my way into the files alongside Elva, so instead I turn my attention to the rest of the room. I'm curious to see how Great Aunt Frances's mind worked, and who she was most afraid of. Because of the green diary, I feel like I'm really getting to know teenage Frances. But who was the elderly version? How did a teenage girl with such a keen sense of self-awareness become such a paranoid woman?

Being betrayed by everyone she felt close to was probably a start.

First I examine the bookshelves, to get a sense of who Frances was when she died. People's shelves can be like a window into their minds. I notice volumes on astrology and tarot popping out from between science books, like weird relatives at a family gathering. Bird figurines are displayed everywhere, and a typewriter that's absolutely ancient sits at the center of a shelf dedicated to plant encyclopedias and flower identification. Flower arranging may have been Great Aunt Frances's hobby, but it looks like murder was her life.

Back at the files, I hear Saxon swearing lightly under his

breath. It's then that I notice something I missed when I grabbed the Crane and Arlington files. One drawer—and only one—has a special lock installed in its front. It's a classic rotary combination lock, and Saxon is trying endless combinations and growing more irritated with each whirl of the dial.

"A crowbar would make short work of this," he snorts.

I walk over to the lock and idly twist the dial. "Where's the fun in that?"

He narrows his eyes at me, but one side of his mouth bends upward in a smirk. "I might remark on how out of order it is that you find this *fun*," he says.

I give him a small smile, because I get the sense that he's exactly the type of person who would find cracking a lock fun. If this whole thing didn't have murder and competition at its heart, I wonder whether Saxon and I would make a good team. He seems nothing like the creepy ten-year-old version of himself that I read about in Frances's diary, and it makes me wonder what made him change from that unsettling little boy into a successful and self-assured man. I also think of Saxon's first comments when he found out about Great Aunt Frances's challenge. *It's rather brilliant, what she's done. Uncle Ford would have been proud of her.* His first reaction was to praise Frances for setting up a clever game, so I'm certain that he appreciates an elegant solution to a puzzle rather than bulldozing through.

So I counter with, "The phrase *where's the fun in that* commonly means *you're missing something if you cut corners.* In this case, whatever set of numbers was important enough to Frances to use for the combination to this lock was probably significant in other aspects of her life." I spare a glance at the fortune written on the wall. "She doesn't strike me as the kind of person who just assigns random numbers to things."

An idea flits across Saxon's face, and he immediately gets back to work on the lock. He has the advantage here, having known Frances the longest. Interestingly, he tells me which sets of numbers he's trying as he's doing it, and their significance. He enters her birthdate, his own birthdate, her late husband's birthdate, the date he died (macabre, but not unlikely given Great Aunt Frances's rather dark fixations), and, in a surprising twist, he rattles off Mum's birthdate by heart and tries that too.

When nothing works, I ask when Rose was born, and Emily Sparrow. "How should I know?" Saxon says sharply.

Mr. Gordon's voice comes through from the doorway, sounding quiet and sad. "Emily was born on the first of December, 1949." A hush falls over the room while Saxon twists the dial to the right to the number one, then left around past twelve to hit it on the second go, then right again to forty-nine. When it doesn't work, Mr. Gordon sighs and continues down the hallway, out of sight.

Saxon turns back to the other drawers, where Elva is still digging. I take the small set of keys to open another drawer, but Elva is making too much noise for me to think properly. She's agitated and rushing through things, and it's like nails on a chalkboard to my methodical mind.

Saxon seems to be getting swept up in her way of doing things, and he dives into the drawers and mumbles to himself, not bothering to keep his thoughts private. "Frances was clearly killed by someone in the village that she dug up dirt on—that was her thing, she was a busybody. That's all this nonsense is."

I decide to come back when they're done, because there are other places in this house I can explore. I grab my phone and snap some pictures of the murder boards before leaving Saxon and Elva to their pillaging.

———

I WANDER THROUGH the kitchen, but there's no sign of Beth. After laying out the brunch spread, I imagine she left to immediately open the deli. I have so many things to do. I want to see the farm—I can practically hear the gunshot from 1966 reverberating in my head—and check out the vet clinic run by Beth's wife, Miyuki, and ask her about the iron. But the more I wander the house, the more I picture the scenes of Great Aunt Frances's teenage writings.

I take a lap through the library and imagine a fire roaring and rain falling outside the window on a dark April night. Just behind the big desk is a set of shelves, and a chessboard catches my eye. There's an intricately made backgammon board next to it, folded closed and latched shut, and I slide it off the shelf and set it on the desk.

I take the photo I find behind it down for a closer look— Ford, Frances, and Saxon, standing in a bright and sunny garden. There's a handwritten description along the bottom— *Paghman Gardens, Kabul. Honeymoon, 1968.* It's the first picture of Ford I've seen. He's handsome, but it's Frances who stands out. She's a little different from the picture on the murder board, the one with Emily and Rose. She was beautiful before, but she's more glamorous here, more sure of herself. The summer Emily went missing, they were all seventeen, so in this photo she'd be around twenty.

My feet wander aimlessly, but it's nice to walk and think at the same time. I end up in the main hallway, and instead of circling back to the left through the dining room, I head to the kitchen to see that impressive solarium again.

There's another sitting room through the kitchen that I didn't notice before, probably because you have to get there through a long corridor. It overlooks the formal gardens and has big French doors that open onto a terrace. The back of the house juts out over steep sloping lawns, and the view over the gardens is perfect from here. I peek through the glass doors and my eyes search the sprawling grounds.

I'm seeing everything through the lens of the diary, so I barely spare a glance for the manicured topiaries and roses climbing up walled sections of the gardens. I'm only vaguely aware of large fountains trickling and a hedge maze far off in the distance. Soon my eyes lock on what I was hoping I'd see.

From here I can just make out the landmarks that Frances wrote about. There is a dense strip of trees that runs along the perimeter of the south side of the grounds. Somewhere along there was the weak spot in the fence. I wonder if Great Aunt Frances ever stood here and thought about how that broken fence had changed her life.

I scan the strip of trees, and I can see a small circle where there are no leaves. I picture Emily and Walt smoking joints, sitting on the Grecian ruins, while Emily taunts Frances about still being a virgin.

I wonder if Emily's baby was actually Ford's, but then . . . Frances was the one who married him. And other than his nephew, Ford had no children. No other children that he acknowledged, I suppose. Mum and I were included in Frances's will because Mum's dad was Frances's brother. We have no blood relationship to the Gravesdown family; it's all through the connection of Frances's marriage. I'm tempted to sit in this sunny room and read more of the diary, but I hear voices coming from the library. Detective Crane must have arrived to question Saxon.

My eyes find the farmhouse out in the distance. It's farther down the valley, over a little stone bridge crossing the River Dimber. It looks like a picture on a postcard, or something conjured in a dream. The waterwheel is actually turning, and the river branches out on one side to feed a large pond that almost fully encircles the house, so that it looks like an island. I try to imagine the house as it was that night, when Walt—Mr. Gordon—hit Emily in the face, and Frances panicked and fired the revolver she found in the pocket of her coat.

Does Emily's disappearance have anything to do with what happened to Great Aunt Frances, or is this a separate mystery that I can't help but be sucked into? One that will waste time I don't have and cost me an inheritance? It's only been two days since Great Aunt Frances was murdered, but already I feel like the task in front of me is too big to fit into the handful of days remaining.

I wander back into the greenhouse that's connected to the big kitchen. Jasmine creeps up one glass wall, with orange trees in pots adding their scent to the air. It looks like every herb imaginable is in here, all well-watered and carefully tended.

I wonder who's been watering these plants since Frances died. Beth and Archie both have access to the house, and I decide to talk to Archie again and see what he can tell me. I try a small door built into a whitewashed wall on the side of the greenhouse, thinking it might lead outside.

Instead it's a dark and rather smelly boot room, but, like everything else in the house, it's large for what it is. Coats and wellies line one wall, and another wall has a teetering stack of suitcases and trunks leaning up against it, though it's hard to really see in the dim light. There's no window, but the murky stained glass of another door lets a weak amount of light in. I picture this entrance through Frances's eyes—it has to be the side door that Saxon led her through, the first night she came to Gravesdown Hall.

It takes me a second, but I recognize one of the trunks I

sent from the Chelsea basement. I notice it because of the crayon drawing on its side—two palm trees crisscrossing against the scribble of a blue sky, their green fronds faded almost completely into the black leather of the old trunk. It's something I drew when I was about seven.

The trunk is in far worse shape than when it left Chelsea. Maybe it was the removal company I used, but it's practically been flattened, and some old black wool is peeking out where the side of the case has split. The removals invoice is taped to the top of the broken trunk. Great Aunt Frances must have made a copy and put it in my flimsy file. I look at my name and signature on the bottom, and at my great aunt's curling writing underneath my own.

Something rattles loose in my brain, and my heart pounds.

But daughters are the key to justice, find the right one and keep her close.

A few days after I shipped these trunks to Great Aunt Frances, she decided Mum wasn't the right daughter. Was it because of my name on this invoice?

A glint of gold catches my eye. It's nestled into the black wool that's sticking out from the trunk, and I don't have time to register the wave of shock that hits me when I see the leaping stag pattern on the button.

I suddenly have to know what's inside.

I turn my attention to the lid, and my hands shake as I flip the metal latches up and lift it off.

I see the rest of the gold buttons first, the leaping stags on them sending spikes of alarm through me as they march down the black wool coat, before my eyes land on the skeletal hand that rests on the folds of fabric.

Finally the breath returns to my lungs, and a scream tears out of my chest.

CHAPTER

21

I'M STILL SCREAMING WHEN ARMS WRAP AROUND ME
from behind, and I nearly fight them off because I'm certain
it must be someone coming to get me. But it's Detective
Crane, talking into my ear in a low, comforting voice. I bury
my face in his chest and try very hard not to think about what
I've just seen.

I don't hear exactly what he's saying, but it's something
like *It's all right* and *You're safe, okay?* He's running a hand
down my back and I'm choking on sobs, feeling overwhelmed
and repulsed. Finally, I draw back and turn so that the trunk
is in my peripheral vision. Saxon is blocking my view, but I
can see he's got a ballpoint pen in one hand and is poking it
around inside the trunk.

"Female, gunshot wound to the head," he says to no one
in particular. "By the looks of the decomposition, this body
has been here for a considerable amount of time."

"Of course it has!" I shout. "It's Emily fucking Sparrow!"

"Calm down, Annie," Saxon says, and he gives me a blank,
clinical stare. It's terrifying, that look. I back up a step, into

Detective Crane. Suddenly the boy Frances wrote about is back—the one who sneaked around and collected information about people to use against them. All at the age of ten.

Saxon pulls a latex glove from his pocket and puts it on. He reaches back into the trunk, and Crane puts a hand out to stop him. "Saxon, this is police business now."

"Do all of you just constantly carry around latex gloves?" I say, and my voice is shrill. It's a nervous, irrelevant comment, and I feel like I'm either going to bubble over with a thousand more or throw up.

"I'll end up dealing with this body eventually anyway," Saxon says, and it's suddenly colder in here. I rub my hands up and down my arms to keep from shivering, but it doesn't really work.

Detective Crane looks at me, concern pinching his forehead. The last time he saw me in this state, I fainted. I can feel hyperventilation sucking away my senses—my hearing, my vision. . . . My stomach roils.

I breathe more deeply, into the side of Crane's shoulder. It's really not the time to focus on how I'm so close to him I can smell his aftershave, or how he doesn't seem to mind that I've curled into his side. I've conveniently blocked out my misgivings over that cease and desist order. That's a problem for Future Annie to remember.

Saxon gives Crane a defiant look and reaches back into the trunk. The wool coat he pulls out matches Great Aunt Frances's descriptions of it perfectly. It's like her diary has come to life, because all the details are there—from the fact that the gold buttons are half-torn from the coat to the revolver Saxon pulls out of its pocket.

"Both of you, out now," Crane says quickly. Saxon shrugs and lazily drops the revolver back into the trunk, and then saunters out of the boot room. It takes me a moment to unclench my fingers from Crane's sleeve, but he gives me a reassuring look.

"I'll come and find you as soon as I can, but right now I need to do my job."

I nod and shuffle toward the door, and when I look back, he's on his phone talking urgently.

Out on the gravel drive, I try to put as much space between myself and the house as I can. I wander in circles for a while and finally settle myself on the lawn just off the drive. I watch several additional police cars arrive, along with an ambulance. I suppose police cars aren't built to transport dead bodies, so Magda and Joe have been called for the second time in as many days to deal with a body at the Gravesdown estate.

I decide to walk around to the rose garden that's off to the side of the house, just to clear my head. When I'm nearly there, I stop short right inside the garden wall when I hear raised voices. On the far side of the garden, from behind a pergola bursting with yellow climbing roses, come the gravelly shouts of Archie Foyle. Oliver's clipped tones interject, and I take a few steps closer to hear more clearly.

"The hell you will!" Archie shouts. "You've no right to parade around the village with your swanky London clients and your oily sales pitch. *Golf course my arse!* That farmhouse is hundreds of years old, it's grade two listed! There's no way they'll let you tear it down."

My heart sinks to my stomach, but I'm also slightly glad to let my mind fix itself on a problem that isn't the corpse of Emily Sparrow.

"We can actually," Oliver snaps back. "We already have permission to tear it down, on account of the hazards in the old building." I hear a rustling of papers, and Oliver says, "You see? Certified permission from the planning office."

There's a moment of quiet while Archie considers this. "You've paid someone off, all this is false," he hisses. "My beams aren't rotting, and the foundation's fine! And no one's been in to look at them anyway. This is blatant fabrication! I'm going to have you and your employer in court for fraud!"

"Oh, you think so?" Oliver's voice is confident and cutting. I peer though the pergola and see him take a step closer to Archie. "You can try, but before the ink on your lawsuit is dry, the police will be knocking on your door with some very damning evidence concerning your recent activities."

Archie steps back, looking worried. He swallows and lowers his voice just a touch. "You wouldn't."

"I absolutely would. Other people in the village might turn a blind eye to your crimes, but I know what you're up to." Oliver gives Archie a look of utter disgust.

I'm in the process of moving closer, because Archie has dropped his voice further still, pleading. But someone surprises me from behind and pushes me out into the path in their effort to get past me.

My cover is blown, but it doesn't matter. Both Archie and Oliver are busy looking shocked as Joe Leroy rushes up and grabs Oliver by his shirt. The radio clipped to the front of Joe's paramedic uniform bleeps, but he ignores it. "If I wasn't the one responsible for first aid here, I'd break your goddamned nose," he growls.

Oliver's at a loss for words, but it doesn't last long. "What problem could you possibly have with me? I've barely spoken with you since I've been here!"

"Do you see the damage you're causing?" Joe is so close to Oliver's face that he's practically spitting in it as he shouts. "How *dare* you try to buy the hotel! Mother's put her heart and soul into that place! With Frances gone, that hotel is *vital* to her mental health! And you've gone and put this nonsense in her head about how she's getting too old to manage it, how she should sell up and move on."

"It's logical, Joe," Oliver says evenly. "Why wouldn't you want her to have the money from the sale? She'd be taken care of for the rest of her life!"

"She has people to take care of her, and you know it's not about the money. Or have you been away from Castle Knoll for so long that you think money is all anyone cares about?"

Joe's radio bleeps again, and this time Magda's voice comes through clearly. "Have you found him yet and said your piece? Because we need to get moving."

Joe exhales sharply and backs away from Oliver. I almost don't notice Archie Foyle slip away through the door in the walled gardens, but he's clearly decided he's had enough. "This isn't over," Joe snaps. He picks up the radio and presses the button on the side. "Yeah, I found the little rat. Thanks for covering, Mags, be there in a minute."

Joe gives me a polite nod as he sweeps past me, out of the gardens. I'm left gaping at Oliver, trying to make sense of the chain of threats I've just witnessed.

"You seem to have a lot of enemies," I say slowly.

Oliver just shrugs and smooths the creases from where Joe grabbed his shirt. "It comes with the job," he says. "To be honest, Joe isn't the first person to say those types of things to me. And Rose isn't the first independent hotel owner nearing retirement I've tried to buy out. She'll cave eventually, and then Jessop Fields will have a main office for our South Coast branch. With the golf course and country club going up nearby, we'll be able to manage them directly and ensure that they're the first of many in the area."

I narrow my eyes. "Classy," I say, my tone disgusted. "Manipulate a grieving woman into giving up the one thing that might get her through the loss of her best friend, all so your company can turn a nice hotel into some corporate office space. I have to say, I'm with Joe on this."

"Well," Oliver says snidely, "then it's a good thing I don't spend my days trying to impress Annie Adams." And he strides past me, his long legs making short work of the gravel paths.

I realize too late that I shouldn't have shot my mouth off. I should have pretended to be appalled by Joe's behavior and sympathized with Oliver.

Because he certainly isn't going to tell me what information he was blackmailing Archie Foyle with now.

CHAPTER

22

I WALK AROUND TO THE FRONT OF THE HOUSE AGAIN. The police cars and ambulance are still parked in the driveway, and the horror of finding Emily's body comes flooding back. I sink down onto the gravel and pull my knees up to my chest. I rest my chin there and focus on the strange ripple of the undulating hedges.

I can hear determined footfalls on the gravel behind me but I don't turn around. My impulse is to keep the house at my back, but even so I catch the gurney coming through the front door in my peripheral vision. They've put the whole trunk on it and covered it with plastic, presumably to preserve whatever forensic evidence might be left.

A phrase whispers through my mind: *Your future contains dry bones.*

"Oh God," I moan to myself. *I sent her that body.* Thankfully I don't say the second part out loud, because Detective Crane sits down next to me.

"How are you doing, Annie?" he asks quietly.

"I mean . . . I've been better?" I say. There's a lilt to my voice that threatens hysterical laughter, or tears, or a combination of the two.

The detective looks at me for a long moment. "Did you know about the body in that trunk?"

My head finds my hands. "What makes you ask that?"

"Your name's on the invoice stuck to the top of it."

I look back up at Detective Crane. "No, I didn't know. I know that sounds insane, but Mum asked me to help clear out the basement in Chelsea, and it was all a bit rushed, so I didn't look in every trunk. There were just so many of them, and after finding the first few were filled with old papers and junk, I asked the removal men to take them all away." I swallow hard and try not to think about how for all those years of my childhood spent playing in that basement, I'd never been more than a few feet away from a dead body.

"And do you think your mum knew that there was a corpse in that trunk? No one noticed any odd smells?"

"Of course not! That trunk was in our basement for years, and we moved in after I was born. Emily Sparrow went missing in 1966, right? So she must have been down there for decades before we arrived!" I was breathing hard now, disbelief coursing through my veins. I'd been trying to write books about murder while there was an actual dead body in my basement.

"Okay, okay. I believe you." Crane isn't facing me; he's let his gaze follow mine, down the rest of the gravel drive, out the gate, and into the patchwork of fields and hedgerows stitching together the countryside below. To our right, I can just make out some of Archie Foyle's polytunnels.

Crane's body language has become distant, and I watch as his mouth opens and then shuts again, as he reconsiders whatever words he nearly said. When he finally does speak, it surprises me.

"I know you've got Frances's file on the Crane family," he says, his voice tight.

I nod slowly, trying to work out the best way to get to the bottom of Great Aunt Frances's problems with the Cranes. But my biggest issue isn't that the detective was upset with my great aunt over her harassment of his dad, it's that his reaction to her death didn't match the angry words in the cease and desist letter.

"Did you lie?" I finally ask. "When you said you were sorry to hear that Great Aunt Frances had died?"

"No." That answer comes out right away, forcefully. But then he lets out a long puff of air, thinking. "I do see how it might look, though. How it would be convenient to my family if she died. I won't deny that she caused us a lot of trouble."

I purse my lips and finally let go of my knees, so that I'm sitting cross-legged. "She broke up your parents' marriage," I say carefully. "Didn't she?"

His face twitches, and it almost looks like he's about to smile, which is confusing. But he doesn't elaborate.

"I'm not trying to pry," I say.

"Yes, you are," he says plainly. But he doesn't seem angry, so I continue.

"But the dates on those photos, and the cease and desist . . . one of the things I've been puzzling over is, why now? Why, after a lifetime of digging up other people's secrets, did someone suddenly decide to kill Great Aunt Frances?"

"And you noticed that my parents' marriage broke up recently, and you deduced that Frances was the cause of this. And you suspect that's enough to push a member of the police force to murder someone?" His eyebrows raise, and I start to feel doubt worming through my stomach. But I hold my ground.

"Honestly, I think someone who investigates murder as part of their job is the most likely person to know how to get away with committing one."

The detective actually does smile at this, and it's open and disarming. "But by Frances's decree, that includes you and Saxon too."

"Yes, but neither of us has ever investigated a murder until now. I'm not saying Saxon's not a suspect, but so far I'm struggling to find a motive for him. He's known for years that Great Aunt Frances had decided he wasn't going to be her heir. So it was in his best interest for her to stay alive, because that way, maybe he could change her mind."

"Unless he knew about her stipulations, and killed her so that he could frame someone else, and then solve his own frame-up in order to inherit," Crane says. His smile has turned playful, and I can tell this is a theory he's not really considering.

"Now *that* would make a great plot for a book," I say. "Maybe I'll use that in my next draft." A pause hangs in the air between us, and I turn my thoughts back to Rowan Crane and what he might've done to protect his dad.

"You're clever, Annie," he says slowly, and looks at me. "But there's something you should know about Frances's files. It's something to keep in mind when any witness is giving information, and they're presenting it as fact."

I raise an eyebrow. "Is this an informal detective lesson, or are you trying to talk me out of treating you as a suspect?" As soon as the words leave my mouth, I'm aware that I don't actually think he killed Great Aunt Frances. But I also know I need to separate my gut feelings from my logic. If Jenny were here, she'd tell me you can't solve a murder based on "vibes."

"Let's call it both," Crane says. "But since those files are going to be a primary source in your investigation, it's important for you to know that sometimes Frances was wrong."

I feel my forehead crease. "But Frances wasn't drawing any conclusions in those files. They're hard evidence. Phone records, surveillance photos. Are you telling me that the pictures of your dad and my mum are . . . I mean, what exactly are you saying?"

"Those pictures didn't break up my parents' marriage. *Frances* didn't break up my parents' marriage. But also, I'm a thirty-three-year-old man, Annie, I understand that people change and some marriages aren't supposed to last." He runs a hand along his jawline, something I'm learning to read as his thinking gesture. He smiles to himself and then continues. "My parents divorced because my dad is a gay man. He and my mum are actually on really good terms. They're both happier people now that they aren't together."

"But . . . those pictures with my mum, and . . . why the cease and desist?" I try hard to put together how all this relates, but I can't seem to make the pieces fit.

"Your mum has been the only person who's known about my dad for decades. They dated as teens, but mostly they were just really close friends. They still are, from what I understand."

"Then why hasn't Mum told me about him?" I sputter. I feel a little sad, but also outraged that Mum has whole compartments of her life that I don't know about. Why hide friendships? I add this to the long list of subjects to broach with Mum when I speak to her next.

Crane just shrugs. "As for the cease and desist, that was because I was worried that Frances knew the truth about Dad, too, and that she might out him before he was ready. But when I discovered she really did think he was having an affair with Laura, I told her the truth, and she dropped it. Dad was safe to come out on his own terms, in his own time."

"Would Great Aunt Frances have done that? Outed him? That seems so cruel."

Detective Crane gives me a considering look. Finally he says, "No, she wouldn't have. But I was afraid, and I wanted to protect him. That generation can be unaccepting when it comes to these things. My own grandad being one example. Frances and Teddy were still friends, so I was worried what she might say, and how he might take it."

I wince. "I'm sorry," I say.

"Thanks," he says. "Anyway, he's got my support, and his friends in the village have been really good. John Oxley—he's the vicar—has helped Dad through some really tough times. And there's Mum, and Laura."

I'm quiet for a little bit, thinking. The detective has given me a new lens through which to view Great Aunt Frances's files. One I should have examined them under from the start—with knowledge that sometimes even the best evidence can lead you to the wrong conclusions.

How many of my other theories are like this one, too flimsy to stand up to any questions? How am I ever going to find out who killed Great Aunt Frances when Saxon knows everyone in the village and Frances's whole history, and when the detective is five steps ahead of me with his cool professionalism?

"Hey," Crane nudges my shoulder with his, "you've got that look on your face."

"What look?" I surface from my thoughts for a second, to narrow my eyes at him.

"Like you're undermining yourself and doubting your methods. You shouldn't. You were right to suspect me. I would've, too, given what's in that file."

"That's something else—how do you know what's in that file? Have you seen *all* the files?"

"After I sent the cease and desist, Frances brought it into the station and showed me. We cleared the air. If you want to double-check that, our receptionist, Samantha, would have listened in on every word, and she can verify."

I put my hands in front of me in a giving up gesture, but I can feel a slight smile on my face. "You didn't tell me you'd seen all the files."

"I haven't."

I feel a growing sense of foreboding. "Are you going to, like, subpoena them and take them away as evidence?"

"If I decide I need to," he says plainly. "We now have a body that's connected to a cold case that Frances was particularly fixated on." He pauses, then corrects himself. "Unofficially. I can't say for certain that this is Frances's missing friend Emily Sparrow."

"But that body was at the Chelsea house," I say.

"Which Frances owned," Crane counters.

My mind kicks into overdrive all of a sudden. Did Frances kill Emily?

Your future contains dry bones. Great Aunt Frances altered her will to include me just after I sent her those trunks. She had to have found Emily's body, with the trunk smashed up like that. It was practically spilling out. *But daughters are the key to justice, find the right one and keep her close.*

"Frances didn't kill Emily," I say plainly. "When she found Emily's body, she chose to change her will to include me, because I inadvertently delivered justice to her doorstep. And I'm willing to bet that after she found it, pieces of a sixty-year-old mystery fell into place for her, and she worked out who killed Emily." I clamp my mouth shut when it occurs to me that musing out loud in front of Crane might not be the best idea. Then I open it again and say, "Did Great Aunt Frances ever ask you about Emily Sparrow? Recently, I mean? Because I'm almost certain that she found that body just before she was killed."

"She never mentioned Emily," he replies. "Do you think Frances confronted whoever killed Emily, and then they killed Frances to keep her quiet?"

I try to keep my face neutral, but I can tell by Crane's small nod that I'm not very good at it. Finally, I decide to try to use his connections, rather than hide my thoughts from him. I just have to trust that I can work this out faster than he can, or that he might actually drag his feet to help save his own village. I hope he's the kind of person I think he is. Or the kind of person I want him to be.

"To find out who killed Great Aunt Frances, I need to find out who killed Emily Sparrow." I turn to look at him, biting my lip. "Can you get me whatever information the police station has on Emily's disappearance?"

Crane actually laughs. "And why would I do that?"

I draw in a deep breath, ready to push some buttons to see if underneath his steadfast just-let-me-do-my-job exterior, Rowan Crane is willing to go a little rogue.

I reach into my backpack and pull out Great Aunt Frances's diary.

"Because I've got proof involving a certain revolver. Proof that one of the times it was fired, a *Teddy Crane* was present."

If the detective were Oliver, he'd make a flirtatious swipe to take the diary from me. If he were Saxon, he'd act nonplussed and then maybe find a way to get Elva to steal the diary out from under me. That's all I've ever seen Elva do— reach out and swipe whatever she wants to be hers.

But he's neither of those men. He scrutinizes me, and

finally smiles. "I'm impressed. I take it you aren't going to show me this proof, though."

"I take it you already know about the incident in question?" I feel so extremely clever that I almost can't contain it. The cleverness pulsing through me is so strong that I don't even cringe at my sudden over-the-top attempts to speak like a lawyer.

I'm gambling on the incident with the gun from Frances's diary being in Emily's missing persons file. They would have interviewed all her friends after she went missing, and while Rose, Walt, and Frances might have agreed to keep quiet, I'm betting honest Teddy Crane would have come clean as soon as he was asked *Do you know if Emily had any enemies?* And a good tactic to get people to spill information is to give them some version of a theory, and often they can't help but correct or corroborate.

"It's in Emily's file," Crane says.

"Victory," I whisper. "So you've already seen this file then, and since I've tricked you into giving me some clue of what's in it . . ."

The corners of his eyes crease as he smiles again. "You didn't trick me. I decided to share information." He runs a hand through his dark hair, making it stick up a little on one side. "Because of who was doing the asking," he says, giving me a pointed look.

I gloss over that, because I honestly don't have room in my brain right now to decide if Detective Crane is flirting with me. He's not my usual type, but he's handsome. He has the kind of face that you know won't change much with age, because the features are so solid.

It takes me a second to notice that Crane is still speaking.

"I had one of the administrators at the station dig it out of storage urgently, and the file was brought straight here.

Teddy—my grandfather—was interviewed after Emily went missing. He described an incident at the abandoned farmhouse, where Emily was hit in the face by Walter Gordon after an argument, and a shot was fired that went wide."

"Did he tell the police who fired the gun?"

"Frances Adams. She became a person of interest after that, but very impressive lawyers were hired by Rutherford Gravesdown to advocate for Frances, and she wasn't a person of interest for much longer."

"Did Teddy tell the police Emily was pregnant?"

Surprise flits across Crane's features, but it's gone in a heartbeat. "No, that information isn't anywhere in the file. Are you sure she was pregnant?"

"Frances seemed to be sure," I say, looking at the journal in my hands. "I haven't read the whole thing, but Frances suspected Emily was using the pregnancy to try to trap Rutherford Gravesdown."

"Yes, there was mention in the file of a sexual relationship between Rutherford Gravesdown and Emily Sparrow, but it was strongly denied by him. And at the time, he was the most powerful man in Castle Knoll, so although he was interviewed regarding her disappearance, it was rather"—he coughs, and I feel like he did it to hide his feelings on something—"cursory."

"Who told the police about a sexual relationship between Lord Gravesdown and Emily?"

"Walter Gordon. He had his own reasons for dragging the Gravesdown family into the investigation, though, because he was the number one suspect in Emily's disappearance."

"Did Mr. Gordon mention any other men Emily was involved with?"

Crane blinks at me. "No. Is there someone else that Frances mentioned?"

The wheels in my mind spin so fast it hurts. "Walt was protecting Frances," I murmur. "Because the other man Emily was involved with was John Oxley, Frances's boyfriend. If Walt told the police about Emily and John, Frances would start to look very guilty indeed."

"What if she was?" Crane says quietly.

"Was what? Guilty? No, I really don't think Frances killed Emily. She has a smaller murder board in that research room of hers, one with Emily at the center. I think she was trying to solve her disappearance in her spare time." My belief in Frances's innocence wavers a little when I think about the fact that I never even met her. So I look at the detective and ask, "Was she the kind of person who seemed twisted by guilt?"

"To be honest, she was twisted by something," he says. I curl the necklace I'm wearing around one finger, worrying. That diary is swaying me toward Frances. I like her, if I'm honest. But I'm keenly aware that I didn't know her.

Still, I make another attempt at her defense. "But could she have killed her friend, honestly? At seventeen years old?" I hold the green journal between us. "I've read these pages, and the Frances in them doesn't strike me as a killer. She's sensitive and smart and—"

"Maybe there are two writers in the family, if she's won you over that well."

"Were," I say sadly. "There *were* two writers in the family."

Crane nods slowly, and I think he gets it. He puts a hand on my shoulder and squeezes for a second before dropping it. He can see that I'm sad to have lost a relative I never got to know. The woman who recorded her teenage exploits in such a way that I wish more than anything to run into her house and ask her about it all. The Frances in those pages is someone I want to be friends with. And I want to know how her story ends.

Not just the story she wrote in the pages I hold in my hand. Her *whole* story.

"I guess it's good that one of us is a detective," I say, and I feel a smirk tug on one corner of my mouth. "Someone has to be unbiased in all of this."

"I never said I was unbiased," he says. He gets up and dusts off his jeans. "Anyway, I'm done playing devil's advocate. I still think someone killed her for a secret she found out."

He reaches out a hand to help me up, so I take it.

"Frances has put us all in a tricky position," he continues. "My biggest concern is that someone was willing to commit murder, most likely to keep Frances from sharing information she'd come across. And with you and Saxon now tasked with digging into that, you both move right into the spot Frances was just in."

"The spot that got her killed."

"Exactly."

"So what do we do?"

"I'm going to monitor the house while all this goes on. A police presence is needed here in any case, because a crime has been committed, as well as a cold case reopened."

"So you're going to stay here?"

"I might have some shift changes with my colleagues, but I'll be here as much as I can."

I nod. "That's both reassuring and intimidating."

He laughs, and the unguardedness of it catches me by surprise. Then his face closes again, and I can tell he's about to say something I won't like. "I'm afraid I need that diary, Annie."

I feel the air squeeze from my lungs, and my hand instinctively flexes around the diary. "W-why?" I stammer. "It's just her teenage ramblings, really, I doubt it's that—" His stern look stops me there.

"I'll make copies," he says, "and get it back to you as soon as I can."

At my shuttered expression, he adds, "Think of it this way—copying the diary is easier than carting all the files away. If I have the diary first, it might show me which files I need, and I won't have to come in and take them all."

"But I haven't read the whole thing! Give me . . . an hour? Half an hour?" I'm scrambling to try to find a way not to obstruct justice here, but when it comes down to it, there's not a lot I can do.

"I'm sorry, Annie, I need it now."

"I didn't have to tell you about it!" I shout. This really isn't playing fair.

He holds his hand out for the diary, and I seethe, feeling like a small child being made to give up sweets they've been caught with.

"Emily Sparrow's murder," I say, clutching at a desperate plan. "What if we help each other, and you can have all the credit for solving it? All I need is credit for solving Frances's."

He pulls his hand back and crosses his arms. "You mean I can close Emily's case in order to distract my bosses from the open—very recent—murder I'm supposed to be solving? That sounds like a lovely way to buy yourself time to catch a killer and win an inheritance."

"Fantastic, so glad you see it my way."

"Absolutely not."

"You mean you don't see it my way? Or you don't want to work together?"

His cheeks puff in frustration as he gives me a long look. "Both. Now, I've been reasonable. I'll copy the diary and give you back the original, which I don't have to do." He gives me a pointed stare. "Or do you want to me to get official about this?"

"All right," I say. I don't bother to keep the surly tone out of my voice, and I can feel the sulk pulling my posture down as I hand it over.

"Thank you," he says.

I start to walk up to the house. "In the meantime, I've got other secrets to swim around in," I remind him.

He winces. "I'm going to have to pull you out of all kinds of trouble, aren't I?"

I scoff back at him. "I'll get myself out, same as Frances did."

But then it's my turn to wince, because of course, Frances didn't get herself out of trouble. Not when it mattered.

CHAPTER
23

SOMEONE HAS BEEN IN MY ROOM. AND THEY'VE NOT even been subtle about it. I left all my blankets in sleepy disarray and my pillow crumpled in a ball. But as I walk in, my stomach tilts. The bed is neatly made.

I'm starting to understand Great Aunt Frances's paranoia a bit better, because once you start thinking about murder, you see potential murderers everywhere. Every detail starts to feel like a threat. I let out a long breath, because there's probably just a cleaner I haven't met. But then I wonder if that cleaner is also Beth. Or someone else whose future relies on the solving of Great Aunt Frances's murder.

I walk over to the bed and cautiously run a hand over the crisp white cotton pillowcase. Then I lift the whole thing gently, and there it is—a small piece of paper, typewritten and yellowed with age.

You little bitch, you think you can stand in my
way? You're so used to getting what you want,
with your perfect pretty face. If you don't stop I

swear I'll ruin that face. I'll put your bones in a box
and send them to your loved ones.

I'll take everything you ever wanted before I come
for you.

A wave of dread flows over me, and I check my surround-
ings. Under the bed is just my backpack and weekend bag,
and the little wardrobe is empty except for my clothes. I even
rattle the handle on the window, but it's a sheer drop from up
here, and the whole thing's locked anyway.

My hand shakes as I pick up the threat again. The line
about sending bones in a box immediately rings true. But
this piece of paper is clearly old, and I remember Frances's
diary mentioning this exact line. *Someone was threatening
me, even before we saw the fortune-teller. I found a piece of paper
in my skirt pocket that read "I'll put your bones in a box."*

And then I think about the last line of that threat—*I'll
take everything you ever wanted before I come for you.*

Emily. That sounds like Emily, and the way she treated
Frances. My hands itch for Frances's diary. But I remember
clearly what Frances wrote about the night she found out
Emily had slept with John. The things she shouted at Emily
in Ford's library: *It's like everything I have, you want. . . . My
hair combs, my coat . . . was my wardrobe not satisfying enough
for you? You had to take my boyfriend as well?*

For a minute I believe in the power of fortune-tellers, because finding this threat feels like inheriting Great Aunt
Frances's fortune. Detective Crane is still downstairs, and I
debate going to him for help. But the competitive edge of our
last conversation makes me hesitate. In books, when the
person investigating a murder starts getting threats, it means
they're close. Or they're on the right track, at least.

I feel a bit of my earlier unease start to fold itself away, leaving space for a raging curiosity. This has to be a piece of evidence from the mystery of Emily's disappearance. If someone was threatening me personally, surely they'd do it in a more direct way, and the threat would be more relevant to me—it would say something about me not belonging here, and that this inheritance shouldn't be mine.

This has to be from 1965, or 1966, around when Emily disappeared. What if someone was trying to help me by putting it here? The more I think this through, the more it feels possible. But who could it be?

I take a picture of the threat with my phone, just in case something happens to it, or Crane comes yet again for evidence I've uncovered. I worry a little that there's some kind of "concealing evidence" accusation that's going to come back and bite me. But I also know that this investigation is going to require more rule-bending and general boldness than I'm used to, so I might as well dip my toe in now.

I read the threat again, and confusion starts to creep in. If this was intended for Frances, why did someone kill Emily instead?

I tuck the paper into what I'm now thinking of as my "Investigation Journal," and put everything back in my bag. The light is starting to slide into that gold-green haze of summer evening, and even though I found a body recently, I'm starting to get hungry. My back is aching from carrying stuff around with me all the time, but this room clearly isn't secure, so I pull my backpack on and head downstairs.

I don't go to the kitchen just yet, because I want to see what files Great Aunt Frances had on the Foyle family. Unsurprisingly, when I get to the little study, Saxon is there again, this time looking at Emily's small murder board. Elva and Oliver aren't around, and Detective Crane is still outside talking to some members of the Castle Knoll Police Department.

"Did you know her?" I ask quietly. "Emily Sparrow, I mean?"

Saxon gives me a long look, and his expression is actually sad. It's odd, given how cavalier he was when we found the body earlier. "I did," he says. "She was . . . quite something. They all were, Frances included. It's sad to think that it's just Rose now, out of the three of them. They were inseparable, before Emily went missing."

Saxon doesn't know that I'm aware of all the drama that happened before Emily disappeared. Before Emily died. I decide to test Detective Crane's theory out on him. The idea won't give Saxon any advantage, and it might prompt him to share information with me.

"Crane thinks Frances killed Emily."

Saxon doesn't give much of a reaction, but he furrows his brow without breaking eye contact with the murder board.

"And why might the good detective think this?"

"That trunk was in the basement of the Chelsea house," I say. "And it's been there for at least twenty-five years, probably longer. It was there when we moved in."

"I'm surprised Crane jumped to accusing Frances. Why not my uncle? Emily disappeared years before he died, and that Chelsea house was his at that time."

I do wonder if Ford might have killed Emily. Saxon has a distinct advantage over me here—I know next to nothing about Rutherford Gravesdown, while Saxon was raised by the man. I decide I'm going to pester Detective Crane to give me the diary back as soon as possible, because I wonder what revelations Frances has made about the man she would one day marry.

But Rutherford Gravesdown has been dead for years. If

Ford killed Emily, it doesn't relate to Frances's murder in any way that I can riddle out. I wonder if I should ask Saxon what he knows about Emily's pregnancy, but I've still got half of the green diary left to read, and I want all the information at hand before I show my cards.

Your future contains dry bones.

Because someone's been threatening me.

I'll put your bones in a box and send them to your loved ones.

An uneasiness is taking over my mind and, as I look at the murder board, a new thought strikes me: Maybe the threat was meant for Emily.

My eyes fall on an old typewriter sitting on one of the shelves.

A terrible thought occurs to me. Frances didn't say where she got the threats, just that she had them. What if she had them because she *wrote* them? *I'll take everything you ever wanted before I come for you.* And Frances was the one who married Ford.

I notice that Saxon is watching me, intrigued. "Frances and Emily did have a bit of a squabble over my uncle," he says.

As I look at Emily's photograph in the center of the board, all the red string shifts and I see the connections in a new way. Who was closest to Emily, and farther out, who was wronged by her. Walt, John, and Rose are on the fringes. Closer I see Archie Foyle, Saxon, and, curiously, my grandparents Peter and Tansy. I'm surprised to see Peter's and Tansy's names up there, but perhaps there's something about them I've yet to read.

Ford isn't even on the board, but logically he could have killed Emily. Based on the diary, he might have had reason to. What if Emily was going to blackmail him over her pregnancy, or trap him into marriage? Great Aunt Frances must have had a reason to clear him as a suspect. Either that, or she fell in love with him and that blinded her to his guilt.

"There's a variable missing," I say, and I forget that I'm speaking out loud.

"And what might that be?" Saxon asks, but he's got a knowing look on his face.

I race out of the little room and through the library. When I get through the front door, Detective Crane is still talking to one of the uniformed police officers there.

"Can I talk to you for a second?" I ask, a little breathless. A look of surprise flits across his face, but only for a second. "It's important," I add.

"Okay," he says. He mutters something to the officer, and then follows me until we're out of earshot. I shrug my backpack off my shoulders and zip it open. I pull out my thin notebook with the mushrooms on it, where the threat sits safely inside.

"I need to see the diary again," I say.

Crane doesn't bother to hide his annoyance; he fully rolls his eyes at me. "Annie, I haven't even been back to the station yet. But it's in my possession, so it's evidence now. I can't just give it back to you."

"Can I just flip through it and check something? Just while you're standing here?" My voice is pleading, but he looks unmoved. "I'll give you another piece of evidence in exchange."

He snorts. "Oh no, that's not how it works. You know that, Annie. If there's something you've found that relates to Frances's death, or the death of Emily Sparrow—not that the body is definitely Emily's, but hypothetically—"

It's my turn to roll my eyes. "I won't take the diary. I just want to look at a page I've already read. You can have the threat; I have a photo of it."

"Threat?" His whole posture changes, and there's a steely edge to his voice.

I explain, in the most casual way I can muster, how I found the note.

"Annie, did I not just warn you about your safety in this house? You should have come straight to me the *second* you found this." He looks angry. His hands have found his hips, pushing back the edges of his blazer in a stance that screams "indignant concern." If I weren't annoyed about the diary issue, I'd be almost touched.

Me babbling my theory about someone clumsily trying to help me win the race to solve Great Aunt Frances's murder only slightly calms him down. Finally, I pull the little piece of paper from the notebook. "Here," I say, handing it to him. "It's all yours. But please, can I at least see the diary now?"

He looks back to where the uniformed officer was standing earlier, only to notice that he's now either inside or patrolling around the back of the house somewhere. "All right," he says slowly. He reaches into his blazer and pulls the diary out from the inside breast pocket. "But you look at it right here, while I think through this whole 'threat' situation."

A grateful whoosh of air escapes from my lungs as he hands me the diary. I focus on finding the passage I need, doing my best to ignore the fact that he's just standing there, scrutinizing me.

My thoughts jump to Saxon rattling off Mum's birthday by heart when he was trying to open the locked drawers of the files. How would Saxon know Mum's birthday? Mum said her parents kept her away from the Gravesdown estate, and Saxon spent most of his youth away at boarding school.

But thinking of the Saxon I met in the pages of Frances's

diary—the spy who gathers information and uses it shrewdly—
I can think of one good reason he might know.

I flip the pages until I'm near the beginning, checking the
dates. Finally, I find what I'm looking for.

September 15, 1966

> *Peter's here and he's arguing with Mum. No one can stand*
> *that Tansy woman he's married, but now that they've got*
> *the baby I suppose there's no going back. . . .*

> *I have to admit, little Laura is the sweetest thing. One*
> *month old and making cute gurgles when I see her.*

Frances didn't write "Now that they've *had* the baby," she
wrote "Now that they've *got* the baby." And when I read it a
second time, the phrase *She does look like her mum, though,*
which is a shame has an entirely different ring to it.

"I need to go back into the house. There's so much I need
to do," I blurt. My expression must be a kaleidoscope of feelings, because Crane's annoyance bleeds away almost instantly.

"I'll tell you what," he says, in that calm tone of his. "Let's
drive to the village and go to the Dead Witch. I'll bring some
files with me, we can get some food, and you can sit and read
the rest of this diary and make whatever notes you want. I
promise I'll just quietly work while you read, neither of us
will bother the other, and at the end of the meal I'll take that
diary back with me to the station."

I only have to think for a second before I accept. It's a better solution than I could have hoped for, not least because
I'm extremely hungry.

He makes a quick phone call but doesn't take the diary

from me as he wanders around on the lawn for a few minutes. Finally, as we pull out of the gravel drive, something occurs to me. "You aren't just trying to keep me out of the house for a while, are you?"

He sighs. "Officer Brady is going to question everyone there about the threat that was left under your pillow. So, yes, that's part of it. But honestly, and this is off the record"— he turns to me for a fraction of a second before his eyes are back on the road—"I just want to see what happens when you have all the right tools at your disposal."

I grin. I think that's as close as he's going to get to admitting he's on my team.

CHAPTER
24

The Castle Knoll Files, September 30, 1966

EMILY TAPPED ON MY BEDROOM WINDOW, AND IT WAS
*well after midnight by then. The rain had stopped but it was still
cold, and she'd found an oversized jumper and was huddling
there like the Little Match Girl. "Can I come in?"*

I set my jaw and stared her down.

*"Come on, Frannie, I really need to talk to you. You don't
want me to cause a scene and wake up the whole house, do you?"*

*And she would. I knew she would. So I lifted the sash window
farther and she climbed through.*

*"What do you want?" I demanded. My thoughts were thun-
derous, and I hoped she could see that on my face. She'd climbed
the tree in front of our house to get onto the ledge under my
window, and I had the vicious urge to push her off it. It was only
a momentary impulse, but I shocked myself with the idea of it. I
forced myself to calm down and swallow the tempest of feelings
whirling inside me.*

*"I'm horrible," she said quickly. "I realize that, Frannie. In the
house earlier, all those things I said—I was just feeling mean,*

none of it was true. Ford doesn't want to know me. I think he sees right through me. And before you get angry about him, all the things I implied were lies. I mean, the thing with John is true, this baby. . . ." She trailed off for a second, when she saw that bringing that up wasn't going to make me feel any sympathy for her.

But I jumped on that, because I didn't want her spinning the conversation her way. She always does this, and it leaves me dizzy. "Why?" I snapped. "I just want to know, why did you have to go for John?"

For a moment her face crumpled. Then she rallied, in true Emily fashion. "John was part of this, too, you know, it wasn't all me! He made the first move, it was him who kept giving me long looks and coming on to me!"

I was ready for this excuse. "I'm not asking about John right now. I'll have words with him later. Right now I'm asking why you had to make that choice." My voice was whip-sharp, and she flinched as if I'd cut her. The effect was rather satisfying.

She opened her mouth and closed it a few times, and I watched her mask fall away. There was something more there, something she wasn't saying. I knew John hadn't forced himself on her—she would have told me that right away if he had. And even though I had a mountain of anger toward John for betraying me, I trusted he wouldn't do that.

"The truth, Em," I prodded.

Finally, she sighed, and it was like all the air had been let out of her. She took a strand of her hair and chewed on it, something I hadn't seen her do for years. I remember once seeing her mum slap her for the habit, when she thought no one was looking.

"I know it seemed like Walt was so in love with me," she said slowly, "but in truth he'd been distant for weeks. I suspect Mother found out we were dating and might have been threatening him. But really I just think I'm trying to deny the truth. . . ." She looked at the ceiling, and I was surprised to see her blinking back tears.

"He doesn't love me, Frances. I think he's been waiting for me to break up with him. I've tried to plan adventures and time alone together, but I bore him. He's gone off me, Frances. Me! Can you believe it?" She gestured toward her face and hair in a way that reminded me of Fiona Sparrow.

"You're lying," I said evenly. "Walt was so angry that night. I've never seen him like that, Emily. I've never seen him violent. Are you forgetting that he hit you?"

"Walt just doesn't like that when he stopped sleeping with me, I found someone else who would." She said this like it was nothing, like bringing up her and John together could be normal conversation now. We were sitting on my bed, and I felt my fists clench the blankets under me.

"I j-just wanted someone to love me, Frances," she stuttered, and then she let her tears fall freely down her cheeks. "I saw the way John loved—loves—you, and I . . . I wanted that. Not John, but just, how he loves you." She drew in a shaking breath, and a sob tumbled out. It startled me speechless, and I forgot the things I was getting ready to say to her. I've never seen her cry like that, ever.

"I've just got so much rage, Frances! Why does everyone around me get blissful lives, parents that care for them and love them, and relationships that show them how special they are? Why do I just get beauty and air and cruelty?"

I pressed my lips tightly together as I tried to work out how I felt. I don't know how I'd have acted if I was raised by a mother like Fiona Sparrow. But I wasn't ready to forgive Emily. And honestly, I wasn't sure why she needed me to.

"Why are you here?" I asked finally. "I've never once heard you say that you're sorry."

"Oh God, I'm sorry!" She grabbed my hand and looked desperate. "I'm honestly so sorry, Frances! And things are about to get really bad for me, at home. You were the only person I felt I could come to for help. Even though I've been horrible to you, we've been through so much together. And now there's an innocent baby in all this. Please. You know more about me than anyone."

The silence stretched out then, because the weight of all the years we'd spent together crept into the room like a third person.

"What about John?" I said miserably. "I hate the idea—it makes me feel physically sick—but you could get married. I think people can get married at seventeen, can't they?" I drew in a sharp breath. I hadn't wanted to face it just yet, but I had to let go of John. Even if Emily never spoke to him again, even if he pleaded with me and gave me every possible excuse to go back to him, I needed to move on. That didn't mean I wasn't going to wallow in my heartbreak for a while, but I knew I had to take the first terrible steps away from my past with him, toward an uncertain future.

Your future contains . . .

My thoughts faltered as my fortune started to recite itself in my mind like a prayer.

The bird did betray me; the fortune-teller was right.

"I don't want to marry John, and I don't want to be a mother. Not yet." Something in her expression suddenly looked more focused. Less desperate.

"I don't see how I can help, Em." I felt heavy suddenly, with the creeping unease of having been outwitted. She'd thought this all through, and it was starting to become clear that Emily had come here with a plan. I was naive to think this visit was just about forgiveness. Ford's words on chess came to mind: You can play without a plan, but you'll probably lose.

Emily was a planner; she always had been. And I worried I was about to lose.

"I just need to find someone who wants a baby, and then hide out until the baby's born and give the baby up."

There it was. A weight hit me when I understood how brilliant her scheme was. It was so perfect it was almost frightening. She'd probably been thinking about this for weeks. "Peter and Tansy," I said slowly. And I couldn't argue with the solution actually. They'd been up and down to London constantly, meeting with adoption agencies, but arrangements kept falling through. Emily had been here when they'd come over to ask my parents for more money, because the adoption fees were getting expensive. They were desperate for a baby, and it was the one thing it looked like they'd never have.

"I can talk to them, but Em, don't let them hope if you don't really mean it. I don't want to see my brother heartbroken if you suddenly change your mind."

"I won't, I promise. I don't want this baby."

I took a deep breath. "Where are you going to stay, then, until the baby's born?"

Emily hugged me suddenly, and it surprised me. "I think you can help me with that too," she said. "So far the only people who know about this are you and Rose, and the boys. I've sworn them all to secrecy, of course, though Teddy's a bit of a liability because Rose is being fickle with him again."

"What about Ford and Saxon?" I added.

"That's the second part of my plan," Emily said. "Ford likes you. I think you can help plead my case."

"You mean, hide out at the Gravesdown estate?"

"Exactly. It's perfect—there are tons of rooms there, and I won't be in anyone's way."

"What's in it for Ford? Why would he put himself in that kind of position?"

"I think we can persuade him," she said. And the look on her face was coy. I didn't like it, so I suggested another idea.

"I think we should get Peter and Tansy on our side first. They might be happy to have you stay with them."

Emily rolled her eyes. "I really don't like that Tansy woman," she said. "And they live in a small cottage right in the middle of town. Not only would I go mad, but my parents would sniff me out in a minute. I just know they would."

We didn't have the whole plan, but we had the start of one. Emily was going to lie to her parents and say she'd been accepted into secretarial school in London. It's old-fashioned, but Emily's mum did one of those courses back when the war was on, and she still thought that's what every woman should do. Fiona also believed that being a secretary would put Emily in the path of successful London businessmen, and that she wouldn't be working for long if she played her cards right. The lie would be one Emily's mum would want to hear.

And that's the thing with lies: They're much easier to believe when it's an idea you like.

CHAPTER

25

I WAKE UP LATE THE NEXT MORNING TO THE SOUND of Archie Foyle clipping hedges. The sun beats at my window, and I'm grateful for the skirt and T-shirt I found in the Castle Knoll Oxfam before it closed last night. The skirt has large pockets and is made of a heavy corduroy, which isn't ideal in the summer heat, but it's a brilliant deep green that pairs amazingly with the fantastic oversized T-shirt I found. It appears to be genuine—it's extremely faded and has the Kinks on it.

I'd popped into the Oxfam while Rowan Crane waited for me at our table. True to his word, he let me read the diary while he paid me little to no attention and focused on his own paperwork. The food at the pub was surprisingly good, and I don't think either of us really remembered that the other was there for most of the evening. It was the most relaxing time I've spent in a man's presence in years.

Walter Gordon came into the pub partway through the evening, but he simply gave me and Crane a small nod before taking a table on his own in a corner. He winced as he sat down, then dug a small pill bottle out of his pocket before swallowing a few tablets. He didn't drink anything but tap water and coffee all evening, and he didn't eat at all. I wondered why he was there, but perhaps he was just lonely and liked the atmosphere.

The only downside to my evening with Crane was that I made so many notes and spent so much time rereading old entries that I didn't get to the end of the diary. When closing time was called, I pleaded for a bit more time, but the detective wouldn't budge. He did promise to get the diary back to me as soon as he could but was conscious of Aunt Frances's deadline, and the lost time was gnawing at me.

This morning, when I look out the window, I can see that Detective Crane's car is still here. It seems he wasn't exaggerating about maintaining a police presence at the estate.

I feel like with every leap forward, I just uncover more tangles in this weird forest of betrayal and murder in Great Aunt Frances's life.

There's a large bathroom at the end of the hall, with a claw-footed tub and stacks of fancy products, and despite the ticking clock, I can't help but indulge in a bath. I come out steaming and smelling of clouds of lavender. I leave my hair loose and damp down my back, because when the summer heat hits it, it'll fall into a messy loose wave that's actually rather stylish. That photo of Emily Sparrow reminded me that my hair does this, but I tried not to think too hard about our similarities when I resisted putting my hair up in its usual bun.

I crave fresh air, and something to distract me from having to face the implications of just how deeply my own history is entwined with Emily's. I wander out of the house and blink furiously at the brightness. I feel like a bat forced out of my cave. I spent half the night on the phone with Mum, talking about Reggie Crane, Great Aunt Frances's will, and, finally, Emily Sparrow.

In typical Mum style, she kept her feelings mostly hidden. When she got the news about Emily Sparrow possibly being her real mum, she reacted much the same way I did to my dad's file. Emily was just some woman she didn't know.

But as I told her some of Emily's story, and about the mysteries that were unwinding themselves all around me, I could hear the pauses in her words lengthening, and the emotions in her voice growing. When I told her about Great Aunt Frances's role in helping with her adoption, she cut me off and said she needed to go. I suppose Mum will have her own way of dealing with all this.

I've come to see the women in my family as lonely pillars. Great Aunt Frances filing everyone else's lives away on her estate in Castle Knoll, while Mum is shut up in the Chelsea house painting out her past. And me, now adrift between them, trying to work out whose story I'm telling and whose story I'm living.

I look thoughtfully at the Rolls-Royce in the drive and then decide I might be able to accomplish several important things at once. I've been so caught up in the diary and Emily Sparrow that I've forgotten to investigate the mechanics of Great Aunt Frances's murder. Saxon could be well ahead of me in his own investigation, and even though it's only been two days, I can feel time slipping by. I need to find out who might've had access to syringes full of a high dose of iron. And I need to find out how the flowers are connected, because I'm convinced they must be. Plus there's Archie Foyle and whatever he's done that's worthy of blackmail. I walk over to the garden shed, hoping to find him there.

"Excuse me," I say, poking my head around the door. "Mr. Foyle?"

"Ah, hello again!" He smiles at me and walks out to join me.

"I was wondering, do you have any experience with the Rolls-Royce in the drive? I was hoping someone could drive me to the village."

Archie looks over at the old car, and for a minute he seems almost wistful. "Sure," he says. "I keep that car going for Frances. Or I did, rather." His face falls, and I try to gauge whether it's genuine. Then I immediately feel horrified, because I hate that I'm looking at every person who knew Frances and trying to see through them as if they're a set of lies rather than a human being.

I turn my thoughts back to the investigation. "Did Great Aunt Frances drive that car around the village?" I ask.

Archie laughs. "No, not really. Once Bill Leroy died—he was the driver on the estate—" Archie looks up, distracted. "Bill married Rose, did you know that?"

"No, I didn't."

"Well, when he died, I did a bit of driving and looking after the car, but Beth actually drove Frances most days."

"Beth drives this car?" I think of Beth in her vintage tea dress and pillbox hat, and imagine she'd look like someone on a film set driving Great Aunt Frances around. I wonder which came first, Beth's 1930s dress sense or her ability to drive the 1930s car.

Archie laughs. "She does! Not in those ridiculous shoes she wears, but she showed a real interest in the car, so Frances had me teach her the ropes about ten years ago."

"So Beth doubles as a cook and chauffeur, all while running her own deli? That sounds like a mountain of work."

"She has employees at the deli, but she does work hard. And if Beth can learn to drive it, you can too."

I wave that remark away. "I'm absolutely not driving that

car, but thanks for the vote of confidence. I do have some questions about it, though, if you don't mind?"

He smiles. "Fire away."

"When we all came to meet with Great Aunt Frances, the engine was open. Had you been working on the car?"

"No, though I noticed she had the bonnet open." He looks thoughtful for a moment. "Come to think about it, I don't know why she would have tried to mess with the engine herself rather than asking me for help. I was here pruning the roses in the early part of the morning."

"She doesn't have another car?"

"There used to be a Mercedes; I used to tease Ford about it a bit. Because you see, *Ford*—" Archie looks at me expectantly, but I let him fill in the rest of the eye roll–inducing joke. "Driving a *Mercedes*? Eh?"

I give him a small smile and force out a little laugh just to be nice.

"Yeah, that was about how he took it too. Anyway, I've worked on half the cars in Castle Knoll." He laughs to himself, lost in thought for a moment. I'm learning that Archie Foyle is one of those people who talks in a constant stream, but changes topic if you don't keep him on track. "You ask Walt Gordon about his old station wagon, I even fixed that a few times for him back in the day. Now that's a car that's seen some things!" Archie laughs again, and I have to bite my lip to keep the slightly scandalized look off my face, because Great Aunt Frances's comment in her diary about Rose and Archie in the backseat of Walt's car comes to mind.

"Do you think you can get it running again?" I ask.

"I'm happy to try," he says. He walks past the passenger side of the car and says, "I'd check the battery, but I put that back in myself, so I know it's not that." He knocks on a wooden box that's resting on the long piece of metal that edges along the underside of the door.

"That's . . . the battery's in that box?" I say.

"No, that's where the car keeps its hopes and dreams," he says, and this time he keeps his face entirely serious.

I laugh. "That one was better," I say.

Archie grins, clearly enjoying the fact that I'm a complete car novice. But I really do want to learn. Because it's not insignificant that Great Aunt Frances had car trouble on the day she was murdered.

"Go, sit behind the wheel, I'll see if there's anything going on with the engine. No, not that way." He stops me as I head for the driver's side. "You have to get in on the passenger's side."

I want to ask why, but he's at the front of the car already, exposing the engine to the morning air. It doesn't take long before Archie is half submerged in the car's innards, and I hear the odd clunk and curse as he investigates.

He comes back and slides in next to me through the passenger door. "Let's start her up," he says. He instructs me in flipping various switches, and I try to commit the sequence to memory so that if I ever need to start the car on my own, I can.

When nothing happens, I deflate a little. "Maybe it's me," I say.

"Nonsense," he says. "I hate to be wrong, but I'm going to check on that battery."

He heads around to the little box he pointed out earlier and comes back in under a minute. "Fixed it," he says. "The battery in this car needs to be taken out and charged, and I guess when I put it back, I didn't connect it properly." But the creases on his forehead deepen, and he scratches his chin, looking puzzled. "Maybe I'm just getting old," he says, but his face is uncertain.

Archie takes me through starting the engine again, and this time it hums and revs when I push the accelerator a little on his instructions. I let out a small whoop. It's a strangely satisfying feeling, being behind the wheel of a big car like this.

"So, let's take her for a spin," he says.

"Oh, wait, you're expecting *me* to drive?"

"Why not? If Beth can, so can you!" Archie smiles reassuringly.

"I guess that's a good point," I say, but nerves are starting to creep up on me. I shake myself a little, though, because maybe this is one thing I can master. And I like the idea that I could be good at this. My countryside experience so far has seen me keel over at least once and panic several more times. So I grit my teeth and decide I'm going to do my best to drive this goddamned boat of a car. "So . . . anything I should know?" I ask over the roar of the engine.

"Well, this is a rather ridiculous car for these country roads. It's a Rolls-Royce Phantom II, and it belonged to Frances's late husband's father. So don't crash it. It's pretty valuable, as family heirlooms go."

"Oh, God, don't tell me that," I groan. "Let's just drive around the bend to your farm, okay?"

Archie's face clouds over. "The village is better," he says. "Need a few things from there myself."

I struggle with the clutch and the gearstick for several minutes, swearing many times. This is nothing like Jenny's automatic, which is the only other car I've driven since I passed my test. Archie seems delighted by all of it. Finally I manage to understand the principles of changing gears in this car, and we roll slowly down the drive. As the expanse of the house grows smaller behind us, it's as if a security blanket is snatched away, and I'm left feeling even tinier behind the wheel. But when I start to get it, I feel a sense of accomplishment, and soon I'm actually enjoying myself.

"I understand Great Aunt Frances got you your farm back," I say.

"Oh, she giveth and she taketh away, that Frances," Archie says. He's looking out over the countryside, and his voice suddenly has an edge to it.

"That's a bit cryptic," I say. I see a turning approaching, where a sign reads Foyle Farms, and I make a snap decision. In seconds, I've yanked the stiff steering wheel to take us trundling down toward the farmhouse.

"Hey now! What about the village?" Archie says. He's annoyed but not angry.

"I just really want to see your farm!" I say, keeping my voice light and enthusiastic. I do want to see the farm, but mostly because Archie seemed to want to avoid the place. I also want to talk to Beth's wife, Miyuki, Castle Knoll's large animal vet.

But as we pulled up to the farmhouse, with its picturesque waterwheel and little duck-filled stream, my mind suddenly empties of all those things. What I think of is a group of teenagers warned to stay away. An argument, a secret revealed, and a gun being fired. And Mum, not yet born, hidden underneath a stolen coat that was ripped apart by a friendship gone sour.

"Come in then." Archie's voice cuts through my thoughts. He sounds tired. "I'll put the kettle on."

I look to the side of the farmhouse, where polytunnels are baking in the sun like oversized caterpillars. Just behind the nearest one is a barn, and I can see a woman in sturdy boots leading a horse from a trailer toward it.

"That sounds great," I say, still watching the barn. "Is that your daughter-in-law?" I ask. "I'd love to meet her."

He nods, but the look he aims toward Miyuki is wary. "You go and say hello, and then come in through the side door when you're wanting tea. Just don't go through the polytunnels—it's a fragile ecosystem in there." He disappears inside.

I walk around the side of the first polytunnel, toward the barn, but I stop short when I see what's growing between the tunnels.

White long-stemmed roses are bursting from rows of bushes, majestic in the summer sun. I feel a sinister chill when I look at the stems. They're the same variety of roses that had the needles in them, I'm certain of it. Whoever sent the flowers to Great Aunt Frances, they started life on this farm.

I step gingerly between the bushes, and Miyuki spots me. She gives me a small wave, and I have to work hard to clear the pinched look from my face. I force a weak smile and wave back.

"You're Annie Adams," she says as I approach. She doesn't make it a question, but then, she doesn't have to. Given her family's connection to the Gravesdown estate, it's no surprise she knows who I am.

"Hi," I say. "It's nice to meet you." She hasn't introduced herself, but I like that we're not pretending we don't already know who the other is. "Miyuki, right?"

She nods and runs a densely bristled brush across the back of the chestnut mare in front of her.

"Client of yours?" I say. I have no idea how to broach the topic of iron injections, and it shows. I'm working hard to resist the urge to run into the barn and look through everything. But I don't see anything suspicious inside, just animal stalls, lots of hay, and saddles hung on the walls.

Miyuki raises an eyebrow at my awkwardness but answers me anyway. "No, this is just my horse. Mostly I make house calls. I've got a clinic back there"—she juts her chin toward the doors—"where I can perform surgeries if needed. It's all state-of-the-art." I open my mouth to ask if I can see it, but she gives me a knowing look and I snap it shut.

"I know why you're here," she says. She looks amused, which is surprising. "I'm honestly wondering what took you so long."

"Sorry?"

"Detective Crane and Saxon both stopped by the afternoon the will was read. You're a bit behind, Annie."

I feel my expression shift, and I hope I'm looking confused rather than letting her see how alarmed I am by this information. "They came to ask about the iron injection, didn't they?" My tone is a bit grim—I've never been good at hiding how I feel.

Miyuki goes back to brushing the horse, which has started to nose her for attention. "They did. And I'll tell you what I told them. We had a break-in about a week ago, and I was a bit late in reporting it, but a report's been filed now."

"Why didn't you report it when it happened?" I ask. She seems very forthcoming, so I don't feel like I'm overstepping too much by pushing the issue.

She winces. "Honestly, I rushed out and didn't lock up properly. So there was some negligence on my part. But before you ask, yes—a whole load of my horse meds were stolen, and it did include iron injections. I only keep those on hand for horses if they get injured; it's not a regular thing. But honestly? At the time, I thought whoever robbed me was just after the ketamine."

"Do you have any idea who did it?"

"If I did, the police would have arrested them by now. But

this is a country clinic—my security isn't exactly top notch. I have no cameras, and locking the doors isn't something that always occurs to those of us who live this far out of the village. I mean, it probably doesn't occur to people who live *in* the village either."

I feel my shoulders sag. Unless Miyuki is lying, finding the killer based on who had access to the horse drugs is going to be a long shot. But this does tell me one thing—it looks very likely that Saxon was right, and the iron that killed Great Aunt Frances came from this clinic.

The roses came from here too. But in a way that makes me suspect the Foyles less, because why would they choose not just one but two murder weapons that would lead right back to them?

Still, something feels amiss here. I think back to Archie's expression earlier; he practically broke out in a sweat looking at Miyuki. So I thank Miyuki and head back to the house to find Archie. I nearly run right into a polytunnel, and a wave of realization hits me. His grim expression might not have been directed at Miyuki at all.

So I decide to ignore his instructions about the polytunnels, and I walk straight into his "fragile ecosystem."

Which, it turns out, is row after row of extremely healthy-looking marijuana plants.

ARCHIE SITS AND considers me for almost a full minute. His tea is steaming in front of him, but he hasn't touched it. He saw me emerge from his weed-filled hothouse—I should have noticed that the kitchen windows overlooked that side of the house, not that that would have stopped me.

But he just stood there looking at me through the window, drying a teacup with a neutral expression on his face. We stared at each other, and finally he gestured for me to come in.

"You seem a good sort, Annie," he says, and finally takes a sip of tea. "And since Saxon and I have a deal, I think it's only fair that I offer you the same."

I nearly let out a groan, because *of course* Archie's helping Saxon. Saxon's known him practically his whole life. I can't picture them being friends, but I imagine they have history.

"Okay," I say. "Color me intrigued. Is this some kind of deal regarding the farm? I'm guessing you've heard about the terms of Great Aunt Frances's will."

Archie seems to relax when he senses that I'm not immediately outraged or calling the police. In reality, I only care about his weed business if it led him to murder Great Aunt Frances. "I have. And I've got a bit of a side business, you see . . . and Frances, she wasn't a fan. Always very keen on following the law, she was. But it's a harmless business, and I've had it going for a few years."

"Interesting," I say. And my brain starts to catalog facts. "And Great Aunt Frances didn't like it because your side business is of the illegal variety?"

"I can put it bluntly." He pauses, and then slaps his knee. "Bluntly! That's a good one!"

Of all the mornings I thought I'd have, drinking tea with someone making grandpa jokes about marijuana wasn't one of them.

"I get your point," I say. "Great Aunt Frances didn't take any sort of action against you over these plants, did she?"

"She liked to give me lots of warnings. Ultimatums, that sort of thing." He waves a hand as if it's nothing. "She even had the farm valued by Jessop Fields and showed me plans for a complex of flats they'd build there if I didn't stop. But it was nothing but intimidation tactics. I knew Frances, and all that was just moves on a chessboard. She only wanted to force me into action, shut down my business and all that."

The valuation by Jessop Fields was probably how Oliver got the information to threaten Archie. Smoking weed was one thing, but it probably wouldn't land Archie in jail for very long, if at all. But growing it and selling it? That was something else entirely.

"So I take it business is booming?" I raise an interested eyebrow at him. I want Archie to think I'm his best bet—that if I solve Great Aunt Frances's murder and inherit her estate, I won't shut him down. But honestly, I have no idea what I'd do. I'll have to cross that bridge when I come to it.

"I'll tell you all about it, but I need your word—no police. You don't want that detective solving the murder, right? I don't want to get my business shut down, and everyone in the village is already flipping their lids with the news of what Jessop Fields plans to do to the place."

"I give you my word I won't go to the police about your side business," I say carefully. This wouldn't keep me from dropping facts that might lead them there, but I'm not in a rush to do that. I'm hoping I can talk Archie out of some of his more illegal choices. I'm about to ask Archie about Emily Sparrow, and his life back in 1965, when I see the ambulance scream down the main road toward the village, lights flashing.

I feel a strange tug of premonition. It's silly to chase an ambulance; some elderly person probably just fell and broke a hip.

But before I can stop myself, the question tumbles from my mouth. "Can you give me a lift to the village, Archie? I just need to check on something."

CHAPTER
26

The Castle Knoll Files, October 1, 1966

THERE WAS ANOTHER THREAT IN MY POCKET, AND IT *was even more horrible than the last one.*

I didn't want Ford to see it—he'd been so kind through every-thing with Emily. He was such a puzzling person, with clever sharp edges that would suddenly fall away when someone needed him. So I kept the note folded in my pocket, next to the first one.

It was the end of April when Ford took us up to his house in Chelsea in that big car of his. It was just the five of us—me, Emily, Rose, and Saxon. Or six, if you count his driver, Bill Leroy. Ford made it clear that the boys weren't going to be tolerated on Gravesdown property anymore, not after Walt hit Emily.

Peter and Tansy were waiting on the steps, looking nervous but excited. They'd come to get Emily settled but would return to Castle Knoll that evening. We helped Emily out with a suitcase and the ghastly plastic and tartan case containing the typewriter her parents gave her as a gift for the secretarial courses she wasn't taking.

"I'll carry that," Peter said, taking the case from Emily.

"Thanks," she replied. "Who knows, maybe I'll even improve my typing while I'm here."

Rose and I exchanged a knowing look. Emily would probably get up to all sorts while in London, but knowing Emily, improving her typing would not be high up on her list of activities.

Emily was going to stay in Chelsea because Peter and Tansy insisted that she have regular doctor's appointments. Emily refused to go to the doctor in Castle Knoll, and she pointed out that giving birth at the local hospital was also a bad idea if she wanted to keep her pregnancy secret. At least two of the women in the church congregation were midwives there, and her parents were regular churchgoers.

So if Emily wouldn't see the doctor in Castle Knoll, having her stay at Ford's other house in Chelsea was a rather neat solution.

It had taken some convincing, and Ford wasn't easily swayed. In the end it wasn't just me pleading Emily's case but Peter and Tansy too. I think it helped when he saw how hopeful Tansy was, and how Peter was doing everything he could to keep her spirits up after all the disappointment they'd had. So Ford relented, and when he did, he said it was because he was warmed by my devotion to Emily. Ford never asked whose baby it was.

Ford opened the door, and we all shuffled inside. "Oh, how elegant!" Emily breathed, and she wasn't wrong. A wide stylish entryway tiled in black and white was polished so well that it reflected the bright chandelier hanging above our heads. The smell of a lovely roast dinner was coming from the kitchen, and I wondered at how thoughtful Ford was being. "You sent your housekeeper ahead of us to get the house ready?" I asked.

He gave me a knowing smile and said, "I wasn't just going to hand over the keys and leave a pregnant teenage girl stranded in a strange city. Mrs. Blanchard will stay with Emily while she's here. I have other staff who can help me manage the estate, and it's not forever."

"No," I said, and smiled back. "It's not forever."

Emily was swanning from room to room as if Ford had given her his house permanently. I had a prickly feeling, an uneasiness I couldn't quite pin down. It felt like Emily was getting a prize for being pregnant. I looked at her standing in the hallway, one hand on her growing belly, giving glowing looks to Ford's back.

All I could think was, Fiona Sparrow would be proud.

I tried to push the thought down as soon as I had it, but it was like a thorn had wedged its way into my mind. It had taken a lot of effort to convince Ford to help—hadn't it? And he hadn't asked who the father of the baby was, because he knew about Emily and John. Saxon would have told him, I was sure of it.

Peter and Tansy spoke with Ford in hushed tones, presumably about how Mrs. Blanchard would make sure Emily took the proper vitamins and not do anything reckless like drink or smoke, and that she'd see her to her doctor's appointments.

But I overheard something I might not have been meant to hear. Something that plucked the thorn of Emily right out of my mind and made me feel much calmer. I folded the words neatly into my memory, to bring out and enjoy in secret moments when I needed to feel their warmth.

Peter said, "This is amazingly generous of you, Ford, what you're doing for us. And for Emily."

And Ford said, "I'm glad to help you all, but I'll be honest. I'm not doing it for you, and I'm not doing it for Emily. I'm doing it for Frances."

MY BICYCLE TIRES made a small crunch on the gravel drive up to Gravesdown Hall, but I'd oiled the chain so that it wouldn't squeak anymore. I didn't want Mother hearing me leave; she thought I was safely tucked up in bed, even though it was only nine P.M. *Unlike Fiona Sparrow, Mother didn't approve of the Gravesdown family. She said something was off about the lot of them, and that anyone who associated with them suffered a string of bad luck.*

I had to work hard to keep Mother's words out of my head, because she wasn't wrong. Archie and his broken home, his father running off with Ford's first wife, the car accident that killed Lord Gravesdown Senior, along with his eldest son and his son's wife . . . even poor Saxon was maladjusted.

I stood at the big door to Gravesdown Hall and wondered what on earth I was doing. Why was I here? Emily was hidden away in Chelsea, but the lift of Ford's words—"I'm not doing it for Emily. I'm doing it for Frances"—and the glowing feeling they'd given me had started to dim when he never tried to see me. He could have come to the village; I wouldn't have been hard to find.

Why hadn't he called for me?

It was that small spark of outrage that led me to ring the bell. A boldness that wasn't really mine, but one which I'd learned from Emily. The logical part of my mind told me to forget everything that had to do with Ford and Gravesdown Hall, to live my life and never visit here again.

But there was the pull now—it felt like gravity. Something so subtle and constant that it lives in your bones and your body can do nothing but obey its rules. Ford had become that for me. And I told myself that the more time I spent there, the greater the chance I might have to pull back the veil. He was just a man, wasn't he? As broken and as flawed as anyone. I'd uncover all those messy pieces, and the spell would be broken.

I was silly enough to believe that hearts can work that way. I didn't know yet how much stronger gravity gets when you see the messy pieces of a person and breathe them in, make them yours.

A maid led me through to the library, to where Ford sat swirling a small glass with a finger of amber liquid in it. He was puzzling over the pages of a newspaper and didn't look up when we entered. He hadn't slicked his hair back today, and it had a slight wave to it but was still neat in an effortless way. Saxon must have been in bed, because Ford was alone.

"Did you send my regrets to the Montgomerys?" he asked. He set down his glass, keeping his eyes on his paper.

"Yes, sir," the maid replied. She shifted from foot to foot, mouth open to announce he had a visitor, but he kept talking and she clearly didn't want to interrupt.

"Good. Their parties are starting to feel like such a bore. All the same people, with all the same daughters."

The maid cleared her throat, and he finally looked up.

His expression was entirely blank as he surveyed me, and he made a little gesture to dismiss the maid. I suddenly felt very stupid, standing there in my handmade Audrey Hepburn trousers and black turtleneck, having parked my bicycle in front of the house like a child. And when I saw his jaw tighten ever so slightly, I got the impression that I had just been a piece in a game he'd played—a game that was over.

That's what anchored my feet to the floor, and I didn't feel stupid any longer, I felt angry. I felt like I'd uncovered the heart of the previous months—a bored aristocrat had used a group of village teenagers for entertainment. He'd sent a spark into a powder keg, just to see if he could predict how it might explode.

I even doubted his words that day. Had he said them loud enough for Emily to hear? Were they just another move in the game he was playing with her?

I dug my nails into my palms. I could feel the spell he had over me cracking, hairline fractures appearing like ice under pressure.

"Frances," he said finally. "To what do I owe the pleasure?"

His voice was even, almost frosty. I noted that he wasn't inviting me to sit down. So I stood there confidently, as if it was my choice not to sit.

"How is Emily doing?" I asked. I could feel my features pinch as I said her name, and I didn't bother to keep the heat from my voice.

His eyes narrowed but he didn't answer straightaway. He folded his newspaper in two quick movements, the pages making a sharp crackle and then a slap as he set it on the end table a little too hard.

"Why don't you just ask what you came to ask, Frances," Ford said coolly.

I crossed my arms over my chest and gave him a level stare. "Is the baby yours?"

One corner of his mouth twitched upward, as if he was impressed at my boldness. "I don't know," he said plainly. He leaned back in his chair and the last of the frost drained away. "Sit down, Frances. You're standing there like Boudicca ready to take on the Roman army." He tilted his head and let out a sardonic laugh. There was a drinks cart on his other side, and he got an empty glass and poured a measure of the amber liquid into it and handed it to me.

I'd never had whisky before, and I was a bit resentful that he didn't ask if I wanted any before pouring me something I'd likely find as horrible as it was expensive. The smell of burned earth, caramel, and extinguished matches hit my nostrils, and I coughed as it set my throat on fire.

He laughed for the second time that evening, but this one was an open and echoing sound, and his eyes sparkled when he looked at me.

That flash of anger pulsed again. "Don't look at me like that," I said.

"Like what?" he asked, and took another sip of his drink.

"Like my wholesome village manners and inexperience are entertaining to you. You who turns down society parties because they bore you, so you go looking for locals to toy with."

He winced as if I'd slapped him, and dragged a hand down his face. "I suppose I deserve that."

I exhaled, a little self-satisfied. "And what do you mean you're not sure if Emily's baby is yours?" I added.

He let out a long sigh and looked at me sideways. "You know, Frances, somehow, whenever we meet, I can't help but suddenly want your good opinion." He stood up and idly wandered to one of the bookshelves. "That isn't like me," he said. He looked back in my direction while running a finger over the polished wood of one of the shelves. "I'll tell you honestly that after my wife left me, I became a society rake. I flitted through glamorous London parties at high speed, going through the women there even faster. Your friend Emily was no different." He looked back at the shelves and pulled out a book at random, as though he wanted something to do with his hands.

"I'd confronted Emily, Walt, John, and Rose in the woods one night, and told them much the same as I did when I first saw you. That they could stay, if they kept out of the way. A week or so later, Emily came up to the house one night, bold as anything. She wouldn't have been out of place at a society party, dressed as she was, and her intentions were clear. And yes, you have the measure of me in one regard at least—I was bored."

I took another sip of my drink and swallowed down my cough this time.

Ford put the book back and pulled out another. "So I let her seduce me. But I'm careful." He looked at me pointedly. "I used protection, I'm not an idiot. And I told her it was a onetime thing. She hated that. I don't think she realized until later that she was no more interesting than any other pretty woman I've met." He didn't look at me.

"What a lovely opinion of women you have," I said levelly. My voice was rough from the whisky, but there was an extra scrape of criticism in it.

He sighed and looked briefly at the ceiling. "Every time I cross paths with you, Frances, I mean to warn you away." His voice sounded tired, with a small edge of annoyance. "You're far too decent for the twisted world I inhabit." He moved back to the chair he'd been sitting in before and finally met my eyes as he sank into it. "So maybe all this information will help. You're right about me, I'm a bored aristocrat who's been desperate to find new games to play."

I watched him carefully for a moment. This man who was only a couple of years my senior but moved and acted like he was from another time altogether.

"That's been your whole life, hasn't it? Not just since you in-herited." I looked more closely at the library and saw that the shelf he'd just been standing at was full of books on war strate-gies. The next one over was industry and economic theory. The more I looked, the more I noticed the library was strewn with the artifacts of victory. Hunting trophies, cups from polo matches, biographies of Churchill and Napoleon.

"This library," I said slowly. "These were all your father's things."

His voice grew quieter. "Father was a conqueror." He looked at the contents in his glass as he swirled it gently. "I was taught to be the same, but it was my brother who excelled at it properly. He and Father were building the Gravesdown fortune to some-thing formidable. They were very good at taking whatever they wanted from people. After they died, I tried to follow their rules." He let out a bitter laugh and drained his glass. "Their rules for winning were the only ones I'd ever known. When my wife left me, I let my heartless streak consume me. I took the farm from the Foyles, scattering their family who knows where."

I didn't know what to say then, so I merely watched him.

"How is it, Frances, that you manage to draw me out so easily? Do you know, you're the only woman I've ever met who won't be led into my games. You break all my rules by simply refusing to play, all while showing me how the framework of my life isn't formidable after all. I'm a house of cards." He bit his lip lightly, deep in his own thoughts. "You've come to knock me over, haven't you?"

The spiderweb cracks in his spell over me didn't exactly reverse themselves, but they suddenly looked different. A thing made more interesting by its fragile beauty.

I'd knocked on Ford's door with the flutters of something starting, some attraction that I knew was a bad idea. And I left that night with something far more compelling. Not a romance, but a friendship that was confusing and faulty and strange.

I was so deep in my thoughts about it all, and a little light-headed from the scotch, that I forgot to be quiet when I crept in through the back door at half past one in the morning. Mother came down and flicked the lights on, her face full of surprise, then anger, then worry.

"Frances, what on earth have you been doing? And don't tell me you just got up to get a glass of milk or something. You're fully dressed, and I can tell you've put a bit of makeup on. Have you been out with John?"

Mother gave me that look—the one where she wants me to tell her things but doesn't know how to ask. But this was something I wanted to keep just for me. I hadn't told her I'd ended things with John; it felt too complicated to bring all those feelings up. And I'm a terrible liar.

So I just sighed and said, "I'm sorry, Mother, it won't happen again."

She looked weary, but she nodded. "No going out tomorrow then, you'll help me in the bakery all day."

"All right."

A week later, Mum caught me coming home at two A.M., even though I'd been sure to be as quiet as I could. That got me put on house arrest for the whole weekend.

My parents are reasonable people—not strict like Emily's or disinterested like Rose's. They're right in the middle, where they let me enjoy my freedoms but will come down hard if I push things too far. She didn't catch me the third time I sneaked out, but when I came back after my fourth visit, I knocked over a water pitcher she'd cleverly set near the back door.

After that I got weekends full of rather creative punishments, under close supervision. I organized the garage all through May, and spent June and July clearing the overgrown back garden. By August I'd run out of gardens to weed, so Mum made me work on Old Lady Simmons's front garden across the road. So, thanks to Mother, I didn't see Ford for weeks.

I started to wonder all over again why he didn't come to see me.

And I started to worry, because I missed him.

CHAPTER
27

THE AMBULANCE IS PARKED OUTSIDE THE CASTLE House Hotel. The lights still flash but the siren is silent. I rush through the heavy double doors, unease bubbling up in my stomach. Archie Foyle's words from earlier echo back to me—*It's sad to think that it's just Rose now.*

Those three friends feel so intertwined in my mind that it almost feels logical that whoever killed Frances would come for Rose next. If Frances worked out who killed Emily, the first person she'd tell would be Rose. And that would make Rose a target—even if Frances hadn't had a chance to talk to her about whatever conclusion she'd come to. I'm confident that Frances's killer was someone who knew her well, and this meant they knew Rose would be a liability too.

The reception area is empty, and as I look around to see where the paramedics might have gone, I can't help but notice that the room is lovely and bright. It has high ceilings and light yellow wallpaper that's designed to look slightly silky. Beyond the desk, I can see two sets of tall bay windows overlooking landscaped lawns. No one is out there either; it's just evenly spaced tables under white canvas umbrellas, dressed with crisp tablecloths. I feel the air leave my lungs when I notice the sad flower arrangements on stands— they're nearly dead, but it's clear Frances did them before she was killed and Rose can't bring herself to throw them out.

I hear voices coming from an open door set in an oak-paneled wall to my left. A man in a hotel uniform comes from the room, and I catch his arm as he rushes past me.

"Excuse me," I say. "I'm looking for Rose. Is she here?"

"She's not well at the moment," he says. "Her son's looking after her, but I can help you."

"Is she okay? I actually came to check on her," I say. "I met her a couple of days ago. My great aunt Frances was her best friend."

"She's fine, she's just had a bit of a scare," the man says. He drops his voice. "Between you and me, I think the whole business with Frances has really rattled her. And I don't blame her. None of us likes the idea that there's a murderer in Castle Knoll."

"If that's Laura," the voice snaps from the next room, "tell her to bugger off back to London!"

I'm a little taken aback by her ferocity. But then I remember the moment when Rose first saw me, when just the sight of me seemed to startle her into anger before she collected herself. It occurs to me that she must have thought for a moment that I was Mum, and I wonder what on earth Mum did to upset her.

"I'm not Laura," I call back, keeping my voice light to try to defuse whatever vitriol might be headed my way. "It's Annie again, Laura's daughter. We met a few days ago, at Gravesdown Hall, remember? I saw the ambulance outside and was worried. I just wanted to make sure you were okay."

Things are quiet, and finally Joe pops his head through

the doorway. His green paramedic's uniform is a little rumpled and his eyes are red-rimmed, and he looks far more disheveled than when I saw him before. "Hello again, Annie," he says, managing a weak smile. "It's kind of you to check in." He comes over to the reception desk and pulls me aside, so that I nearly walk into one of the potted ferns next to it. "Mum pricked a finger on a thorn in one of the flower arrangements that Frances gave her." His eyes dart to the wilting flowers on the reception desk. "She had a panic that she'd been poisoned, but she's fine. She's been distraught about Frances and worried for her own safety. Then that snake Oliver didn't help things," he says quietly. "She'll see you, but please, if you can just be gentle with her, I'd appreciate it. Frances was Mum's whole world, and Mum's mine. I just don't want to see her hurt anymore."

"I understand," I say. I'm even more curious about what Rose has to say now; I have so many questions I want to ask her. But I don't want to push her too far, and I don't want to be the cruel great niece who didn't even know Frances, coming in with questions just to win an inheritance.

Joe leads me into a smart parlor with oak-paneled walls and Chesterfield sofas. A waitress follows us in with tea and a three-tiered stand overflowing with tiny cakes and sandwiches, and Joe and I hang back for a minute while she sets everything out. Joe motions me toward a wingback chair across from the sofa where Rose sits. He joins her and takes her hand, watching her as if she's a bomb about to explode.

Rose looks at me then, for a long time. The look she's giving me is one of recognition, but it seems that anything familiar she sees in me makes her angry.

"Breathe, Mother. You need to breathe." Joe is rubbing

her back, and I'm so shocked I don't know what to do. I can't bring up the murder, not when she's like this.

"It's just, she looks so much like her," Rose says to Joe. She lets out a small burp, which is startling. It occurs to me that she might've been drinking. She turns to me. "Laura never appreciated Frances. But you know, when I see you properly..." Rose's face softens into a smile. "You remind me more of Frances than of her. That's a good sign, I think." This is interesting, because Rose knows I'm not related to Frances. She knew Mum wasn't Peter and Tansy's biological daughter. I wonder again what Mum did to upset Rose, but I suspect it was just her personality. Mum has a way of insulting people without knowing she's doing it.

Rose reaches out and pats my hand, which is holding one of my notebooks and a pen. "Frances liked to write in little books too," Rose says. Her eyes crinkle at the memory, but I can sense it's a fond one. Then Rose shakes her head and looks at the ceiling, her eyes watering.

"I wish I could have known her. It sounds like she led a fascinating life. Saxon and Walt haven't told me much about her."

Rose's expression instantly sharpens. "Saxon? Don't listen to Saxon. He's always been a liar and a snoop."

"All right, Mother, let's ... Annie, can we change the subject?" Joe's face is pleading, and I nod.

As her tears fall, I see her contained grief boil over, and the sob that comes out reverberates with heartbreak. She points to the far wall, which is lined with decorative bookshelves. "Bring Annabelle that scrapbook, will you, Joe? She should see it. The one in the top corner, on the right."

Joe gets up and heads to where she is pointing and returns with a large photo album. "Are you sure, Mother? We've talked about this—there are too many of these albums around, and it's best for you not to look at all this."

"That's why I'm giving this one to Annabelle," she says. She looks at me again, and at my hands, which are nervously toying with my notebook and pen. "Joe's always been there for me in the ups and downs of my friendship with Frances. Even when he was a little boy," she reaches out and squeezes Joe's hand. "If Frances canceled a luncheon or, oh, there was that year she didn't make it to my birthday party—"

"She was ill that year, Mother," Joe says evenly.

"I suppose," Rose says, her eyes downcast. "I have too many copies of these photos. The ones from the old days. I just have to have a book of them around wherever I am, that's why there's one here at the hotel. I've got another at home. Frances hated that I had these, she always said we needed to move forward and look to the future." Rose smiles weakly. "Always so concerned with her future, that Frances. But we were so alike, you see. Frances spent as much time as I did thinking about our youth, maybe more. Because we all never really got over losing Emily."

"I'd love to see them," I say. Joe gives me a slightly worried look, and I get the impression that Rose is one of those people who burned bright in her youth and everything since then has seemed a little dim. Or maybe it's a mixture of pleasure and pain, because Emily is the scar that won't heal.

She hands me the book, and her hands shake as she grips it. It's difficult for her, giving it to me, and I don't know how I should react. I don't want to deprive a grieving woman of mementos from her past, but she's acting like giving them to me is some sort of positive step in a therapy program.

"There," she says as she releases the book to me. "That's done. You keep that, okay?"

Joe reaches into one of his pockets and pulls out a pack of

tissues for her. "This is upsetting Mum," Joe says firmly to me. "I should get her home."

"No," Rose says, gathering herself together in the way that only determined old ladies can muster, like pulling a drawstring bag closed. "I have things to do." She pats Joe's knee. "It'll help my mind process everything if I'm busy. You stay and have some tea and cakes, don't let this all go to waste." Rose stands and Joe makes to follow her and fuss over her further, but she waves a hand to him to sit back down. She walks out of the room briskly, just as Magda enters.

"How was the call?" he asks Magda, standing up to go.

"Hey, Annie." She gives me a small wave, then looks back at Joe. "Stressful, but manageable. An elderly man had a fall, so I've taken him to Sandview. I suspect he needs a new hip." Magda sighs. "But while you were here, another call came through about a toddler choking. That was resolved, so I didn't radio you, but with just the two ambulances, it's spreading our emergency resources a bit thin."

"Got in trouble with dispatch again, did you?" Joe says.

Magda just shrugs. "They've got a whole team in Little Dimber, and it's not like it's in the next time zone. They can send people here no problem, they just don't like my style."

"There are two ambulances?" I ask.

"Yes, though we're almost always out as a team," Magda says. "So one ambulance sits in our little local dispatch in Castle Knoll a lot of the time. But this is boring talk, you don't want to hear about all that. Plus, Joe, we need to get going."

"Right," he says. He turns to me as if he's about to say something more, but thinks better of it and shakes his head as he and Magda leave.

I'm left clutching a photo album that brings so many of

the images of Frances's diary to life. A quick flip through and the scraps of Frances's story start to live in color in my mind.

The photo on the cover is particularly striking—it's Rose and Frances, in their late teens or early twenties, smiling, with two men, in front of the shiny Rolls-Royce. I recognize a young Ford, from the picture in Great Aunt Frances's study, but I've never seen the other man before. His mop of curly hair and the affectionate way he gazes at Rose lead me to think that this is Joe's father. I pull the photo out from the plastic covered pocket on the front, and sure enough, it's there on the back: *Bill Leroy, Rose Forrester, Frances Adams, Rutherford Gravesdown. June 1966.*

Emily was still away in London at that point, and I wonder when Rose met her future husband. The parlor is empty, and the tea is still hot. No one touched the cakes, so I gingerly take one and immerse myself in the photo album. Maybe there is some clue as to who killed Emily hidden in one of the pictures, something Frances knew that I haven't seen yet.

I pause over a picture of Emily, sitting in the garden of our Chelsea house, her belly absolutely huge.

"Mum," I murmur as I run a finger over the bump in the picture.

CHAPTER
28

The Castle Knoll Files, October 5, 1966

"IT ISN'T THAT BAD, FRANCES," ROSE SAID.

We were in the baking August sun, and Rose was sitting and chatting to me while I did my weekly punishment. I could see Mum periodically twitching the curtains from across the street, checking that I was doing the work and not just talking. Rose was allowed to visit, so long as she didn't help or distract me too much.

"It's horrible," I said. "I'm sweating, and I think Old Lady Simmons must cultivate these weeds on purpose. Or maybe she's a witch and she uses a spell to make everything I pull up grow back in triplicate."

"Let's turn it into a game," Rose said, smiling. "I'll pull some up and you watch the curtains. Any sign of your mum and you shout a code word. Like, daisy or something. Then we'll run and switch."

"That sounds so stupid, Rose," I said. "But I'm willing to try anything that makes this more fun."

And it was fun actually. Rose is good at that, even though she seems icy and faraway sometimes. She's not daring like Emily, but she can take simple things and make them special.

And while Emily was up in London, we'd filled more and more of our summer days like this.

Finally it was getting too hard to keep our laughter quiet, so we stopped to calm down before my mum came and shouted at us. If Rose got banned from visiting, I'd be dealing with this punishment alone, which would be even more awful.

"Have you seen the baby yet?" she asked.

"No, but Peter and Tansy are in Chelsea now. Ford is letting them stay in his house for a few days so that they have his housekeeper's help as they find their feet as parents." I paused, not wanting to ask Rose about what Emily was up to, but not being able to help myself in the end. "You haven't bumped into Emily yet, have you?" I asked. "Now that she's back?" As soon as Emily was well enough to leave Chelsea, she apparently headed straight back here, eager to pick up the threads of her old life. The knowledge that Emily was free to wander around Castle Knoll again made me uneasy. I told myself I was over John, that any feelings I'd had for him had evaporated, but there were shreds of bitterness that I still couldn't let go of.

"Oh, you didn't know?" Rose said. "She went back to Chelsea this weekend. She said she left something at the house and was going to stay for some appointment or other." Rose's mouth twisted, and I knew she was just as sour over the whole thing as I was. "I didn't seek her out. Archie Foyle told me."

I picked up a stone and threw it at a tree, hoping it might make me feel better. It didn't, really. "God, I can't wait for this all to be over! Joking around with you just now, it almost felt like old times. Like this whole mess with Emily and John never happened."

"Almost," Rose said. "But I know what you mean. I want things to go back to the way they were. Or not quite. At least we

240

learned our lesson with the wrong kinds of boys. And the wrong kinds of friends."

I rolled my eyes and swatted at some dandelion puffs. The hot dull air gave them nothing to travel on, and their seeds barely floated up an inch before settling on the grass.

"Are Ford and Saxon still visiting boarding schools?" she asked.

"Yes. They go almost every weekend these days, and I miss visiting the house. But you've been going there, haven't you?" There was mischief in my smile, because Rose's romance with Ford's driver was something of an open secret between us.

Rose blushed a little as I asked her questions about Bill the chauffeur, but when we chatted there was a sort of grown-up feel to it all. We'd moved on from spotty and fickle teenage boys, and it felt like our futures were falling into place.

"This feels like a good direction," I said. "None of Emily's crass games and underhanded antics."

Rose smiled and took a breath to say something, but her expression changed to shock and anger when she saw something just over my shoulder.

"Oh, you've got some nerve!" Rose shouted at John as he came out from behind the shadows of the overgrown weeping willow on the side of Old Lady Simmons's house.

John put his hands out in front of him, as if he could protect himself from her words. "I just need to talk to Frances," he said. "It's important. I know she's going to want to hear what I've got to say."

"Absolutely not," Rose sputtered. "Frances has far better prospects than the likes of you!"

"Please, Frances," John said.

Fury overtook my thoughts at the sight of John standing there. My blood boiled to think that he'd not even bothered to fight for me after I'd ended things.

"Why should I give you even a second of my time?" I spat at him. "When you just moved on with your life, when you knew there was a baby coming into the world, and leaving Emily to rely on us to help her sort it out! Rose and I have had to pick up the pieces of your mess, when all we wanted to do is cut Emily out of our lives forever!"

John just looked at me, his eyes pleading. "I'm sorry, Frances. I promise it was hard for me to stay away. I thought it best if I respected your wishes, and I heard from Walt that you'd been seeing Ford Gravesdown, and I . . . I thought maybe you'd be better off. You know, with someone like that."

I sputtered, not knowing where to start. "Why is Walt even speaking to you? You slept with his girlfriend. And Walt doesn't forgive easily."

John nodded and bit his lip. "I know it's hard to believe, but Walt and I worked things out. I explained to him about Emily, because . . . there's something not right, Frannie."

"Frances," Rose snapped. "You keep her nickname out of your cheating mouth."

I nearly smiled then, because Rose defending me was such a satisfying feeling. Emily would never have been so fierce just to protect a friend.

But John looked so worried, and I could feel that something was wrong. If Walt had forgiven John . . . something about this felt strange.

"Just hear me out?" he said gently. "Let me talk to you alone." His eyes flicked to Rose, then back to me. "After that you never have to see me again if you don't want to." His sandy hair was going blonder in the sun, and it had fallen a little into one eye. My hand flexed by my side, so strong was the impulse to reach up and brush it across his forehead.

"Fine," I said. "But after this you have to promise to leave me alone."

He nodded and bit his lip again. He walked back under the tree, putting some distance between us and Rose. I turned to Rose and whispered, "Just shout the code word if you see Mother twitching the curtains."

She gave me a serious look and nodded.

"I don't have ages, John, so you'd better cut to the chase," I said, once I was standing next to him under the tree.

"Okay. Thank you, Frances. I just, I have to tell you this while I have the chance." He took a deep breath and paced a little, as if he was trying to choose his words carefully.

I didn't make it easy for him. "Out with it then," I said.

"All right, it's like this. I know you're getting involved with Rutherford Gravesdown, and I know I've no right to say this, but I do still care about you, and I want to protect you. There was something about the time . . . God, this is awkward and horrible." He pulled at his jaw, the color rising in his neck. "About the time Emily and I were together." He looked at his feet but rushed on. "I'm not so dumb as to have been led by her little imitations of you, Frances, even though she was really trying that night. She had your handbag, and she was wearing your perfume. She'd even started saying some of the things you say, little phrases that I didn't notice until later. But the thing is, she was determined for us to sleep together that night. She kept saying it over and over: I need to be with you. It has to be tonight. I had a box of condoms on me, but she insisted we didn't need them. Said she was safe and I shouldn't worry."

I looked away, not wanting to show John how much that rattled me. But my stomach turned at the thought of them together, even though my brain had been torturing me with these thoughts for months. It was like poking a bruise, every time.

"I know it's horrible to hear this, especially from me, but you need to know. I think she was trying to get pregnant. I think she'd been with Ford and she wanted to trap him. Either to blackmail him or to trick him into marriage. And she needed a bloke to use."

243

"If that's true, why not Walt? Why'd it have to be you?"

"I tried to work that out, and that's part of why Walt and I are on better terms now. All his anger is directed at Emily, because . . . I think it had to be me because that was part of her whole obsession—and she does have an obsession, Frances, and not with Ford. Her obsession is with you." John let a few beats of silence pass while those words hung between us.

"Anyway," he rushed on, "why else would Ford put her up in his house in Chelsea, and visit her every weekend, unless he thinks she's carrying his child?"

"He's not visiting her. He's going to look at boarding schools with Saxon."

"Is that what he told you? Because I saw Saxon with the new chauffeur in the village, and he told me they'd been staying in Chelsea."

I took in a sharp breath through my nose, steadying myself.

"Why does she have to ruin everything?" I spat the words out, and my voice shook.

"That's why I'm here. I'm trying to make sure she's not able to ruin anyone else's life. I don't want Emily messing with us ever again. Because, Frances, if she meant to get pregnant and she wants to trap Ford into some kind of marriage or financial arrangement . . ."

"Peter and Tansy," I whispered. "She doesn't intend to give up that baby, not if it's her ticket to something bigger. But then why involve them at all?"

"Emily's a planner," John said. "They're probably insurance, so that if he rejects her completely, she won't be stuck on her own with no money, no help, and a baby at seventeen."

"Peter and Tansy are in Chelsea now. They're staying there with the baby, and Emily had come home. Except . . ." I felt my heart sink into my stomach. "Rose said Emily went back this weekend. She said she forgot something at the Chelsea house."

"I think she's gone to confront Peter and Tansy. She's going to demand her baby back. Because when I saw Saxon, he also implied that Ford was giving in to Emily."

That bitch! Outrage coursed through me. I didn't want to think about the warring emotions I had when it came to Ford and Emily, or whether I believed the baby was really his. I packed away my feelings on whether he'd actually fallen for her games, even after all the conversations we'd had.

But I couldn't think about that. Because throughout my swirling anger, one thing floated above all the others. Something far more important than these stupid games.

And that was Peter and Tansy.

"She's going to crush them!" I said. "What the hell am I supposed to do? I can't let this happen!"

"Walt's got his car around the corner, and he's on the warpath. I'm worried about what he'll do to Emily." John faltered for a minute. "He's my best mate, but he's not good at controlling his anger, you saw that. So I'm going to go with him, to make sure he doesn't do anything stupid. And besides, I don't know whose baby that really is, but I'll be damned if I let Emily Sparrow ruin any more lives, the baby's included. You deserve the final word, so do you want to come to Chelsea with me and Walt?"

"I'll cover for you," Rose said as she appeared under the tree. "Go in and tell your mum you're using the toilet, and grab a bunch of your old clothes. Make sure you include that godawful sun hat she makes you wear, so I can cover my hair with it. I'll be out here all afternoon with my back to the house, and your mum will hopefully just think you're trying to avoid a sunburn. Grab a dress or a shawl or something if you can, so I can cover myself up."

"Thank you, Rose," I said, and I hugged her fiercely. "I only have to weed the garden until five, you just have to fool Mother for ten more minutes, then you can leave. Christ, this is such a mess!"

It was a bit of a panicked blur, but I grabbed a heap of things that I'd put in the back of my wardrobe that I no longer wore, not even bothering to sort through what was there. I found the hat, thankfully; that was the important part. Then I dumped the pile of dresses, ponchos, and coats under the weeping willow tree, and Rose changed into me as quickly as she could.

"God, sorry, half these things are winter clothes, you'll roast if you wear them."

"It's okay, I'll take the rest of the stuff with me and get it all back to you later. You did what you could. Go. Emily needs to be put in her place."

WE WEREN'T EVEN out of the village, and I yelled for them to stop when I saw Peter's car parked in front of their house. Walt pulled off the main road but refused to go down the long drive. He wanted to get to Chelsea as fast as he could, and he told me I was lucky he'd pulled over at all.

"We're too late," I said, looking at Peter's car. "They're already back. Emily's already done her damage." As if to prove my point, Ford's Phantom II roared past us, his chauffeur not even looking our way. My heart wanted to collapse, as all the growing feelings I had for Ford had turned on me. My affection for him was broken glass in my chest now that I'd witnessed him driving off to be with her.

"This is about Emily, Frances," Walt growled. "She's up there in that townhouse playing heiress. I want them all to know what she is. She's a whore and a liar. Ford's on his way to see her—don't you want some justice?" He slapped the steering wheel and looked at the road with thunder in his eyes.

I did want justice. But as I looked down the drive toward Peter and Tansy's house, I realized that my teenage heartbreak was a small thing compared to what theirs would be if Emily sent them packing after giving them all that hope. Because Ford was clearly rushing up there to be by her side. It was inevitable; Emily always gets whatever she wants. I was stupid to trust those little conversations I'd been having with him, when all the while I'd never stopped being just another game piece. Just another source of entertainment.

I didn't need him. I knew where my family was. I had my brother, and I had Rose.

"I have to see Peter," I said. "If you want to go, then go without me."

"Are you sure, Frances?" John asked. "You might not get another chance at this, once this all blows up."

"I'm sure. And I think the thing that will bother Emily the most is me losing interest in everything she does."

The look John gave me was so tender it made me want to break into a thousand pieces. "You're the best of us, Frannie," he said.

"Don't do anything stupid, okay? Walt?" I called out as Walt revved the engine, eager to set off. "Maybe try a little forgiveness?"

"You are far too forgiving, Frances," Walt said through clenched teeth. "It's not natural. I hope one day you learn to be more of a fighter." Then the car tires kicked up dust as Walt sped off.

When I knocked on the door and Peter answered, I'd expected him to look devastated, but he was the happiest I've ever seen him. He bubbled with pride and adoration, with baby Laura in his arms.

"Oh, God, I was so worried Emily had changed her mind!" I said.

"She did," Peter said, and his expression clouded over for a minute. "But I took care of it." He smiled and kissed Laura on her little head.

CHAPTER
29

DETECTIVE CRANE CALLED ME THREE TIMES, BUT I had my phone on silent while I was looking at the photos. I finally noticed it flashing on the fourth call, and his voice was urgent when I picked up.

"Annie, thank God. I worried when you weren't at the house."

"Enough to call four times? I'm okay. I just went into the village to see Rose."

"Well, someone's taken a crowbar to Frances's locked drawer and done some heavy damage. And Saxon and Elva are nowhere to be found."

"What about Oliver?"

"He's here, sitting in a corner looking stressed out and occasionally taking phone calls to be shouted at by his boss. He says he spent most of the morning wandering around the gardens on the phone and trying to manage his workday remotely."

"Did they get the locked drawer open?"

"No, and whoever it was felt pretty pissed off about it. It looks like someone took their frustration out on the library: The windows have been smashed, the books thrown off the shelves."

"Saxon," I say.

"Or Archie Foyle. He was out clipping hedges earlier. But yes, I'm almost certain it was Saxon."

"Archie was with me, teaching me to drive Great Aunt Frances's beast of a car."

"Oh, you took *that* car?" Detective Crane actually laughs.

"You doubt my driving skills?"

"No, it's more the image of you behind the wheel of that thing."

"Let's move away from insulting me and back to why you think Saxon attacked the library. I agree with you, but I'm curious what your reasoning is."

"The forensics came back on the body. It's been confirmed as Emily Sparrow, and she was shot with the revolver found in the pocket of the coat from the trunk. Annie, it's looking like my theory about Frances might be right. I think she might have killed her friend."

"How sure are you?" This doesn't match what Frances wrote in her diary, but then if she'd actually killed Emily, she might have left out another visit to the Chelsea house.

"Frances had the body of her missing friend sent to her, and she hid it in her boot room rather than calling the police, for one. Saxon confirmed to me that the coat from the box had belonged to Frances; he recognized the stags on the buttons. When he made that connection, he looked ... crushed. Whoever attacked the library specifically went after photos of Frances. Saxon knew Emily when he was younger, so I'm guessing he was pretty upset. He even told me a very interesting story about his uncle and an old love triangle."

"Whatever Saxon told you, it was to confuse you. Remember, it's not in his interest to help you solve anything."

"It's not in yours, either, but you've been giving me decent facts."

"That's because I have a limited grasp of my own self-preservation. And in the spirit of that, you've got to remember Frances's diary. I don't think Frances killed Emily. I think Walt or John did, or possibly even Ford. I'm coming back to the house because I want to have a look at those locked file drawers. The combinations are a puzzle I can't get out of my head, and whatever's in there is extremely important, I know it."

"I'm nearly at the village—I'll pick you up. Tell Archie to leave the old car parked wherever it is. Beth will drive it back to the house. Or if you see Joe around, he knows how to drive it too. His dad taught him the basics years ago."

"I just saw Joe, but I think he's still working. I'm glad someone else will deal with the car," I say, letting relief flow through me. "I don't want to drive that thing again anytime soon. It was character-building, but I think my character is fully formed now."

I add the photo album from Rose to my bag, and within a few minutes Detective Crane pulls up in front of the hotel.

When we arrive back at Gravesdown Hall, I can see he's not wrong about the state of the library—the place looks ransacked. But it's a very deliberate violence, as every photo with Frances in it has been smashed, and her face has been scratched out of the pictures. It's so unhinged that it seems to me like the behavior of a killer.

My mind circles back to the outlandish theory the detective had about Saxon. What if he'd found out about the challenge in Great Aunt Frances's will, killed her, and framed someone else so he could "solve" her murder? It was the perfect plan to make sure he inherited and nothing was left to chance.

"I think . . . I think the police should look for Saxon," I say slowly. "Though he could be anywhere in the house or on these grounds. He knows this place well. He knows where to hide."

"There was one more detail from the analysis of Emily Sparrow's body," Crane says. "She had two envelopes on her, with *Emily* handwritten on the front of them. They were full of a very large amount of cash. Thousands of pounds. Does that ring any bells for you?"

"Someone killed her, but didn't take the cash?" I say. "For the baby," I whisper. I walk over to the smaller murder board, with Emily at its center. "Here." I point to a line of string that leads to a picture of my grandfather, Peter. "At one point Great Aunt Frances suspected her own brother of killing Emily because my grandpa Peter and grandma Tansy were going to adopt Emily's baby. Great Aunt Frances thought Emily would change her mind, because she was using the baby to blackmail Ford Gravesdown. But near the end of her diary, Great Aunt Frances went to her brother's house, and he was there with newborn Mum, and he told Frances, *I took care of it.*"

I look at Peter's name, there on the murder board. There's a thick, fresh-looking black line striking through it. Tansy's as well. "Frances ruled them out," I say. "She must have found the cash when she found the body, and put that all together."

Detective Crane blinks hard, trying to take in this new information. "So you're telling me that when Frances found the body after you sent it to her in that trunk"—I wince as he says this—"she checked the coat pockets? And then put the money *back*?"

"Yes! And that act more than anything should clear her, because if she killed Emily in 1966, she'd have known what was in those coat pockets, because the killer stashed the revolver in there, right? So after all these years, Great Aunt Frances finally struck Peter off her list of suspects. She found those envelopes and recognized his handwriting. She realized that when he said *I took care of it*, Peter hadn't meant that he'd hurt Emily to get the baby. He'd just paid her off."

What I don't wonder out loud is why Emily would've done that if she'd known Ford was on his way. Why take the cash and give up the baby, her biggest bargaining chip, to convince Ford to stay with her? I'm close to figuring this all out, I can feel it.

"I need to go away and think," I say.

"I'll walk you up to your room," Crane replies.

"I'm fine, honestly," I say. I just want a bit of space, but he's hovering next to me like a bodyguard.

"This isn't a game, Annie," he says. "No matter what Frances might have intended." He's getting stern now—his arms are crossed, and he's using what I'm starting to think of as his "detective voice." The tone that says, *Don't forget that I'm in charge here.* It's actually kind of appealing, and because of that I ignore him and head off to my little bedroom.

"Lock your door," I hear him say behind me, but I'm already running up the stairs.

THIS TIME THE threat isn't even under my pillow—it's right on top.

My throat goes dry as I nervously check the little wardrobe like I did last time, then under the bed, in case someone might be lurking there, ready to pounce the moment I close my door. I exhale when I see that there's no one there, and then I walk back to my bedroom door and lock it.

It's the same paper as before, yellowed, with old-fashioned typeface.

> You stupid bitch, you think you're so worthy? You deserve nothing but a hole in the ground. You're a whore and a liar, and I swear if you don't stop this I'll snap your scrawny neck like a twig.

Although I'm still fairly certain that someone isn't using these threats to scare me, the words on the page still make my blood run cold. I think of teenage Great Aunt Frances reading this with shaky hands. Then the images of the crowbar damage to the filing cabinets come to mind, and all the glass smashed around the library.

Violence, aimed at Frances. Or the memory of her.

I read the note again, working harder to put my mind back to 1965. *You're a whore and a liar*—Walt. Those are Walt's words. In Frances's diary he said he wanted to make sure everyone knew what Emily was, and he'd called her both those names.

I pull out my various notebooks, my hands shaking as I pile them up on the bed. Finally, I pull out the book of photos from Rose.

I start flipping through the pages quickly, trying to find the one murky image I know has to be in there. The color-saturated glow of 1960s Kodachrome becomes a blur as I scan each page. There's Great Aunt Frances, with figure-hugging tops or blouses tucked into patterned cotton skirts, her long hair loose and always shining. Rose, linking arms with her future husband, Bill Leroy. My hands start to steady as I look at the photos, and whatever vague idea of a clue I thought I'd find there slips away. There's only one photo of Walt, and he's smoking and scowling at the camera, as if he loathes having his picture taken.

How much of the violent teenager still lurks underneath the surface of that meek overworked lawyer? Why did Great Aunt Frances trust him so much, making him the executor of her will, when the clue in this threat is so obvious? *A liar and a whore.*

Because of the time of her death, Walt himself is more or less cleared, but what if he wasn't working alone?

Oliver. He was just late enough to that first meeting, the morning Great Aunt Frances was killed. And if Walt killed Emily back in 1966, Oliver would be the perfect accomplice to make sure that secret never got out. Because he'd have the benefit of scoring a professional victory when Great Aunt Frances left her estate to him to sell off.

I touch a finger to a picture of Great Aunt Frances standing with an ice cream at the seaside, and I feel a pang of grief for never having known her. And the injustice of how her life ended starts to twist my stomach, because all she ever wanted was for people to take her seriously.

And it seems that after Emily disappeared, Frances was the only one still looking for her. Frances never stopped looking for her for sixty years, even though Emily made her teen years a mess and betrayed her at every turn. Frances moved forward, she really did look to the future—and everyone just thought she was nutty. Everyone from Elva Gravesdown to the receptionist at the police station had a story about something superstitious Great Aunt Frances had done.

"The future," I murmur to myself. "What is this whole

exercise for?" I muse. "It's a task set by Great Aunt Frances, but it was important to her. She wanted justice. She wanted to be believed, the letter in her will was clear about that. . . ."

I open my mushroom notebook and look at my list of small things that have been getting to me, my unanswered questions list:

The flowers—who sent them, and why?
The lock—xx-xx-xx, left and right standard rotary lock

I flip to where I've copied Great Aunt Frances's fortune, and I cross off the same parts she did:

~~Your future contains dry bones. Your slow demise begins right when you hold the queen in the palm of one hand. Beware the bird, for it will betray you.~~ And from that, there's no coming back. But daughters are the key to justice, ~~find the right one~~ and keep her close. All signs point toward your murder.

I add my reasoning for why she felt each part had come true.

Dry bones = Emily's body recently discovered, the bird's betrayal = Emily cheating, the queen = Ford's chess piece, find the right daughter = me, because I sent the body.

The issue of the lock starts to gnaw at me, and I think about those old rotary locks. I had one on a locker at a gym I used to go to, back when I had the funds for things like gym memberships, and weird impulses for things like exercise. You basically just go right, then left for a whole circle, then right again. The numbers only go up to forty, clockwise, with zero and forty using the same space. When Saxon was entering birthdates as the combination the other day, he was doing it all wrong, turning the dial too many times.

If I hadn't flipped to the page where I'd copied the fortune, I might never have seen the pattern.

The word *right* sticks out to me, twice. And the number one. "But there's no *left*," I murmur to myself. "And no numbers but one."

Thoughts click against one another in my mind, pushing me toward a conclusion. Finally, it hits me, and I rush back downstairs. I look over my shoulder as I go, making sure nobody is behind me.

I start when I notice Oliver is blocking my way down the stairs. He's not on his phone—he's just standing there, looking up at me. I slow down as I reach him, and with each step it occurs to me how much taller and stronger he is than I am. He could overpower me in seconds, before I could even scream. I push the thought down and keep my expression carefully blank.

"Can I . . . do you mind?" I say. I try not to seem wary of him, but I don't think I'm convincing.

"Making good progress?" he asks quietly. He doesn't move aside, which is unsettling.

"I, um—" I clear my throat, unsure what to say.

He leans in and drops his voice further. "I'll give you a tip for free," he says. "Don't fall for the detective's good-guy bullshit. I can already tell he's getting way more information out of you than he should."

"Excuse me?" The undercurrent of fear that was flowing through me is replaced by indignation. But then his words really hit me, and the fear rushes right back. Oliver's been watching me. And closely, if he's been keeping track of my conversations with Crane.

"Annie?" Detective Crane calls to me from the hallway, as if my thoughts have summoned him. Oliver finally moves aside, but not before giving me a smug look.

"You all right?" the detective asks as I pass him, but I wave him off as I head straight to the filing cabinets. He follows me, looking concerned. "What's going on? Have you found something important?"

I ignore Oliver's warning and make the choice to talk through my thoughts with Crane. I feel rattled and decide that being reckless enough to get hurt is worse than sharing information with Crane and having him on my side. "What's the one thing that people failed to take Great Aunt Frances seriously for?"

Crane's eyes go to the fortune written on the wall, but I'm using the pen in my hand to underline words in it.

"It's so silly. Upstairs I was just thinking about the lock, left and right and all that. But Great Aunt Frances really believed in this fortune. It was at the center of all the decisions she made."

Soon I've underlined all the words we need.

Your future contains dry bones. Your slow demise begins <u>right</u> when you hold the queen in the palm of <u>one</u> hand. Beware the bird, <u>for</u> it will betray you. And from that, there's no coming <u>back</u>. But daughters are the key to justice, find the <u>right one</u> and keep her close. All signs point toward your murder.

"I was so angry that there weren't any other numbers," I say, a little breathless. "But then I saw *for* and *back*, and I thought, what if that just means *four to the left,* once you've turned up to one?"

"Zero one—thirty-seven—thirty-eight," Detective Crane says out loud, twisting the dial. There's a click as the mechanism in the old lock trips.

I let out a victorious stream of air. "Right," I say. "Let's see what it was that Great Aunt Frances only wanted her cleverest and most loyal of relatives to know."

The drawer is bent where it's been hammered at with the crowbar, so it takes me a bit of tugging to get it open.

When I finally do, my forehead creases with confusion. I was hoping inside would be her conclusions about who killed Emily, and maybe even her theories concerning her own potential murderer. But then Great Aunt Frances said it herself—if she knew who was going to kill her, she'd have been right down to the police station warning them all about it.

When I look at the contents, I know it was Saxon who tried to break in. Because it's more of Great Aunt Frances's discoveries. Specifically, the dirt she had on Saxon. He must've known what was in here.

I pull out a file on Saxon that's mostly surveillance photos, and not just of Saxon—it's Saxon and Magda, with time stamps that range from months back to just days before Frances's death.

"What am I looking at?" I say, passing the file to Detective Crane.

He flips through and is quiet for several minutes, examining them. While he does this, I reach back into the drawer to check if there's anything else in there. There's just a very small canvas, one of Mum's from when she first became a big deal in the art world, though it's not one that looks like it was ever for sale. It's probably something Mum painted and gave to Frances as a gift one year. I nearly blink back tears then, because it shows that Frances kept something of Mum's safe, maybe even treasured it.

I take one of the photos back from Detective Crane, and he lets me. "The drugs from the vet's clinic," he says.

"Excuse me?"

"I know you'll be aware by now that Miyuki's vet clinic had a break-in, and someone stole a bunch of horse drugs."

"Yes, but how do these photos relate to that?" I ask.

"This photo shows Saxon passing boxes to Magda . . ." Crane trails off, flipping through pages of notes in Great Aunt Frances's writing. "Frances's notes indicate that Saxon's been supplying medical drugs for recreational sale, and using Magda to transport them to various locations."

Magda. I think about Dr. Owusu's appointment book, and Great Aunt Frances's appointment that morning. "Is there anything in the files about Dr. Owusu being involved?" I ask.

Crane is quiet for a moment as we both look at the pages of information. Some of it's been typed, and it reads like it was provided by someone else. "It looks like Dr. Owusu was trying to help Frances get to the bottom of Saxon's dealings."

"Does this prove that Saxon stole the horse drugs?" I ask.

"There are no photos of him at the clinic, but the boxes he's handing to Magda here contain opiates, so that's incriminating enough, even if it's not evidence that he killed Frances. It looks like whoever took these photos was already onto this whole operation, and alongside Frances's notes . . . If her information is good, then this is pretty damning."

Crane looks at some of the typed notes. "These were done by a local PI," he says. "I recognize the letterhead. I know him; I can have him confirm all this. He's solid, and I'm not surprised he was on Frances's payroll."

"Look," I hand him a page. "She added to these notes on

the day she died. See, here." I point to her writing, underneath the date, and my heart squeezes in recognition. It's similar to her teenage handwriting, and every time I see it, it feels like I know her. It feels like she's right here.

"Frances's notes from the morning she died," he says, scanning them quickly. "She visited Dr. Owusu and learned that Saxon's been using Magda to get medical-grade opiates from her clinic. It looks like Magda told Dr. Owusu that the ambulance dispatch in Little Dimber was asking them to have their supplies ordered through the local surgery, for convenience's sake. Magda even produced an email from dispatch and an official inventory sheet for them to use—look." He points. "Frances made a copy of that when she visited Dr. Owusu that morning."

"Why didn't Dr. Owusu immediately blow the whistle on them? Or on Magda at least?"

"Maybe Frances didn't tell her everything. She simply asked the right questions and then went home to act on the information, or double-check it?"

The clicking feeling in my brain returns. It's satisfying, working through things even when I can't see the end result.

"Saxon was on an earlier ferry, right?" I say. "He was in Castle Knoll when Frances was killed. I saw Magda in Dr. Owusu's surgery. She came in when Dr. Owusu was patching up my blisters. But . . ."

Crane doesn't speak. He just gives me a questioning look that says, *Go on.* It's that look that brings me to my senses. I shake my head and let my expression relax. It doesn't make sense; there are too many missing pieces. I think of my unanswered questions list, and while I've ticked off the lock, the flowers are still bothering me. And Emily's killer. Walt is my prime suspect, but could Saxon have killed her at ten years old? I thought the murders were connected, but if

Saxon killed Frances over her discovery of his role in drug dealing . . . maybe it *was* Frances's dirt-digging that had gotten her killed after all.

I decide to leave Detective Crane with the photos and notes—I feel like I have to, because it's evidence that Saxon has been up to something criminal.

"I'm going to run this over to the station," he says. "Annie, please go up to your room and lock your door. I'm going to come right back, but I'll radio for a PC to come straight here while I'm dealing with this."

"Okay," I say. He gives me a brisk nod, and he's off.

I head back to the little bedroom and turn the skeleton key to let myself in, and immediately lock it again from the inside, taking the key with me as I turn around. But when I survey the room, my stomach twists. I forgot that taking my backpack everywhere with me was vital. I'd left it in the bedroom because I'd been in such a mad rush to crack the code on that locked drawer.

The laptop I've barely touched since coming here is smashed to pieces, probably with the same crowbar that did the filing cabinet in. But the thing that really makes my chest squeeze in on itself is the sight of all my notebooks shredded to pieces. My entire investigation gone, ruined by a single lapse in judgment.

I put the key on the bedside cabinet and kneel among the pieces of paper. It's stupid to cry over a torn-up notebook cover that used to have friendly drawings of mushrooms on it. I blink, take a deep breath, and try not to feel so forlorn. All the notes are in my head, really, and paper is paper.

Then it fully hits me, how much of a target I've become. Whoever killed Great Aunt Frances won't hesitate to kill again to protect their secrets.

Just as my feelings overwhelm me, I hear a thud from the

other side of the room. I scramble for a weapon—a letter opener, a hairpin, anything. I finally find a fountain pen and uncap it so that the sharp end stands at the ready. If I weren't so scared I would laugh at how absurd this is, but instead I back slowly toward the door.

I try the handle, ready to burst back out into the hall, but it won't budge. I look across the room to the bedside cabinet and swear inwardly. The little skeleton key that unlocks the door is right there, next to the wardrobe, from where a second thud sounds.

There's someone in here with me, and I've locked us both in.

CHAPTER
30

I SCREAM, LONG AND SUSTAINED, THOUGH I KNOW there isn't anyone around to hear me. Oliver, maybe, but then again would he even try to help if I was in danger?

"Oh, that's quite enough!" Saxon shouts at me as he emerges from the wardrobe. When I don't stop, he lunges at me and claps a hand over my mouth. The fountain pen is knocked from my hand in one small slap, and I'm overpowered in seconds. He's got both my arms pinned to my sides, with his other hand still covering my mouth. I use all the strength I have to try to wriggle out of his grasp, but he's surprisingly strong for someone so lithe.

Saxon holds on to me calmly, waiting for me to stop. Finally I do, because he's not trying to hurt me, but I'm still thinking through every self-defense move I know in case I need it. I'm extremely alarmed by the fact that he was just quietly *waiting in the wardrobe*, and I wonder how long it will take for Detective Crane's PC to arrive and knock on my door. Will I be dead by then?

"Annabelle," he says calmly. "I'm not going to hurt you.

I'm sorry I startled you, but I didn't frighten you on purpose, I promise." He takes his hand away from my mouth but keeps hold of my arms. "If I let you go, can we talk? Calmly, no violence?"

I nod. There's not a lot I can say, and I don't trust my voice.

"Good," he says, and releases me. I immediately move to put my back to the door, even though I'm still helpless without the key. "I'm not responsible for that, by the way," he says, pointing to the shredded notebooks.

"What about the library?" I ask, my eyes darting to the window, where I hear the faint crunch of gravel. Is it the PC? Or Oliver? I consider screaming again but draw in a shaky breath instead. If Saxon wanted to hurt me, he would have done it already. "And *why the hell were you hiding in my wardrobe?*"

"The damage to the library wasn't me," he says, and he gives me a slightly self-conscious smile. "And I was in your wardrobe because I was looking for something I stashed there, years ago. I heard you coming up the stairs and shut myself in, thinking you might not be in the room long, and I could just leave later."

"What were you looking for?" I ask. It's something to focus on, to distract me from the fact that my pulse is still hammering in my head.

He waves a hand. "Doesn't matter. But for future reference, there's a false bottom to it. It would make a better place to store one's murder theories." He picks up some of the shredded paper, and I see the words *poison* and *Saxon* in my careful cursive before he lets the fragments flutter to the floor.

"So who trashed the library?" I ask. And I shudder, because I still feel violated by Saxon's creepy apparition. But I suppose that's his thing—it reminds me of what Great Aunt Frances wrote, about how she turned to see him just standing there, watching her and John under that tree.

"My guess would be one of the Gordons."

"One of? Walt or Oliver?"

"Either. Both. It doesn't matter much, because unfortunately we're both rather screwed. And I don't think we've got a way out unless we work together," Saxon says, keeping his voice light.

"Go back and explain the screwed part, because I've been doing just fine on my own," I counter.

"Why, because you've read Frances's diary? It's a good read, that one. I had a browse myself, when I stumbled across it years ago, just to see how she remembered everything that happened. Because you forget, I was *there*."

"You were where? At the Chelsea house? When Emily died?"

"No, by the time Uncle Ford and I got there, the house was empty. I have no idea who killed Emily; if I did, I would have said so years ago. And honestly, I expected her to show up one day, having spent time as a chalet girl in the Swiss Alps or something."

He's just spinning thoughts around and telling me nothing. "What do you want, Saxon?" I ask. My voice is tired now. "If I were anyone else, I'd have hit you with a candlestick just for coming out of my wardrobe." I glance at the bedside cabinet, and there is in fact a heavy brass candlestick there. Why didn't I grab that when I needed a weapon? Did I learn nothing from all those rounds of Clue with Jenny?

"But you're not anyone else," he says, and his smile grows teeth. "That's why I think we won't be so screwed if we work together."

"Did you kill Great Aunt Frances?" I ask. I watch him

closely, looking for signs he's lying. All he does is watch me back.

"No," he says finally. "I'd never do such a thing."

"But you'd steal drugs from a vet's clinic, to sell?"

Saxon doesn't say anything; he just examines his fingernails.

"Where are the drugs now, Saxon?"

"Are you going to team up with me or not?"

"You've not given me any reason to. What information could you possibly have that would make me want to form an alliance with you?"

"It all comes back to the Gordons." He stares at me for a long time, then raises an eyebrow.

"What do you mean?" I ask.

"Walt has the final say in this competition—don't you find that odd? He's also the executor of her will. He's been one of Frances's closest friends all these years, one of the only people who'd listen to her going on and on about Emily Sparrow, chess pieces, dry bones, all that rubbish."

"It wasn't rubbish to her," I say.

"She's in your head!" he says, and laughs. "I suppose that's a good thing. One of us needs to peel away the layers of her bizarre psyche. Walt's setting this up, he's playing ringmaster."

"How?"

"I wasn't on the eleven o'clock ferry, but I couldn't tell Walt that. When Frances died, I was at the bank. The same bank in Castle Knoll that manages Frances's accounts. I have a trust fund there, set up when I was a child, and I've never bothered to take Frances's name off it. When I asked for a printout of the amounts left, the employee there accidentally printed recent information from Frances's accounts as well. Her legal fees tell an interesting story."

"Are you saying that Frances was overpaying Walt?"

"And then some. I took the printouts without saying a word, and when Elva called me about Frances, I needed to buy some time, so I lied and said I was still in Sandview."

"Why was she overpaying him?"

"I don't know, but I suspect she didn't know that she was. I think he was defrauding her."

"Why didn't she notice?" I ask. "She noticed everything else. . . ."

"Because of who her accountant is. Frances uses the same accountant the law firm does. It's run by an old friend of both of them, someone who, like Walt, doesn't seem to want to retire yet. Even though he's also well past the age of retirement. Isn't that curious? Seventy-five years old and still going. I know times are tough these days, but these two don't like to trust anyone else with some of their clients."

"Who's the accountant?"

"Our old friend Teddy Crane."

"The detective's grandfather?"

"You bet, and I'm planning to use this information as leverage to get a certain set of photos removed from the detective's possession."

"You think Walt killed Frances," I say slowly. It fits with my theory, but not entirely. I still think Oliver killed Frances, with Walt's help. After Frances found out Walt killed Emily.

Saxon nods, his face pinched.

"But how did he get the drugs to do it?"

"That's the last piece of the puzzle, isn't it? Go halves on the inheritance with me, and I'll tell you."

"Why do you need me?" I ask. And he finally shifts, looking guilty. He stares out the window to avoid my eyes. "Ah," I say. "Because you're going to go down for this drug business."

"Not if you help me," he says, his eyes snapping back to me.

"I'm not covering for you!"

"I don't need you to, because I'm not bloody dealing them! It's Magda, working on her own. But I'll go down for writing false prescriptions for her, and for stealing from the vet. Those pictures of her and me together—it's clear I'm supplying her with drugs she doesn't need, but I've got plausible deniability when it comes to the dealing. I'll lose my medical license and my career, but my life won't be over."

"What about Oliver? Do you think he's an accomplice, if Walt killed Great Aunt Frances?" I'm curious whether Saxon suspects Oliver of anything.

"No." Saxon's tone is steady as he paces the room. "But I don't trust Oliver as far as I can throw him. That's the thing about all of us—all of us except you. We're all guilty of something."

"Right now I'm just concerned with which one of you is guilty of murder."

"Well, I've told you." Saxon shrugs.

"You've told me why you suspect Walt, but I still need to know how you think he did it," I say.

"Are you going to split this inheritance with me? It's a good move to play, Annie. And my uncle had a favorite saying about chess."

"*You can play without a plan, but you'll probably lose,*" I say, half to myself.

If Saxon is surprised to hear me quote his uncle, he doesn't show it. "How's your investigation been going so far? Or have you just been crashing around, getting swept up in Frances's teenage adventures?"

I give Saxon a long look. This place was his home, and he was close to his uncle. From his standpoint, me inheriting all this must seem insane. A place I've never been to, from a great aunt I'm only getting to know in death.

"Frances put that clause about a prison sentence in her will for a reason," Saxon says. "I think she wanted me to think long and hard about my misdeeds. I *could* get prison time, with a bad lawyer and a harsh judge. I don't plan on letting that happen, but if I do get put inside, it won't be for long."

"But you'll be discounted from inheriting. Unless I agree to split it with you," I say.

"I'm not a bad person, Annie," Saxon replies.

I let out a long breath, considering. "I'll make you a deal, Saxon. I'm going to consider sharing some of this inheritance with you, but I need you to know that I'm the one holding all the cards here. You've tried to make me think I'm failing at this along with you, but I'm not. So you tell me what you know, help me beat Oliver and the detective to the truth, and you'll just have to hope I'm feeling generous at the end of it all."

Saxon's expression sours a little, but he nods. "Fine. Walt would have had access to the drugs because he's one of Magda's Castle Knoll customers. In the village, if you want to get something from Magda, you call her number and she comes in an ambulance and 'treats' you."

"God, that's so wrong," I say. I throw him a dirty look to underline my feelings on his role in all this. But I remember seeing Walt taking painkillers for his back when Detective Crane and I bumped into him at the Dead Witch yesterday.

Saxon at least has the good sense to pretend to look ashamed. "I'm just passing on the facts."

"But by that logic, any of Magda's 'customers' would've had access to her stash."

"True, but because of my involvement I know the rest of

her Castle Knoll clients, and none of them had any reason to kill Frances."

"So what do we do to prove it?"

"That's where our teamwork really comes into play." Saxon's back to smiling again. "The two of us collaborate. And then we win."

CHAPTER
31

I DECIDE TO TAKE A WALK AROUND THE GARDENS TO clear my head. Before I leave, I grab the photo album Rose gave me, which was mercifully undamaged by whoever ransacked my room. I stop at the big desk in the library and dig out a pen and some loose plain paper from one of the drawers. The PC that Crane sent over is in the kitchen talking to Beth, so I double back and go out through the boot room, even though I shudder a little as I step through. I don't think that room will ever not be creepy to me.

Jenny picks up on the second ring. "Annie, finally!" she says. "You know when you don't call me back I start to worry that something gruesome has happened to you in that murder house."

"Well, it turns out I grew up in a murder house, so maybe that explains my resilience."

"Tell me everything. And leave nothing out, because I'm taking notes on all this and trying to solve it too."

"Why? Are you angling for a sprawling estate in a town that is utterly *rife* with crooked people?"

"No, I just want to play along. Like when I watch *Bake Off* and try to do the challenge, but with murder. And I might be helpful!"

"Jenny, you always fail the *Bake Off* challenges when you try them. Remember those madeleines?"

"That was my oven's fault. And this is far more my speed, so spill."

I find a stone bench in the walled rose garden, and this time I notice bright gravel paths that make patterns around the box hedges. An ornate lily pond sits at the center, and an understated fountain provides a slow trickle. I missed all this the first time I was out here, but then again, I was very focused on spying at the time. As I catch Jenny up, I make notes on the fresh paper. Soon I've got pages full—I've added my unanswered questions list from memory, and I've even redrawn the murder board from my notes. Though I stop short of pulling photos out of Rose's album to stick on it.

"Saxon sounds like a snake-oil salesman in an old-fashioned cartoon," Jenny says. "Did he show you the printouts he talked about? The ones that prove Walt is stealing from Frances? Because he could be flat-out lying."

"No, but I'm going to try to get him to. Because I don't trust him either. But it *is* weird that Mr. Gordon is still plugging away at that law office, and his old friend is still his accountant."

"I hate to say it, but it's a good point," Jenny says. "And they've got something important in common—they were both friendly with Emily, Rose, and Frances the summer Emily disappeared. Also, they currently work for Frances. Sorry, *worked* for."

"The one thing I can't figure out is what was up with those flowers? The hemlock bouquet," I say. "For the life of me, I can't see how it matters."

"Maybe it doesn't," Jenny says plainly. "Maybe it's just a coincidence."

"Yeah, I suppose," I say. My brain is starting to get foggy, and I feel like this is all just circles within circles now. "I think Walt makes the best suspect for both murders, with Oliver as his accomplice for killing Great Aunt Frances. But I want to know what you think, because I might be getting too close to this to see all the details clearly."

"I'm imagining this is like a TV police drama," Jenny says matter-of-factly. "The simple explanation is usually right. I mean, why do people kill?"

"Um, greed?" I offer.

"That's one reason. . . ." Jenny's got a teacher voice on, as though she's trying to help me come to my own answer on a tricky math problem.

I roll my eyes, even though I know she can't see me. "You've googled it, haven't you? You're on some website that's devoted to serial killers or murderous housewives or whatever, and you're—"

"So what if I am? It's actually really interesting! And serial killers are the outliers; they kill because they're psychopaths. I don't think you're dealing with that, or people would be dropping like flies. Anyway, the most common motives for murder are greed, revenge, passion, and self-preservation, according to this website that has . . . crap. Very likely given me a virus."

"Well, I don't trust your sickly website then, but okay," I say. "Just for the thought experiment, I'm making four columns. Let's put the suspects for Great Aunt Frances's murder into these columns, and then I'll do some asterisks for people who had access to the murder weapon." This is why I like talking things through with Jenny—she's always up for discussing my weird plot ideas and never hesitates to tell me when I go too far. And I'll usually emerge from the conversation looking at everything in a completely new way.

"Which in this case is . . . what again? Horse tranquilizers?"

"Not exactly. It was an iron injection, stolen from the vet's clinic along with a stash of other drugs. Okay, now let's fill in the first column: greed." I like the idea of the motives and columns—I should have done this right from the start.

"Ooh, this is fun, I'm playing the game with you. Wait, I'm writing people down and then let's compare."

"You should design board games, you know," I say flatly.

"Oh, you joke, but this would make a *good* one! Like Clue, but you have to solve a fortune-teller's puzzle to beat your friends to an inheritance. But you're all also guilty of a secret crime, and—"

"Jenny."

"Right. Okay, I've got my greed column. Who did you put?"

"Saxon, Elva, Walt, and Oliver," I say slowly, trying to think if I've missed anyone.

"Me too, but I also added that accountant you just mentioned."

"Teddy Crane. Sure, okay, let's put him there too. Next column: revenge," I say.

"Okay, that could technically be all of Castle Knoll if it was common knowledge that Frances was ready to sell off her estate to the highest bidder, or that she kept evidence of everyone's secrets. But let's think conservatively. Because here's the thing with collecting gossip about people: It only ruins people's lives if you spread it. Or use it for blackmail. And I don't think Frances was a blackmailer, was she?" Jenny asks.

"There was an incident with the Crane family, actually," I say. "But I talked to the detective about it and it turns out Frances was wrong, and it was all cleared up."

"Are you sure? As much as I don't want to suspect the sexy detective of murder, it's possible, right?"

"I suspected him for a while," I say. "But I've cleared him. And I think Reggie Crane, and Frances's interest in him, was an outlier; it's likely she just gathered and filed secrets here at the estate and kept quiet about what she found. I mean, she was logical, and keeping secrets hidden would be the best way to prevent yourself from making tons of enemies."

"Yeah," Jenny says slowly, and I can tell she's reading the website again. "So, in the revenge column, even though it's a dish best served cold—"

"That's on the website, isn't it?"

Jenny snorts and says, "I've got a special T-shirt for you that says LITTLE MISS SARDONIC."

"Perfect, I'll wear it when we play your new board game."

"Anyway," she drawls. "Stay. On. Topic. I think anyone killing Frances for revenge would only be doing it in retaliation for something she did recently."

"John, maybe? I'd put him in the passion column, but again, that's all old news," I say.

"Not necessarily," Jenny counters. "I mean, people rekindle old flames all the time. And he's a vicar now, right? And the pins in the roses . . . this is all starting to feel very passionate to me. You said she arranged flowers for the church, right?"

"That's what Walt told me on the first day, and . . . wow, I didn't think of that. And I guess I should have, because a love affair gone wrong is a classic reason for murder. It's actually the motive in my most recent novel," I say a bit sheepishly. My plot was probably way too predictable.

"Maybe he flew into a rage after she seduced him, and his heart was heavy with sin. . . ." Jenny says. She has a tilt to her voice that makes me think she's suppressing a giggle.

"Maybe John was rejected by Frances again, after all this

time. But then there's the problem of the murder weapon," I add.

We're both silent for a while, and then Jenny chirps, "All right, who's in your revenge column then? I'm thinking Elva."

"Good point, Elva can go in two columns," I say. "She might have wanted to kill Frances out of anger for disinheriting Saxon."

"Yeah, but didn't Saxon find out about that a while ago?" Jenny asks. "I mean, why kill her now?"

"True. I think we also have to consider the Foyles, Beth and Archie. Frances recently found out about Archie's weed-growing enterprise and threatened to kick him off the farm if he didn't shut it down. Archie seems like the stubborn sort, and Beth would have had access to Miyuki's horse drugs easily. She'd have even known when it was unlocked. The only problem is the photos Great Aunt Frances has of Saxon and Magda, implicating them in the drug theft."

"But then all someone would need to do is just buy the drugs from Magda, right?" Jenny asks. "Wait, do you think Magda knows who killed Frances?"

"I think she's also a suspect, for sure. I bet Crane's onto that now," I say, groaning inwardly. "Because he took that whole surveillance file with him. But according to Saxon, Walt was also a regular customer of Magda's. He could have stolen the iron from her when he went to buy something else."

"Makes sense," she says. "Otherwise Magda's your murderer, and she did it to silence Frances when she found out the info Frances had on her."

"I just thought of something," I say. "When you mentioned Elva, and asked *Why now?* The timing of Emily's body arriving at Great Aunt Frances's estate."

"Yeah, well done on sending that, Annie."

"I had no idea there was a body in there! But of course the irony is not lost on me. I know that body set something off, and I think it revealed the true identity of Emily's killer to Frances."

"Yeah, that's the connection," Jenny says. "And we're on to the self-preservation column."

"And back to Walter Gordon. He's the only one connected to both crimes. Let's say he killed Emily, and then Frances found out and must have been devastated, so rather than turn him in immediately, she tried to talk to him. They must have gone back and forth for a while, but on the day of that meeting, something snapped for Walt. What if that meeting was Frances's big reveal—you know, she wanted to get everyone in a room together and finally prove who killed Emily after all these years. Agatha Christie–style."

"And Walt faked that phone call moving the meeting because he knew she was already dead. And he wanted to get off the hook for it, so he said she'd called him while he was still in Castle Knoll. God, you've cracked it, Annie."

"I'm uneasy at the idea that Saxon was right," I say, chewing my lip. "I agree that it all fits, but I'm struggling to believe that Saxon genuinely wants to work together to solve this. I'm sure he lied about ransacking Great Aunt Frances's library, I just feel like there's something going on with him that I'm missing." I sigh. "And there's one big issue with Walt now."

Jenny's silent for a couple of seconds. "You've got to prove he did it," she says finally.

"Exactly. Proving it will be the hard part. Because I suspect something else about Walt: that he learned to play games from a master." I stand up and leave my stone bench behind, pacing to stretch my legs.

"Which master? Ford?"

"Frances."

CHAPTER
32

"ALL RIGHT, SAXON," I SAY. "WHAT KIND OF A PLAN DO you have in mind?"

We're in a dimly lit corner of the Dead Witch, where I'm having a pint of IPA and Saxon's got two fingers of the most expensive single malt on the menu, which still isn't particularly fancy. Great Aunt Frances's Rolls-Royce is parked out front, so I guess Archie decided to spend his day at the pub as soon as he dropped me off earlier at the hotel to see Rose. Saxon parked his sports car next to the Rolls when we arrived and tossed a questioning look at the old car. I just gave him my best enigmatic smile.

Archie tried to join us when we came in, but Saxon shooed him away as if he were an annoying terrier. I watched as Archie shrugged and walked off, but I didn't have time to smooth over any hurt feelings.

I have my hair in two long French plaits, and I'm wearing a battered black leather jacket over a light blue floral dress that sweeps down to my ankles, again care of the Oxfam shop on the high street. Saxon sits across from me with one ankle resting across his opposite knee, an argyle sock visible under his tailored trouser leg. It gives him a friendly grandad vibe, which is surprising.

We've got an uneasy alliance, and I'm still very unsure about him. Although I'm more convinced than ever that Walt killed Great Aunt Frances, Saxon is undoubtedly still a potential suspect. Thinking about that moment when he came out of my wardrobe still gives me the creeps, so I keep it at the surface of my mind. Whatever game he's playing, I'm not just a piece on his board. I'm still his opponent.

"How do you feel about being bait?" he asks, and his grin makes the question feel like a dare.

"Can't say I'm a huge fan," I reply, giving him a stony look. "Could you be the bait? And how does this relate to our plan to take down Walt together?"

"I'll get to that in a moment, but the drugs are the murder weapon, don't forget. And unfortunately I can't be the bait, because in the first part of my plan we're trying to reel in Magda."

"Oh no. No way."

"We need to see if she's still got those drugs, for one. And even better if one of us can steal the container from her. It's a sealed plastic box, similar to the ones you store leftovers in. Airtight but see-through."

"Can't we just break into the ambulance or something?"

He gives me a tepid stare and lets the silence stretch out.

Finally I say, "So my job would be to call the number her drug users have, and when she shows up in her ambulance I go in there for a . . . a fix, or something? You do realize I'm the *worst* person for this. I can't handle blood, hospitals make me panic, and even the smell of the cleaner medical professionals use can be enough to set me off."

"So you need a little ketamine to curb your anxiety. Magda will believe that, especially if you've got a wad of cash."

"Which I don't."

"I'll get you some."

My unease grows. This box of drugs won't help us conclusively solve Great Aunt Frances's murder, and Saxon's logic is stretched far too thin to make it seem like it's key to the whole thing. He's most definitely playing me. I'm being set up, and I don't know why he doesn't see how obvious it is.

I could call him out, but I want to know more about what he wants to achieve with all this. Does he want me out of the equation so that he wins the inheritance? Given a prison sentence, so I'm disqualified? Or does he want something worse—a chance to incapacitate me so that I can't look any deeper into what his own involvement in Great Aunt Frances's murder might have been?

"So how am I supposed to get hold of this box of drugs then, if I'm sitting there pretending to be a customer?" I ask.

"Classic diversion. Magda will be on alert because she won't want to get caught with that stuff, so I'm going to tip off the police."

He has to know how transparent this is. I decide to test him on it, to see what excuse he has ready. "Oh, great, so not only will we not get the evidence we need, but I'll come off looking like a drug user. Great plan, Saxon."

"You forget that there are two ambulances. Magda will be listening to the police scanner, but she's always got the volume low. So it'll be vital that you get the box of drugs when she pops into the front to turn the volume up. When I call the police, I'm going to use a few words that she'll know refers to her business, so she'll suddenly be paying much more attention when those start coming through on the police scanner. But I'll tip them off about the wrong ambulance, and I'll be waiting in the car for you when you make a run for it with the box."

"All right." I fold my hands in my lap and watch Saxon carefully. "Let's *say* this works, and we get what we want. How are we going to prove that it was Walt who actually injected Great Aunt Frances with the iron?"

Saxon leans back and swirls the amber liquid in his glass, one arm lazily flopped over the side of the chair he's sitting in. His face is measured, careful. But when he lays out the rest of his plan, my heart starts a worried pulse that quickly turns to a hammer.

"Walt's organized in some ways, but he's not great at covering his tracks. The bank records are an example of that. I can practically guarantee you that he didn't wear any gloves to handle the box."

"So you're certain his fingerprints on the box will be enough?" *They won't,* I think. "I mean, Magda's will be on it too." And it's not like the actual discarded syringe will be in there—he wouldn't have put it back in the box after injecting Great Aunt Frances. That murder weapon is probably long gone, thrown down a storm drain or buried in a trash bin two towns over. It's been three days since Great Aunt Frances was killed; it's likely even made it to landfill by now.

"But Magda doesn't have the motive to kill Frances that Walt does," Saxon says.

"I want to see the printouts," I say. "The bank records you mentioned, that show that Walt's been taking money from Great Aunt Frances."

Saxon shrugs but pulls out the leather briefcase he has resting on the floor next to his chair. He riffles through some papers for a minute, and then hands me several sheets of A4 that appear to be genuine printouts from Great Aunt

Frances's accounts. The name Gordon, Owens, and Martlock LLC comes up several times, charging £500 each time. Interestingly, the payments start right around the time I sent Emily's body in that trunk.

"I'll want those back in a minute," Saxon says, watching me.

I look at him sideways, but then pull out my phone and snap several photos of each page. "How do you know he was defrauding her? Lawyers are expensive, so this could just be his normal fee."

"It's not. I called and talked to their secretary under the pretense of hiring them to handle my own probate paperwork. She sent me a full list of their fees when I asked about other legal work as well, just as a potential client."

I look at the papers again. This isn't a huge amount of money given how vast Great Aunt Frances's fortune is, but maybe over time it could add up. And no matter what, if Walt's been overcharging Great Aunt Frances, it's still stealing. "So what do they charge for probate?"

"Three hundred pounds for the whole package. They have an hourly rate of a hundred pounds an hour for other work, and some flat fees as well, but daily repeat payments of five hundred pounds? That's a nice round consistent number, don't you think?"

He's right, but something still feels off. Walt and Great Aunt Frances were extremely close, and if he needed money and she refused to help him, would that push him to steal from her? I feel like there might be more to the story here, but I can't figure out what.

The thing that's bothering me the most is, if Great Aunt Frances found out Walt was stealing from her, would that be enough for him to kill her?

I think about his violent past, how he hit Emily and then

drove up to London in a rage to confront her in Chelsea. If Walt wanted Great Aunt Frances dead, it wasn't because of the money. It would have been because she found out that he killed Emily. All those old demons would have come flooding back, things he'd been hiding from for years.

But the way the murder was carried out . . . it was carefully planned, it had to be. I look at Saxon. He was the one caught in the surveillance photos passing the stolen drugs to Magda. He learned to play games from his uncle, and he strikes me as a careful planner.

He's got medical knowledge, motive, and the means to carry out the crime. And he was one of the people who wasn't in Walt Gordon's office at the time Great Aunt Frances died.

Finally I hand the papers back to him. I don't want him to know that I'm onto him, but I have two choices: I can play along and hope that I get more evidence that way, or I can just politely refuse and go back to Gravesdown Hall and try to find enough evidence there to prove he did it. The second option is safer, but the first option gives me more power to push Saxon into giving himself away.

You can play without a plan, but you'll probably lose. I decide to form a plan of my own, and beat Saxon at his own game.

"I just—" I start, and then nervously look out the window as if I can't find the right words. "There's got to be a less dangerous way to expose Walt, right? Maybe we could start with this paper trail of fraud? Can we show the printouts to Detective Crane?"

"Now that's just stupid, Annie. We can't have the detective solving this first!" Saxon looks at me like I'm a silly child, which is a good thing. I need him to underestimate me.

"True," I say slowly. I down the rest of my pint.

And, as if summoned by my thoughts, Detective Crane

walks right into the Dead Witch. I watch Saxon stiffen, and then look extra languid to try to hide his alarm.

Saxon has seen me and the detective around the estate, so he knows we've been comparing notes. Given Saxon's habit of lurking and listening at doorways, I'm betting he's heard a lot of what we've been discussing. Detective Crane gives us a curt nod, and then heads straight over to Archie Foyle.

I stare back into the bottom of my empty beer glass. How can I outsmart Saxon? I'm riddling this out when a group of teenage girls passes through our corner of the pub. They're arguing about normal things, clothes and makeup. It wouldn't usually stand out to me, but my head has been so deeply immersed in the summer of 1966 that I can't help but picture Emily, Rose, and Frances. I overhear one of the girls as the group walks by: "Claire, you've got to give me my dress back, you've had it for weeks! I need it for Andy's wedding!"

I shake myself out of this momentary daydream and make a decision. "All right." I smile back at Saxon. "Let's do it. You tell me when and where, and we'll take Walt down together."

CHAPTER
33

THE SUN IS SINKING BEHIND THE HOUSE BY THE TIME we roll back up the gravel drive, and Saxon bids me a quick good night before shutting himself up in his room. A golden strip of light shines under Oliver's door, and I hurry past it, keeping my footfalls as quiet as possible.

Back in my room, I look at my unanswered questions list and find that I forgot to add the typewritten threats to it. So I scrawl:

Threats—who sent them originally (1966) (Walt), and who put them in my room (unknown)?

This is where my heart starts pounding, but in that exciting *I'm really getting there* sort of way. The first threat reads like it's for Frances—*I'll take everything you ever wanted before I come for you.* And it sounds like it's *from* Emily, the person who took John from Frances, and was nearly going to take Ford, as well as the baby Frances's brother so desperately wanted.

At first I was convinced (like Great Aunt Frances was, I'm certain) that someone was threatening her by slipping the notes into her pockets when she wasn't looking. But what didn't make sense was the content of the threats. It was all so specific in terms of what ended up happening to Emily, and then there was the language used. *Whore* and *liar* weren't words that described Frances—she was teased for being the least experienced of the group, and the most honest.

So the second threat reads like it's *for* Emily. But in reality, both threats were for Emily, sent by the same person. I wouldn't have wondered why elderly Great Aunt Frances had them—it could have just been part of her evidence gathering in her own investigation of Emily's disappearance. But teenage Great Aunt Frances referenced them in her diary. So how did teenage Great Aunt Frances get them?

When I overheard the teenage girls at the pub arguing about clothes, it jogged my memory. One of them was asking her friend to give her back the dress she'd borrowed. And I thought of Emily, always wearing Frances's clothes, imitating her to a curious extent.

The threats were definitely meant for Emily. Frances only got them because Emily had put them in the pockets of whatever she was wearing on the day she received them. And both times, she was wearing something that belonged to Frances.

Instinctively, I put my hands into my own pockets, even though my leather jacket is something I bought today. But the reflex reminds me—there were things I took from Elva's blazer pockets that first day. Post-its she tore from the murder board, and extra papers. My heart starts to race because this could be evidence against Saxon. I'm betting Elva shredded my notes and smashed my laptop. Both of them have been looking for whatever it is I took from her pockets, and I'd completely forgotten I'd even done that.

I dash across the room to the wardrobe. I think of Saxon hiding in there, telling me he was looking for something from years ago. They'd both been searching my room for something—I just hope Saxon didn't have time to find it.

I see my old jeans balled up in a corner in the wardrobe, looking rather smelly.

"Please," I whisper, "let Saxon have ignored those. . . ." I dig into my pockets and my fingers pull out the folded papers. "Yes!"

I sit on the bed and look at what Elva took. Two Post-its in Frances's writing, and a sheet of paper also written by Frances.

It's an inventory of missing household items:

silver heirloom necklace (bird)
silver flatware—seven pieces missing
rare antique edition of The Snow Queen *by Hans Christian Andersen*
bone china tea service—four pieces missing

I feel myself deflate. Elva wasn't protecting Saxon. It looks like my first instinct was right, and she was protecting herself. Near the bottom of the list, in a rather hasty scrawl, Frances has written *Elva*. The Post-its confirm this. One lists dates and times next to the words *Elva visits*, and another is Saxon's holiday schedule.

I think about Saxon again. I know, without any shred of doubt, that if I get in Magda's ambulance to attempt some theft operation, I'll find myself caught by the police trying to buy drugs. And whatever I say, I won't be able to talk myself out of a prison sentence—Saxon will have "evidence" that will damn me and disqualify me from inheriting. Great Aunt Frances's will is clear on that.

I pull out my phone and look up previous cases where doctors have been caught writing bad prescriptions, and none of them were given prison time. They lost their licenses and were slapped with heavy fines and put on some kind of watch list, but they didn't go to jail. I suppose it depends on the circumstances and how good your lawyer is, but it's enough precedent to show me that Saxon's confidence isn't misplaced. Saxon knows he'll come out of all of this okay, as long as they can't tie him to the break-in at the clinic.

So I'm left trying to outsmart him, and it's going to take a large amount of courage. I've got some checking to do before I really commit to the plan that's forming in my mind, but I can already sense what I'm going to find out. My plan is probably dangerous and stupid, but staying in this house like a sitting duck is far worse.

So I ring Detective Crane because he's the first person I've got to check on. Even though it's late, he answers on the first ring.

"Crane."

"Hi, Detective, it's Annie Adams. Sorry for the late call, but I wondered if I could ask you a question about the day Great Aunt Frances died."

"Of course. I'm nearly at the estate. I'm going to take over from PC Evans for the night. Has everything been okay? Have you been safe? I saw you at the pub with Saxon—be careful there."

The concern in his voice is sort of touching, so I'm certainly not going to tell him that I was in the Dead Witch plotting to out-double-cross Saxon.

"I've been fine, thanks. Saxon just wanted to chat, nothing serious." I try to keep my voice light and breezy, but I'm in desperate need of some acting classes. "I just called because there was something I was curious about, while I'm trying to get all my ideas straight."

"Always a solid plan in any investigation," he says. "What can I help you with?"

"This is going to sound silly, but you know the meeting that Great Aunt Frances set up with everyone? The one she invited me, Saxon, and Oliver to?"

"Yes, I know the one."

"Did she invite you as well? Or anyone else from the police?"

"Me? No, she didn't. Do you think she'd have reason to?"

I pause, choosing my words carefully. "If she didn't call you, then she didn't need you there," I say. "That's all I wanted to know, thanks. I'll see you later, maybe in the morning."

"Okay, Annie, good night."

I hang up and bring out my notes again. I put a big *X* next to Walter Gordon.

If Great Aunt Frances had set up that meeting to expose him, to do the classic reveal of all the ins and outs of a case she'd solved after sixty years, she'd have invited the police. After all, that was a cornerstone of her personality—she had a very firmly defined sense of justice, and a conviction in her fortune that was practically religious. If she was planning a classic murder mystery wrap-up scene, Detective Crane would have been called upon.

I decide to tuck my notes under the mattress overnight for safekeeping. I consider doing the same thing with the photo album, but it's far too thick. I leave it in my bag and crawl into bed.

I try to sleep, but when my eyes find the wardrobe, I can't stop thinking about what Saxon said earlier, when he'd just emerged from inside it. I jump out of bed and switch the side lamp on, feeling a bit silly about my compulsion to check the false bottom in the wardrobe.

My fingers find the loose board in the base easily, and it pops up on a small spring when I press on it.

It's actually a rather big space, probably about the size and shape of a medium-sized Amazon box. But inside is a bundle of items wrapped in several dish towels. I inhale sharply as I pull out an antique book and seven pieces of silver cutlery. The only thing missing are the tea cups. I feel around the dusty boards for something more, and finally my hand closes on a small velvet pouch. My breath catches as a silver bird necklace slithers out into my palm.

Saxon must have known this was Elva's hiding place. She's been stealing from Great Aunt Frances, that much is clear. Possibly stashing things here to come back for later, when the coast is clear? But then why would Saxon tell me about the false bottom in the first place?

Perhaps he doesn't care. These thefts seem like a minor thing, and I suppose they technically aren't even thefts, as nothing has left the house. I can't think why Elva would be taking these things, but my main conclusion is that while Elva might be shady, this isn't a motive for murder.

I put the items back and replace the loose board. Finally, I crawl back into bed and switch the light off, but footsteps outside my door keep me awake. It's probably Detective Crane just making sure I'm here, since he said he was on his way. Still, I check that the key to the door is safely on the bedside table next to me.

I fall into an anxious sleep, where I dream of footsteps, whispers, and someone rattling my doorknob.

When I wake to use the toilet just after midnight, I nearly trip over a small package that's been put outside my door. A little book-shaped object wrapped in paper. I shred the paper immediately, and Great Aunt Frances's green diary falls into my palm.

I sink back onto my little bed and hungrily read to the end.

CHAPTER

34

The Castle Knoll Files, October 7, 1966

A SAD FACT OF EMILY'S DISAPPEARANCE IS THAT IT shocked the town, until it didn't.

For weeks afterward, it seemed everywhere I went I heard gossip and theories. Emily ran off, or Emily got mixed up with the wrong man. The phrase they started using most was Got *herself* killed.

My hands would curl every time I heard someone say that. And as I walked around town, hoping her face would just float out of a crowd, I started to care about Emily more, and Castle Knoll less.

Because the more I listened and the more I watched, the more I learned. And everything I learned was vile.

We all had times when we hated Emily, but it seemed she was the glue that bound our little group together. And once she was gone, we saw less of each other. The only exception to this was Rose and me.

I refused to talk to Ford, but Rose was like an electric cable connecting me to the Gravesdown estate. Bill, the driver, started spending more and more time with Rose. And then, after all this time, Rose became the upbeat one. And I was the one with clouds hanging over me.

I trusted no one, especially the men connected to the estate. John and I even reconciled for a time, but it wasn't the same. It would never be the same.

Ford wasn't pushy, but he sent me small things through Bill. A book about Afghanistan. A chess set. Every gift he sent made me more determined never to speak to him again. Because the events of the summer had changed me, and opened my eyes to just how much everyone around us keeps hidden. Three months earlier, those gifts would have had the desired effect. They would have flattered me and impressed me. But now I saw them for what they were—they were all about him. He wasn't thinking of me, he was thinking of himself, and he wanted to see his image reflected in my eyes.

I hated it.

And I had reason to hate it even more, when John finally opened up to me about the day he and Walt left me at my brother's house. The day everyone was racing up to see Emily in Chelsea, only for her never to be seen again.

It was when we were trying to make another go of things, John and me. He had been making a lot of effort to take me to civilized places, and we were having coffees on the terrace at the Castle House Hotel. The subject of Emily hung between us like a ghost. For weeks, neither of us wanted to bring her up, but we were unable to move forward with so much left unsaid.

John's stilted and formal attempts at courtship just came across like pantomimes of what he thought Ford might do if Ford were to take me out. Not that Ford would have done that; he knew he'd gotten me into trouble at home. Mother made it clear that she'd finally pieced together where I'd been sneaking out to, and that she found it inappropriate. And it was more than just her superstition talking, though she reminded me that the Gravesdown family had always had bad luck. But she said that no matter how much money a man has, if he's a gentleman he waits until a lady is eighteen and then he takes her out properly.

"Shall we order some cake?" John asked, and he reached across the table and took my hand.

"I'm not particularly hungry," I said. I gave him a weak smile and sipped my coffee, because he really was trying.

We were quiet for a while, and finally he said, "Did you know that Walt's been thinking of applying to study law?"

That nearly made me spit my coffee out. "Walt? Our Walt, who I last saw nearly unhinged by Emily's betrayal?"

"I've wanted to talk to you about all that," John said quietly, and it was like a hammer falling. "That day was such a horrible, backward day. I waited for you to ask about what happened when we got there."

"I've been scared. I've been scared that you might tell me something I can't un-hear."

"I know. And I've wanted to tell you the truth of it, but no matter how I put the words together in my head, it just comes out making implications about someone I know you care about. But Frances, you need to know that we never made it to Chelsea."

I blinked in surprise. "What?"

"Walt's old car died on the A303, and we had to push it to a nearby garage. We hitchhiked the rest of the way back to Castle Knoll, and the hatchback's been up at the garage ever since. I think being stuck at home these past few weeks is what's inspired Walt to do something more with his life, because you know his family."

"Yeah," I said. "They're as crooked as the rest of this town."

"But the point is, I didn't want you thinking that we were the last people to see Emily before she disappeared. Because we weren't. We never saw her at all."

"And we all saw the Rolls-Royce heading out of town." I put my head in my hands, because I knew why John hadn't wanted to tell me this. The last people to see Emily were either Peter and Tansy or Ford and Saxon.

"I always look like a bitter sod when I talk about Ford, and it's worse because I've no right to be angry about who you've been seeing, given everything I'm guilty of. But I've noticed you've gone off him lately. Is it for good, do you think?"

"Rose doesn't think I'm being fair. She thinks I should give him another chance, but she doesn't see through his little gestures like I do. And you're right, John, this information—it makes it worse."

John nodded. "Because, Frannie, what if he killed her? He's a powerful man, and men like that, they just do what they want. And no one bats an eye."

"You think if Ford killed her, there won't be any justice?"

John's mouth became a thin line. "I've thought about that day so many times, Frances, but you know what stands out the most? More than Walt's rage or Emily's manipulations? Your kindness. Just before we drove off, you mentioned forgiveness. And your words, and the generous and calm expression you had—it was a moment of peace that has resonated in me like music, for weeks. I've been chasing it ever since.

"There's a child in this world, and I don't know if she's here because of Emily's scheming and my betrayal, or because of Ford's lust, but you put aside any feelings of ill will toward all of us and let that baby be the gift it could be for someone you love."

I'd never heard John talk like this. It made me warm to him even more, because who knew he was so eloquent? I could see him making speeches, maybe running for the local council one day.

But then I had a thought that made my hands start to shake, because the love John talked about—it had been given to people *who might have just taken it and twisted it. Finally, I said it out loud. "Or I was part of a chain of events that ended Emily's life."*

"If it helps, I trust your brother's good character more than that of Rutherford Gravesdown's. And you did everything you could, Frances, given the circumstances. You acted with grace. I can see that. And I just wanted you to know."

A tear escaped my eye and traveled down my cheek, and John reached out and wiped it away with his thumb. "It keeps me awake at night, you know," I said. "It's . . . it's not knowing what happened to her, but it's something more too. She was a deeply flawed person, and she treated me badly, but she was a person. And watching the town exchange stories about her, everyone pulling out things they think they know, all of it salacious and all of it gossip . . ."

"Some of it's true," John said, but he looked ashamed as soon as he did.

"Even if it's true, it's appalling to hear the way they pick her apart with their words. Walt gets to be a lawyer if he wants to—Walt, who stole porno magazines from the off-license, and who cheated on exams constantly. Walt drinks and smokes and swears, but he'll have a chance to be whatever he wants. Emily could have too. Her life could have moved on. But now it's like she's just a gruesome story people tell."

"Frances," John said, and worry creased his forehead, "there's a lot of goodness in you, but be careful this doesn't eat up your ability to have faith in people."

But I was lost in thought. "Laura was born on the eighth of August. Did you know Emily named her? Peter told me. He said she insisted. She's Laura Frances Adams. Laura is Emily's sister's name, so she's named after her. But there's me in there too."

John did that frustrated motion of his, where he runs his hands through his hair to the point where he's practically pulling it. "I can see that you feel flattered, Frances, and I know I just told you not to lose your faith in people, but that name could also have been meant to be cruel. Naming the baby she had from sleeping with two men who care about you after you? Don't forget she was unpredictable and obsessive. And her focus—it was always fixed in your direction."

"I know, you've said it before. Emily had one obsession, and it wasn't Ford and it wasn't money."

"It was you."

"Maybe it's only fair, then, that she's all I can think about now."

"It's possible that someone did you a favor then."

"John! That's heartless!"

"I know, I'm sorry, but it had to be said!" John's hands curled and flexed and then curled again. "As much as you might hate to hear it, Frances, Emily wouldn't have grown up like the rest of us. She would have kept on hurting you. Walt has a future in the law, and I'm— You're going to laugh, Frances, but I'm really considering the church."

"The . . ." I blinked a few times, not sure I'd heard him right.

"I don't know about a career in ministry, but theology . . . I want to study it at least. It's the one thing in all my life that makes me feel anchored. I'm sure you'll have something like that too. And Rose has a job here at the hotel, though she hasn't told you yet. Act like you're surprised when she does, okay?"

My coffee had gone cold, but I took a sip of it to have something to do with my hands. I would be eighteen in the spring, and I was drifting toward an anchor too. But it was one that John wasn't going to like. It was the anchor of the unknown, of questions and theories. It was the anchor of puzzles and predictions. And it was the anchor of a fortune that I was determined to outsmart.

When I looked up from my coffee cup into his eyes, his trusting, clear eyes, I could already feel myself being drawn into the dark. And I could see the hope in him. He was so beautiful.

Your future contains dry bones.

The day I'd been to that fortune-teller had been such a complicated day. Was there something in that fortune that I should have listened to more closely? I wrapped a finger in the chain of the bird necklace I still wore, which I couldn't stop wearing.

Was Emily's fate meant for me? Had fate killed the wrong girl?

I kissed John then, just because I wanted to one last time. He was older than me, nineteen by then, and spinning his wheels in Castle Knoll. Perhaps the church would end up suiting him. Or some university somewhere.

Another tear fell as I drew back from the kiss, and I felt like something was ripping in my chest. It was more than just saying good-bye to John; it was the knowledge that I was turning away from the parts of me that he thought were the best.

My choice was to follow all the threads of unpleasant stories about Emily, to weave myself in and out of the fabric of Castle Knoll, learning everything about everyone until I found the truth.

Because I knew, deeper than I've ever known anything, that our fates were intertwined—Emily's and mine. I couldn't shake the belief that underneath everything, I was really just Emily in disguise.

So I'd find out what happened to her, even if it killed me. And I accepted that, given my fortune, it probably would.

CHAPTER
35

MORNING LIGHT SLAPS ME IN THE FACE AS I LET IT flood the room with a jangle of metal curtain rings. I hardly managed any sleep; I'd been too busy reading the diary. Once I reached the end of it, I looped back and read sections of it again, this time pausing to flip through Rose's photo album. This way, it was almost like Frances was narrating the photos, until a disturbing pattern emerged. Until something in the pictures didn't match her words.

And finally, with the chilling clarity that only comes at three A.M., I know what Frances had figured out when she found Emily's body. After that, the pieces wouldn't stop coming together in my mind, and I spent the rest of the early hours frantically adjusting my own plan to solve the mystery.

I dress quickly and nod nervously at my reflection in the little tarnished mirror on the wall. I'm going to do this, I really am. Saxon and I have arranged to meet later tonight, and I know it's going to be hard work keeping my nerves at bay until then.

The delicious smell of cooking wafts up from the kitchen, and my stomach rumbles. I take the carpeted stairs down two at a time.

"Beth," I say when I reach the kitchen. The bright smile that finds me is genuine.

"Annie, hi! I've just made muffins. Would you like one?"

"They smell amazing," I say. I don't know if my nervous stomach can handle breakfast, but I'm so hungry that I decide to try. Beth pours me coffee without my having to ask and puts milk and sugar next to the steaming mug. I ignore both and take a long sip. It fortifies me a little.

"I'd ask about your investigation," Beth says cautiously, "but I don't want to be too nosy."

I nod and try to give her a reassuring look. "You're in a nerve-wracking position, and I don't want you to worry. I'm doing everything I can to get justice for Great Aunt Frances, and to make sure things are secure for the future of the estate."

"You mean if you win this game Frances created, you'll keep things running as they are? Let us keep the farm?" She leans forward to put a muffin in front of me, and I look across the table at the china tea service she's set out, presumably waiting for the others to wake up and come looking for a hot drink. That list of missing items I found in Elva's pocket comes to mind, but there must be several bone china tea sets in this house. Still, I notice six cups and saucers, which seems like a full set to me.

"Beth," I say as I reach over and pick up a cup. "This might sound like a silly question, but have you ever noticed any of the teacups go missing?"

I look at her carefully. Her cheeks color, and she doesn't try to hide the guilty look on her face. "I've put them back now," she says quietly.

I don't bother trying to hide my surprise, because her admission makes me worry all my conclusions about who killed Great Aunt Frances might be wrong. Beth has keys to the house, access to Miyuki's clinic . . . what if I've completely misjudged her? I assumed she was just helpful, and worried about the state of her family's farm. All the while she's been a thief, taking things that meant a lot to Great Aunt Frances.

I look at her carefully. "I found a whole list of missing items, actually. Elva tried to take the list and hide it, probably just to meddle with whatever pieces of Aunt Frances's notes she could."

Beth sinks into a chair across from me. "I was just trying to protect Frances from herself, honestly. The things I took—they were things that were causing her stress, things she related to her fortune. Even some of the forks were making her nervous because the design started to look *too regal,* she said. She'd been eating with them for decades; I don't know why she was getting so much more paranoid. But anyway, I thought, out of sight, out of mind. None of those things ever left the house. I only hid them." She pauses, considering me. "I'm guessing you found the rest of them, seeing as you decided to stay in that room?"

I nod.

I consider Beth. She seems open and honest, and I don't think she would have killed Great Aunt Frances. I feel my three A.M. revelations fall firmly back into place, so I see no harm in giving her my honest answer in terms of what I'll do with her farm if I inherit. "Beth, I don't want to take your family's farm. And I know just what your grandad's been growing up there." Beth's eyes widen a fraction at that, but she doesn't say anything. "I'd need him to stop, but I'd be willing to set him up with some other—legal—moneymaking enterprise. I was already planning to give you guys that Rolls, because I don't have any use for it."

Beth's expression lifts. "You would? It would mean a lot to us. We love that car."

"Of course," I say. "I mean, as long as none of you killed Great Aunt Frances."

Beth laughs, but I'm only half joking. But either way, my words have cleared the air a bit. I find that I'm able to eat a little breakfast, and I decide to take a gamble on Beth.

"Can you do me a favor?" I ask, and I desperately hope that my instincts about her aren't misplaced. "Can you take my bag to Mr. Gordon, please?" I reach under the table and bring my backpack out from where it's been resting near my feet. I need all my progress in his hands, in case anything goes wrong tonight. "It's just some boring forms I had to sign because we got behind on our electricity bills for the house in Chelsea." It's a weak explanation, but there's too much at stake for me to tell her the whole truth.

"Sure," she says, and takes the bag.

I just have to hope that she not only delivers the bag, but that she does it soon, and without looking inside.

"Thanks," I say, and I go to find a private spot in the garden to make some phone calls. It's time to implement another phase of my plan.

I pull up the number for the doctor's surgery in Castle Knoll from their website, and it rings twice before Dr. Owusu answers.

"Hi, it's Annie Adams," I say.

"Oh, hi, Annie. How's that rash? I assume it would have healed up days ago."

"It has, thanks. But I'm actually calling for another reason. I don't know how much Great Aunt Frances told you about her investigations before she died, but she had proof that

Magda was dealing prescription drugs. I know she comes through your surgery for supplies, but from Great Aunt Frances's files, I can see that Magda cooked up a genuine reason to obtain certain things through you. So I'm not phoning to accuse you of being involved."

The other end of the line is quiet for a second, and I hear what sounds like soft swearing. When Dr. Owusu speaks again, her voice is full of controlled anger. "Magda told me there were changes in how things were being ordered and stocked," she says. "She had order lists and invoices, and everything looked fine. And it wasn't like she was just ordering oxytocin or liquid morphine—most of the supplies were standard things needed in an ambulance. EpiPens and insulin, that kind of thing." She pauses. "You're sure?"

"Pretty sure, yeah," I say.

"Then I need to call Rowan. He'll have to deal with this."

"He already knows," I say, and I have a sinking feeling in my stomach. I wonder how far Detective Crane has gotten in finding Great Aunt Frances's murderer. So much has happened in only three days, with only four remaining to solve this. But those days won't matter if Crane is closing in and solves it today. I can't even bring myself to wish he was a bad detective, or to sabotage him in some way. I just have to stick to my plan and hope that means I get my answers faster. "But I have a favor to ask. And it involves you talking to Magda, without letting on that you know what she's up to. Is that something you'd be willing to do? It's for Frances."

"You aren't putting yourself in any danger, are you, Annie? Because I have no qualms calling Rowan and telling him to rein you in if you're getting in over your head."

"And let him solve the murder before me? You'd let Jessop Fields turn that land into whatever makes the most money, earning the anger of the whole village?"

"I think you need to give Rowan more credit than that," she says. "He's walking a very careful line, Annie, trying to keep everyone safe while still doing his job, all while giving you room to conduct your own investigation. But if you turn up dead, that's not helping anyone."

I do my best to swallow my nerves again, because the more I think about my plan, the dumber it sounds. "I need you to spread a little gossip for me. Just to Magda. Let her know I've solved Frances's murder. Can you do that?"

"Have you worked out who the murderer is? Because I'd think Walt Gordon should be the one you're calling, if that's the case," she says.

"I think I've solved it, but I need a few more things to prove it. So can you just do that one thing for me?"

There's another long pause, and then a sigh. "All right," she says finally.

"Thank you."

"But I'm also going to do everything in my power to keep you safe, and that includes telling Rowan about this conversation."

I wince. "You do what you have to do," I say.

"You too," she says, and hangs up.

CHAPTER
36

I WRING MY HANDS IN TIME WITH THE CHURCH bells, realizing just how nervous I am to meet John Oxley. Time was crawling by up at Gravesdown Hall, and I couldn't just wander the rooms any longer. So I called a taxi, deciding it was time to stop avoiding the church and my own family connections there. The church is perched on a small slope, like a little echo of the castle ruins on the larger hill at the other end of town. I make my way up slowly, weaving between lopsided gravestones and sprawling yew trees.

A stream of people is leaving the church—women in hats of lilac and robin's-egg blue chat with men in rumpled suits. I glance behind me to the bottom of the hill and see the quick flash of a voluminous white dress before the door closes on a smart black classic car. It feels like the wrong moment to walk up to John and say, "Hi, I'm Annie, am I your granddaughter?" so I find a bench off to the side of the church where I can watch for a bit. It doesn't take long for the people to thin out, and I notice that the stream of cars only drives to the other end of the road, to the Castle House Hotel.

I see John as he's chatting to an older lady, but he isn't looking at her—he's looking at me. He looks just like the photo on the church website, with his white hair neatly combed and his lean build suggesting he stays active. I can't say why, but he strikes me as a tennis player, or someone who rows. I try to picture him at eighteen, sneaking around with Emily, living the teenage stereotype of a rogue and a cheater. I try to picture him as a murderer, and feel satisfied when I find it next to impossible.

But the second thing that strikes me are the flowers—roses, all of them, and of a very particular type. The front of the church has two large displays on stands, and I surmise that the inside is decorated with them too. They are all, down to the very tiniest bud, the roses I saw on Archie Foyle's farm. Archie must have kept up the tradition after Frances died, and delivered roses to the church himself, because these are fresh.

Finally, the vicar finishes his chat, and makes his way toward me. I fold and unfold my hands, wondering how much to tell him about my knowledge of his past.

"I wondered if I might run into you," he says, and his face is friendly. "I heard you were in town, but I was certain you wouldn't find a reason to visit me. Laura and her parents never set foot in church. May I?" He gestures to the bench beside me. He smiles, and it's warm, but almost shy. He must have a thousand things running through his head. He gives me a long considering look.

"Of course," I say. I wonder what he sees when he looks at me. My blond hair, wide-set eyes, and high cheekbones—does he see Emily Sparrow when he looks at me? Or just the odd feature that's familiar? And now that I really look at him, I see that my cheekbones and eyes could come straight from John. This might be why, when I saw Emily's photo, I couldn't see the resemblance between Mum and her. The blond hair is the one thing we share with Emily, but our faces favor John. Warmth floods through me, because I never knew Peter and Tansy or my father. And here is this kindly old man who regards me with such amazement that I feel remarkable even though I'm doing nothing but sitting here. He's looking at me as if I'm exceptional just because I exist.

It's a new feeling for me, and it's like the cheerful crackle of logs when you first light a fire, or the comforting smell of baking bread. Both are things I've never really experienced in my life. It's a different feeling of *family*, I decide. The unconventional life Mum has given me isn't lessened by this, but a new dimension has suddenly been added to the word for me.

I decide to dive right in. "Peter and Tansy were probably worried that Mum would find out, about you being her real father, I mean. Aren't you?"

If he's shocked at my candidness, he doesn't show it. He lets out a sigh that actually sounds relieved.

"Peter and Tansy . . ." He puffs his cheeks out, considering his words. "They were very careful with Laura. I think that as their only child, she represented a fine balance of happiness for them and, looking back, they did everything they could to make sure that balance was maintained. They never went to church once I was ordained and had the position here. They paid more than they earned to send Laura to the private school in Little Dimber, so she had very few friends in Castle Knoll. Reggie Crane was probably her only friend from here, but that was because he briefly went to the same school as her. And when Peter and Tansy visited Frances, it was always short, pleasant, and supervised."

"How do you know? About school, and visits to Great Aunt Frances, I mean. And the truth about you being Mum's dad?" I couldn't yet bring myself to say the word *grandfather*.

"I found out I was Laura's real father because Ford paid for a paternity test right after she was born. It was a relatively new science back then, but he wanted to know for sure. It was Frances who told me, and I was glad she did. Frances and I met weekly for coffee. We did that for years, actually, and she kept me updated on Laura, and on you. We went to the Castle House Hotel, sort of a tradition." He smiled fondly. "I was so very sad to hear of her death, and even more outraged at the circumstances of it." He blinks several times as his eyes water, but he doesn't look away. "I never stopped loving her."

I don't really know what to say to that, so I don't say anything for a bit. I see no ring on John's hand, and there's a cracking feeling in my chest as I picture him spending years loving Frances but watching her live a life slightly removed from him. At least they continued their friendship.

"I was sad I never told Laura I was her real father," he says eventually, "but I made a promise to Peter and Tansy, and I understood why they wanted things that way."

"I'm sure Mum would love to come and visit, and hear the truth from you," I offer. I've got a lot to catch Mum up on, but now that her new exhibition has opened I don't have an excuse to keep her at arm's length.

"I read all about her success in the papers," John says, and he smiles almost proudly. "And when you were born, Frances brought photos to our weekly coffee chats." He pauses, and his voice hitches. "It's silly of me, but I'll miss those coffee mornings so much."

"I know I can't replace Frances, but maybe you'd like to have coffee with me?" I say weakly.

"Are you planning on staying in Castle Knoll?" he asks. His whole face lifts, and the tug of *family* pulls at me so deeply that I know just where I want to be.

"Yes," I say, and with conviction. "I am."

CHAPTER
37

WHEN I RETURN TO THE HOUSE, I PHONE MUM FROM Great Aunt Frances's file room.

"Sorry I haven't called sooner," I say. "How did the show go?"

"Oh, it was great!" Mum says. "Honestly, the reviews are amazing, and the art has been selling really well. I have money to start renting my own studio, so I won't have to resort to using the basement anymore. Oh! That reminds me, Annie, can you tell Aunt Frances's lawyer that he really doesn't need to keep sending me that maintenance? I think something must have glitched with the accounts last week. Another check came through for two hundred pounds, and that's just not necessary."

"Wait, the maintenance checks from Great Aunt Frances always came through Gordon, Owens, and Martlock?" I ask. I think of the bank records, and something starts to get a little clearer.

"No, they always used to come directly from Aunt Frances, but about a week before you got that letter—you know, about that meeting?—they started to come from the solicitor's office. I didn't question it at the time; funds were low, and money's money, right?" Mum sounds upbeat, almost breathless. "But Annie, you won't believe what one of my paintings sold for. It was even in *The Times*! But it's not just the money. My career's back on track. I was so worried this show would flop, but it's so nice to see that people really understand my art, what I was trying to convey with this show."

I smile, because it's good to hear Mum feeling positive about her work again. "That's amazing, Mum, I knew it would go well."

"Anyway," she breezes. "How come you're still in Castle Knoll? Is Saxon trying to contest Aunt Frances's will? Or is the estate being split up?"

I don't have the energy to tell her about my situation, about how I'm stuck in a twisted game with Saxon, trying to outwit him in order to keep our house in Chelsea and the Gravesdown estate out of the hands of property developers. There's too much emotion tangled up in Great Aunt Frances's last wishes now. Having learned about Emily, and all the ups and downs of what happened that summer they were seventeen, I have to be the one to win this. And I want my head to be as clear as possible.

"It's still being argued over. I'm going to stay here and see this through, and I'll do everything I can to make sure we get to keep our house," I say. "I'll call you again soon, okay?"

I hang up and open the pictures I took of the bank records. Mum confirmed what I noticed when I first saw the printouts—the first overpayment for legal fees came a week before I got that letter. The day Great Aunt Frances received the trunks I sent. The day she found Emily's body and everything changed for her.

She must have been in such a terrible state, having found Emily after all those years of searching. I picture her, frantically moving around her murder room, reciting her fortune to herself and fully letting the horror of it all take over.

Changing her will had been an act of desperation, a superstitious move to try to fend off a death she thought was imminent. Cutting Mum out when she did nothing wrong would seem like a cruel move to anyone but Frances, and I can picture Walt trying to talk her out of it while Beth hid books with *queen* in the title, teacups made from bone china, and even forks that didn't look right, all to protect Frances from her own paranoia.

And when Walt couldn't talk her out of changing her will, he decided to find a way to keep supporting Mum. Mum, who didn't even know Walt that well. Those last few payments would have gotten her through her final paintings and bought the supplies that made her show possible. My eyes sting, and I blink a few times to clear the welling tears. Great Aunt Frances was right—Emily never got the chance to become any better, but everyone else who made mistakes that same summer did. And I think Walt could see that. Helping Mum seems like Walt's way of showing he still cared for Emily, forgave her broken promises, and realized just how much was stolen from her.

I think of Rose's photo album. There's a particular picture of Great Aunt Frances wearing her wool coat—the one she ripped off Emily the day they all found out about her pregnancy. That, plus the information that John and Walt never made it to Chelsea, with the Phantom II blazing past them . . . I just hope I'm not wrong. Saxon just wants to destroy my progress and slow me down and make me feel discouraged so I'm easier to manipulate. But Walt didn't kill Emily. Walt wasn't even there.

"Ready?" Saxon's voice floats over my shoulder, and I turn

to see him watching me, in hiding for who knows how long. He steps into a slice of early evening light that's fighting its way through the little door to Great Aunt Frances's office.

Saxon doesn't question why I don't have my backpack with me. I don't know if it should give me confidence that I might be succeeding in outsmarting him, or if he's just waiting until the right moment to move his own game pieces. But the contents of that bag are my insurance, and I've planned ahead. I can't risk all my work being destroyed again, and my notes are the key to everything—so long as they find their way into the right hands.

All I've got is my phone, with voice activation enabled, and a burner I got from a shop in the village. I loved going and buying a burner phone; it took all my restraint not to walk in and say excitedly, "One burner phone, please!"

Jenny is waiting until exactly eight P.M. to call the Castle Knoll police station and fill them in on everything. I wanted to give them just enough information to keep me safe, but not so much that Detective Crane will fill in the blanks and get to the finish line before I do. But hopefully by eight, Walt will have everything he needs from me to satisfy the conditions of Great Aunt Frances's will.

"Ready," I say. I've got my battered charity shop leather jacket on again, and I can tell Saxon hates the sight of it. He's trying hard to keep his face impassive, but he's eager to get me out of the house. For good.

We settle into his sports car and drive in silence for a few minutes. I check my decoy phone for the time—it's 7:25. The burner isn't your typical basic Nokia, because I couldn't take a chance on a phone that didn't have a whole lot of memory and a top-of-the-range mic built in to record properly. My overdraft screamed when I bought a brand new iPhone, but I could link it to my already active iPhone account as a second phone and have it working within minutes. I suppose this technically means it's not a burner, but I like using the terminology anyway. And I'm counting on switching the phones right under Saxon's nose, so I need them to look the same. I start the recorder while mumbling fake text messages to myself as a distraction. *See you for brunch on Sunday, Jenny, xx,* I mutter as I click the red start button. Saxon has his eyes on the road, his expression steady. I slip that phone into an inner pocket and pull out my real one to click on, as if nothing's changed.

I'm wondering now about my timing. I might have to drag this out, and I'm hoping the mic can pick up sound through my pocket. Once I'm in position I won't be able to just pull it back out to get a better recording. I'm also panicking that I've got everything wrong and that the evening will end with me being busted for buying drugs.

I'm tempted to test Saxon some more and to ask him just *how* me stealing these drugs will point to Frances's killer. But this plan was never about Frances for him; it was just about taking me out. And if I press him too much, he'll know I'm on to him.

"Open the glove box," Saxon says. "You'll find the cash in there. Magda will ask for that up front, before she even lets you into the ambulance."

A wad of notes falls into my palm, rolled up and secured with a rubber band. It looks grimy and dog-eared and just like the sort of thing TV drug addicts would carry, but as I remove the rubber band and Queen Elizabeth's face peeks out at me, Great Aunt Frances's fortune ignites in my mind:

Your slow demise begins right when you hold the queen in the palm of one hand.

I shudder and bat down any superstitious thoughts before they can take hold and feed my anxiety.

I tuck the money into the pocket of my jacket, sparing another side glance at Saxon. I bet there isn't a single fingerprint of his on this cash, and he's gone out of his way to make sure mine will be all over it. No envelopes or plastic bags here.

"Once you're in there, she'll ask what you want. Don't go off script and ask for something that won't be from the stash of vet supplies. You've got to ask for ketamine."

"Got it," I say. *Don't think of needles, don't think of syringes. . . . Keep it together, Annie. To do this, you've got to be Annie the main character. Annie the detective.*

We reach the village, and he pulls into a small car park behind the off-license. It looks like it's used only by employees, and although there are a few cars parked here already, Saxon isn't bothered. I suppose the ambulance is hidden in plain sight, really. Even if someone were to come out to their car, they'd just see a parked ambulance and not think twice.

He backs the sports car into a gap behind a dumpster, where we can see the car park but not be seen by anyone unless they're really looking. "I'll be here, ready to drive us off as soon as you've got the box. If the police scanner diversion doesn't work and she's got her eyes on the box the whole time, just put the ketamine she sells you in your pocket and play it off like a normal sale, okay?"

This is where he must think I'm extremely thick. "Why wouldn't I just have a sudden change of heart and ask for my money back and leave without any drugs?"

"Because Magda will get suspicious. That's the thing with illegal activities—it needs to be reciprocal. If you're in just as deep as she is, she'll know you're not just going to rat her out."

I want to scoff at the flaws in that logic, but he needs to think I'm confident in him.

"Okay, I guess that makes sense." I nod and bite my lip. I hope Dr. Owusu has spread the word about me solving the murder. Everything depends on that information getting to Magda.

"That's good, look a bit anxious," he says. "Play up the whole panic-attack thing, because Magda's going to assume you're not usually the drug-using type. Let me see your phone. I'll put the number in for you."

He holds out his hand for it, and here's where I knew things might go a little sideways. He's smart, and he wants to check I've not got the recorder on. He's also going to hang on to it when I get out of the car.

I give him an expression like hardened cement and unlock my phone. I look him dead in the eye, and hand it to him. His mask slips a little, because he was expecting some sort of hesitation from me.

He dials the number and sets it to speakerphone—he wants to monitor this conversation with Magda, but it's going to be me doing the talking. I don't doubt Saxon's got his recorder going on his own phone somewhere in this car.

It rings a few times, and then Magda's voice comes lazily down the line. "Magda's minor injury line," she says, and the small lilt of singsong to the words makes it obvious this line is anything but casual.

"Hi, Magda, it's Annie Adams. I heard this is the number to call if I need, uh . . . a bit of chemical help?"

"This is the one," she says cheerfully. "Are you looking for something right away? Depends on what you're after. I've not got a huge selection at the moment. . . ."

Saxon is nodding at me encouragingly, so I try to show some commitment to my role. "I'm losing my mind over all this stuff with the murder, I'd love something to really calm me down. Do you have any K?" Urban Dictionary tells me that people don't ask for ketamine by name, and I suddenly feel like the uptight law-abiding citizen I am when saying "K" comes out stilted and wrong.

"I think I can sort you out with that, sure," she says. She gives me an amount and asks if I need time to get to an ATM. When I tell her I don't, everything starts to happen more quickly.

"A good spot for treatment for a minor injury," she says, "is in one of the car parks in town. Are you in the village?"

"I am," I say. "I've just left the off-license. Is there somewhere near there?"

"The car park around the back is a perfect spot. I'll meet you there in ten."

"Okay, great."

Saxon ends the call and then pockets my phone. "Magda won't allow you in there with a phone," he says. "I'm sure you understand. She's just trying to keep herself safe. But don't worry, I'll be here watching, and the worst that can happen is you just end up buying some K." He sounds much smoother when he says "K."

I swallow, my throat suddenly dry. "Yeah," I say. I try to hide my nerves because the atmosphere in the car is feeling tense now. The more nervous and scared I seem, the more plugged in Saxon gets. I tell myself it's just that he thinks he's winning, but alarm bells are ringing in my head.

"You'll do great," Saxon says. "But you'd better get out and wait there, because we can't let her see that I'm parked here."

I get out of the car like it's about to explode, but I manage to rein it in as soon as the evening air hits my face. I walk about thirty meters into the car park, and when I turn around I notice I can only see Saxon's car when I'm at the far corner. I walk to the other side, where I'm hidden from his view, and reach into the inside pocket of the leather jacket. The recording might not have caught any of Saxon's instructions through the muffle of the leather, but there aren't any other places to keep the spare phone, so I'm just going to have to pray this works. I look at the clock on the phone; it's 7:45 now. Fifteen minutes, and Jenny's going to implement phase two. If I don't get what I need in those fifteen minutes, I will have revealed my whole hand, and Detective Crane will swoop in and the case will be his. Or worse, I'll take the fall for something I didn't do, and the game will be Saxon's when he works out who really killed Frances. Because he will.

I take a deep breath and remember that while Saxon may think he's trapping me, I'm trapping Great Aunt Frances's murderer. I'm pushing us all into the endgame.

I'm counting on the fact that gossip fuels this town. I'm also counting on Magda's business being an open secret, especially among people she spends a lot of time with. If I've overestimated either of those things, I'm going to be in some serious trouble.

"Where are you?" I mutter through clenched teeth. I need this ambulance to get a move on, because I need to be inside it before my timer goes. I probably should have taken lateness into account.

Finally the ambulance rolls into the car park and I can't help it—a small satisfied smile twists my lips when I see that I've gotten some things right. Saxon must be cursing in the little sports car right now, confused as hell. I quickly check that the recorder is still on and tuck the phone into my pocket.

"Hi," I say, and Joe Leroy gets out of the driver's seat. "I called for Magda," I add, pretending to be confused.

"Oh, I know," he says. "But I said I'd see if I can help you. She said something about a minor emergency, a panic attack? You seem okay," he says, and his face is friendly.

"I, uh, did some breathing exercises." I try to get more strain into my voice, and it isn't hard to do. I look at the bright blue gloves on his hands and the carefully set mask of his expression. My plan doesn't seem so carefully laid now. I'm being reckless, but I can't think of a way out. *Fifteen minutes.* I just need to keep him talking for fifteen minutes, and hopefully I'll get what I need and be able to get out of here. "I'm still a little dizzy. Is there somewhere I could sit down?"

Joe goes around to the back door of the ambulance and opens it. The fluorescent lights flicker before they settle into that feeble hospital glow, and my stomach turns. "Sure," he says, and he takes one of my arms, helping me into the back of it. His surgical gloves squeak on the leather of my jacket, and I can smell disinfectant mixing with his aftershave. He's the fox, leading a scared little rabbit into the jaws of his den. I'm already shaking as I sit on the paper-covered stretcher in the back of the ambulance, but my mind clears a bit as I notice the plastic box under a pile of supplies across from me. It's exactly as Saxon described it, but then again, I knew it would be.

I hear the doors swing closed, and Joe's voice turns professional as he says, "Well then, Annie." As my eyes snap toward him, it occurs to me that I did actually get my timing all wrong. Because Joe is not wasting a second. He's already got a syringe in his hand when he says, "Unfortunately you're in for a drug overdose tonight."

CHAPTER
38

The Castle Knoll Files, January 10, 1967

IT WAS THE FIRST CHRISTMAS AFTER EMILY DISAP-
peared, and I must have been feeling generous because I finally
agreed to go with Rose to Gravesdown Hall. I could tell Ford had
been scheming with her, because his gifts had stopped in September and he'd started sending me letters instead. They were
eloquent and interesting, and he was curious about me and my
dreams for the future. Each one softened me just a little, and by
the end of September I tentatively started writing back. Nothing
too personal, at first, but he had this way of drawing me out that
felt almost erotic at times, even though his letters weren't overtly
like that. Oh, it's so hard to explain!

When we went to the estate for Christmas I felt the full force
of his affection, but from feet away. It was as though he was
handing me that chess piece all over again, saying, "Here, you
hold the queen." But I realized that when he'd said that he'd been
opening up a space for me at his side, rather than simply quoting
a line from my fortune. I'd chided myself when I first met him,
because I thought it was silly to think he'd be interested in me in

that way. And after I knew he'd been with Emily, I used the image of them together to help burn him from my mind.

Throughout October, I was still afraid he might have killed her. And then it occurred to me that I could take the queen and place it on the board. Because getting close to him could mean finding out what really happened to Emily.

But I knew it was vital that I kept my head through it all. So whenever he'd reach in and stroke my heart, I'd picture him and Emily on the big rug in front of the fireplace. The one in the dining room was best, because it was fur and I'd always wondered what it would be like to luxuriate on it with him. It was my most shameful daydream about Ford, so I put Emily right at its center to kill it stone dead. I pictured them there together, a tangle of arms and legs, Emily always scheming. It kept me cool toward Ford, and focused on how Emily might not have had the control over him she'd hoped.

Because if he'd wanted another wife, he could have had one.

And here he was writing to me about loneliness. In such beautiful words, too, his handwriting masculine and neat, with clear effort in every line. Of course, I kept every single letter.

Rose did her best through November to keep me from thinking about Emily. I suspect John had written to her from the university where he was studying, explaining that I was talking too much about fortune-telling and murder.

So I stopped talking to either of them about it, and I grew lonely too.

By December, my reservations had started to slip, and the letters became a void into which we could spill our secrets. Ford reassured me that he and Saxon hadn't been staying in Chelsea with Emily, as Saxon had told John last summer. Saxon had lied; they were in fact away visiting boarding schools.

He started signing his letters "Affectionately yours," and addressing them to "My Darling Frances." He said that he longed to see me but that he was nervous, after all this time. After every-thing that had happened. I hadn't seen him since that day in April when we'd left Emily at the Chelsea house. As time passed, it became harder to puncture my own imagination with thoughts of them together. The more I got to know him, the less plausible it seemed that he would ever have found her interesting.

I became more convinced that he saw right through her. As he saw right through me. And that was what really pulled the final thread of my fate and wound me around him.

"Don't fuss with your hair, Frances," Mother said as she watched me trying to pin it up. "If he likes it down, wear it down." Mother had changed her tune once the letters started; she found it respectable of him. It was old-fashioned, but it reminded her of her own past. She talked about how she and Father wrote to each other during the war, and how young people these days didn't appreciate a proper slow romance. So I let her read one (an early one, where he asked me about my favorite walks and what kind of flowers I liked), and you'd think Ford had romanced her too.

"I'm trying to make it look a little fancier," I said. "It's a Christmas party, after all."

Mother fussed with the hem of my green velvet dress, upset that I'd shortened it, but trying her hardest not to say anything.

"If he asks you what you'd like to drink, ask for a champagne cocktail," she said. "But don't have more than one. There will likely be wine with dinner, and you shouldn't get too tipsy. I want that driver bringing you back by midnight—I don't care if you're of age now. All that business last summer . . ." Her frown deep-ened. "If you're going to carry on a romance with a man with that much money and a title, it's got to be aboveboard."

"Yes, of course," I said, and a warmth rushed through me.

Rose rang the bell, and soon she was next to me, gushing over my hair, my dress, the color of lipstick I wore. When Mother went to get my coat, I handed Rose the tube and she carefully applied some, fledging her lips in my mirror to make sure it didn't smudge.

"Kiss Ford with this lipstick tonight, Frannie, and when I kiss Bill it'll be like twin echoes," she said.

"You are so over the top, Rose!" I said, but I laughed.

"He asked me to marry him, you know." She kept her voice low, but her cheeks were glowing.

"Rose!" I smiled at her, and she let out a small squeal and squeezed my hand.

"And you said yes, right?"

"I said I would, but only when you and Ford get married."

I kept my expression measured, because I knew how Rose was. She was happy, so she wanted to pull me into that happiness with her. It was sweet, really. But she didn't understand all the things I was going through. I thought in that moment that no one did, but something told me that wasn't quite true.

"Rose, please don't hang your happiness on mine, okay? I don't know where I stand with Ford. Things are really complicated."

"They'll iron out soon, I can feel it," she said. "And in the meantime, Bill will come and drive you up to the estate anytime. Ford lets Bill drive me whenever I want, it's fantastic! It almost feels like it's our car. And just wait until you see the Christmas tree Ford has had put up. I think he went a little overboard for us, but it's because he's seeing you for the first time in so long. He's nervous, Frannie. He loves you, he really does."

"Is it just going to be us? Isn't it strange, having a Christmas party and inviting your chauffeur?"

"Ford didn't bat an eye. As long as you were happy, he was happy. And he knew you wouldn't come without me."

I nodded. "I'm glad you'll be there," I said. "And Bill will round out a nice little group."

"It may be a little unconventional, but Ford's really making every effort, Frances."

Mother came back a little flustered, holding my beige mac. "I can't find your winter coat, Frances. The one with the gold buttons."

"Oh," I said, trying not to think of it. "That one's been lost for ages. I can't think where I left it."

"What have you been wearing in this weather?" Mother asked suddenly. "I could swear I've seen you in a coat."

"That one was Rose's, but I forgot it at the hotel when I went for coffee yesterday. I'll be all right."

"I suppose your other one was getting old," Mother said. "And it was never the most flattering cut—it hung far too loosely. Well," she said, handing me the mac. "You won't be outside for more than a minute anyway. I'll think about finding you something more tailored, maybe with a nice belted waist."

"Thank you, Mother," I said, and I kissed her cheek before Rose and I linked arms and headed out into the warmth of the Rolls-Royce, with Bill stepping out to help us into our seats.

Rose was right about the Gravesdown Christmas tree—it was a tower of elegant lights right in the center of the dining room. It stood almost as tall as the vaulted ceiling, and the crystal star on the top of it kissed the bottom of the chandelier in what was most certainly a very careful design.

The fires roared on both sides of the room, but it wasn't too hot. Bill had disappeared with the car, and then to change clothes. "He insisted," Rose said. "He wanted to make sure he was seen as a guest, even though Ford told him not to bother with the driver's uniform when he came to get us."

I noticed new staff coming and going silently. One took my coat, and another wordlessly offered me champagne from a silver tray. Rose and I each took a glass, and we stood gazing at the tree.

"I could get lost in there," I said.

"I'm glad you like it." Ford's voice came from behind me, gentle enough not to startle me, but with enough electricity in it to quicken my pulse.

When I turned, his eyes were bright but his smile was soft. I could see his nerves in it, and flutters of hope in there too. It was disarming, and when he kissed my cheek in greeting, I couldn't help but breathe in the scent of his aftershave and give him a whispered "Hello."

The evening became easier after two glasses of champagne.

I suppose that's why people like champagne, isn't it? But soon the formalities and fanciness of things like canapés and caviar felt almost normal. Conversation was livelier than usual; it crackled with the twin fires in the fireplaces. Ford's hand found the small of my back as we passed from the dining room into the library after dinner, to coffees and petits fours waiting on silver trays. Two sofas had been arranged around a low table there, and it felt like a very deliberate shift in the layout. Ford had decided it was a place to entertain instead of a place to hide.

As if he could read my mind, he asked, "How do you like the way I've changed the library, Frances?"

I looked around, taking note of the flowers he'd had arranged near the windows, and the colors of the new curtains. It startled me to see what was really different. I was reflected in this room. The pieces of myself I'd revealed in those letters—he'd settled them into this house. Rose beamed at me, and I let my feelings shift across my face. It was a little jarring to feel so seen. And when I looked at Ford, I found that he also made me feel desired.

"It's lovely," I said. "I've always felt most at home in this room."

Ford leaned in and kissed me then. It was just a quick gesture, but it was sweet and surprising. I heard the echo of Rose kissing Bill from the sofa opposite, and I felt oddly annoyed by it. This was my moment, not Rose's. I should never have let her use my lipstick.

When Ford leaned back, relaxation finally settled across his shoulders. He closed his eyes for a moment, a satisfied smile on his face. He had one arm resting casually across the back of the sofa, behind me, but not touching me.

"I have a gift for you, Frances," he said, finally opening his eyes again. He gave an almost imperceptible wave toward the door of the library, and one of the staff came in with a large rectangular box. Thick gold ribbon was tied neatly across the lid, and I hesitated when it was set in my lap.

"Go on," Rose urged. "Open it." She gave me a reassuring smile.

I lifted the lid, and under layers of tissue so thin they were like butterfly wings was a perfect fur-lined wool coat. It was deep green, and I knew looking at it that it had been chosen to set off my eyes.

"It's beautiful," I breathed. And I meant it, it really was. I pulled it from the box, and it felt weighty and warm, but I could tell it was stylishly cut and would be elegant to wear. Not too old-fashioned, but classic.

Ford smiled at me and raised his glass in my direction. "To replace the one you lost," he said, and he drained the contents of the glass in one long swallow.

CHAPTER

39

"DON'T WORRY, ANNIE, I'LL MAKE SOME FEEBLE AT-tempts to resuscitate you," Joe says. "But as an inexperienced drug user, you just took too much too quickly. Poor thing. If only we'd known and had gotten to you sooner."

I reflexively back all the way into the ambulance. The double doors behind Joe look like a wall, blocking us in. I'm suddenly aware of just how little space there is in here. Be-tween the gurney and the drawers of supplies, the IVs and oxygen tanks, there's nowhere for me to be in here that isn't within arm's reach of him. My throat constricts as I see that my only escape now is through the front doors. I try not to look at the syringe in Joe's hand as he takes another step to-ward me, but I've got to keep track of it if I want to avoid it. I had no idea he would resort to this, but I should have known. If you're trying to corner a killer, the odds of getting yourself killed in the process skyrocket. And an injection is exactly how Joe committed murder before.

It was the flowers that finally led me to him. That, cou-pled with the details from Frances's diary about who she saw driving the Rolls-Royce up to Chelsea the day Emily was last seen. Those things showed me just how connected the two murders were. Great Aunt Frances was so emotionally tangled up with Ford and whether Emily was going to win him back that she simply made the leap that Ford was rushing up to be by Emily's side.

But all she really noticed was Ford's chauffeur at the wheel. Bill Leroy.

It was Rose's words in Frances's diary that put the final pieces into place in my mind. *Ford lets Bill drive me whenever I want, it's fantastic! It almost feels like it's our car.*

Panic threatens to consume me, but I try to keep my head clear. If I hyperventilate because of the needle, the smell of the ambulance, and the very real threat to my life, I'll pass out and make this even easier for Joe.

I think of Great Aunt Frances, and my anger at what Joe did to her keeps me focused. I lean into it, poke at it like a scab, and use it to steady myself.

"How's Rose?" I say. My voice is strangled and shrill, but it's important that I get Joe angry too. Angry people talk. "How is she coping with what you did to her best friend? Frances was her *whole world*, right, Joe? But more than that, Frances was Rose's obsession. Far more so than Emily's."

"I've set Mother *free*, Annabelle," he spits his words at me like a venomous snake. "You have no *idea* what years of living with this fixation on Frances did to her. How it killed her a little every day to see Frances obsessing over Emily goddamned Sparrow. Mother did Frances the biggest favor of her life—she made sure Emily would never hurt her again. That's what strong people do! They protect the ones they love! And Frances was destroying Mother. It was time for me to be the one to protect her." He lunges toward me and grabs my arm, but the thick leather jacket allows me to wriggle free. I pull one arm out of my jacket, and when I'm free of it, I try to get farther into the front of the ambulance, looking for the horn or the radio. I hear the phone fall from my pocket and clatter to the floor.

A hand wraps around my bare arm and jerks me backward, and I find myself in a headlock, pinned against Joe's chest with a syringe aimed at my throat. I try to swallow and nearly choke.

"Joe," I manage, "they're coming."

"You're full of shit," he says, but he starts to work more quickly. He's decided I'll never be still enough to let him inject me, so he puts the syringe to one side and opens another box of medical supplies. He keeps one arm locked tightly around my neck, and no matter how hard I struggle and pull at him, I can't get free of it. "Frances at least sat still!" he roars. "Don't make me knock you out!"

"Frances thought she was poisoned by hemlock!" I rasp. His hold slackens a little as he reaches for something in the box. "You sent her that bouquet knowing that she'd panic and call you! You knew she'd make it easy because she was so paranoid about being murdered! You used her biggest fear against her." I finally get an elbow into Joe's ribs, but he just pulls me around to face him and shoves me onto the stretcher. His knee slams into my chest so hard that I think a rib cracks.

"Just stay still, Annie. It'll be over soon." His voice is horrifyingly flat, and I let out a scream that is far feebler than I expect. I should have screamed minutes ago, but I was so focused on trying to get evidence out of Joe for Frances's murder that I let my good judgment slip.

"I've sent my findings to the police," I say. "They're on their way. That wasn't a lie."

"I don't see how you could have worked it out," Joe hisses. My arms are free, but his knee is pressing all the air out of me. I scratch at his leg and try to claw his arm as he catches one of my wrists. I kick my legs but reach nothing but air—his other leg is steadying him and gives him even more leverage to ram his knee harder into my breastbone. "You guessed. You've got nothing! I don't believe that you figured out what Frances took sixty years to uncover, and then you connected her death to me."

"So let me go," I gasp. I see the telltale glimmers of white spots creeping into my vision and know I'm going to faint. The pain is horrifying, I also think I might be sick, and I feel my limbs growing heavy as Joe's knee keeps pressing down. His other hand goes for my throat, and I pull feebly at the back of it. I realize with horrifying certainty that I might have less than a minute to live. I'm like a rag doll, my small frame giving me zero advantage. Tears stream down my cheeks and I feel stabs of outrage at how easily overpowered I am. All he has to do is start squeezing and I'm done for.

"It's too late for that now," he says. "Mother is going to heal from this, finally. She's been through too much over the years—that bitch Frances put her through hell! Always Emily, everything about Emily. Frances never saw how much Mother did for her, how wonderful their lives could have been if only Frances had given up her stupid quest for justice. Mother remembered every birthday, every anniversary, every little event that meant something to Frances, and Frances gave her *nothing* back. It was my mother who held Frances's hand as she grieved her husband, but when Father died? Frances just sent one of her stupid bunches of flowers! *Flowers!* After all they went through together! After everything Mother sacrificed in getting rid of Emily and making sure Frances didn't obsess over stupid Laura and her overblown paintings! Do you know Frances used to stare at this messy canvas Laura did for her, practically losing her mind looking for the symbolism that 'the right daughter' could have put in there?"

My thoughts are drifting to strange places as I fight for air, but Joe getting distracted in his rambling has loosened his grip on my throat for a moment. The memory of pulling Mum's canvas out of the locked file drawer floats through my mind and drifts back again in a tide of other images. But it hits me that Great Aunt Frances *did* care for Mum. It occurs to me how much damage Rose might have done to Mum and Great Aunt Frances's relationship.

I retch as Joe's grip tightens again.

"And don't think I'm naive enough to believe Frances wouldn't have turned her in! She was days away from it—it was only a matter of time."

"How . . . how did you know? That Frances . . ." Every word feels like a bruise now, but I'm praying it's nearly eight o'clock. I just have to hang on until Detective Crane gets that call. And Saxon! If Saxon had planned to set me up, to put me out of the running for this inheritance by having me arrested for buying drugs, the police could already be on their way. But I wince as my lungs are crushed further, because I could have been wrong about him. And all Jenny's telling Detective Crane is what I've found, and where I am. She won't know how dire the emergency is. And even if the detective learns of the dangerous situation I've put myself in, it'll still take him several minutes to get here. Minutes I probably don't have.

"She told Mother. Frances actually went and told Mother all about what she'd discovered. It was the beginning of the end for Mother; she started to unravel. I knew then that as long as Frances was alive, Mother would never know peace. *And she deserves peace!*" He shouts these words in my face, and fury rises in my throat that his hot disgusting breath might be the last thing I experience as my life slips away. "Mother hasn't been able to rest easy since she was seventeen, when she could see that Frances didn't appreciate what she'd done in getting rid of Emily. My whole life, Frances has dominated Mother's worries, all her thoughts. And it needed to stop." His voice cracks and his face contorts with emotion. "I had to make it stop," he says, and his words are quieter now, but the sob constricting them feels almost as dangerous as his shouts.

"Your fingerprints, on . . . battery," I choke out. And Joe's eyes widen, and his knee actually gives a fraction. "You're a chauffeur's son." I cough. I gulp air through my lungs in a rush as his hand slips from my throat. I steal another shaky breath and struggle to push more words out. "You knew how," I pant. "You cut off her escape with a simple disconnected battery. She'd tried the car already that morning and called Walt to tell him to bring us to the estate. They'll check, and your prints will be there."

"No, it'll be impossible. I had my gloves on," he says. But he looks worried all the same. It only makes him move faster. His knee presses down again, harder, and I try to cry out, but the sound is so tiny.

"Who . . ." I just want to know one last thing, the one piece I couldn't figure out. "Who did you get to deliver the flowers?"

Joe's face is inches from mine, the look in his eyes practically burning into me. "Elva," he says.

I can't breathe, and I think of how stupid I've been. I feel something wrap around my upper arm, like a rubber band cutting off my circulation, and all those horrible times I've had to have blood drawn come into my head. My vision swims, and I try to move my arm to avoid Joe's needle, but my whole body feels leaden. The last thing I hear is Joe saying, "Just like Frances, Annie . . . you brought this on yourself."

I feel something puncture my skin, and interestingly, that's when my familiar needle phobia finally feeds a spark of panic through my body. The jolt of it is quick, and I feel the wooziness threatening to lap up my consciousness right on its heels. So I don't hesitate. I act.

Joe is so focused on my arm, on keeping that still enough to administer his overdose, that he's leaning over me off-balance and has slackened his grip on my other arm. His knee has even slipped off my chest, and I'm able to get one leg up under him in a lightning-fast kick. And because he's already tilted to balance over me on the stretcher, it's enough to topple him over the other side of it.

I know he won't stay down for long, but that kick used up all my strength and my mind is sinking into blackness. I wonder if I imagine the groan of the ambulance doors opening before the darkness swallows me.

CHAPTER

40

WALT'S FACE IS THE FIRST THING I SEE, THOUGH I feel like I'm looking through foggy glass. I'm still on the stretcher in the ambulance, but Joe is on the floor. He's scrambling to get up, so Walt puts an arm under my shoulders, trying to get me out of there. My head is facing the rear of the ambulance, so Beth helps him pull me free of the doors before Joe can get back up. I don't see who slams the ambulance doors, shutting him inside.

I was right about Detective Crane—the minutes it took him to arrive were just that little bit too long. Police cars roar into the car park as I sink to the pavement. The relief of seeing them cuts through my panic a little. But my arm is oozing blood, and the sight of the long scrape where the syringe was dragged down my arm is what sends me out cold.

I've never fainted twice in such quick succession, and the sick feeling it gives me is horrendous. I hear the rumble of the detective's voice as I come to a second time, because my ear is pressed to his chest. He smells like clean laundry and some earthy cologne that's mostly worn off. Someone is arguing with him, and I stir a bit.

"Just not the bloody hospital, why the hell would you—Oh, sorry, Annie—" Beth looks a little stricken. "I didn't mean to say *bloody*." She winces when she realizes she's said it again. "I'm just lobbying for them to take you somewhere comfortable that's not going to make you panic."

"It's okay," I say, though my mouth is dry and, as I move my head, bile rises in my throat. I don't have time for the humiliation to hit me, because in seconds the detective is holding my hair back as I'm sick in the car park. I'm still sitting in his lap, which makes the whole thing much worse.

"You can rest assured that you've not been injected with anything," he says steadily. "The first thing we did was find the syringe Joe was trying to use on you, and it was still full."

"Please don't say the word *syringe*," I whisper, as Beth produces an actual ironed cotton handkerchief from her bag. I shake my head at it, because I feel too gross for something so fancy. Shaking my head turns out to be a terrible idea, and I get to experience round two of Detective Crane cradling me like a wounded deer as I'm sick a second time.

The whole car park is lit in the blue flashes of police lights, and I can tell they're going to be examining the ambulance for hours. It's the scene of more than just the attempted murder of Annie Adams, and I see Magda in the back of one police car, and Joe in another.

"What's going to happen to Rose?" I whisper to Detective Crane.

"We'll talk about all that once you're feeling better," he says.

Beth is walking around talking on a mobile phone now, and she catches my eye mid-call. "Dr. Owusu has agreed to come and check you out wherever you feel most comfortable," she says.

"Can I go back to Great Aunt Frances's house then?" I ask.

"Of course," Crane says. I swing an arm up around his shoulder with the plan to use him as a crutch on my way to someone's car, but he's stronger than he looks, and he lifts me instead. I'm annoyed at being cast as a damsel in distress, but there's not a lot I can do about it. He gently deposits me in the passenger seat of Beth's car, and she drives me back to Gravesdown Hall, with Walt and Crane following behind. I do make a point to limp on my own into the house when we get there, and I refuse to lean on anyone as we all shuffle into the library.

It's only then that I notice that there's no sign of Saxon. Once Joe and Magda were arrested, I expected him to make a play for his half, citing the very nonbinding deal we made when he offered up that fickle partnership. I wonder if he's in another police car, care of Detective Crane and the photo evidence of Saxon's involvement in Magda's drug business.

Meanwhile, Beth finds seemingly every pillow in the house and piles them on the sofa in the library, where I'm ordered to lie down. Walt sits at the big desk again, his briefcase open and my backpack next to it. I have to endure Dr. Owusu checking me over, ordering a chest X-ray, and insisting I don't go without proper medical care just because I don't like the idea of it.

Even Archie Foyle is here, with a very conflicted-looking Oliver Gordon sitting next to him.

"Annie," Walt says, "I'd like to think that Frances never intended for anyone to put themselves in danger trying to solve her murder. Perhaps she saw the whole affair playing out in the classic way—at the end of the week we'd gather everyone in a room and the killer would be revealed. Or the detective would swoop in and put a halt to everything when he beat you all to solving the case."

Walt gives Crane a smug smile, because in the end, it was

his own quick thinking that saved my life. All I did was ask Beth to take him my bag. "But I knew Frances well enough to know how deep her paranoia ran, and I should have seen that in the days before her murder, when she rushed to change her will to include you, that she had convinced herself you were the invincible savior in all this. The *right daughter* who would bring her justice. I'm sorry it nearly cost you your life, and if I could go back and change things, I would."

"It's not your fault," I say. "And I don't blame Great Aunt Frances either. I got fully stuck into all this simply by being me. And Great Aunt Frances didn't suspect Joe would kill her until it was too late. I think she assumed he didn't know about Emily, about what Rose did. I didn't have any physical proof it was really Joe who killed Frances, so I had to confront him. I couldn't just accuse him in front of you all; he'd have simply denied everything."

"Can you rewind a bit, Annie?" Detective Crane asks. "How did you know it was Rose?"

"The diary mostly, but also the car, the coat, and the photo album."

"Can you explain a bit further? Because other than maybe Walt, I don't think anyone has the inside track on Frances's mind."

"The important question wasn't who killed Emily Sparrow, though that mattered too. The key was why Great Aunt Frances was able to work it out all of a sudden," I say. I take a drink from the glass of water that Detective Crane hands to me. "One thing I kept coming back to was how often Frances's clothes came up in the diary. Rose was always talking about Emily stealing Frances's things, imitating her. And in the diary, the focus on clothes started to reveal that the three friends had a toxic sort of closeness. Emily did take Frances's coat, and being Emily, she got hold of a revolver. Ostensibly this was out of boredom, but I think underneath that she wanted to protect herself, because she'd been receiving threats from an anonymous person for months."

"Threats from Rose?"

"I'll get to that, but yes. Anyway, the thing that got to me was that coat—Emily was killed with the gun that had been left in the pocket of Frances's wool coat. Then, when Rose gave me the photo album, it finally dawned on me. *Rose* was the one wearing all of Frances's things. Specifically, a pile of winter clothes Frances had handed to Rose on the day she was trying to sneak off to Chelsea instead of weeding the neighbors' garden. Her mother was keeping track of her as she worked, because it was Frances's punishment for sneaking off to the Gravesdown estate to see Ford."

"So Rose had the coat, but how could she have got to Chelsea?" Beth asks.

"When I first read the diary, I thought that when Ford's car was seen driving past Peter and Tansy's house on the road out of town, it would automatically have been Ford and Saxon in the back. But Frances mentioned it was Bill at the wheel, which was nothing out of the ordinary, until I read about how Bill was allowed to drive Rose in that car whenever she wanted him to. He took *her* up to Chelsea that day."

"Do you think Bill was complicit in the murder?" Crane asks.

I bite my lip as I think about that, but Walt cuts in. "I doubt Bill knew what Rose was up to. I imagine if she'd asked him to wait with the car he would have, given what I know of their relationship," he says.

"So Bill drove Rose up to the Chelsea house, where she killed Emily and hid her body in that trunk in the basement, along with the coat and the murder weapon," I say. "The one variable I couldn't work out was Ford and Saxon, because

Saxon told me that by the time they got to Chelsea no one was there. But then I remembered—Ford never drove the Phantom; he had a more modern Mercedes he preferred. Saxon was doing everything he could to mislead me when it came to Emily Sparrow." I look at the detective, who gives me a small nod. "And I understood just how hard Saxon was working to keep me off track when it came to Emily. For a time I thought it was because he was protecting his uncle's memory, or perhaps protecting himself, but really he was just trying to keep me confused."

"But Emily also told John that she forgot something at the Chelsea house, which is what set this whole thing off," Walt says. "In your notes, that was still unanswered. Did you work out why Emily went back?"

"John believed Emily really meant she wanted to take Laura back from Peter and Tansy, but it was far simpler than that. She forgot her typewriter, the one her parents had given her to take up to London. And I know that typewriter never made it back to Castle Knoll because I found it years ago and brought it to my room to mess about with. The descriptions of the case in Great Aunt Frances's diary match the one I found—it was plastic and tartan-patterned. I think Emily's mother had questioned her coming home without it when she first came back to Castle Knoll, and when Emily rushed back to Chelsea, the housekeeper was just packing up and getting ready to lock the house. Rose had the perfect excuse, because Bill was waiting with the car, and this meant Mrs. Blanchard could drive back to Castle Knoll with him instead of getting the train. Rose would have sent her out to wait with him in the car while she talked to Emily, promising to lock up."

"But then why didn't either of them question why Emily wasn't with Rose when she locked the house?" Oliver asks. I'm surprised he's interested at all, but he's watching me with a look that's almost like awe on his face, as if I'm a magician performing a trick. I wonder whether Castle Knoll has his heart after all, and if he's been hiding behind a veneer of nonchalance just to get through the terrible situation he was put in by Great Aunt Frances. So I pause, and I look at him.

"The parking at that house," he says slowly.

"Now you're thinking like a property developer," I say, and grin.

"The parking's restricted, and it probably was back then too. Bill Leroy couldn't have pulled up in front of that house for more than a minute, if he did at all. He'd have had to park all the way down at the far end of the road."

"Exactly," I say, and it's satisfying to watch how Oliver sits up a little straighter now, pleased with himself. "That gave Rose time to lock up and come back to where the car waited, alone, with a story about how Emily had decided to go and do whatever sounded like Emily. Go to a show, go shopping, get the train back later, whatever."

"But how did she get rid of the body so quickly, and clean up whatever mess was caused by the murder?" Crane asks. I feel a little of the wind flag from my sails as he watches me. He's not trying to derail me—his expression is simply interested—but I keep forgetting that I'm not really in charge here.

Then Walt jumps in: "This is just a guess, and the detective will have to examine the basement of the Chelsea house to get the full picture, but I'm thinking Rose killed Emily in the basement. Only Rose knows why they were down there, if that's the case, but it's the most likely scenario."

"There's a drain in the basement floor," I remember suddenly. "It's one reason Mum was so keen on using it for painting. If there was blood when Rose killed Emily, a few buckets of water could have taken care of it pretty quickly."

Everyone is suddenly quiet, because I've run out of things to say. I feel used up, but glad that there's some justice coming around for Great Aunt Frances and Emily Sparrow. And I feel almost proud that I'm the reason for it.

Then I look out the window at the rolling lawns in front of the house, and I feel a pang of guilt for Archie Foyle and his family. "I'm sorry," I say to Beth. "I tried my best, but I had to get the police involved in the end. I'm afraid that's ruined everything for everyone now. Jessop Fields will come, and all this will be turned into a golf course."

"What do you mean?" Oliver says, before Beth can even react.

Walt clears his throat, and we all watch him carefully as he shuffles through the papers in his briefcase. "I think you forget, Annie, that Frances gave me the final say in who has officially solved her murder first. It should go without saying, but it's undoubtedly you."

Beth lets out a happy gasp, but all I can do is blink while trying to come to terms with an inheritance this size really being mine.

The first thing I feel is a wave of relief that Mum can keep the house she so dearly loves. And I find I feel protective over that house too—I spent my childhood there unearthing strange things from the backs of cupboards, like old tins of hair wax and cuff links, and it was then that I started making up stories about the ghosts of whoever left those things behind. Now, with hints of the true story, I feel even more compelled to preserve it.

We just might have to shut the basement off for good, and Mum can get a professional studio space somewhere else.

But I'm also surprised to find that I feel a little sad about winning the inheritance, because it feels like Great Aunt

Frances is truly gone now. When her murder needed solving, she was my constant companion. I looked at everything in this house as clues to her life, as much as her death. I didn't know it at the time, but I don't think it really was the mystery of Emily Sparrow that sucked me in, or the task of finding out what happened to Great Aunt Frances.

I was drawn in by the mystery of Great Aunt Frances herself—her life, her loves, and her many obsessions. She spoke to me with her guarded temperament and her keen observations. In her I saw someone who was so self-aware it was catastrophic, a tendency I share. And for a moment, I nearly did inherit her fate as well as her fortune.

I exhale slowly as the realization hits me that I am, in fact, the right daughter. I've brought justice for Great Aunt Frances. And for Emily, my real grandmother. That gives me a peaceful sense of satisfaction, even if I've now also inherited the pinch of Emily Sparrow's loss, along with the outrage of how her life was cut so short.

Everyone in the room is congratulating me, though I can feel Detective Crane watching me carefully. I feel comforted by the fact that at least one person in the room realizes I'm taking a moment to grieve that this is over. Because I only knew Great Aunt Frances after I'd already lost her.

I cross the room to the shelves behind the desk, where the chessboard is sitting. I take the queen from its place and walk back to where Walt is looking at me from behind the desk. I set it down in the very center, and I draw a breath and blink back tears as I try to get the right words out.

"The first order of business will be to say good-bye properly," I say. "And I want the whole village to be here. I want them all to know—I want everyone to know—how wrong they were about Frances. How special she was."

CHAPTER
41

"GOD, THIS PLACE USED TO GIVE ME THE CREEPS,"
Mum says as we stand on the lawn in front of Gravesdown
Hall. It's been two weeks since I solved Great Aunt Frances's
murder, and the sun has decided to bake its way out of August and into early September. I crave crisp autumn days, and
I feel invigorated knowing that I'll be in Castle Knoll to experience them. I picture this lawn strewn with yellow leaves,
then coated with frost as winter hits. "I only came here a
handful of times," Mum continues, "but it looks nicer now."
She twists one of the long chains she wears, and the charms
on it clink a little, like her own personal wind chimes. "I suppose it helps that I'm not seven years old anymore, convinced
Archie Foyle will use his hedge trimmers to clip my fingers
off if I misbehave." She shudders. "Saxon used to feed me all
kinds of lies whenever I was here. He was a very strange teenager."

"Ugh, what a horrible thing to say to a child," I reply.

"Well, from what Aunt Frances wrote, Saxon never got to
be a child himself, so I feel a little less angry toward him

now." She rubs her arms as if there's a chill in the air, even though it's so hot I'm wishing for sprinklers to run in, like a child.

One of the first things I did after I filled Mum in on everything that had happened was give her the diary to read. She took her time over it, and when she finished it, she refused to discuss it with me. But lately she's been starting to unpack her own history in all of this. I think it helps that she has her art to work through it all. She's not one to talk about feelings; she visualizes them and shares them that way.

"Though the fact that he tried to frame you for buying drugs was pure evil," she adds.

Elva was cleared of any involvement in Great Aunt Frances's death, but that was simply because she had plausible deniability. Elva claimed that Joe had given her the flowers in passing, saying they'd been mis-delivered to the hotel and were meant for Frances, from some anonymous sender. This was clever of him—Elva would have been around the estate a lot, so Frances would have assumed the bouquet was from her. I imagine Elva treated Frances with reverence, sucking up to the woman who could give her husband his proper inheritance, and wouldn't correct Frances's assumption. That's also why Elva didn't call the police when we found Great Aunt Frances—she was worried about being implicated when she realized what had happened.

I'd expected Saxon to avoid me and this house, but he hasn't. After being arrested for his drug-related crimes, he got out on bail and is awaiting trial. He's made a point to visit me several times, and I'm keeping a close eye on him because I don't think he's done playing games with me yet.

I stayed true to my word and gifted the Rolls-Royce to the Foyle family. Archie cleared out his polytunnels, though I decided not to ask too many questions about what he did with all that weed. He's chosen to retire from gardening—he says he only really kept going because the flowers meant so much to Great Aunt Frances. He's having one of the other barns converted into a workshop for his hobby, restoring vintage cars. I was happy to invest in his new business; I think all he really wanted was for someone to back a venture of his. He just picked the wrong one to win Great Aunt Frances over with.

"Don't worry about Saxon," I say. Mum doesn't know the full details of how my scheme to outsmart Saxon nearly got me killed; I didn't want to worry her. Mum has her own brand of reckless, but it's adventures like sneaking into West End shows during the intermission, or daring me to put on a French accent to flirt with a bartender. Nothing that would get her killed. She wouldn't understand how dedicated I was to rooting out Great Aunt Frances's killer. "Detective Crane is watching him very closely these days."

"Speak of the devil," she says. The detective's car is crawling up the gravel drive, and I notice Walt in the passenger seat.

"Are you sure you don't want to come?" I ask. Detective Crane is taking me to the facility where Rose is living, after she was declared unfit to stand trial. I debated going at all, but I think it might help me feel like this whole story has the right ending. I guess it's what some people would call closure, but Crane was careful to warn me that seeing Rose might not give me that.

I know what he means. There's nothing satisfying about a woman whose life fell apart in quite the way Rose's did. She killed a friend, and then her son killed her best friend. I don't know what I expect to get from talking to Rose, but I still feel like I should do it.

"I'm sure," she says. "I'm going to meet John instead. It feels like the better path forward for me."

"I understand," I say quietly. "Oh, I almost forgot," I add, and I root through the canvas bag slung over my shoulder. In it I have some pens and notebooks, just in case I need to write down my thoughts on meeting Rose. I've started chronicling my own experiences in much the way Great Aunt Frances did, and it's helped me see that my own story is a living thing. It unfolds and turns and folds itself over again. When you write it all down, you can go back and find meaning you'd never noticed was there all along.

I hand Mum the thick file with Dad's name on it. "For you," I say. "You asked me to retrieve it, and I did flip through a little, but I think this is something I'm not so curious about right now."

She looks at the folder, and a sad smile flits across her face. "Okay. I'll keep it until you are, because, Annie?"

"Yeah?"

"He's out there, your dad. He's not a very good man, and now that we're both making the news, I expect he might turn up again."

I've wondered about this, but I don't say anything. Mum bursting back onto the art scene would have been noise enough, but my story has made international headlines too. Me solving two murders and becoming an heiress in the process is news on its own, but the murder of a grandmother I previously didn't even know about? The headlines practically wrote themselves. ANNIE ADAMS: HOW THE SECRET GRANDDAUGHTER OF A TEENAGE MURDER VICTIM TURNED HER TOWN UPSIDE DOWN.

"Will you come to the house after, for dinner?" I ask Mum.

She sighs. "I'm keen to get back to my new studio," she

says. "So I'll just head home if that's okay. But I'll be here in October, for the funeral. I promise."

Walt approaches us carefully, and he has a wistful look in his eye when he sees Mum. I can't say I blame him. Mum could represent the daughter he never had, or an echo of the woman he loved and lost. When he turns to me, his eyes widen a fraction at my secondhand T-shirt. I'm in the outfit I found on my first trip to the Castle Knoll Oxfam—the corduroy skirt with the faded retro concert T-shirt tucked into it. You can just make out the words *The Kinks: Live at Kelvin Hall, Glasgow, 1967.*

"I thought I'd got rid of that shirt," he half mumbles. He actually blushes a little.

"I found it in the Oxfam shop," I say, pride in my voice. "I always liked that song, you know, 'You Really Got Me.'"

Walt laughs, and nods. "I'm glad it found its way to you, then."

"If you have any more, I'll gladly take them off your hands," I offer, and smile.

"I might have a Pink Floyd T-shirt around somewhere," he says. "Oliver wouldn't appreciate it properly. I'll see if I can dig it out. It'd be good to give it new life."

I want to thank him for sending money to take care of Mum and me, even if it was only for a handful of days. He went behind Great Aunt Frances to do it, because he didn't agree with her choices. I think he just wanted to help Emily's family in some small way. But I decide it's better that he thinks I don't know it was him.

There's an awkward pause, and finally Detective Crane looks at me pointedly. "We should go, Annie, if we're going to be on time. They set us up with a special appointment, we don't want to miss it."

"Okay," I say.

———

ROSE IS HUNCHED and timid as she sits at the small table opposite me and Detective Crane. She looks at the detective most often, and her eyes are oddly trusting. She's decided she likes him, it seems. Every time she looks at me her features twist, but no expression ever settles on her face for long. It's as though she can't tell who she's looking at; which one of the women who wronged her I actually am.

A therapist sits next to her, a man in his forties who I imagine is there both to advocate for her rights and to keep her calm.

I don't know how to start. I'd say, *Thank you for seeing us*, but she didn't have a choice. I'd say, *It's good to see you*, but it's not. Thankfully, Crane senses this and takes the lead. I'm only here because he's letting me tag along, after all. And he's only able to see Rose because he's the detective in charge of closing both murder cases.

"Hi, Rose," he says. "We thought it might be helpful if we could all have a chat. Just to check in and clear the air. No one's going to be asking you to share information you don't want to. Now that you've confessed, and there's not going to be a trial, we thought this might help heal some old wounds. What do you think?"

Rose's eyes flit to me, and her posture shifts, deflating. "I wanted to like you," she says. "I tried, but you made it really difficult." I'm not sure if she's talking to Emily, Mum, or me. I thought I might feel angry toward Rose, but my feelings are so mixed they're hard to sort out. She was seventeen when she killed Emily. I think I just want to know if she's sorry.

"I enjoyed looking at the photos in the album you gave

me," I say. This, at least, is true. I treasure that book, though it makes me a little sad too. I've had the photo of Emily, pregnant with Mum, framed and put in the library with some of the other memories Great Aunt Frances has there.

Rose looks into the distance, but then her gaze snaps back to me, and her dark eyes bore into mine. "You want an apology," she says suddenly. "You aren't going to get one. Emily had to be stopped."

This, at least, clears up some of my mixed feelings. I don't hesitate to tell her what I think after that.

"Rose," I say, keeping my voice calm. "You do understand that if you hadn't killed Emily, Frances might have forgotten all about her fortune? I've read her diary. Her belief in her fate started because she found the threatening notes *you wrote* in the pockets of her skirt. And then, when Emily disappeared, it just fed her fear. She wondered if someone had meant to come for her but found Emily instead. You thought you were protecting Frances from a life ruined by Emily, but she ended up living with a fear that *you helped cultivate*."

Rose starts as my words hit her, and she blinks. But there aren't any tears in her eyes, and as I watch the expressions change and shift on her face, I can tell she's remaking my words into a story that she likes better.

Detective Crane gently takes hold of my elbow, under the table where no one can see. The sparks of my anger dim, and I'm left with only the embers of an animosity toward Rose that I can tell will smolder there for years.

But I suppose that's what happens when you solve a murder. The outrage of the crime itself doesn't go away just because you've put the pieces together. That's a sad fact I've learned, and it makes me look at my life and my writing differently.

"I think that's probably enough for today," the therapist says.

I take one last look at Rose before she's led back to her room, but she doesn't bother to take one last look at me. I suspect my face is burned into her memory, blurred with Emily's now.

CHAPTER
42

I CHOSE OCTOBER FOR THE FUNERAL BECAUSE FRAN-
ces's will specified autumn. And I can see why—the estate is
glorious in the golden light, with the strip of woodland that
edges the grounds putting on a riotous show of oranges and
reds.

I stand and watch everyone after the speeches are over,
sipping the good champagne from the Gravesdown cellars
and feeling glad to be on the fringes of everything for a moment. John Oxley made everyone cry, but in a heartwarming
way, and I feel content as I watch everyone eat the food that
Beth has provided.

The wake is being held on the large lawns in front of the
estate, which is a good thing, because the entire village has
turned up. The house feels like the perfect backdrop to say
good-bye to Great Aunt Frances. The re-creation of her little
study in the center of the lawn is being admired constantly.
Jenny created the whole tableau, and it's a very fitting piece
of art. Oriental rugs sit underneath the whole thing, with
the floor-standing Tiffany lamp and Great Aunt Frances's

leather armchair at the center. I wanted to make sure that in all of this—with the news reports and town gossip swirling—everyone remembered there was a woman in the middle of it all who was missed.

A selection of her books—all murder mysteries—are arranged in teetering stacks, and Jenny has artfully packed flowers into all the crevices of the armchair, and in the top of Emily's typewriter (which Mum brought with her from Chelsea, under my instruction). It sits on a plant stand on its own, along with a photograph of Emily in a silver frame. I wanted to make sure we said good-bye to Emily, too, especially because I feel like it's what Frances would've wanted.

Emily's sister, Laura, has come from Brighton, and she's standing serenely at the edge of everything. She approached me before the speeches started, and she hugged me and whispered "Thank you" before melting back into the crowd. Every time I spot Mum, though, she's chatting to her namesake, and I find that to be a heartwarming development.

Saxon and Elva are here, wandering around with everyone else, complimenting Beth's food and drinking more than their share of the champagne. Miyuki helps Beth ferry platter after platter from the kitchen to the long tables we've set up in a wide square around Jenny's centerpiece on the lawn.

I notice Oliver standing close to Jenny, trying to engage her in conversation. Jenny's looking mildly interested in him, so I approach them with the idea of rescuing her from herself. Jenny has this in common with Mum: If someone is a car crash of a man, Jenny's pulled in like a magnet. Thankfully she has me to step in and repel that magnetism, like a proper opposing pole.

"This is wonderful, Annie," Jenny says as she sees me.

"Thanks," I say. "I owe a ton of it to you, though, you know that," I add, and I smooth a hand down the front of the coat I'm wearing. I feel my forehead crease as I look around me.

"Why do you look so worried?" Oliver asks.

"I just . . . don't like loose ends. And seeing everyone in one place, thinking about all the events that led us here . . ." I sigh. "I never worked out who left me those threats."

"Oh." Oliver scratches the back of his neck, looking grim. "That was me."

"You . . . *you*? Why? And where did you find them? Wait, did you smash my laptop and rip up my notebooks?"

"No! I didn't smash anything. That was Saxon; if he told you he didn't do it, he lied. But I get that me leaving those threats in your room without any explanation was a weird move. I just felt like I needed to do something rather than stand around and watch everything unravel around me. I couldn't decide if I should do something to intimidate you or to help you. And when I found those notes in Frances's office, if felt like they . . . sort of did both. Which they did, didn't they?"

Oliver's face looks so open and unassuming for a moment that I almost don't say it. But then I do.

"Oliver, I felt like I was being watched—it was really creepy!"

He looks a little deflated, but then nods. "Sorry, Annie. I just couldn't see any other way of doing things. . . . Honestly, I've always hated my job. I just wasn't brave enough to find a way out. But I knew that if you solved the murder, I wouldn't have to make any hard choices. They'd all be made for me. Which"—he stops and then sighs—"I know is extremely cowardly, but it was all I could manage while being endlessly ground down by my boss."

I nod, because looking back, I can see how Oliver was constantly stressed and on his phone during those days in August. "I mean, you did help," I say slowly. "But I really think you should quit your job."

"Oh." He laughs, but it's got a cynical edge to it. "I was fired. But it was sort of what I was aiming for anyway, so I guess it worked out."

I hear a polite cough behind me and turn to see Detective Crane patiently waiting to talk to me. Jenny raises an eyebrow in my direction, so I throw her a look that says, *Stop being so obvious and ridiculous.* She and Oliver make their excuses and walk over to a crowd of people admiring the food Beth has laid out.

"Annie," Detective Crane says, putting both hands in his pockets and rocking lightly on his heels. He's dressed more smartly than usual, and is wearing pale chinos and a tie that's sitting slightly to one side, as if he's been pulling at his collar throughout the day. His dark beard is cropped a little closer than normal, and his hair looks neatly trimmed. I suspect he went to the barber specially just before coming here.

But looking at Detective Crane, who is so carefully trying to find a way to break some kind of news to me, suddenly makes me aware that I'm being a little cowardly in not following through. So I meet his dark eyes and take a deep breath.

"I need to give evidence at Joe's trial, don't I?" My voice is stony, because I don't like thinking back to that whole experience in the ambulance.

Detective Crane's shoulders relax, because he's the kind of person who likes to be candid, and skirting around something important would almost feel like a lie to him. I smile to myself, because I'm starting to understand how rare that kind of honesty is.

"The prosecutor called this morning," he says. "She suspects the defense is going to come for you, for trying to bait Joe into confessing. But our case is so strong there's not a lot of chance that will work. But she wants you to be ready to face that in court."

I nod. "Thanks for the heads-up." I find that most of my conflicted feelings about Great Aunt Frances's murder are wrapped up with Rose. But Joe fits in my mind like a straightforward villain, someone who thought he could control a situation with violence. I have no conflict with helping put him away, so when the time comes, that's what I'll do.

Detective Crane reaches out as though to take my hand, but the moment is so quick I might have imagined it. His hand moves to my shoulder, and he squeezes it once in a brief pulse, and then lets his arm drop to his side.

The October sun is strong, but the chill in the air is enough that I've layered up. My new coat is a smart brown mac, which Jenny picked out. I did find Great Aunt Frances's dark green wool coat that Ford gifted her, hanging in her wardrobe next to the green velvet dress she wore that Christmas. I was tempted to wear it, but because borrowing clothes played such a role in my investigations, it didn't feel right. Plus, my first instinct on seeing the coat was to check the pockets for weapons or threats.

The fact that Great Aunt Frances seems to have saved every item of clothing she owned since 1966 has me wondering as well. There are several other leather journals filled with her writing; I found them in a different spot in the house. I guess because they don't concern Emily Sparrow or murder, Great Aunt Frances kept them separate. But looking at her wardrobe, wondering what to wear, I decided I didn't want to risk wearing something that could have been part of another crime she investigated. Because that would have been just like her, to get mixed up in solving another murder while trying to prevent her own.

But I did stumble on something that felt like Great Aunt Frances was expecting me, after all this time. In the cedar chest in her bedroom, where I found the other journals she'd filled, were several blank leather-bound notebooks, all empty and waiting for someone to come along and add new words to them.

Just before I came outside for the funeral, I cracked open the nearest one. Putting pen to blank paper, I started writing.

ACKNOWLEDGMENTS

A lot of excellent people have put an unbelievable amount of hard work into getting Annie's and Frances's voices out into the world. When I think of where this book started—and if you keep reading my acknowledgments, you'll see what I mean in a moment—I feel such conviction in saying wholeheartedly, this was a team effort.

I have to start by thanking my wonderful agent, Zoë Plant, because it's really down to her that this book took any decent sort of shape. In 2021 I was mid-pandemic, homeschooling two young kids, and my writerly brain decided to fragment into tiny pieces and I started sending Zoë half-drafts of every wild idea I had. She patiently fielded everything from picture books to middle-grade comedies about vampires, and even though most (all) of my pandemic writing was objectively terrible, she never stopped encouraging me to keep at the ideas. I eventually sent her a huge chunk of a YA novel where a sassy New Yorker named Annie went on a road trip in England to solve a murder because of something a fortune-teller once told an estranged relative. Zoë held fast through three different versions of this book, and at any moment could have said, "Really, that's enough now," but she didn't. And I am beyond grateful for that.

A huge thank-you goes to Jenny Bent, and the amazing team at the Bent Agency, who helped bring this book to the US and to so many territories beyond. Jenny is such a fantastic champion of my work and I feel so well looked after with her in my corner. I also want to thank Emma Lagarde, Victoria Cappello, and Nissa Cullen for their support, as well as Gemma Cooper, and anyone on the TBA team who looked at early versions of this draft and joined the chorus of "I think there's something here."

And thank you to my fantastic film agent, Emily Hayward Whitlock, and her team at the Artist's Partnership, who have done such a wonderful job making sure Annie and Frances have landed in the right cinematic hands.

I have been amazingly fortunate with my editors, two phenomenally talented individuals whose enthusiasm for this book overwhelmed me in the best way. Anytime I felt myself flagging in my work, I just thought of all the energy and excitement these two had for my book, and I was ready to take on the world. Florence Hare at Quercus in the UK, and Cassidy Sachs at Dutton in the US, I feel like I landed the editorial dream team with you both.

The UK team at Quercus—Stefanie Bierwerth, Katy Blott, Ella Patel, Lipfon Tang, Emily Patience, Khadisha Thomas and Charlotte Gill and their hard work shouting about my book and being so impressively creative in the ways in which they've done it, thank you all so much. A huge thank-you also to the UK copy editors, cover designers, and anyone working hard to make such beautiful promotional materials for my book; you've all done such stunning jobs.

The US team at Dutton—Emily Canders, Isabel DaSilva, Erika Semprun, John Parsley, Christine Ball, Ryan Richardson, Susan Schwartz, LeeAnn Pemberton, Ashley Tucker, and Tiffany Estreicher—and the US cover designers, copy editors, and team members I've yet to meet: I love everything you've done with this book, it's been far and away beyond my expectations.

I have some wonderful writing friends who helped me shape up this book, and I am so grateful for the support, sharp eyes, and invaluable advice of my Texas ladies—Lisa Gant, Tyffany Neiheiser, and Mary Osteen. A huge thank-you also to Ashley Chalmers, my fellow American Londoner, whose friendship, sparkling conversation, and spot-on feedback has propelled me through several books now.

I had some lovely help with a few details in this story, and I'd like to thank Roger Sweet for educating me about old cars —even if the Rolls-Royce Phantom II might not be his favorite car, he had some great insight into what it would be like to drive one and how they work, and was overall just a delight to talk to. Any mistakes in the facts relating to Rolls are mine and mine alone.

To Hannah Roberts, my long-standing critique partner and friend, who has held my hand through so many ups and downs in publishing (and in life!), I am forever grateful for you. It is so rare in this world to find such a genuine friend who will celebrate your wins, listen to you complain, geek out about books with you, and read all the random non-drafts when they are so rough they are actual garbage and still make you believe in yourself. So much love and gratitude to you.

My amazing husband, Tom, whose patience, love, and support have made my whole writing career possible. You know how much you mean to me, I don't need to put it here, but I will say that I appreciate beyond words how hard you work, and I feel so grateful to have someone who gets me so perfectly. For our two amazing children, Eloise and Quentin, of course you won't read this for many years, if you do at all (and I won't mind if you don't), but I'll put it here in print that I couldn't have asked for two better kids. You both amaze and inspire me daily.

I'd like to thank the booksellers who've shown such enthusiasm for my book and have worked hard to physically put it in people's hands. I see what you do, I know how special your work is, and I am always awed by your knowledge and passion for books every time I set foot in a bookstore. Equally, the translators, who do such complex and nuanced work shifting my words into multiple languages—I'm forever in awe of all your talents.

And lastly, because you are so important you deserve to be saved to the very end (like the best awards given at any awards show), my thanks go to all the readers, for picking up my book. You're why I do what I do, and I appreciate you.

ABOUT THE AUTHOR

Kristen Perrin is originally from Seattle, Washington, where she spent several years working as a bookseller before moving to the UK to do a masters and PhD. She lives with her family in Surrey, where she can be found poking around vintage bookstores, stomping in the mud with her two kids, and collecting too many plants.